Advance Praise for *The Arrows of Fealty*

"On the one hand, who could have known that a novel about peasant unrest in fourteenth-century England would be so relevant today? On the other hand, what Jill MacLean demonstrates so resoundingly in *The Arrows of Fealty* is that the nature of power and the power of resistance are perennial—and perennially fascinating—subjects.

"Gripping and nuanced from page one, *The Arrows of Fealty* is a marvellous tapestry of unshowy-yet-encyclopedic historical knowledge, deep insight into human nature, and profound wisdom. An absolute triumph. I loved this book."

– Anne Fleming, author of *Curiosities*, shortlisted for the 2024 Giller Prize

"Deeply immersive, *The Arrows of Fealty* pierces the heart. The novel's world, at once strange and familiar—yet ultimately different—coaxes us into what the best historical fiction can do: form deep empathetic connections at once created and strengthened by the very strangeness. Paradoxical? Not in the hands of Jill MacLean. A treat for history fans, *The Arrows of Fealty* also welcomes every reader with universal themes of longing and love. Quiet and often subtle, written with great care, *The Arrows of Fealty* shines with the brilliance of fire at night."

– Michelle Butler Hallett, author of *Constant Nobody*, winner of the 2022 Thomas Raddall Atlantic Fiction Award

"In this stunning sequel to her equally powerful novel *The Arrows of Mercy*, Jill MacLean asks us to consider questions about where we pledge our loyalties and why, and whether the efforts of one person can ever make a difference in the fight against injustice and tyranny—issues as pressing in our own time as they were in fourteenth-century England. Her vivid portrait of Haukyn and his experiences of the horrors and resounding effects of war is deeply affecting and thoroughly convincing."

– Sarah Emsley, author of *The Austens*

"Most historical fiction either parachutes a character with modern attitudes and beliefs into a historical context, or uses broad stereotypes and clichés that have little depth or subtlety. *The Arrows of Fealty* threads this needle beautifully: MacLean's characters are complex, diverse, and fully human, richly medieval in beliefs and attitudes yet able to think against their context and social norms. The English Peasant's Revolt of 1381 is brought to life in all its intricacy and complexity. Meticulously researched and sumptuously detailed, *The Arrows of Fealty* nonetheless demonstrates that the fight against tyranny and the power of individuals working together is universal."

– Kathy Cawsey, author and professor of Middle English literature, Dalhousie University

"The best historical fiction manages a double feat: It depicts a world distinctly different from our own, so that the reader truly feels like a time-traveller, while at the same time creating characters who belong in that world yet are relatable to readers today. By these standards, *The Arrows of Fealty* is great historical fiction. Haukyn's world of soil and serfdom, battles and brutality, feels like a foreign country, yet his desire for freedom feels as immediate as today's headlines. This is a beautifully written visit to medieval England that will linger with me for a long time."

– Trudy Morgan-Cole, award-winning author of The Cupids Trilogy

"A beautifully crafted novel that immerses the reader in the lives of ordinary English people during the perilous fourteenth century.... MacLean leads us with compassion and sure-footedness.... *The Arrows of Fealty* is a testament to the hearts of our forebears who refused to tolerate injustice, and an inspiration as to how we may live our best lives, honouring each other and the earth that nurtures us."

– Julie Strong, author of *The Tudor Prophecy*

Praise for *The Arrows of Mercy*, finalist for the 2023 Whistler Independent Book Awards; a Best of 2023 from *The Miramichi Reader*; and Editor's Choice, The Historical Novel Society

"Richly imagined and compellingly realized, *The Arrows of Mercy* draws the reader into a story of the past that is imbued with the urgency and immediacy of our own time."

– Anne Simpson, author of *Speechless*, winner of the 2021 Thomas Raddall Atlantic Fiction Award

"Gripping, immersive, and penned with wisdom and a fiery prescience, *The Arrows of Mercy* is a story of human desire that pushes the boundaries of language to make a powerful statement on the passions and impulses that shape morality itself. A story for the ages."

– Carol Bruneau, author of *Purple for Sky*, winner of the 2001 Thomas Raddall Atlantic Fiction Award

"I love a good historical novel, and this one absolutely swept me off my feet. Engaging, thought-provoking, and thoroughly satisfying, it is one of those books you can't put down yet want to savour for its beautiful prose, compelling story, and rich characters.... The story is firmly planted in the past, but the emotions are timeless, fresh, and relevant. I only hope Edmund's story doesn't end here. I want more!"

– Heather McBriarty, *The Miramichi Reader*, July 2023

"This is an unflinching portrait of a harsh and violent age...yet amidst the darkness, there is light.... The issues confronted still resonate in our world today.... An impressive performance. Highly recommended."

– Ray Thompson, The Historical Novel Society (US and UK), 2023

THE ARROWS OF FEALTY

BY JILL MACLEAN

First published in 2025 by

Halifax, NS, Canada
www.ocpublishing.ca

OC Publishing is based in Kjipuktuk, Mi'kma'ki, the traditional territory of the Mi'kmaq.

Edited by Marianne Ward

ISBN - 978-1-989833-54-4 (Paperback Edition)
ISBN - 978-1-989833-55-1 (eBook Edition)

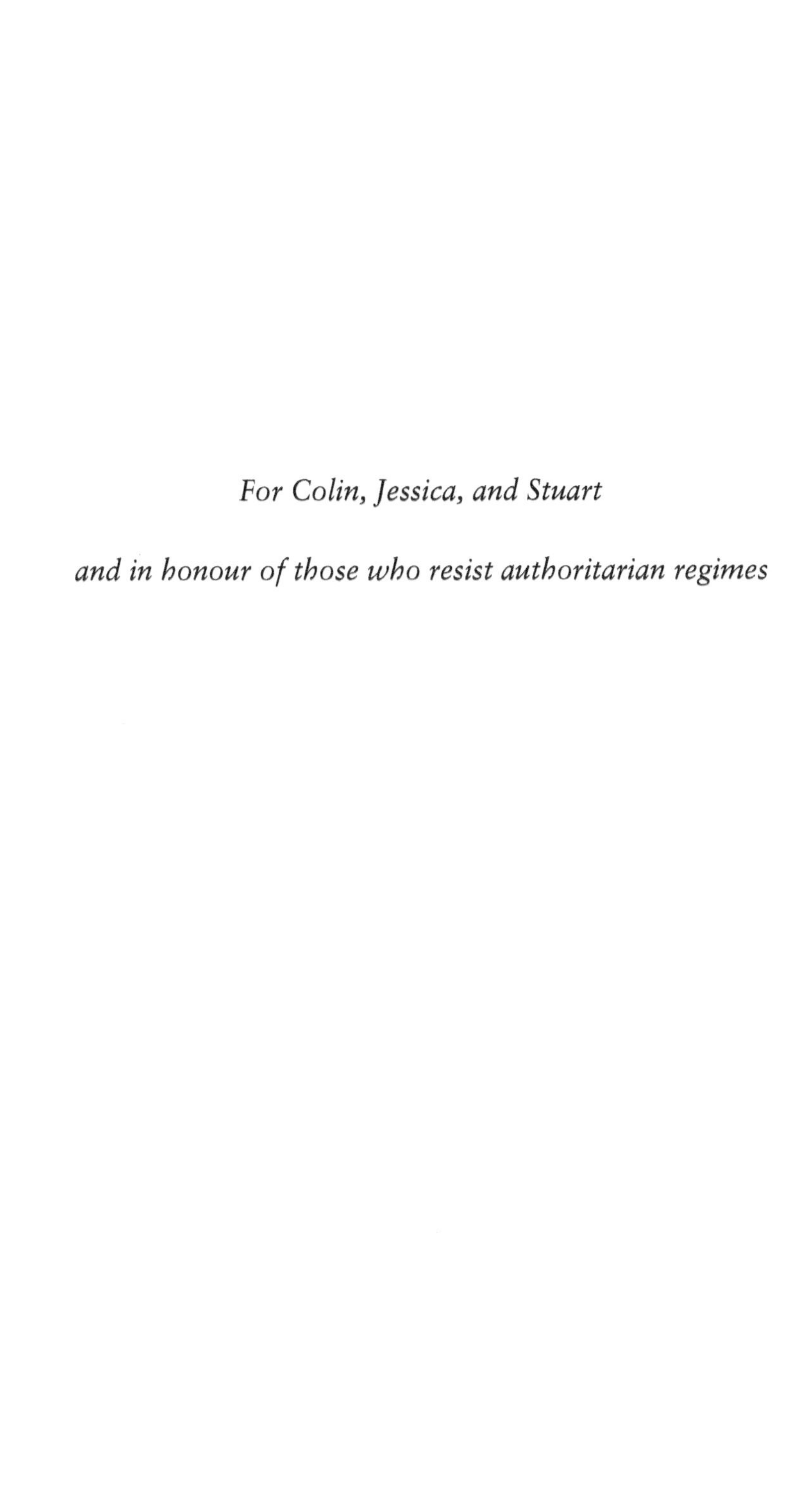

For Colin, Jessica, and Stuart

and in honour of those who resist authoritarian regimes

Contents

PART ONE
1373

...a day of thievery...

He'll not forget this sight til the day death claims him.

Blare of trumpets, heartbeat thud of drums, and in the distance, the army's vanguard stirs into motion. Bright-hued banners flaunt themselves in the wind off the Channel. Pale sunlight dances on the polished steel of armour. Horses snort, curvet, and fart. The captain of his retinue bellows, "Giddup!" and he, Haukyn of Flintbourne, is riding in John of Gaunt's army, leaving Calais for an unknown world to the south, a world of adventure, where he'll take part in something of far greater import than himself and his small village. This war will be one long raid on the French countryside, Calais to Bordeaux, a *chevauchée* that rounds up beasts to feed the army and grain to make its bread, and burns everything else. Battles, too, which they will win, for English archers are unbeatable. And for the victors? Loot, from dukes to lowly varlets.

Eighteen winters to his name, and he'll go home rich.

Two dukes, three earls, knights, and squires, he's ranked them in their proper order already and is in awe of their magnificence, the sheer splendour of their vivid coats of arms and of armour whose cost is so far beyond his reach as to be unimaginable; he's but a humble serf, a villein, lowest of the low. By craning his neck, he can see John of Gaunt, Duke of Lancaster, son of good King Edward. The duke's red and blue jupon is emblazoned with gold lions and *fleurs-de-lys*, his very vestments laying claim to France. He's astride his destrier, a huge black horse bred for war. Haukyn bends forward and rubs his mare's sleek chestnut coat. Modge is a cob, sturdy and much loved, although he tries not to display the bond between them for fear of jests.

As a little boy, he'd trembled at the very word *war*, for he'd heard his father's choked screams in the night and had listened to his mother say softly, "Wake up, Edmund, tis only a nightmare 'bout France."

A nightmare? Did herds of mares run through the darkness?

He'd never dared ask.

But now? He'll not wallow in nightmares.

Modge swishes her tail. The smell of close-pressed horseflesh fills his nostrils—tis how Heaven must smell. His friends Piers and Willem are riding to one side of him, and a smile stretches his face. Harnesses jingle, armour clanks (a noise he hadn't expected, a somewhat undignified noise), and the trumpets cry *Victory! Glory! Aquitaine for England!*

All day they ride, then camp for the night in an open field, guards posted along its perimeter. At dusk, half their retinue is assembled by their captain, Fulk of Hertford, a stocky, slab-faced man whose gravelled voice Haukyn had quickly learned to obey. Ten archers and two scouts will leave at first light and ride east with empty packs. Two waggons in the rear. Burn the standing crops. Poison the wells. Kill the serfs that get in your way. Oxen, cows, pigs, sheep, bring 'em back alive along with any sacks of grain. Loot if you can carry it, up to you. No attacking of towns or churches. Twould displease the Duke of Lancaster, and we wouldn't want that, would we.

Nigh dark and Fulk is about to dismiss them when shambling toward them comes a knight in mail and jupon; he has the smallest head Haukyn has ever seen atop a man's shoulders, his nose netted with purple veins close-hued to Gascon burgundy. Fulk shouts, "Attenshun!"

They snap to attention. The knight says, "And what transpires here?"

"A raid before dawn, Sir Nigel. To the east."

"Ah. Good. And you'll return with vittles for the army?"

"Aye, sir, God willing."

"The ways of God are ever inscrutable," Sir Nigel says sagely and to no purpose that Haukyn can discern. A snicker rises in his throat.

"You and your men will do well—er, I've forgotten your name?" He looks around vaguely, as though a name might spring from the campfires.

"Fulk, sir. Fulk of Hertford."

"Of course, of course." He nods earnestly, his wisps of greying hair nodding with him, and wanders off in the direction he'd come from.

Fulk raises his voice. "Rouse yerselves afore dawn. Dismissed!"

Haukyn frowns at Piers. "Er, your name?"

"Piers, sir. Piers of Hungerford."

Willem snorts. "Better to follow a gaggle o' geese than that dimwit."

"Fulk should be knighted for putting up with him," Piers adds.

Haukyn draws himself to his full height and nods so that his hair flops over his forehead. "The ways of knighthood are ever inscrutable," he says.

The three of them throw arms around each other's shoulders, laughing, and head for their bedrolls. But Haukyn is slow to sleep. So Sir Nigel of Winchester heads their retinue and six others besides, Fulk all deference though he is a man ill-suited to defer to anyone, let alone a pea-brained noble. God help all seven companies should Sir Nigel ever lead them into battle, and how can such a dolt be a knight banneret?

No matter. Fulk will be giving the orders on the morrow's *chevauchée*, and already he trusts Fulk, a soldier as tough as last year's jerky. A thrill streaks his nerves, edged with apprehension. On the hard ground, his bedroll argues with him most of the night, although his mare sleeps peaceably enough. Dark when they're roused. He pisses, chews bread and hard cheese, fills his waterskin, wraps Modge's harness in soft cloth, and they set off, Willem on one side of him, Piers on the other, the filthy-faced archer called Benedict riding nearby, a felon who'll be pardoned for partaking in this campaign and who, given the chance, would throttle the blessed Virgin.

As they speed to a trot, Haukyn's chain mail rustles and his heart hammers at his ribcage. His hard leather helmet, iron-rimmed, digs into his forehead. Bowstave, two quivers, each with a sheaf of ash arrows, sword and dagger at his waist, and he's grateful for the warmth of his quilted leather doublet.

From the black trees a crow flies straight for them. Willem says, "A bad omen."

"If the river's full, Willem, you bemoan the fording," Piers says, "and if tis empty, you're thirsty."

Haukyn adds, "A crow'll steal the bread that's twixt your teeth and the snot from your nose. A good omen for a day of thievery."

Willem grunts. Always he's doleful until Sext. No day should begin at Prime, he says, unnatural to expect sensible speech of a man at that ungodly hour.

Haukyn's muscles loosen as he urges Modge forward. While it was Piers who taught him the medley of heel, knee, and hand that gave Modge her nimbleness, her swiftness of foot, it was Willem who taught him how to shoot from her back. In Hungerford's fields, reins dangling against Modge's neck, he'd learned how to guide her at a canter with knees and heels, his body leaning into the turns, stirrups short, his bowstave brushing her flanks. Only later had Willem taught him to add the snap and whirr of an arrow's release, nor had the lessons ended until he could shoot a target on the approach, at the level, and from behind. A rare skill, highly valued by an army, most certain by Fulk; and how deeply he grew to cherish his trust in the mare, their slow-gained, mutual delight in this new game.

They travel as fast as the waggons will allow, sun in their eyes, scouts ahead and behind, and within two hours sweep down on a village whose barley is ripe and whose serfs have not been warned of a hungry English army. Belligerent serfs, armed with pitchforks, axes, and daggers and unwilling to flee to the woods. Fulk spits out his orders. "Piers, Haukyn, shoot 'em. Willem, keep 'em away from the barn. The rest o' you dismount and empty it. The scouts'll watch for French soldiers. Go!"

Haukyn's bow already strung, arrow to hand. With knee and heel, he wheels Modge, his bow at a slant. Three fingers to the string, lightest of pressure on the shaft, his first arrow loosed at a serf in ragged hose and the man drops, arrow in his chest, and in utter shock Haukyn thinks, *I've killed him.*

Another serf is running toward Piers, pitchfork raised. Haukyn looses a second arrow, the serf bowled backward by the force of it. *Christ, two men dead at my hands.*

This is war, this is what I'm here for. I'll count each one of my kills, I'll remember them so that at least they don't die unnoticed. Then, in true horror, he sees Benedict savagely stabbing a skin-and-bones lad against the barn wall. Fulk yells, "Haukyn, keep shooting, don't let 'em hide in the woods! The rest o' you, fire the barley."

Serfs shouting and screaming, and as Modge skitters, Haukyn forces his attention back to his mount—does he want to land on his arse in a French field? He strokes her shoulder, murmuring, "Easy, girl, easy, there's naught to fear." But a torch has just lit the ripe grain, and the breeze whips the flames through the barley with horrifying speed: fire, the terror of every horse. Modge whinnies, high-pitched, and breaks stride, switching her rump from side to side so he has to fight to stay in the saddle. He clings with one hand to the pommel, clutching his bow with the other. A serf is swinging a staff, too close, and somehow he manages to loose an arrow—*nay*, to the man's gut, cruellest shot of all. "Easy," he says again, and with knee and body turns Modge against her will so he can put the poor bugger out of his misery.

Flames and scraps of charcoal whirl in the air, a cow bawls louder than Fulk, and from the back of a horse whose coat is sweat-streaked and who wants nothing but to flee the scene, Haukyn weaves this way and that, shooting again and again, off-hand when he has to, until not a serf is left standing. By now, the waggons have oxen and cows tethered to them, the stout boards loaded with barrels of grain, chickens squawking their indignation inside heaving hemp sacks. The barley has burned to the ground, the charred, smouldering stalks making him wheeze.

"Move fast," Fulk shouts, "surround the waggons and keep watch."

Haukyn tugs on his left rein and glances back. A scene of devastation, smoke drifting in the air, everything else still. Uncounted, uncountable, bodies litter the ground, and the field is as black as any crow.

Only then does he begin to shake.

When they rejoin the army with their booty, Stephen Sadlere, the squire under Sir Nigel, is waiting for them. On his jupon three red foxes bear down on three blue hares. He's square-jawed, young, his manner with a lively hint of levity; he'd need a goodly dose of levity to put up with Sir Nigel, Haukyn thinks, a knight as sober as a serf on Sunday, though with fewer wits. The squire says, "You've done well, Fulk, you and your company. No casualties?"

"Benedict lost a fingernail to a cockerel, sir."

Sadlere laughs. "Haukyn of Flintbourne, Fulk told me you carry herbs and have some skill with them?"

"Aye, sir. I do."

"Tend to his finger then. Our archers need all ten of them. And Fulk, dole out a hen or two for your men."

Benedict, whose tunic is stained with dry blood, a helpless lad's blood, is unappreciative of Haukyn's ministrations. "Herbs? Tied up with linen? Tis but a nail gone."

"Sadlere's orders. Yarrow will make it heal quicker. You could have slit the lad's throat, one clean stroke."

"Where'd be the sport in that?"

"Hold still!"

"So you be Fulk's wise-woman? Where be yer skirts? I wouldn't want t' spread me legs nor lift me arse in *his* bedroll."

Haukyn's face reddens. He fastens the bandage and he's not gentle. "Let me know if it shows signs of infection." Benedict chucks him under the chin and strolls away. Haukyn gazes after him. A waste of good yarrow.

He's always been fair-skinned and blushes like a girl; tis a curse that goes with his hair, chestnut, though darker than Modge's, and curly as any girl's. Still, on the sunny day their cog had finally set sail across the Channel, Piers had said, "Your nose got a bump in it where it got broke, but your eyes be the colour of the waves, Haukyn, blue 'n' green mixed. Girls like blue eyes," he'd added complacently, his own the deep blue of a summer sky in a face undeniably handsome. "They like a man to be tall too, you be in luck."

Despite his father's stoop as he ages, Edmund is still taller than most; yet Haukyn tops him by a hand-span and his mother by three. "Better fed, you were," she once said, grumpily. "Don't think 'cause you can tuck me under your arm that you be the cock o' the coop."

Thoughts of his father are also best tucked under his arm. He heads into the French king's woods that edge their campsite to gather branches for a fire, and that evening, he, Piers, and Willem sit cross-legged and silent around their stone-edged hearth, bellies full of fresh-plucked chicken roasted on a makeshift spit, Willem absently scratching the stubble on his chin. Haukyn says, finally, "Twas both easier and harder than I'd thought to kill a man."

"A goodwife charged me after I'd shot her husband," Piers says. "I had to kill her."

Willem flicks a scab into the fire. "Sodding lice," he says. "A serf in the barn, a grey-beard, not much to him, but he come at me with his dagger. Killed him, didn' I, used m' sword and done it quick… Heloise wouldn't dub me knight for that killing."

His wife, Heloise, a lusty woman who's caused him to corrupt many a saint's day, likes his breath sweet and his nails clean, neither easy in the midst of an army, and that she is in Hungerford and he in Artois makes no difference—he frets anyway. Haukyn had asked him on the way to Plymouth why he'd left Heloise for the dangers of France. "She wants a little-un 'n' little-uns need a cow 'n' good grub. War the only way to gain hard coin. Nor I wouldn't mind a little-un m'self, now would I, sarding being the way to get 'em." And he'd winked.

When Haukyn first met Heloise, he'd been baffled to find such a mousy little creature. How was a man to guess what he'd discover on his wedding night?

The coals pulse and throb. Silence falls over them again, and this time Piers breaks it. "Sixpence a day, the duke pays us. A farthing a serf?"

Haukyn says, "What were they doing, those serfs, but defending their livelihood—you know how I feel about farming, but would I not do the same?" Without much conviction, he adds, "Don't forget, we'll be taking plunder back with us."

"Can't go home soon enough for me," Willem says.

"Back home, I had an eye on the bee-woman," Piers says, cheering up. "Willem, you know Ilotte, the one who'd rip your throat out were you to snatch a kiss. But I'll have silver enough that she'll look my way."

"She'll marry Hungerford's constable, him with silver to hand 'n' you with your pretty face far away killing Frenchies."

Piers cuffs him on the shoulder, chuckling. "He got a face like the arse end of a sow. She won't stand on no church steps with him."

Wanting to keep laughter around the fire, Haukyn says, "Remember the popinjays, Willem?" He can still picture how Willem, half-standing in the stirrups with his cob at a canter, horse and man perfectly balanced, had loosed five arrows at the stuffed bird fastened high on a pole at the Hungerford market, the air a sudden storm of small feathers.

"Never could loose more 'n four feathers, could you," Willem says, "'n' that only once."

"Maybe I needed a better teacher."

Willem swats him. "Pass me that last wingbone."

The chicken naught but bones when they're done.

Piers, whose bedroll is beside Haukyn's, snores like boar with bellyache. Haukyn pokes him in the ribs, his eyes burning, sleep elusive...how old was he when he first heard his father use the word *chevauchée* to his mother as they talked by the hearth? Five winters? Six?

He and his elder brother had been in bed, Robert asleep, Haukyn wide awake and listening. He liked listening. A good way to learn things his parents didn't want him to know. *Shev-oh-shay* was what he heard, and knew it was a French word and thus must concern his father's war, the one before Robert was born, before his parents had even met. He'd sat up, cupping his ear. A raid, armed men on horseback, fire and steel their weapons, serfs who screamed and fought back with pitchforks (he's a serf, but an English serf—French serfs must be different), bodies left on the ground, cattle rounded up, barns in flames, and he, aghast and fascinated. His father had done this. The same father who never struck either of his sons, leaving the slaps to Hawise, their mother, and hers only rarely with the power of her elbow behind them. Other boys in the vill were beaten with belts or switches, whichever came to hand; he'd seen the welts on the smith's boys and knew he was lucky that his misdeeds—there were a lot—weren't punished by leather or withy.

Does his father scream at night because he thinks he's a French serf? Haukyn eased down to the straw mattress and curled into the warmth of Robert's back. He can't ask. He's not supposed to know about those French serfs.

When the hens were scratching in the dirt in his mother's herb garden the next day, he stole a live faggot from the hearth and set fire to the coop, watching as the withies caught and crackled, the flames a pale flare in the sun. The posts were soon charred, but they stayed upright, proud as soldiers. The wattle fell, snap of sparks, glow of coals.

"Haukyn, what—"

His father dashed to the rain barrel, filled a bucket, ran back, and threw the water on the fire. It hissed, like the serpent in the Bible. The coals went black and soggy. "Oh," Haukyn said sadly. "Oh."

Edmund grabbed his shoulder. "Did you start the fire?"

Haukyn nodded. Of course he did. Robert was helping Ma in the garden.

"*Why?*"

Haukyn kept his gob shut. If he said *shev-oh-shay*, his father would know he'd been listening and there'd be no more talk in the darkness. Edmund shook him. "Tell me!"

"Wanted to," he said.

Disappointment darkened his father's face. Haukyn sighed. His father never looked at Robert that way, because Robert liked weeding and picking flint and running beside the oxen with the goad. Edmund said, "We are not put in this world to destroy. You will weave the withies to repair the coop. Now. And you will do it well."

Haukyn nodded again. It was hard poking the branches in and out, harder still pushing them down tight. His fingers bled, his knuckles soon raw. His father didn't offer to help. He just stood there, arms crossed, til the task was finished. Then he said, "If you set any more fires, I'll send you for two nights to Jorden Smyth's."

Haukyn has watched the two Smyth boys play slingshot in the woods, bold, foul-mouthed Warty Ivo and older, milder Slug-Arse Sim, both of them running like rabbits if their da was in a rage, sleeping in the bracken or in someone's byre til Jorden was too busy pumping the bellows or shoeing the lord's palfrey to bother with them. "I won't," he said.

He's had his own *shev-oh-shay*. He doesn't need another one.

And now? He should have remembered how fast the coop caught fire. He should have prepared Modge for flames leaping through a field of barley.

The days pass, one after the other under the August sun as the army marches south—St. Omer, Aire, Arras, raid after raid leaving a swath of destruction two leagues wide. Three thousand archers had disembarked in Calais, three thousand men-at-arms, and fifteen thousand horses, together with ox-pulled waggons loaded with weaponry, carpenters' supplies, and tenting, barrels of salt fish, dried meat, and mouldering flour; the provisions are untapped, for the summer countryside must feed men, horses, and oxen.

The banners and trumpets can still thrill Haukyn, as do the knights in their steel breastplates and bright jupons. Lions rampant, crossed swords, half-moons, spiked suns, all in colours whose names he learns by asking: *argent, gules, azure, sanguine, vert*, a world of mystery and ceremony from which he is ever excluded. He hears tales of gallant and courageous knights, tough-minded men who live for war. Across the unbridgeable river between noble and villein, he admires them.

As for the raids, always they darken his mood. The serfs left after the killing is done—the old men, the women, the children—will starve before winter, and he knows, from bad harvests in Flintbourne, how hunger shackles the belly. Not all the women and girls are spared; at night, when he lies awake, the screams of the raped ring in his ears, and aye, his tarse can harden as quick as the next man's, and he longs to know how it must feel to empty himself inside a woman, but not like that, not with cruelty yoked to lust, never that way.

And then there are the little-uns, stabbed, axed, broken-necked, tossed aside like rubbish on a midden.

Gules, azure, vert, could they be but a gloss over the unspeakable?

More leagues, more raids, Santerre to Rémigny. Harvest season in this fertile land of Champagne, vines and crops left in flames, scorched earth and the blackened rafters of houses and barns, and the waste of it all unmans Haukyn, shame clinging to him like the mud stuck to his pattens in Flintbourne's fields. God knows, he has no love of farming. But to burn every crop in sight, poison wells, slaughter beasts, his every deed one his father would detest?

Uncountable, the deaths from arrows he has loosed, although with each comes a pang of recognition: *I have ended a life.* He senses a change in himself. He's not so quick to laugh and is, perhaps, beginning to understand the mindset of those warrior knights.

Without making it obvious, he watches his friends. Willem was never prone to laughter, and Piers is unaltered, mercurial as ever. Though today, not so. Today Piers is naught but misery because Piers has the squats. Fulk also. Unfit for service, neither of them going on today's *chevauchée*, for cramps and shite glue them to the privy's rough wooden seats. Their squire, Stephen Sadlere, is leading them instead, villainous Benedict part of their retinue.

Sweat trickles down Haukyn's forehead, and has his mail ever felt so heavy on shoulders and arms? He spurs Modge forward, his lively, obedient Modge, so named because his twin brothers were too young to say Margery, her real name, and Modge it is to this day. Margery, daughter of their lazy reeve, was the prettiest girl in Flintbourne. For many months he'd worshipped her from afar, blushing if she as much as glanced his way and discounting all gossip of her ill-temper, until the afternoon near the well, when he overheard her laughing with her friends. *Me, with moony Haukyn? Pink-cheeked as a girl, balls like berries, 'n' tarse like a twig?*

She'd married the bailiff's son from Swallowbend, and word was she'd become the worst scold in the valley. He'd fled to his hideaway by the river that day, and aye, on the way he'd scrubbed tears from his chin. Her scorn still had the power to sting.

He pats Modge's shoulder. Sadlere on his gelding keeps them at an easy trot, and after a while he and his small group sight a barn on a slope surrounded by fields. Haukyn rests one hand on his quiver—twenty arrows in this sheaf and his other quiver full. With any luck the barn will house pigs, goats, chickens, anything edible for the army now two leagues east of them.

He prays there are no serfs in the barn.

The scout yells, "French! To the west."

Haukyn's head whips toward the slow-sinking sun. Fifty or sixty soldiers cresting the hill, too many to fight and too close for comfort. "Head for the trees, fast," Sadlere shouts. "Haukyn, Willem, see if you can pick any of them off."

As Modge swivels, Haukyn pulls an arrow free, raises his bow, puts his back into the draw, and aims for the soldier in the vanguard. The man topples from his horse. Willem's arrow fells another. The French speed to a gallop. He risks another shot, another man down whose horse panics, scattering the riders behind it. Willem, dour Willem, gives a jubilant whoop and looses a fourth arrow. "The trees," Haukyn cries, heels to Modge's ribs. "Now!"

Modge leaps a fallen stump and weaves through beech and birch, Willem ahead of him, the sun at their backs. He hears a crash of branches as the French soldiers enter the woods. Shouldn't he halt and shoot more of them, for there needs be some gain from this expedition now that there's no hope of forage, and too rarely do they come across men armed with aught but pitchforks.

Sadlere calls, "Hurry!"

He's lingered, a good leader watching over his two best archers. Willem surges out of sight among the trees. As Haukyn, with regret, spurs Modge forward, a lone rider bursts through the beeches, gold *fleurs-de-lys* on his doublet, battle-axe upraised. Sadlere unsheaths his sword, too slow, the axe cuts through mail and buries itself in his shoulder; he's not armour-clad for a clandestine raid. The sound he makes is dreadul. He sags over his pommel. The soldier jerks the axe free and raises it to strike again. Haukyn, with no knowledge of how he got there, is upon the Frenchman, sword thrust into a leather-clad chest and as swiftly tugged free. The axe thuds to the ground.

He doesn't wait to see the man fall. Grabbing the reins of Sadlere's gelding, he kicks the squire's boots free of the stirrups, right side then around to the left, hauls him across the gap between the two horses, and jams a leg each side of the saddle, his own arm around the man's waist. He turns Modge south rather than east and urges her into the woods, struggling to keep Sadlere upright in front of him, praying for concealment, praying also that Willem won't realize he isn't following.

To his dismay, the gelding is trailing them. Short of shooting the beast, he'll have to trust it to keep quiet, a worry soon dispelled by the thick carpet of pine needles muffling their passage. Modge plods around some rocks. Blood drips down her foreleg. Sadlere's blood. In the distance he hears a French soldier shout a command, unintelligible, followed by the diminishing thump of hoofs. When he's sure he's not being pursued, he dismounts, grunting from the squire's weight as he eases him to the ground, face up, a face that's too white, eyes closed. The faintest of pulses beats at the base of his throat. Blood stains his jupon, its red foxes and blue hares; the soldiers call him Ol' Saddlebags, even though he's young, the name a sign of respect for fair dealings.

From his canvas pouch, Haukyn takes out a clean cloth and smears it with calendula; his mother had knotted the pouch to his saddle the day he left, with instructions on the remedies it contained. He slices the laces of Sadlere's doublet and lifts the shattered mail so he can apply crushed plantain leaves to the wound—tis deep, torn muscle, splinters of bone, and his stomach swoops. With unsteady fingers he ties the cloth around the squire's shoulder. He's seen blood before. No need to feel muzzy, and plaintain will stem the bleeding.

Hoisting the squire back over Modge's shoulders takes strength, ingenuity, and his mare's accord—a relief the man's unconscious. They pick their way through the woods on a southerly course, all his senses alert, he trusting Modge to find the path and the gelding to follow.

Blood has soaked through the bandage.

No sightings of English or French, so he turns the mare east, the only sounds the soft huffs of Modge's breath, the scrape of the gelding's hoofs, and the occasional cheep of a small bird. Then, far away but infinitely reassuring, comes the rumble of an army on the move, the sound he's lived with for nearly a month. The rumble grows louder, the trees thin, and across the width of a field he sees the army, his army, hears the clink of armour, waggon trains groaning and creaking. He heads for the midguard, where John of Gaunt's standard flaps on its pole.

A knight sees his approach and trots toward him, two archers in his wake. Crook-nosed Sir Gardrad, a knight whose parlous reputation precedes him. His pale blue eyes rest on Haukyn with disfavour. "Where are the others?"

Haukyn gapes at him. "Did they not return?"

"You and Sadlere. No one else."

"Christ."

Sir Gardrad orders one of the archers to fetch the surgeon and the other to lift Sadlere down. "Lay him flat—careful, he's not a sack of grain. What happened?"

Haukyn slides to the ground, holding the reins loosely, and says to the second archer, "Fetch Sir Nigel, will you?"

"Pay attention!"

"We sighted dozens of French soldiers who pursued us into the woods. I'd waited so I could shoot the men in the vanguard. A lone Frenchman attacked Sadlere. I killed him and brought the squire here. Sir."

The surgeon hurries toward them, kneels down, and moments later says, "Dead."

"He lost so much blood," Haukyn says helplessly. "I did my best to quench it. I can't believe I'm the only one to return alive."

"You would contradict me?"

"The rest were travelling fast and due east, but I veered south because of Sadlere and kept the horses at a walk. They should have been back long before this." Willem, gone? Peter, Adam, Jonah,

Tybald? Benedict the felon? Why didn't he leave the squire to bleed out and fight to the death beside his friend and fellow archers? "I'll take some men and search for them."

"If they're not back by now, they're dead. Or prisoners."

Prisoners? Only the nobility are worth holding for ransom; common archers own no property, no stables or castles. The archers, his troop-mates, are dead. "We must send a search party anyway. Some might only be wounded."

"No straying from the army, have you not heard the duke's orders?"

Haukyn wavers on his feet, more weary than he ever remembers being. "*Chevauchées* stray from the army, or are you forgetting that?"

"A bad day's work," Sir Gardrad says sharply.

"Five soldiers dead by Willem's hand and mine," he answers with equal sharpness, "and who knows how many more? Our archers wouldn't have died without taking Frenchmen with them, they'd have wielded sword and dagger to their last gasp."

Sir Gardrad's eyes are hard as pebbles. "How dare you speak to me in a manner so greatly above your station?"

Haukyn shrugs. "I can read and write too. Better than many a knight."

Pure meanness in those eyes now. "Were you in my retinue, I'd have you flogged for insubordination."

"Then I'm glad I am not."

He turns on his heel, almost expecting to hear the knight's sword drawn from its sheath. He's fed hatred, not a wise thing to do.

Wisdom, according to his father, is not one of his attributes.

Before he can go in search of Piers, he has to repeat his story to witless Sir Nigel with his purple-veined nose, whom Benedict claimed was married to an heiress twice his age, *more 'n' enough to make any man drain the bottle*. Benedict wouldn't have surrendered to a clutch of French soldiers, he'd have hacked his way to Hell.

Willem, dead. Unshriven and unburied.

Sir Nigel frowns prodigiously. "So you fled French soldiers and your own retinue. I suppose that was for the best…though the duke ordered no straying, no straggling."

"If you were wounded by a French soldier, sir, would you want me to abandon you to your fate?"

"I…er…nay. Yet without a successful raid, we go hungry."

We. Sir Nigel means himself and his fellow knights; he doesn't give a sow's hock for the hunger his archers suffer. Haukyn's jaw drops. Knights don't go foraging to fill their bellies, they send archers led by commoners like Fulk. Sadlere, a squire, only went because Fulk was wedged over the privy. Why has he never realized this before? And which of the knights in this army would lower himself to herd mucky pigs and wild-eyed goats, to grab indignant chickens by the throat and dodge their shite?

But is that not as it should be? The possession of armour places a man beyond certain tasks. Tis the way of the world.

Unsettled by questions that have lodged themselves in his mind and will not conveniently be forgot, unwilling to loose his grief in front of any knight, he goes in search of Fulk, and in the stench by the privies relays his story for the third time. Fulk grunts. "You did yer best, lad. But I should've been there with m' men. God curse them Frenchies, 'n' the Devil take the gripe in m' guts. Tell Piers 'n' the rest."

"Yes, sir. Sir, they came over the hill so fast—"

"Willem a fine archer. You'll kill for vengeance on our next raid."

French as enemy. Aye, he feels that now as he hasn't, fully, til now. He has to tell Piers about Willem.

Tis as gruelling as he'd expected, and when Piers weeps, it releases his own tears. After a restless night, Willem's absence a wound as deep as the gash in Sadlere's shoulder, Haukyn untangles himself from his bedroll, and on his way to the privy in the grey light is hailed by a man of noble bearing. "An archer told me you are Haukyn of Flintbourne?"

His heraldry is two tidy rows of helmets, sable on pale green, a shade for which Haukyn doesn't know the proper term. Rubbing his eyes, he says cautiously, "Aye, sir."

"I am Sir Geoffrey Stratton, cousin to Stephen Sadlere."

Red blood soaking white linen. Haukyn winces. "God rest his soul. He'd lost too much blood, sir, herbs and a bandage not enough to staunch it."

"I'm not here to chide you but to express my gratitude that you did your best to save him and brought his body back. The duke's priest buried him last night with due rites. It gave me solace."

A knight thanking him, as no other ever has. Haukyn offers the only consolation he can. "I slew the soldier who killed him."

"I thank you for that also." He adds, with some difficulty, "Stephen and I grew up on adjoining estates in Kent; he was like a brother to me, and I will miss him sorely…Should you ever be in need of help, Haukyn, seek me out, in the rearguard."

"My thanks, sir," Haukyn says, and means it.

"God's blessing."

Haukyn watches him walk away. Blood and grief, they flow together, neither easy to staunch.

...underlain with wildness...

Dusk. Haukyn and Piers gaze into the coals of their little fire, lighthearted Piers reduced to a shadow of himself, dull bruises under his eyes. He groans in his sleep, and although he chews his rations, Haukyn can tell they have no savour. Mind and heart, Piers is with Willem.

Haukyn mourns his friend in his own way, tormented by images of Willem's body after French axes were done with him, a body left for wild creatures of the woods to further savage. Yet had he himself not stopped to save Sadlere, had he ridden in Willem's wake, he would have died himself, outnumbered by a band of soldiers bent on slaughtering invaders. To be dead, when your life stretches in front of you...he shivers, wrapping his arms around his chest.

Ineptly, twice, he tries to break Piers's silence, and fails each time.

Meanwhile the army rides steadily southward, burning, looting, and raping, in their wake the same blackened trail of devastation. Arras, Bray-sur-Somme, Cappy, the names meld one to another, as do the dead peasants. One evening, gulping pilfered ale with Haukyn, Piers bangs his mug down. "I want to kill soldiers, not sodding serfs."

"The French army marches a league or two east of us and has ever since we set out from Calais."

"Scurvy cowards."

To keep him talking, Haukyn risks saying, "Do you think John of Gaunt would care that Willem, a serf from his Hungerford manor, has died in his cause?"

Piers flinches. "Him? Nay. Always more serfs."

"Are we of no more value, then, than a winter-fed cow?"

"Did Gardrad send out a search party for Willem 'n' the rest? We ain't names to him nor to our lofty duke—why d' you think I got bailiff 'n' steward in m' sights? Stewards can own land, free-hold."

"Stewards are freemen, like you. I'm only a serf."

For a moment Piers's mockery surfaces. "With a serf's choices. Plant parsley or cabbage in your garden? Poach the lord's rabbits or go hungered? Just don't leave the manor nor try to join a guild nor tramp to the king's court for justice."

Haukyn says slowly, for these are new notions and he worries speech will give them too much heft, "Deference, obedience, starvation when harvests are bad…is that a serf's lot? Unending, unchanging?"

Piers downs more ale. "Don't have to be. Last thing in *your* sights is to be a farmer. Stay in the army, Haukyn, become a captain like Fulk. Or a mercenary with your own company. More than one way to flay a cat."

Killing is not the way Haukyn wants to spend the rest of his days. But neither is farming, and why did his father never talk about the ills of serfdom? He says gloomily, "Another raid on the morrow."

"Haukyn, I'll have to tell Heloise. Willem's widow." Piers's voice breaks. "His old ma too."

"I'll go with you."

"God's bones, me the one who persuaded you to join this stinking army."

"Not much persuasion needed. I was desperate to get away from Flintbourne."

Slurping another mouthful, Piers says, "M' sweet doughty Willem."

"Bed, Piers."

On a level patch of ground Piers subsides into sleep. Haukyn touches his bow to Modge's foreleg, and obediently she sinks to her knees, then lies flat with a whoosh of air so like a man's heartfelt sigh that he finds himself smiling. Bedroll out, his head on her belly. It won't stay there long, but for now he needs her closeness. *Desperate*, he thinks. A strong word. Of Edmund's four sons, he the only one who takes no pleasure in—nay, say it true—the only one who loathes seeds and crops and weeds, shovels and rakes and scythes; and as such, was he not a continual, and not always unspoken, disappointment to his father? Aye, he was desperate to get away.

What use dwelling on sharp-spoke orders, old arguments and resentments, his own short-comings as a son? The comforting rumblings of Modge's gut relieve the soreness in his own; he breathes in her scent, lays his palm against her rough hair, and goes backward in time.

Willem and Piers were friends years before Haukyn met them at the Hungerford market, where they'd all three gone to shoot at popinjays. On foot, not on horseback. "I challenge you," he'd said with the brashness of youth, "but fair warning, should you wager coin you'll go home the poorer."

"That won't be the way of it," Willem said, "'n' who be you whose gob spouts so fine?"

Piers said, "Ignore him, Willem. Cocky bastard."

"Ignore me at your peril." Haukyn shot fast at the popinjay and three feathers drifted downward.

As quickly, Willem loosed an arrow. Four feathers. Piers, two, and Haukyn starts laughing. "My gob spouts so fine because my father, a Flintbourne villein, years ago learned a similar manner of speech in France and foisted it on his children. I shouldn't have been so hasty with talk of coin." He doesn't tell them why he never rebelled against his father's speech, how even as a little boy, although he couldn't have put these words to it, he'd found its accuracy, its expansiveness, somehow freeing.

Willem tugged on his ear. "Should I turn m' back, I'd think I were shooting with one o' them Oxford priests. You better take lessons from him, Piers, since you wants to be bailiff of our manor."

"No woman I've yet bedded has yearned for what hardens below a priest's cassock," Piers said, grinning. "Best shots of five?"

After a close contest, accompanied by more laughter, a contest Willem won by a mere feather, they invited him to the manor of Hungerford where they lived, with its well-kept demesne belonging to an absent nobleman called John of Gaunt. Piers looked after the manor's horses, while Willem, a villein, was content to keep his wife happy, his breath sweet, and his acres ploughed. They drank ale, ate fish stew, and then Piers had guided him around the stables.

The horses. Those great hoofed creatures, rounded, restless, and inquisitive, as different from Flintbourne's ill-bred and overworked plough horses as they could be. They'd bemused him with their glossy coats, heads tossing, ears pricked, and the smell of them, a smell underlain with wildness; were your eyes shut you'd never mistake them for cows or oxen. Their muzzles, soft as...he'd never felt velvet. The lord entered the church every Sunday in a velvet doublet—if this was what velvet felt like, why wouldn't the lord clothe himself in it? And Haukyn had sensed from the beginning that each of the horses knew its own worth, had...*dignity*, that was the word, and him searching for words like his father.

Will he ever forget that day? He'd heard of revelations, as would anyone who attended Mass year after year, but he'd never understood the force, the awe behind that word, how it could enlarge you, make you more than you'd ever thought of being.

He slides his head to the ground and closes his eyes.

From too much ale, Piers breaks wind the night long. But the next day he gets his wish to kill more than serfs, for they are ordered to take the town of Roye on the banks of the river Avre, and Roye has a garrison, soldiers who grimly and futilely fight to their deaths. Just as Willem and his fellow archers must have done, Haukyn thinks breathlessly, ducking a sword's swipe and seeing Piers, to his left, gut a hapless soldier. Mace and axe, spear and sword, the noise horrendous, the brutality at such close quarters appalling; he's never felt proper gratitude for the distance an arrow's range confers.

In the midst of the melee, he sights Sir Nigel swinging his sword with gusto, if little accuracy, his helmet a smaller target than most. A spiked pollaxe whips past his own shoulder, its victim's scream worse than a stuck pig's. *Pay heed, Haukyn. If you're driven to your knees you're done, your bowels will join the mess under your boots,* and he sees Sadlere's cousin Sir Geoffrey hauling an English archer upright, his back to a mace-wielding French soldier. Haukyn yells a warning and slices the soldier open, and Sir Geoffrey gasps his thanks, laughing breathlessly, his face running with sweat under his helmet. Haukyn would like to have laughed back—a knight who saved an archer and an archer who saved a knight—and finds he cannot.

Too far away for him to prevent it, too close for him to turn away, an English axe descends on a soldier whose helmet is askew, a man's face sliced from his skull. *In nomine Patris…* He trips over an amputated arm, parries a dagger, skids in the mingled blood of Frenchmen and English, who's to tell the difference. Citizens unable to reach the sanctuary of the great stone church are cut down as they run, prayers and howling rising to the heavens, and then the town is torched, flames and smoke Heaven-bound also. The smell of cooked flesh makes Haukyn's gut heave. Climb the army's ranks and do this for his living? He'd as soon plough Berkshire from west to east.

Piers all day has jabbed and slashed as though each victim was the murderer of Willem, and that night beside their campfire again gets thoroughly drunk. Although the sights and sounds of hand-to-hand fighting, of burning and rape, are seared into Haukyn's brain, he stays sober. He has some inkling now of why his father used to scream at night.

His sleep is too broken to be of much good to him—was he afeard he'd wake to his own screams?—and early the next morning, Mass is served by every priest in the army and confessions heard. Haukyn watches the Host raised heavenward and forbears confession. For as long as he's been old enough to question, he's regarded God as a riddle whose answer hovers between a wraith and a rabid boar. If you try to touch a wraith, tisn't there. You retreat from a rabid boar, feeble weapons raised, heart a-thumping. Who's to know the mind of God, be it vengeful, protective, distant, or loving?

Confession must herald more than another *chevauchée*. Archers, shriven and unshriven alike, fill their quivers, sharpen daggers and swords, and avoid each other's eyes. Then the orders are relayed, duke to knight to squire to captain, and they are arrayed on the plain of Vermandois beside the Avre, battle-ready. Scouts, French and English, are regularly crossing the two-league gap between the opposing armies—the challenge cannot go unmet.

For nearly a week they stand beside their mounts and wait, an interminable week of heat, dust, and thirst, of flies, which, Haukyn swears, tear chunks from his face, bare beneath his helmet...a week for images of death, Willem's among them, to play on his mind. Modge is as restless as he, nudging him, whickering, her white blaze bright in the sunlight, and he recalls the second time he went to the Hungerford stables with Piers, a year after his first visit. A horse was for sale that day, this same restless chestnut mare, and within the hour he'd pledged to purchase her even though he'd not once been astride a horse; he wanted her as he'd never wanted anything in his life, and back in Flintbourne he had coin saved from good harvests, with silver enough to buy saddle and harness, and he, for once, grateful that his prosperous father had drilled into him a farmer's skills.

The mare recognized a man who knew neither how to mount her nor what to do when he had, and that first day bucked him off twice, playfully. Each time, he rode through the air and landed with a whump that emptied his lungs, his face to the grass and the late-blooming speedwell. After picking himself up the second time and heeding Piers's amused instructions, he managed to stay in the saddle, although with an alarming tendency to tilt from side to side.

On the Vermandois plain, Piers is stationed to his right, as usual sunk in silence. Haukyn says, "Do you remember how Modge threw me when I first tried to ride her?"

Piers rouses himself. "Your hair sprouting blue flowers 'n' your nose like the Green Man's. Twice, weren't it?"

"Not thrice though. You taught me well."

"I ne'er saw a man so fixed on glueing butt to saddle."

"A fortnight later I rode all the way to Flintbourne without once landing in the ditch." And with no idea how he was to explain his purchase to his father, a thought he keeps to himself. "Then Willem took Modge and me in hand til I could shoot from the saddle and she'd stay steady as any destrier. God help us, but that took some doing."

"Willem more patient than I ever were. Wiser, too, in the way o' horses…Them was the days, Haukyn, nor I didn't value them like I should've."

Haukyn swats the fly that's crawling up his bare neck. Memories, what good do they do? All too clear in his mind is the day he took Modge home with him, his father peacefully carving shavings under the shade of the walnut tree. Then he'd looked up, Haukyn and Modge ambling toward him, sun and shadow wavering over the mare's chestnut coat. Of a sudden, his face was shuttered against them and his eyes went blind—his body there, the rest of him far away. When Haukyn was a little-un, this gone-back-to-the-war face had made him scurry behind the nearest bush, his only wish to run as far and as fast as his galloping heart would let him. He was grown that day, yet his heart still raced to see his father so easily undone.

Anger had followed, anger on both sides.

To his relief, Haukyn is jerked back to a dusty plain, to John of Gaunt approaching on his black destrier; he nudges Piers and stands to attention. The duke inspects them regularly, this seethe of restless men and restless horses under the late summer sun. Rumour whispers how strongly he craves a full-out battle; his reputation needs it. A haughty figure, John of Gaunt, long-nosed and long of face, tis difficult to imagine he needs anything. Owner of twenty-eight castles, Fulk told them, scattered over five countries. Haukyn, who is not allowed to own anything but his chattels, and those can be seized should the law on a rainy Monday decide upon it, wonders what possible use you could make of twenty-eight castles. A man can only sleep in one bed at a time.

John of Gaunt sleeps in a large square tent, his banner at the peak, guards on each corner, pelts of wolf and bear softening his mattress. According to the army's ever-wagging tongues, he has a lusty mistress back home, a redhead, along with a fiery Castilian wife.

If the duke so desired, he could have twenty-eight mistresses. One for each castle.

The afternoon passes. No cloud of dust on the horizon, and then the news streaks through the retinues that the French have passed them, heading south, a living barrier between the duke and Paris. "Must irk him," Piers says, "stinking rich son of our king, brother of that mighty warrior the Black Prince, his standard raised 'n' not a speck o' glory to be gained."

"No loot either." Loot that was to have filled Haukyn's purse with coin.

His father had returned to Flintbourne weighed down with silver.

September a litany of names, one blurring into the next, one *chevauchée* into another, Ribemont, Laon, Rheims, Plancy-l'Abbé, then, finally, Troyes, a botched attack on the suburbs, the French again skirting battle. Three days the English wait this time, war as boredom, Haukyn thinks, as tedious as the passage of the seasons on his father's land. Was it that tedium, that predictability that kept him from farming, from all the tasks that are a villein's? Spring for sowing, summer for weeding, autumn to stook and winnow, winter to slaughter beasts and measure out food, then, during February's hunger, plough and harrow for the next crop? On and on, until a man laid down his ploughshare and was given last rites.

When he met Modge, he understood what those tasks lacked.

After Troyes, they head south again, Gyé-sur-Seine, Châtillons-sur-Seine, three leagues a day so the waggon trains can keep up with them, the hours of daylight shortening, the evening light an autumnal gold. The countryside they pass through is beautiful, its sloping fields and groves of oak and beech a sharp reminder of Flintbourne and the family Haukyn had so blithely fled: his mother's green eyes from which no escapade was ever hid; his elder brother Robert's tidy brown hair and close-cut beard; the twins, Ralf and Gil, unalike yet so much alike, mischievous without malice, already grubbing in the soil because that was what soil was for. He misses them all, painfully, tis worse than a gripe to the gut. He even misses his father, although learning to shoot arrow from bow was the only thing he's ever done to win praise from him.

He nudges Modge to one side of a deep groove in the road. What he wouldn't give to hear Robert's slow voice, to see the smile that so often lurked in his eyes, to witness his patience. Yet hadn't he been astonished by his own patience when Willem tutored him and Modge in the strenuous skills of horse archery, he who banged buckets against the well, cursed chickens, and despised the very word *plough*? A month or so after he'd ridden Modge to her new home in Flintbourne, he tried to explain this oddity to his brother. Robert said in his deliberate way, "Da and I love the soil and what it gives us. You've found another path into the world, and I'm happy tis so."

"He wants me to love spade and harrow!"

"The pair of you, like sparks to tinder." He smiled, easing a thistle from the earth. "Me, I'm doughy wood, slow to burn. Give him time."

"Aye. The rest of my life."

"Your patience with your mare, extend it to him. Haukyn, you were born with a need to butt against everything in your path, I see this and cannot understand it."

"Ma's the same," he said defensively.

"She's learned to walk around things. As you will, I trust. For your own sake."

Sighing, Haukyn brings his attention back to the road. How far away is Flintbourne, and how close.

The Nivernais, the Charolais, cross the Loire at Marcigny, and into the Bourbonnais, too late for harvests, the countryside bare of grain or grape, the nights colder. He begins to ration Modge's hay, risks thefts of horse bread from carelessly guarded stores, and hides the flat brown loaves in his pack. As a small boy in search of fun—or was he, once again, butting against any who would tell him *nay?*— he'd become adept at theft, beans from Maud Cat-Skinner's garden, sweet baby turnips from Simon-by-the-Lane's, faggots from Bony Mabel's woodpile. He'd only been caught once, his cheeks jammed with cherries from their priest's tree. "Tell me who else you have stolen from," said Father Mortimer.

"Course I won't. Stealing's a secret."

The priest's nose turned bright red. "Stealing is a sin. Your father spares the rod of discipline!"

A vigorous shaking that left bruises on both his arms, a lecture on the tortures of Hell, then flight to his hideaway, where he ate the cherries he'd hidden in his pouch and saved the pits to spit into the river. How could God be loving if he burned people alive, them with no hideaway to run to?

He still has no answer to that question.

Slowly, unease spreads through the army, archers standing in groups at night around their fires. Bordeaux is still far to the southwest, but where else can they go? Not back to Calais through territory they themselves have devastated. Besides, Calais would mean the loss of face for John of Gaunt. Unthinkable.

Three leagues a day, so Haukyn tells himself, is a goodly pace because it means their provisions travel with them. The time will come, and come soon, when they'll need the precious contents of the waggon trains.

The terrain worsens as they enter the foothills of mountains farther to the south, horses, men, and oxen toiling up the slopes and slithering down them, river upon river to cross, each swollen by rain, the exhausted carpenters building bridges then dismantling them to save the planks for the next river. A name races through the army, a river called Allier, a mighty river that must be crossed if ever Bordeaux is to be reached. Another rumour, of a solid stone bridge over the Allier at a place called Moulins, a lifting of the army's mood, followed swiftly by alarm—Moulins is surrounded by marshes, and the scouts have brought dire news. Three French armies are converging on the bridge; should they arrive too soon, the English will be slaughtered to a man and the duke's craving for battle end in dishonour and death.

Modge ploughs through water and mud up to her knees, stench of sulphur and decay, fear a miasma that rises with the gases. Haukyn squelches along at her side, Piers and his gelding close by as Fulk shouts himself hoarse at men too weary to curse him. Crossbow fire, stragglers shot, is this how his life will end, facedown in muck and rushes, a bolt in his back? "We should be shooting the scuts," he mutters to Piers.

"Too far away."

Slurp and suck of mud, closer and closer to the bridge. Modge jerks on her harness as a crossbolt hits a horse behind them, Haukyn trying to close his ears to its ghastly shriek. Wounded men add their screams, a distant trumpet sounds, French, he praying tis too far away to mean a charge. Grimly he forges through close-packed reeds as sharp as swords, wades a deeper, colder rivulet, his wet thighs aching, and glimpses over the helmets of the archers ahead of him a solid earthen embankment. Fulk yells, "Up the bank and over the bridge! Move yer lazy arses."

Up the bank he goes, boots slipping and sliding, Modge following in an ungainly scramble. An archer tumbles backward, and as Haukyn pivots, his hand reaching for an uplifted hand, he sees—and will see, over and again—a face distorted with terror, eyes bulging, he hears a choked cry as the man is trampled under a relentless tide of English boots and English hoofs. Sickened, he grips the reins, pushes himself up onto the bridge. A wide bridge, hard stone underfoot, the road ahead empty of French dukes and French armies.

Modge pauses and lifts her tail, plop of dung. The Allier slides between the abutments; on the mossy parapet of the bridge, a slug is leaving a trail of slime. Haukyn breathes deep, a futile attempt to loosen his taut nerves, mounts his mare, and glances at his companion. Piers, who on Hungerford's manor prized his one silk shirt and the jewelled clasp on his mantle, is dripping weeds and sludge and stinks like a dead weasel. Haukyn starts to laugh, a laugh that hitches between relief and a sudden, horrible weakness. "You're in need of preening, like the peacock you once were."

"A peahen'd run for cover if I courted her now. Haukyn, will we ever see a pretty woman again?"

"When I meet one, you must keep your distance. She'll favour you without a second thought."

"Not if she be round the next bend lusting for a well-scrubbed troubadour." Piers gives a weak grin. "Dunk you in the Allier with a tonne or two o' lye soap 'n' you'd do well enough. The bump in your nose…t'ain't that bump the girls'll have their eyes on."

For once he doesn't blush. Maybe the marsh drained him of blood.

Piers rouses himself to describe the charms of Ilotte, the bee-woman, and his hopes that she not be wooed by the ugly constable. Haukyn musters a smile, for Willem's death had ousted Ilotte, and now she's back. The pale sun sinks westward and, briefly, is upheld by the tops of the trees.

Fulk rejoins his retinue, his mouth a hard line, and for once speaks without obscenities. "All our waggons was abandoned on the Allier's east bank," he says.

Haukyn and Piers look at each other in consternation. Dried beans, flour, salt herring, carpenters' gear, weaponry, everything in the greedy hands of the French. Piers says with a smile that doesn't reach his eyes, "We'll have to tighten our belts."

Poor harvests in Flintbourne only three years ago; Haukyn does not smile back.

They camp near St. Pourcain beside another riverbank, where he strips and scrubs himself in the current, wishing he could as easily sluice away the face of a doomed archer and rinse his ears of that atom of silence after a bolt pierces the flesh of horse or man. At least soldiers understand what is happening. How can he explain war and its ways to gallant, loyal Modge? Shivering, he puts his clothes back on, grateful that all day the clouds had clung to their rain. After they eat dry bread smeared with fat from the piglet he shot two days ago, he burrows into his bedroll. Piers soon begins snoring. Haukyn lies awake until dawn.

All Hallowes and All Saints, October merging into November and no one seems to know where they are. Massif Central, some say, others bandy words like the Limousin and Puy de Dôme. *Puy*, so Haukyn learns, means volcano; they ride past strange conical hills and peasants' houses built from black stone. To live inside a black-walled house, Haukyn thinks with an inward shudder, the shutters closed, the door latched against the marauders of night, he would go mad in such a place, he'd be gibbering like Flintbourne's idiot, Wortle Dill.

Foreboding settles on the archers, heavy as their damp bedrolls. Hunger is their constant companion. Day by day there is less jesting, their bread rations cut, no hay for Modge's net, the dwindling stocks of horse bread too close-guarded for Haukyn to risk thievery and the noose. Belts are indeed tightened. Cinches are tightened on the horses. They clamber up crumbling limestone hills to plateaux where an unceasing wind numbs their fingers and makes their eyes water. They clamber down to valleys whose rivers are gorged with currents that tumble a horse from its hoofs and an archer arse-over-ears. Gamely the carpenters fashion bridges. Forests swallow the English soldiers, pine roots trip them, remnants of the French army kill foragers and stragglers who have disobeyed John of Gaunt's orders to keep in formation—an impossible order, Haukyn thinks sourly, given the terrain. All the same, he strives to stay close to his fellow archers. He pisses where he stands. He trains himself every dusk to use the pits dug for privies, never to head into the woods when his bowels grumble. He notices the men who take chances and boast of them, and avoids them. He listens for stray noises, vigilant as a hunted stag.

I am become a cautious man, a man of prudence, he thinks with as much amusement as is possible when slogging through the woods on an empty belly. *How disconcerted Father would be, he who once shouted at me for gaily waving my shirt in the same field as Solomon the Small's red-eyed bull.*

It has never occurred to him that recklessness could be curbed.

Tis wise to curb it, for worse than the soldiers are the local peasants. They know this God-forsaken land as he knows Flintbourne's hillocks and coppices; they attack at night, in silence, their faces blackened with soot, black as the walls of their houses, the whites of their eyes the only warning. English archers are beaten to death, hung from trees, hamstrung. Their throats, their wrists are slit, they bleed onto the thick carpet of needles. The army posts guards. The guards disappear.

Then it begins to rain, and the rain does not cease.

He doesn't remember Edmund ever mentioning rain in France, although it must have rained or he'd have mentioned drought, and here's his father roving his head again, haul one boot free of the mud, plop it down, haul on the other. His father once said to his mother—a boy listening in the dark—"We gave our son a name that sounds like a hawk, after your father, was it not?" and her reply, "Da were more raven than hawk, charcoal being his trade, but Haukyn be the name of our son in memory of m' father and his slow-burning fires."

"Naught slow-burning about Haukyn," was Edmund's answer. "Cockerel a better name, for he came crowing and clawing from the womb, and upheaval in the coop has followed him ever since." His mother, he remembers, had sighed.

Raven? Hawk? Cockerel? In his father's mind, he was always the misfit of the family, the cause of misery and strife.

Boot up, plop it down. Boot up, plop it down. He's leading Modge now, she bearing only his sodden bedroll, his meagre supply of rations, and the canvas pouch of herbs, much lighter than it used to be. Piers and his gelding are always close by. In daytime, from streams murky with mud, they ladle water into their helmets for their mounts to drink. The familiar lollop of Modge's pink tongue. At night they anchor helmets in the mud to collect fresh rainwater. Fulk pushes his retinue forward, his language ever more foul as men and horses begin to drop.

At least every second day, John of Gaunt mounts his black destrier and inspects his army by riding its flanks, ducking low-hanging branches, himself flanked by guards, his banner dripping. He pauses now and then to speak to a soldier, his cultured tones penetrating rain and the slop of hoofs and boots, *do not stray, rain that starts must stop, we make progress, soon the valley of the Dordogne with its friendly towns, do not stray, do not stray...*

Men with the squats in the ditches. Dead horses in the ditches. Dead men in the ditches.

Huddled in their bedrolls against their mounts, quaking with cold, he and Piers talk of the river Kennet that meanders through the town of Hungerford and through Flintbourne's fields, its clear water, brown trout, and stately swans; they recount Willem's flair with bow to hand and even raise a chuckle over his inventive curses when he was woken before the sun awoke, curses that could rival Fulk's.

On yet another cold, wet dawn, most of the archers still asleep, Piers one of them—why call it dawn when day after day you don't see the sun, only a faint leavening of darkness?—Haukyn unties his braies to piss against a tree whose trunk trickles with rain, its fallen needles drowning in the water cupped by its roots. His wet hose sag against his thighs. Hell is not fire, he thinks, Hell is rain, endless, icy, needled rain. He'd argue it with any priest in the land.

Or is Hell hunger? The archers have taken to calling their leader Gaunt John because even he has had to tighten the gold buckle on his belt. Haukyn listens to his own stomach growling for bread warm from the oven, for his mother's pottage thick with beans and oats, growling loudly enough to conquer the incessant splash and splatter of rain, and how his spirit longs for the simple cheer of flames crackling in a hearth.

He cocks his head, every nerve on alert. That sound, in the distance...growls? Or imagination? Naught to do with his belly, it comes from deeper in the forest. With care, he picks his way over the roots and through the puddles, farther and farther from the camp. Someone shrieks, making him jump, shrieks again, a sound he's come to dread. He takes his dagger from its sheath, its blade whetted, and skulks through the trees. To one side of a boulder, two shadows materialize. Motionless, he lets his eyes adjust to the gloom. His heart jolts. Two peasants, their backs to him, are watching their mastiff rip the flesh from another man, an archer who's writhing in the mud, his weakening screams an assault to the ears. One of them says something; the other laughs. Edmund, his father, his face torn by a French mastiff, tis not to be borne. Silently Haukyn creeps up behind the first peasant, jams his knife between his ribs, hears him groan, a death-groan, pulls the knife free. The dog has swerved, snarling. He parries the bloodstained jaws, knees it, and plunges in his blade. The mastiff collapses with a yowl that sounds human, and the second peasant rushes him, a stupid move. Haukyn sticks out his boot, grabs him by the hair, cuts his throat with a single vicious stroke, then flings him aside. The man's head—Christ, near-severed from his shoulders—thunks against the nearest tree trunk.

I have avenged you, he thinks.

The archer's eyes are wide-held, his body in spasms.

Die, for the love of God, die. Haukyn crosses himself with trembling fingers. "May God forgive you for your sins, *in nomine Patris et*—" and the man, choking on his own blood, gives one last gasp and dies.

Chest heaving, red-hot blood surging through his veins, Haukyn circles, ears strained should there be more of those filthy peasants.

Only the drip of rain on head and shoulders.

The deep furrows in his father's face, how can he ever forget them—and a memory, buried so deep it took a blood-hungry French mastiff to disinter it, inflicts itself on him. He, a little-un of three or four winters, had woken, whimpering, to the echo of screams in the dark. He'd lain rigid on his mattress, blackness pressing him down, his heartbeat a worse racket in his chest than Solomon the Small's geese as they waddled to the pond.

Whispers, a candle lit, shadows moving like demons ever closer, too close, he whimpering again, for demons live in Hell and Hell was more to be feared than aught on earth, Father Mortimer said so, and a man's face loomed over his bed, eyes like holes in his head, his face black-ridged, his ear nigh gone, and he'd screamed, "Nay! Nay, go away!" and broken into noisy sobs. When the man tried to lift him by the shoulders, he punched at him with his fists, wriggling and squirming until the man let go, tears dribbling into those ditches in his cheeks and falling onto his own face and now, deep in a French forest, Haukyn understands how he, the man's son, that night dealt a deeper wound than any mastiff could mete out.

Forgive me, Father, he thinks, and knows not if he's addressing his earthly father or his heavenly. If ever he gets back to Flintbourne… of course he'll get back, he's not going to die in this blasted forest. He kneels beside the archer, grimacing at the hideous injuries, glossy with sluggish blood, says a prayer to the Virgin—she more approachable, more merciful, or so he believes, than the God whose Son she bore— and smooths the man's lids shut. How easily his father could have died from a mastiff's fangs.

Then he edges through the trees toward the camp. A guard's voice quavers, "Be you friend or foe?"

"One of our archers dead and two peasants who will no longer kill Englishmen."

He could have killed a hundred peasants, he thinks, such was his rage, and how deeply his father is engrained in him. In the dull light, he holds up his dagger and watches the rain wash it clean.

...all here around the hearth...

In Flintbourne, Edmund sleeps uneasily, mastiffs with bloodstained teeth snarling through his dreams. He wakes with a start at first light, his fingers seeking out the ridges on his cheek. Hawise says, "You was wrestling with summat, had to dodge your elbows, I did."

"A skill you've learned over the years," he says, kissing her by way of apology. "So many years since I first saw you in the woods, a wild rose in your hand. A dirty hand, as I recall, and have you noticed I go backward in time more, now that I have...is it forty-five or forty-six winters, how's a man to remember?"

"More 'n m' hands was dirty, and you was a lucky man to happen upon a woman who'd put up with you and your elbows."

He draws her closer, her body as well-known to him as his own. Seven children she's birthed, each of them loved, three of them no longer living. Her monthlies gone now. They're lying bare skin to bare skin, and he slips inside her, smiles into the smile in her eyes. "Tis all show," he says, "I hear the twins chattering near the hearth."

She moves her hips, chuckling. "A fine way to begin m' day, husband."

"So it is." He kisses her again, lifts his head. "The dog's barking. Was that a knock at the door?"

"Tis Ivo," Gil calls.

"Wants you, Ma," Ralf says.

And he, Edmund, limp as a dead fingerling. As he reaches for his braies and Hawise hurries into her clothes, he says, "Ah well, the last of the hazelnuts to gather and I'm helping Solomon slaughter a sow."

Scab-chinned and shifty-eyed, Ivo Smyth is standing on their step. "M' da needs salve for his scorched arm."

Although Hawise prefers to be called herb-woman, she's been Flintbourne's wise-woman for the last twenty-five years. Jorden the smith no favourite of hers. She says, "I'll come once I've ate m' porridge."

Fear flicks across Ivo's dirty face. "Now, he said."

Edmund says, "Come in, Ivo, and I'll get the fire going. Have some oats, then the two of you can walk to the smithy together."

Ivo ducks his head. "Got work to do," he mutters and disappears into the chill November mizzle.

Edmund closes the door. His friend Ralph was the smith until plague took him, and a sad day that was. Absently he scratches behind the dog's ears; all his dogs have been called Ranulf after Ralph, this one thick-chested, blunt-nosed, and protective. The smithy stood empty until Jorden arrived many years ago, an incomer from Wiltshire with a scrawny wife and three grimy children; Ralph would deplore how oxen snort and sweat when driven into the forge for shoeing.

Hawise says crossly, "This ain't no time to daydream, Edmund. Feed the fire, will you?" She starts mixing water and oats with dried apple and a small dab of honey as Edmund lifts the cover from the hearth, lays it on the floor, and hurriedly sets twigs to the coals, watching the flames catch. "He could do with a square meal, that lad," he says, a lad Haukyn always called Warty Ivo, for Haukyn hated Ivo, and with good reason.

Feeling the draught, he looks up when his eldest son, Robert, opens the door and walks in. Gil throws a mock punch at him, Ralf winds himself around him, and Ranulf wags his tail. "God's blessing," Robert says. "Da, will Solomon want my help too?"

"Not today. Maybe you and the twins could deepen the ditches around the back of the assart."

Robert presses the muscles in Ralf's arm. "I'll oversee these two," he says. "Five winters to their name? Shovels in hand? You'll have the deepest ditches in Flintbourne. Any oats to spare, Ma?"

"None at your house?"

"Johanna's finding the last few weeks hard."

He looks careworn, and not for the first time Edmund wonders about Robert's marriage, a marriage that took place last spring after Haukyn left, Johanna already with child. *A grandchild come Christ's Mass,* he thinks, *our first.*

"A belly laden with a little-un be heavy enough," Hawise says and passes Robert a bowl of oats. "Edmund, when I takes that salve to the smithy, I'll make sure I'm paid in coin, 'n' I'll dunk it in verjuice. Jorden's wife's a sloven."

Her smile is as fierce as the day he married her. Her herbal sits on the shelf in pride of place, the herbal she wrote herself, with careful ink sketches of each plant, its flowers, leaves, and roots. His book of verses beside it, two of their four children able to read and write as well as any steward, and the twins learning these skills fast. Twins, what a surprise that was.

Robert, Ralf, and Gil, all here around the hearth. Haukyn, his second son, in France, gone to war, and why? To worry me, Edmund too often concludes, for worry he does, and why wouldn't he when he knows the cheapness of life in enemy territory. His son is somewhere between Calais and Bordeaux, there will be no word from him, and should he die, no body to bury. Little wonder he, Edmund, has grey hairs in his beard and white hair over his ears—one ruined, one not. The scars on his face, they haven't changed.

Haukyn the horse archer...Ten years since King Edward's decree was read from the pulpit by Father Mortimer, Father Thomas long dead, God rest his soul, a decree that ordered all sons over the age of seven to be provided with a bow and two arrows. Edmund had purchased Haukyn's from old Dunstan up the hill. "I don't want a bow," Haukyn said.

"The younger you start, the easier shooting will become." Smiling, Edmund put the bow, already strung, into his son's hand. Haukyn, a sturdy boy, threw his weight onto the elm stave, arching it until the nocks almost touched. The wood snapped into two pieces and fell to the ground. Edmund slapped him on the cheek.

They stared at each other in mute horror. Haukyn recovered first. The marks of Edmund's fingers white on his furious face, he cried, "I'll never go to war, I'll never scream in the night like you!" Then he ran.

Edmund knew where he was going, to his hideaway near the big oak in the hollow. He'd followed him there one day and gone back later, while Haukyn was feeding the chickens. The encroaching hawthorn and blackthorn made a small cave, its interior rimmed with a tidy circle of flintstones from the river; he didn't understand why those stones should hurt him deep in his chest.

The day of the broken bow, his son came home at dusk. "Haukyn," he said, "you will learn to shoot. King Edward wants a nation of archers and you'll be one of them."

Hawise thunked a bowl of soup down in front of the boy. "Do what your father says!"

Haukyn ducked his head into his bowl and said nothing.

Soon afterward, early one morning when dew glittered in the grass and a blackbird carolled from the oak tree near the lord's manor, the two of them walked to the butts by the river, St. Edmund's church casting its long shadow, the jackdaws that lived in its tower out foraging in the fields. Edmund stooped to position his son's fingers around the new stave, showed him how to nock the arrow left-handed, then guided the bow toward Haukyn's ear and helped him draw; his voice, he noticed, had an unaccustomed hardness.

On the first loose, the arrow buried its tip in the straw that surrounded the mark. Haukyn blinked and looked down at the bow. "I want to do it on my own."

Edmund watched him trying to remember everything he'd been told. His second arrow hit just outside the mark, the third just inside, and from then on Haukyn and his bow were as one. It was clear the boy was enraptured by that unity, and it wasn't long before Edmund knew Haukyn would be a better archer than himself, he who had championed the shire.

His shame for being a man who still screams in his sleep, years after his return from France, is as nothing beside his shame for hitting his son in anger.

Robert scrapes his bowl. Edmund hastily finishes his own oats. Robert and the twins leave for the assart, Hawise takes salve and departs, and he should rouse himself, feed chickens and sow, and walk up the hill to Solomon's.

The hens and the cockerel sprint to the trough. He didn't hit Haukyn the day his son set fire to the wattle walls of the chicken coop, then stood like a lump watching them burn to char, though twas no accident, that much Edmund knew. But why did Haukyn do it? What purpose did it serve? Downcast eyes in a sulky face, *wanted to* the only words Edmund got out of him.

Hasn't there always been a barrier twixt the pair of them, an ill-made wall of ill-fitting flint? Robert now, he and Robert stand in the same sun-washed field, scythes swinging in unison and no words needed.

Wanted to… Ten years passed and Haukyn was still neglecting his chores, fleeing to the Hungerford manor every chance he got; if he did condescend to pick up shovel or axe, it was with a silly smile on his face and no care for the work at hand. And then, on a day when the grass was green and the speedwell blue as the heavens, he came home from Hungerford.

But not alone.

Ranulf, Hawise, and the twins elsewhere, he himself sitting in the shade of a willow tree. Piled on the table, pine branches and curled shavings, which, once dry, would kindle their fires; he'd always found this a satisfying task that freed his mind for wordplay. And then he'd looked up, and the rhymes that had been tantalizing him vanished. His son, who looked so like himself before the *chevauchée* where a French mastiff had torn open his face—Haukyn with his cropped curls, his eyes a mingling of his father's dark blue and his mother's green—Jesu, this same son was leading a chestnut mare with a white blaze and—*a page in bloodied livery, little more than a boy, trapped beneath a chestnut mare, the horse sweat-drenched, flailing its head with its red-flecked blaze, front legs smashed, he steps over the boy and with his dagger cuts the mare's throat, gush of blood, he can't shift the weight of her so two other archers help him roll the mare off, a snapped-off arrow in the boy's belly and he dies as they watch and he leans over and brushes the boy's eyes closed and whispers a prayer—*

The dagger dropped to the table, the haft clattering against the wood. Heaving in breath, Edmund scrubbed at his face with hands that shook. Haukyn planted his feet, fingers clenched around the mare's reins. He said flatly, "She'll never go to war, Father."

To Haukyn, he is *Father*, almost never *Da*. Edmund picked up his dagger and searched for his voice. It came out colder than intended. "You will pay for her feed."

"I will. Solomon the Small has offered a manger in his byre, she'll be no bother to you."

"We have an ox for ploughing. This horse, she's a whim of your new friends in Hungerford."

"She's strong enough to pull Solomon's plough, and I'll pay for the rent of the stall."

As Haukyn clucked to the mare and led her away, up the hill toward Solomon's, Edmund swore under his breath. Wrong-footed, why was he always wrong-footed with his second son?

If Haukyn comes home from war—when Haukyn comes home from war—they will do better, the two of them.

I pray you, Father, in your blue heavens, keep my beloved Haukyn safe.

...all that fine armour...

Haukyn now wakes before dawn each morning, lifts himself from the wet curve of Modge's ribcage, nods at the guards, and slides into the forest, where three more peasants die from his dagger. Piers says nothing. Fulk nods.

He kills from a rage he doesn't care to examine.

Gaunt John has new lines scored in his face. John of Gaunt, king of Castile and Leon, duke of Lancaster and Aquitaine, earl of Richmond, Lincoln, Leicester, and Derby, lord of Beaufort, Nogent, Bergerac, and Roche-sur-Yon, steward of England; Haukyn overheard Sir Nigel reeling off the titles the day after their first *chevauchée*, the knight's small skull able to hold each of them in order. What they mean to Gaunt John as the days drag by is a mystery.

While the duke might be thinner, he's in no danger of joining the dead soldiers in the ditches. Gaunt's personal waggons of food, wine, tent, bedding, clothes, weapons, armour, who knows what, trundle along in the very centre of the army; they made it across the marshes of Moulins and are guarded night and day in order that a king's son may be coddled. No opportunities for thievery there, Haukyn thinks, telling himself tis contempt he feels toward Gaunt John, and only contempt.

Gaunt's surgeon calls the squats dysentery, a dread sickness that slinks through the army, the shite and cramps deadly no matter the name. Piers and Haukyn, mercifully free of it, slog on. Modge, his dear Modge, her peaked hip bones, her ribs a cage of curved bars, the knobs of her knees. When she nudges him with her soft nose, looking for hay, his heart nigh breaks. He feeds her the crumbs of a loaf, strokes her white blaze, and coaxes her forward. Many of the knights are now on foot, their horses staggering beside them, their pages and varlets trailing behind, heads bent against the rain. Those in the vanguard of an ever-shrinking army have dropped their armour in the ditches, back-plates, greaves, and gauntlets, and though armour is of high value, no one stoops to pick them up. Carcasses of horses another matter, haunches and shoulders flayed, raw flesh gouged out by soldiers snarling like dogs, teeth bared, gums bleeding. Haukyn averts his eyes. He'd rather starve than eat horseflesh, nor will he ever allow such mutilation to Modge. They trudge across another hastily erected bridge—is France naught but rivers, nameless, swollen, turbid rivers, and why would any king want to lay claim to such desolation?

They fan out onto one more mud-churned track, Piers and his grey gelding at his side. Ahead of them, near the bottom of a steep slope, a knight still laden with armour is leading a skeletal destrier, Haukyn taking consolation that Modge is in better shape...could it be Sir Nigel, purple-nosed Sir Nigel, his shoulders bowed under a jupon too soiled to pick out any design? His head is down, a head that, if tis he, would be adorned with the smallest helmet made by any armourer. Haukyn watches him, feeling, oddly, no pleasure should the leader of their retinue be brought so low.

God's balls, another river.

The knight with the soiled jupon drops the destrier's reins, gives a wild cry and runs headlong toward the river, toppling down the bank into currents that tumble him before his armour weighs him down and he disappears beneath the rough-hewn bridge and the brown-curled foam. The men around them, shocked out of their apathy, stop in their tracks, and the word races back through the ranks: *twas Sir Nigel, Sir Nigel of Winchester.*

Piers crosses himself. "The mouth of Hell will gulp him quicker than I'd gulp a dried herring."

"All that fine armour," Haukyn says thoughtfully, "and naught inside to hold it up."

The destrier is put out of its misery, and the pressure of the men behind them pushes Piers and Haukyn across the bridge. Not even an hour passes before Piers's gelding gives a deep groan and collapses, limbs sprawled, eyes dim with the film of death. As two archers help them roll the corpse into the ditch, the rest of the army parts around them, inured to such a common event. "Blessed Saviour," Piers says, his voice unsteady, "a good horse, mine for four years, and how long before someone cuts into the pitiful flesh that's left. This infernal march, will it never end?"

Everything ends, Haukyn thinks, tis the only certainty a man can cling to. He twines his fingers into Modge's mane. "Come, Piers, wipe your eyes and before long we'll share our mouldy bread ration." They push forward, step by arduous step, pass a knight crouched in the ditch, his page hovering over him, and Haukyn says impulsively, "From the lowest varlet to John of Gaunt, shite comes out of our arses. Yet we are told by king and archbishop that there is a great gulf twixt us and them. A puzzle to me how that can be."

"Tis God-ordained."

"So they tell us."

"We feed 'em with our labours, they protect us with their swords 'n' shrive us with their Latin."

"Or do their swords and sermons put the fear of God in us so strong that we dare not rebel? Their laws, courts, judges, and gaols, aren't they designed to keep us in our place?"

"You be witless as Sir Nigel," Piers says with some of Haukyn's impatience. "Become a freeman, tis better than a serf, I tol' you that before. P'rhaps your lord will let you purchase manumission."

"Aye. With the riches I'll be carting home from France."

Piers actually laughs, a weak laugh but nonetheless a laugh. "If you flee your manor and stay hid for a year 'n' a day, the law says you be free. Or if you be bastard, you was born free. And neither of 'em costs a farthing."

"*Bastard?* You mean it? Why have I never heard that before?"

"The lord o' the manor ain't going to tell you."

"Piers, my father was born a bastard. So he is free? And I, as his son, would also be free?"

"It must be proven first."

"He's well-known in Flintbourne, such proof should be easily had."

"All you has to do is get back to Flintbourne." Another laugh, wry. "Not so easy done."

Haukyn picks up his pace. "We'll do it together. You and I."

"Slow down. M' legs totter like an old-un's, 'n' your mare falters."

In swift compunction, Haukyn rubs Modge's muzzle and does as he's told. When they bed down that night, he lies across the mare's bony ribs, both of them under the same blanket, and stays awake for a long time, not just from the gnaw of hunger. Freedom, he thinks. Free to leave Flintbourne without paying chevage, free from tallage and the bailiff's strictures, no longer the property of the lord of the manor to be disposed of as the lord sees fit. This freedom the gift of a bastard father.

The army stirs around him, stirs like a great mastiff, chained and hungry.

The skin of Haukyn's wrists is wrinkled like an old man's. He's hollowed to a husk, he thinks blearily, hollowed by hunger. If he steps on a rock, it jars his head like fist to skull. The jingle of harness sounds like ill-tuned jugglers; the squelch of mud tears at muscles wasted to gristle; his jaws munch his teeth. He staggers through a weariness that urges him to make each step his last, to lie down, the ditch will be your shelter, your place of rest where you can close your eyes and hunger will no longer swallow you.

He's afeard he'd kill were he to see bread in another archer's hand.

Hunger devours the soul, that much he has learned. Had Sir Nigel lost such soul as was beneath his rusted armour? *God*, he thinks—or is he praying?—*feed me and I am Yours.*

And yet...he picks up his left leg, puts it down, picks up his right leg, puts it down, too bone-headed to do other, is that not what his father would say?

Be damned if his corpse will rot in a ditch in this land of Cain, this place of exile.

Piers stumbles along beside him. Haukyn is afeard for his friend too, for Piers lacks his own cussedness. With what energy he can summon, Haukyn makes fun of Flintbourne's priest, shrill-tongued Father Mortimer, and Hungerford's unctuous Father John, honey-tongued, as more than one widow could testify. As they wait for the latest bridge to be constructed, he mimics Wortle Dill's flailing arms, his feet that jounced like a puppet's, his sobbing laughter— Wortle Dill, who had once come to Haukyn's rescue from Warty Ivo, to his own cost and Haukyn's also. Today not only Piers laughs; Haukyn is gratified to have lifted, even fleetingly, the black mood of his retinue. But as if God had been judging the cruelty behind his play, punishment comes a league or two beyond the bridge. Modge's hoofs falter, then sink into the mud, her head hangs, and none of Haukyn's pleading, with its undertone of desperation, will make her move forward. Piers steers the other archers around the mare, to grumbling and half-hearted curses. Haukyn strokes her shoulder, whispering endearments. A fit of coughing seizes her, it lasts and lasts, and to his horror fresh blood drips over his boots. When he wipes her mouth with his sleeve, spatters of red soak into the wet leather. She quietens, her muzzle drooping.

A light tap to her knees with his bowstave, a signal he taught her at Willem's urging, and, groaning, she lies down. "Piers, will you keep everyone moving," he says and takes out his dagger, kept sharp, he can acknowledge now, with this in mind. He sits on the wet ground close by, and with some difficulty lifts her head and lays it across his lap so he can rub her ears and stroke her blaze, a ritual begun soon after she moved into Solomon the Small's byre. Bending double so he can rest his cheek against her mane, he breathes in her scent, the knife behind his back so she can't see it. Priests say that to pray for a beast is sinful, for beasts, being without souls, are barred from Heaven. "Modge," he whispers, "I pray the Virgin Mary will lead you into fields lush with grass, where you will never again know hunger."

His fingertips find the spot in her throat. He bunches his muscles and slices deep, severing her windpipe and the great vessels that lie beneath. She stiffens in shock, the sound she makes—blood gushes over his hand. The white hairs on her muzzle quiver. Her hoofs kick at the mud. Then, slowly, her eyes glaze over, the weight of her head a dead weight. He's shaking as though he has the ague.

The blood of a horse, the blood of a man, the reek is the same. He'd hoped the end would come by a river and he could topple her into the current, away from flensing knives and starving soldiers. Instead, Piers, an archer named Javyd, and Fulk, who'd stopped when he saw what was happening, help lever her into the ditch. He bends again so he can slice a hank from her mane. Fulk says gruffly, "She were a good horse, Haukyn, 'n' deserved a better end."

Unashamedly wiping tears from his cheeks, he says, "Aye, sir, she was a good horse."

Fulk buffets him on the shoulder, no force behind it. "C'mon, lad, we got to keep moving."

So Haukyn leaves his mare where she lies, walks on, and does not look back.

He'll tell the twins she died from a French bolt to her heart.

That night he can no longer curl his bedroll into her flanks, her warm, bony flanks. Sorrow racks him, twinned with guilt. "She'll never go to war," he'd said to his father, and for months he'd kept his word. But by the time his arrow could hit a target with Modge at full gallop, it was spring again, and on a bright day in March, buds bursting, birds an urgent chorus from dawn to dusk, Piers had come to Flintbourne. He found Haukyn spreading dung. "Throw your fork to the ground. The steward of our manor, a squire called Stephen Sadlere, he been in London the last week and sent news: John o' Gaunt wants archers for a *chevauchée* in France. Archers like us, for how many c'n shoot with any accuracy from horseback? You, me, 'n' Willem'll start off for Plymouth on the morrow as part o' the duke's retinue, Sadlere'll meet us along the way. We'll be paid sixpence a day, 'n' there's rich plunder to be had in France."

"I'll come," Haukyn said.

His mother was weeding her herb garden, his father repairing the fence nearby. When he'd told them of his plans, his father had gone silent, his face stricken. The little boy tucked inside Haukyn, who'd learned from a father who screamed in the dark that war was the stuff of nightmares, had that little boy wanted his father to stamp his foot and insist Haukyn stay home? Big feet, his father had, as big as his own. *They keep me in touch with God's good earth*, Edmund was apt to say, *with its bounty and its blessings*, and he'd smile, rubbing kernels of wheat between his fingers.

Feet are meant for stirrups; and his father, that man of words, offered none that spring day. His mother, green eyes ablaze, offered plenty. "You'd leave the peace of our valley 'cause the king wants fancy archers to kill Frenchmen? The king wants his Gascon wine, that's what he wants, and you the fool to get it for him. Senile, ain't he, besotted with that greedy mistress o' his."

"John of Gaunt is our leader, Ma, he's one of the king's sons. A son isn't always like his father."

"You'll break *your* father's heart."

"I need to go! I can't be a farmer, it isn't in me, I'm not like Robert."

"A few screams in the night and you trit-trot off to France, abandoning your birthright. I knew there'd be trouble the day you rode that ram-skyte horse into our yard."

He'd never doubted the bond between his parents, for it was the foundation on which he and his brothers rested. But to have it thrust in his face like this, to have doubts assail him when he'd just mouthed an unassailable truth. "Freedom is what I want," he said wildly and felt deep inside the chiming of a distant bell. "I'm going to Hungerford with Piers and Willem. We'll leave from there on the morrow."

So he'd fled dung, plough, and family, and gone to war. To this day he can't bear to remember the way his father had held him close then pushed him away, tears shining in his eyes.

Once home, he'll gain his freedom, a gift of that same father, who was born bastard. But Modge, his sweet Modge…he the cause of her suffering these last weeks as her body ate the flesh from her bones.

The next day, as is his wont, John of Gaunt rides past, *do not stray, do not lose heart, we are ever-closer to Ussel, a town friendly to the English, provisions there and we will rest…*

They have not been paid for weeks, a fact the duke chooses to disregard. Sixpence a day, why would a king's son bother his head over such a paltry sum?

Haukyn nurses his anger, for it is easier to bear than grief or guilt. In the grip of that anger and a satisfaction that, distantly, shames him, he counts knights as they drop—Sir Guy, Sir Richard, Sir Bartholomew, Sir Gareth, armour cast off, bodies rolled into the ditches, and when they joust in Heaven, will the commoners with their lice and fleas be permitted to watch from afar?

Fulk has fewer archers to harry; between agonizing bouts in the ditch, he lets fly obscenities and threats and swats his men on their backsides to keep them moving. "There be bread 'n' ale a-plenty in the Dordogne," he says. "The Frenchies in that valley got the sense to welcome good English soldiers. Move yer stinkin' arses."

When Fulk draws level with them, Haukyn says, "Sir, Piers and I still have a small chunk of salt beef, tough as the soles of my boots, but edible—you need to eat."

"Nay, lad, it'd go in one hole 'n' out t'other quicker 'n you can say *squats*. Javyd, Roger, you shiftless buggers, this ain't Sunday on the village green, pick them boots up."

And so they stagger on toward a town called Ussel, and what if there's hay to spare in Ussel, hay Modge could have eaten had she but lasted a few days more?

The rivers are fewer, to the relief of carpenters and soldiers, the water less turgid and more palatable, to the relief of all. Even the rain has eased off, and the thought skitters through Haukyn's brain that he and Piers might reach Bordeaux alive. Buoyed up by the sight of a sturdy bridge already in place across the next river, he almost smiles as a knight, his armour clanking and creaking, limps past him to drink. A surprise the man has survived, for most knights, sensibly, have abandoned their armour, some bashing the steel plates with rocks so no French soldier can use them. This knight has lost jupon but naught else. He kneels awkwardly, wavers, grabs for the bank, and with a screech overbalances. Haukyn dumps bedroll and bowstave, darts forward, drops to his knees, and grasps the slippery, steel-clad ankles, halting their slide toward the racing waters of the river. Bracing himself, he tugs with all his strength, not enough strength. He puts his back into it and the knight babbles, "Save me, save me, Almighty Lord, save me."

"Dig your gauntlets into the bank—push backward!"

Piers and Javyd seize the knight's shoulders. Grunting with effort, they lever him back on level ground. He raises his head in its heavy helmet, and only then does Haukyn realize that the knight he has saved, the knight leaking water from every seam, is Sir Gardrad. He says breathlessly, "You nearly drowned the three of us, you stupid bastard!"

From behind him, a voice he would recognize anywhere, a cultured voice, says, "Stupid I might agree with, but bastard, nay. His antecedents are impeccable, his mother a second—or is it a third—cousin of mine."

Haukyn stands up, rubbing his back. "Sire," he says.

"*Your Highness* is the correct term," the duke says drily. "What is your name?"

"Haukyn of Flintbourne...my father an archer who fought beside your father at Crécy," and why those particular words?

"I have no doubt he did well that day, as you did this day, Haukyn of Flintbourne, and your friends also. Gardrad, you will toss all but your breastplate in the river."

"Your Highness," Sir Gardrad says. His sunken cheeks flushed with humiliation, he scowls at his rescuers. "You and you, help me up."

Haukyn and Javyd lift him, Haukyn saying blandly, "A word of thanks would not go amiss, and you'll feel better when you're not lugging all that weight."

If a man's eyes could throw daggers, he, Haukyn, would be covered in gore. Sir Gardrad twists his face into an obsequious smile, bowing so deep that more water gushes to the ground. "Your Highness, I had to mortgage my Berkshire demesne to purchase my armour—"

"I recognize two of these archers. When they had horses, they could shoot mounted, an exemplary skill. The matter is closed, Gardrad." He raises his voice. "Make way so I may cross the bridge."

Speaking more to himself than to his fellows, Haukyn says, "We have a rare leader," his admiration unwilling because the same leader has cost him Willem and Modge. Or does his admiration stem from a duke recognizing a villein?

Javyd is a short man, black hairs sprouting from his ears. He says dourly, "What our rare leader gobbles to break his fast would feed me 'n' m' sister fer a week."

"You're not wrong. Yet he keeps his army on the move."

"Easy to rule on a full gut, and what else c'n we do but follow him?" He raises bushy black eyebrows. "Us don't get choices, ain't you worked that out yet?"

"Does it have to be that way?"

Javyd grins, revealing the gaps in an array of oversized, yellowing teeth. "Has been since I were born and will be til I drops."

Gaunt John rules by the steel of his will as much as by the power of rank and vast wealth, Haukyn thinks, a thought he does not share. He understands willpower. If his has its way, he and Piers will tramp into Bordeaux and board the first ship back to England.

...a world wider than the vill...

On the last day of November, the Feast of St. Andrew, after Father Mortimer celebrated Mass, Edmund lingers in the church, his spirit on edge. Before Mass, his wife had lost her temper. Hadn't Robert taken an hour—an hour!—that morning to bring back a pot she'd loaned Johanna because he got talking to Solomon the Small about seed and crops and hay, and hadn't Gil at None the day before left herbs on the ground for the ants to chew, and hadn't Ralf burnt the porridge to cinders two days ago because he was playing with Ranulf, and how was a mother s'posed to put up with such negligence, such waste when every kernel of their oats come from their father's hard work.

Although Edmund has heard variations of this tirade for years and should have shrugged it off, Hawise at his side with her green eyes burning hadn't been a peaceful companion as the Host was raised and the little bells chimed; he'd stayed on his bench when everyone else filed out—Hawise, Robert, and the twins among them—and silence now settles on his good ear.

Worse by far than any mishaps with oats or herbs, they've had no news of Haukyn. The bench digs into his thighs. He can gain no solace from verses, for they have deserted him since Haukyn went to war. The paintings on the church walls, the white lily floating above Mary's rapt face, the solemn-eyed donkey witnessing the birth of the Saviour—solace eludes him there too, and his prayers are worn from repetition. *Keep my son from harm, I beg You, merciful Father, keep him safe.* My impetuous, hot-headed son, who rushes through life hungry for whatever is beyond his reach. So unlike Robert, whose demeanour calms the oxen, whose patience coaxes shoots from soil and digs poppies and cornflowers from the wheat. Too patient, perhaps? Johanna, daughter of Waryn atte Water and one of the vill's alewives, would have married Robert two years ago had he asked; but he'd waited until his younger brother had gone to war. Johanna now ponderous with pregnancy. The thought of a grandchild warms him, and eventually he pushes up from the bench.

Outside, not yet ready to go home, he gazes across the river at his fields. He doesn't own them—how could he, when the king owns all the land in England?—yet he does own them in a manner that no king can. The poor drainage in the assart's back acre, the wide band of clay in the south field that always makes the oxen stumble, the fertility of the Southwaters' acres near the river, which he leased after the plague's first wave, all are his. As also the meadowlarks perched on his fence posts, the first haze of green after the spring sowing, the clouds in the sky that bring rain or hail. His two and a half virgates, his to cherish. As Robert cherishes them, and the twins, nearing their sixth winter, show every sign of doing—farmers to the core, though young, happy with his acres and the earth's yearly promise.

But not Haukyn. Never Haukyn.

A jackdaw swoops low overhead, *chakchak...chakchak*, and he admits to himself something he's never admitted to anyone, not even Hawise: at times he is relieved to be free of the daily sharkskin-rub of Haukyn's presence. Sharkskin smooths wood to a fine finish. But a father's skin? Tis scrubbed raw and heals slow.

Haukyn the boy who'd climbed the highest tree in the lord's woods, been unable to climb down, and was not discovered until his frantic parents had combed riverbanks, fields, and woods in the encroaching darkness. "I wanted to see the world, a world wider than the vill," he'd said, not in the least grateful to be lowered to the ground.

Haukyn the boy who a few days later had run away to Windsor Castle to see the king and been brought back by a tinker on his cart, a man, luckily, of Christian charity.

Haukyn the boy he'd glimpsed climbing the fence that enclosed Solomon's red-eyed bull, jumping to the ground and waving his shirt to gain the bull's attention, then darting to one side of the bull's charge with an agility Edmund more than matched as he'd raced toward the fence and leaped it. Him brandishing his pitchfork, Solomon rattling the feed can, and the bull had been diverted, nostrils flared, light catching on his horns. Another rescue, another scolding.

Haukyn the boy deaf in both ears.

Beneath the fitful sun, as he stands like a stick on the green, he becomes aware that someone is hailing him, a merchant on his way to Bristol, who asks for the name of the nearest inn. From him, Edmund learns the Chancellor lately informed Parliament that John of Gaunt's forces have inflicted much damage on the French, by valiance and astute leadership. Head bent, Edmund fords the river and takes the river path back to his house. Damage involves fighting, and fighting involves death. But if Haukyn had fallen, would he not know, would he not feel the fatal wound in his own flesh?

On a day in late summer, ten years ago or more, he was rounding the corner of his byre when Haukyn ran full tilt into him, both lips split, blood dripping from a nose crooked on his face. Hawise dosed her son with betony and reset it as gently as she could, Haukyn slept the rest of the day, and only then did Edmund sit him down, Haukyn squirming and in no hurry to reveal that there'd been months of blows, taunts, and cruelties, either dealt by Ivo alone, two years older and strong from his work at the forge, or with the help of one or more of the Cat-Skinner brothers, the vill's reprobates. His son stubbornly silent when it came to reasons for the attacks, and Edmund ignorant of all of them, because Haukyn had always run wild and always had excuses for his cuts and bruises...*slipped on the rocks at the ford...tripped over a stump in the woods...fell out of the oak tree...* "I should have known," Edmund remembers saying.

"Wasn't your business," Haukyn had mumbled, and hurt had mingled with the guilt in Edmund's chest.

After that, he undertook to teach his son a number of lowdown tricks that he'd learned from his serjeant in France. Ten days or more of throwing punches, grappling, tripping, and wrestling, and all the while he was aware of the anger behind his son's fists, the force behind his kicks, the hurt far greater than warranted by a few blows.

He hopes Haukyn has remembered every dirty move on the long march through France. Wrestling, though? Punches? Of no value when arrows fly, and why did he stay silent the day his son left for war? Why didn't he protest to the very heavens? *Listen to me*, he should have said. *I never knew my father, my mother couldn't stand the sight of me, and when I was your age I had to scavenge for pottage, steal milk from a cow's udder, eat raw mushrooms. I had to sleep under bracken and the cold stars, rags on my back. Barefoot as oft as not. You have a home, a loving father and mother, food in your belly, a warm hearth in winter, yet you dare run away from that home?*

And why didn't he recount his oath that, because of the atrocities of an earlier war, he never again would kill man, woman, or child? The temptation had been there all too often when plague ravaged Flintbourne, robbing him of his friend Ralph, of Beatrice, the little girl who had been like the sister he'd never had, of Bart, his half-brother, his complicated, brutal, loving half-brother—oh, aye, he'd been tempted to end the horrendous suffering plague brought with it, to kill for the sake of mercy.

But he had not. Nor would he kill again, regardless of what the future held. Why hadn't he impressed upon Haukyn that war makes commonplace that most dread of all acts, the ending of another's life?

Instead, he had kept silent and his son had gone to war.

The army enters the Corrèze in early December, emerging from those hellish forests to the foothills of a plateau called Millevaches. The hilltop town of Ussel, enclosed by two rivers, is held by men loyal to the English cause. From it, raiding parties are sent out, stealing bread, slaughtering French oxen and French sows. The duke's men eat. They burn logs that do not hiss water from the cut ends, the flames flickering over their haggard faces. They are supplied, grudgingly, with hay for their remaining horses. Haukyn, heart-sore, cannot watch. They then muster for John of Gaunt, who is not quite as tight-lipped as a week ago and whose destrier swishes its long black tail and breaks wind with magnificent disdain. Rumour now has it that their leader, after reaching Bordeaux, plans to fight in Spain, to become King of Castile in actuality as well as in name.

Haukyn wants nothing to do with Spain.

After the muster, the army bedraggled but an army nevertheless, Piers kindles another small fire and they roast the ribs of a Corrèze piglet. Javyd belches. "Tulle be west of us 'n' Frenchies hold it, we might have to fight for it," he says, he who keeps both hairy ears to the ground. "Wouldn't mind loosin' an arrow or two—ain't that what we ain't being paid for?" and he cackles at his own wit.

Fulk sits by the fire and is offered a rib bone. "I got news. 'Cause Sir Nigel's dead, we got a new master of our retinue. Sir Gardrad.

Stole hissself a horse north o' here, in Quercy. Gaunt John must've been drunk the day he took that sod on. The last one I'd've chose, but they don't ask me, do they."

"I'd best keep my head down," Haukyn says.

"May his guts rot afore he's dead. All three o' you watch yer backsides, 'cause he don't have no love for any o' you."

"Bluster beneath a breastplate."

"Meanest scut-arse in the army," Fulk says vigorously, "but he be related to our duke, so you heed what I say." He puts the rib bone down. "On the morrow I has to pay fealty to him, kneel down 'n' put m' hands twixt his. Enough to make you puke."

He's left out the oath of fealty, Haukyn thinks, and remembers how some years ago he and all those in the vill's tithing had sworn fealty to their new lord, Sir Mauger, soon discovered to be marvellously lazy and lazily benevolent, as few lords are.

The flames lick the darkness, and Haukyn's belly is full. *Sir Gardrad, with or without breastplate and pilfered horse, is no different from me,* he thinks, *no different from Fulk or Piers or Javyd. We are all men, born under God, we all watch the same sun rise and set, we can all die from a sword-thrust or an arrow in the back, we eat and shit, we laugh and weep and curse, and where's the archbishop or king who can deny it?* Thoughts that have been brewing for days, he realizes, picking a shred of meat from his teeth. He did right to join the army and endure that awful massif; even the loss of Willem and Modge seems less severe, for now he knows how easily knights can be denuded of armour, he knows how their leader has failed to entice battle or seize plunder.

Heady thoughts and exhilarating, nor do they stop there. When he's back in Flintbourne, he'll be a freeman because of his father's bastardy, he'll take up a trade of one kind or another and move to Kintbury, Hungerford, or Newbury, near enough to Flintbourne for visits, yet far enough to live his own life. Tis hard not to blurt all this to the night wind and the two rivers, but a splinter of wisdom warns him to keep his insights close to his chest. Time enough to tell Piers later; in the meantime, he'll decide which trade would please him and where he'd go to learn it.

If only he could board ship for England on the morrow.

Spain? Never.

His resolve hardens as the valley narrows and steepens and their food runs out. The stout gates of Tulle are surrounded by a slow-wreathing mist, through which the army looks impressive: Gaunt John has placed his mounted knights and archers in the fore, banners held high, the trumpets only slightly dampened by that same mist. Haukyn, Piers, and Javyd are in the midguard, their bows strung and swords sharpened. Haukyn's toes are cold. He flexes his fingers to keep them pliant. Javyd says, "Our leader better talk his way through that gate. We might look fearsome in the fog, but we ain't."

Soon enough a white flag is hoisted from the top of the stone walls and hangs limply. A ragged cheer echoes through the army. Yet Tulle yields too little in the way of food, and because the town surrendered, plunder is not allowed. They leave, following the Corrèze to Brive-la-Gaillard, which throws open its gates, its citizens thin as twigs. From there, they traipse down the valley of the Dordogne. Rock and forest and no food to be had. Souliac, Sarlat, men and horses falling by the roadside into the ditches. Piers is in worse shape than Haukyn, muttering incomprehensibly under his breath, his eyes dull with exhaustion. Haukyn urges him onward. "We'll soon be in Bordeaux—Gaunt John says so. Bergerac before Bordeaux, his own possession. You mustn't give up, Piers, not when we're so close and have come so far."

Piers grunts. Haukyn has no way of knowing if he understood, and here he is, offering Bordeaux as though its streets are flowing with milk and honey. What if its inhabitants are like those of Brive-la-Gaillard, and he without a penny to his name?

They pass a small dark chapel, its square tower reminding him of St. Edmund's tower in Flintbourne, houses clustered nearby, another nameless place among so many, and soon afterward make camp.

Pitiful bread rations are apportioned, not enough to keep body and soul together. Piers chews, swallows, rolls himself in his blanket, and closes his eyes. Haukyn lies still, waiting for the darkness to be punctuated only by the snores and fidgets of hungry men, and ponders fealty: tis about obligations, serf to lord and lord to serf, and, according to every lord in the land, represents devotion. He and Modge, each time he swung himself on her back, each time she neatly lowered herself to the ground so he could sleep against her warm bulk, was that not true fealty, acknowledged by each, beneficial to each, and alive with devotion? He feels the prick of tears, blinks them back, and cautiously leaves his bedroll.

Stars overhead, cold and distant, and as always his night vision and sense of direction are blessedly acute. Hood forward, each step placed with care amongst the mounds of sleeping archers, and he's adept at passing between the guards and their little heaps of glowing coals. He retraces the last of the day's journey, and very soon the square-towered chapel looms ahead of him. If he has to, he'll use the point of his dagger to pick the latch, a useful trick taught him, in a rare moment of amity, by Warty Ivo; as a young boy years ago, he used to follow Ivo at dusk, imitating the placement of his feet, his stealth, and twas worth the whap on the ear from his mother when he'd tried to sneak, just as stealthily, into his bed.

The chapel door opens on well-oiled hinges. He freezes, then very quietly slips inside, a palm flat to the door behind him so it closes just as quietly. The red sanctuary lamp hangs over the altar, and with a leap of his pulse he sees, positioned on the altar, a metal chalice. Even from here, he can discern the dull gleam of jewels. Real? Real enough for barter in Bordeaux, he thinks, and steps forward, pouch open. His hand is wrapped around the chalice when a man's voice, coarse, aggressive, shatters the chapel's dusty silence.

Another leap of pulse. The man is, of course, speaking French, words Haukyn has no hope of deciphering.

He doesn't let go of the chalice, though tis a near thing, and slowly turns his head. A priest is standing in the shadows, dark-robed, stocky, a silver crucifix dangling on his chest. Hands moving just as slowly, Haukyn puts the chalice in his pouch, pulls the string, and sifts through his scanty store of French. "*Mon ami…malade…très faim…l'armée faim…*"

Anglais the word for *English* and better omitted.

The priest steps forward, barks a command. *Put the chalice back*, would be Haukyn's guess, and this he will not do; he switches to Latin. "*Absolvat me Deus*," he says and eases his dagger free of its sheath. The red light overhead, which signifies the presence of the Host and therefore the presence of Christ, plays along the blade. He quells a shudder, rams the weapon back where it belongs, and backs away from the altar, feeling for the roughness in the stone floor with the heel of each boot. The houses are too close to the church, one shout from the priest and he'll be in trouble.

"Willem and my beloved horse," he says, "both dead, so many deaths, uncountable deaths, I can't let Piers die, don't you see, I can't—this chalice will buy food in Bordeaux, a passage home, in Christ's name, understand! And in Christ's name, Father, I beg your forgiveness."

In Christ's name…a gabble of anguish loosed to darkness. The crucifix lying against the black habit catches a flash of red as the priest takes another step, this time toward the brass gong suspended from a rope, its hammer lying on the altar. A gong, a warning signal in times of war, one stroke and the vill will wake, its men pour toward the church, and he'll be castrated, beaten to a pulp, torn to pieces. As the priest's hand makes a sudden grab for the hammer, Haukyn lashes out, the punch thrown before he has time to think, terror powering his fist. Crunch of bone to flesh and the priest lurches backward, his harsh cry echoing from the crude stone walls, his head hitting the carved stone that supports the corner of the altar and he lies still, a stillness that Haukyn recognizes all too well.

I've killed a priest. A man of God. I'll be cast into the inferno, into the everlasting flames of Hell, beyond any hope of divine forgiveness.

Blood, dark in the semi-dark, pools on the stone floor.

He whirls and runs for the door, almost expecting an arrow to bury itself in his back, shot by demons hungry for his soul. Open the door, glance left to right, the houses slumbering in the night, and he races for the trees, where he trips over stumps, bare branches slapping face and shoulders, the chalice banging against his thigh. Edmund, his father, his eternal disappointment in his second son, and now the Father above—all he's earned in this world is condemnation, tis all he's worth. He's sobbing, loud, messy sobs, and what's he going to do, rouse the English camp and be hung for thievery from the nearest tall tree?

Piers. Remember Piers. This chalice will save his friend's life, and together they'll board ship in Bordeaux and sail home.

He leans his forehead against the trunk of an oak, the leaves still clinging just as they do in Flintbourne, and tries to still his breathing, the judder of his heart.

I didn't steal for gain, I stole for the sake of love.

Only when his hands are steady enough for him to trace the curves of the chalice in the pouch does he start sneaking between the trees, alert for the guards' banked fires. The tears have dried on his face. Nine years ago, or was it ten, twas after Easter, he sneaking between the lord's trees when he'd heard someone sobbing, ugly sounds as desolate as any he just loosed. He'd edged around a beech tree, crept closer, and peered through the new leaves. Warty Ivo, his back to a hornbeam, one arm nursing the other, the burn on his forearm—tis the shape of a horseshoe. Horrified, Haukyn ducked. Jorden dealt out this punishment to his son, who else.

Ivo'll kill me if he catches sight of me.

He backed up, keeping low, and when he was a safe distance away, ran as if the hounds of Hell were after him. How could a father do that to his son? Doesn't Father Mortimer preach that God, the Almighty Father, is love? On Good Friday that same year, the day of Crucifixion and he curious, he'd held a shiny new nail to the top of his foot and banged it with a hammer til the skin broke and he'd cried from the pain. With nails through hands and feet, hadn't Jesus cried out, at the end, that his Father, his loving Father, had forsaken him?

God as love or Hellfire, wraith or rabid boar?

He feared the answer then, and still does.

When he reaches his bedroll, Piers is lying still. Too still. Kneeling, he pushes back the blanket, hand to Piers's throat, skin warm, pulse faint but there, and in deep relief he gulps from his waterskin, transfers the chalice to the pack he carries over his shoulder, better hid that way, and covers himself in his musty blanket. In his ears, a priest's last cry echoes from a chapel's stone walls.

They pass Limeuil and Piers weakens before his eyes, his mithering decipherable only to Haukyn...*bread, in the name of our Saviour, give me bread...*but when he puts his own scanty ration in Piers's hands, Piers gobbles it then retches, spasms that rasp his throat and produce naught but a thin, yellowing slime. By now, Haukyn walks with one arm around his friend's waist, encouragement all he can offer: "Only Lalinde, so Javyd said last night by the fire, then Bergerac, a place to rest and eat for it belongs to John of Gaunt. After Bergerac, Bordeaux and home, think of Hungerford, think of beauteous Ilotte, you can't let that scut of a constable put his hands on her...home, Piers, home."

His handsome, mercurial friend reduced to bones, a travesty of a man.

They are within a league of Lalinde when Fulk orders him to treat an archer's infected ankle with the last of his mother's herbs. "Piers, I won't be long," he says, "are you listening? Just keep moving, one foot in front of the other. I'll be back as soon as I can."

Hastily he ministers to the archer, whose name he doesn't catch but who mumbles gap-toothed thanks. Haukyn the wise-woman, he thinks, not a trade he'll pursue, and hurries forward, searching for Piers among the ranks of men trudging head down; unable to sight him, he scans the ditch in dread that he should find him there and comes alongside a familiar face. "Javyd, have you seen Piers?"

Javyd is grey-faced. "Dunno. Had to shite, though I ain't eaten a morsel raw or cooked all day. Got to be round here, don't he."

Another archer says, "Staggering along talking to hisself? Headed into the woods, he did. Back past that rock."

Haukyn shoves his way through the army's flank. Beside the rock, Piers's bowstave with its carved nocks lies abandoned. "Piers," he shouts and scrambles up the slope. He shouts again, stops to listen, hears brutish groans. Hand on the haft of his dagger, he bursts into a clearing. Piers is on the ground, legs thrashing at a cluster of young beeches. Haukyn falls to his knees and sees, poking up among the beeches, the torn stems of mushrooms, dark brown caps, pale warts erupting from their surface. In horror he cries, "You didn't eat them, tell me you didn't!"

Fragments of white flesh are scattered on the duff. Piers jabbers something incomprehensible, kicks out, clutches his belly, groans again. Haukyn tries to jam his fingers down his friend's throat and is bitten for his pains. He wrenches his hand free, uncaring if he breaks a tooth, grabs his waterskin, and dashes water in Piers's face. "Open your mouth, you fool, open it!"

Behind him, footsteps. Javyd? "Take his shoulders, we'll lift him and pry his mouth open."

"Leave him where he lies."

He knows that voice. He jerks his head around. Sir Gardrad in his breastplate, accompanied by four archers, two on each side. Haukyn says, "He's dying—help me lift him."

"Let him die. Go back to the army."

"I'll not leave him, you must help me!" He looks straight at one of the archers, a big man with a dent in his helmet and a nose that's been broke. "I beg you, take this arm and I'll take the other."

The man stays where he is, eyes as cold as the French sky. Piers shrieks, clutches his belly, and doubles over in pain, teeth clenched. Frantic, calling on a strength he didn't know he possessed, Haukyn hefts Piers's chest over one knee, pushes his head down, and jabs at his mouth with two fingers.

The knight barks an order and Haukyn is seized from behind. Piers thuds to the ground, writhing in agony. Sir Gardrad says, "Hell's demons have his soul, stay away from him! Take the archer back to Fulk's retinue. In Bordeaux, I'll have him branded and gaoled."

Men roughly tugging at his arms, his shoulders, he can't leave Piers, he won't. Somehow he tears himself free, pivots, knees the broke-nosed archer in the crotch. The man drops, bellowing in pain. Haukyn pulls his dagger from its sheath and crouches. "I'll gut the first one who tries to take me anywhere."

Three more daggers drawn and the men circle him warily. One rushes him, howls as Haukyn's knife slices through his doublet. Before Haukyn can brace himself, his legs are knocked from under him and he's face first in beech leaves, the smell of Flintbourne, he thinks hazily, and kicks out in retaliation. A yelp, a knee digs into his back, his face ground into the dirt, he can't breathe, is this how he'll die, choking on duff? His head spinning, he gets his fists under him and heaves upward.

A boot hard to his ribs. "Get him to his feet."

Haukyn finds himself upright, though his legs aren't convinced they'll keep him there. Piers is still breathing, short hoarse gasps; of a sudden he gives a great cry and convulses, knees to his chest, face unrecognizable. Haukyn says in desperation, "For the love of God, sir, let me go to him. Then lock me in the first gaol we come to."

"Take him away."

One last glimpse over his shoulder and he's being dragged down the slope toward the ditch. The mud is slippery; the archers loosen their grip. He hauls one arm free, swings his fist at the nearest jaw and connects, bone to bone, then he's thrown to the ground, another boot to his ribs—he'll kill these sods first chance he gets.

"What happens here? English soldiers fighting an English archer?"

"Desertion, Your Highness. And disobeying my orders," Sir Gardrad says.

"Let him stand." A pause while John of Gaunt, high on his destrier, surveys Haukyn's filthy face. "Gardrad, this is the man who saved your life."

"I'm no deserter," Haukyn says hotly. "My friend is in the woods, he's dying, he ate the mushrooms we call deadwarts, and your idiot knight won't let me stay with him."

"Go back to your friend, and if he's dying, dispatch him. You," he indicates one of the archers, "go with him and make sure he returns. I shall wait here. My horse is restless, be quick."

Haukyn races up the slope and into the clearing. Piers's body is distorted in the dirt, his face a rictus of pain beyond bearing, his eyes blank. Haukyn crosses himself with fingers that tremble. "Piers, may God have mercy on your soul," he whispers. "*In nomine Patris, et Filii, et Spiritus sancti.*"

Whatever the nature of God, the words bring him consolation.

He kneels down and, as he's done for many others, strokes the sightless eyes closed. Then he scrabbles in the dirt with his bare hands because he won't allow badgers and ravens to tear at his friend's body; Gaunt John can wait for once, it'll be good for him. He dumps the dirt over Piers's shoulders, digs deeper, and hits a sharp-edged rock with his nails, his own yelp shocking him. Blood drips to the ground. None of his mother's herbs left to quench its flow, and he didn't think he had a drop of blood left in him.

"Stop, lad, not even the knights who've died in the ditches've warranted a grave."

He looks up. This archer is older than the other three, his beard grizzled; he'd stood back when the others were dealing out punishment, and now he scoops up an armload of duff, spreading the leaves over Piers's ankles. Beech leaves whose veins are straight as arrows. "You cover his head," he says, "I'll cover his feet 'n' legs. Tis all we can do."

Haukyn stares at him. The archer adds, "We'd best hurry else our mighty leader'll be out o' patience."

"Sir Gardrad also."

"Him? He ain't got none o' the seven virtues. Get to work now."

Haukyn gathers an armload and lets it spill over Piers's head. Together they collect more dead leaves, blanketing the dead man's body with the damp smell of decay. "I...my thanks," Haukyn says huskily.

The archer nods and they slide down the slope toward Gaunt John, who still sits high on his destrier. Heart afire, Haukyn gazes at the reins, their tooled leather, their design of ivy leaves whose stems are intricately interwoven. Had he thought the duke would dismount so they could meet eye to eye?

John of Gaunt says, "Look at me."

Hours of work to engrave those leaves. "Look up, you mean."

"Your friend is dead?"

"He died without me at his side, thanks to a knight who lacks both gratitude and Christian charity."

"I happen upon your deeds too frequently, Gardrad," the duke says, steel sheathed in his voice. "There will be no reprisals for this episode. Now, move up the column to your assigned place." He turns his attention back to Haukyn. "You speak well for an archer."

For a serf, that's what Gaunt John means. "My father was tutored in grammar and speech by a squire at the siege of Calais. I can both read and write."

"And shoot French soldiers at a gallop. An archer of many talents. Gardrad has manors in your shire, you will be neighbours when you return."

"Have you other bad news?"

Hauteur at his levity thins the duke's lips. "Allow me to tell you that Gardrad has two sons only, one born with crooked legs, the other a crooked back—a sorrow to him and his wife. If you have any compassion, you might forgive his...excesses."

"My friend Piers was from your manor in Hungerford, he died far from home, alone and in agony. I have no more compassion for Sir Gardrad than he had for Piers. As for his sons, villeins thus afflicted would be reduced to begging in the streets."

"You are impertinent!"

"When truth is regarded as impertinence, we all become court jesters." He sounds like his father, playing with words; he's unsure which is uppermost, admiration for his own audacity or discomfiture from the likeness.

Gaunt John flicks his reins against the destrier's shoulder. "You'd best contain your fires, Haukyn of Flintbourne, or you will be scorched. Return to your retinue."

"You'd best check Bordeaux's gaols, Your Highness, where your knight's branding iron would have me scorched."

"Go!"

So, finally, he's punctured that noble hide. Haukyn turns away and merges without haste into the column of men. His torn nail is still bleeding.

Red of blood, a sanctuary lamp glowing red, a dead priest in a dark stone chapel. *Nay*, he thinks, *nay*. But Piers, no matter how hungry, was a man of the countryside. What would have driven him to eat deadwarts if not the vengeance of Almighty God?

...foot up, foot down...

Fulk catches up with him before they reach Lalinde. "I heard what happened to Piers from one o' Gardrad's archers. Hell's mouth'll gulp Gardrad, you wait 'n' see."

Violently, Haukyn sweeps his arm so it encompasses knights in rusty armour, skeletal horses, and stumbling men. "Sir, what is all this *for*?"

"For?" Fulk frowns. "Tis war, you ninny. 'Gainst the Frenchies. You obeying me and me obeying Sir Gardrad and him obeying our good duke. What else d'you think it's for?"

"I'm done with obedience. And with war."

The frown deepens. "None o' that talk."

"Bow, dagger, sword, I'll not lift them again! Throw me in gaol before Sir Gardrad does, brand me as coward, chain me as deserter—I don't give a rat's arse what you do." He grips his captain by the wrist. "Fulk, don't you see the folly of this march, its futility? No battles, no plunder, no ransoms. No garrisons set up to hold the territories we've raided. For certain, no French throne for our king. We've accomplished naught from Calais to Limeuil, and at what cost? Half the men and most of the horses." His voice catches in his throat. "If this is war, you can keep it, you and the mighty Duke of—"

With his free hand, Fulk slaps him hard across the face. "Keep yer voice down! You want to be hanged for treason?"

Stupefied by the blow, Haukyn gingerly rubs his nose and lowers his voice. "I tell you, I'm done."

"You'll fight at Lalinde or I'll have your balls on a platter for m' dinner."

"Only *your* dinner? You think them so small?"

"You be too clever for them boots o' yourn. Obey my orders at Lalinde's gates 'n' don't think o' desertion—though if you did, French peasants'd be quick enough to make a girl o' you, which'd save me the trouble."

Haukyn watches him stride away and, reluctantly, begins to think. He knows the reasoning behind the *chevauchées*: destroying crops and livestock means fewer taxes for the French crown and therefore smaller French armies. When it comes to English archers, those left in his retinue owe their lives to Fulk, who's harried them from one coast in the north toward another in the south. Mother hen with her chicks, he thinks with wintry humour, the captain a good man—he's not so far gone he doesn't realize that. He peers down at his sore nose and wonders how he'll comport himself at the gates of Lalinde.

The river Dordogne flows wide and shallow at Lalinde; stone walls surround the town, crossbowmen line them, and the six gates are locked. Haukyn stands with his troop, Fulk nearby, and discovers when they're ordered to shoot that he cannot purposely miss bowmen who have as targets his fellows, men who have travelled with him since late summer and many of whom he knows by name. *I'm naught but a bag o' wind*, he thinks, *and holy Mary, I wish Piers were beside me.*

He aims, an archer on the ramparts topples, and he aims again.

The engineers breach one of the gates. The army streams into the town, close-pressed French soldiers facing them who know there'll be no quarter should they surrender. A soldier charges him, sword raised; Haukyn parries, thrusts, and the man's down. A pollaxe whips through the air, misses his shoulder by a feather's width, another jab with his sword, another man down, and as battle-noise deafens him, he sees Javyd cornered by five Frenchmen. He rushes forward and with bloodied sword slaughters two men, Javyd kills the third, and the two left alive take to their heels. Javyd grins at him, black brows bristling. "I could've killed 'em all, but you was a help—I'm going after them two we missed."

Among the houses and warehouses the burning has started.

Smoke stings Haukyn's nostrils. From the corner of his eye he sees a little boy dart into an alley, an English archer chasing him. He races after them. The boy is trapped by a pile of chicken cages, he's the age of the twins but emaciated, scabby, his eyes huge with fear. The archer raises his sword. Haukyn throws himself at him and knocks him to the ground. "Run!" he shouts to the boy, and the boy pushes himself off the cages and runs, though how far Haukyn has no way of knowing. He says unevenly, "For Christ's sake, kill men not little-uns," and pulls the archer to his feet.

"I got two daughters 'n' a son, but Sir Gardrad tol' us to kill every Frenchie on legs. This sodding war," the archer says and heads for the gap in the alley.

Left alone, Haukyn sags against the pile of cages. Men on the battlefield can wear two faces, he thinks: the ferocity to survive at any cost, or the absence of all humanity, replaced by something he's never been able to name. Or are the two faces one? Into his mind drops the image of a millwheel, driven by unseen currents, crushing the ripeness of grain to dust.

Has he, by saving a little boy, offered atonement for a priest's death and for his many other killings?

He'd give ten bushels of wheat to be back in Flintbourne.

Sword in hand, he leaves the alley, enters another narrow street, swerves past some steps, and nigh trips over three dead bodies, one an English knight. No one watching. He hauls off the knight's jupon and tugs it over his leather doublet, listens for the worst screams, and hurries that way. A woman is being dragged by the hair from her house. He shouts, "You're to surround the church, go!"

"Sir!" The soldier drops the woman and runs.

Haukyn picks her up and props her against the wall. She's young, as thin as the little boy, and might once have been pretty. "The gate—*porte*."

She gawks at him. Gripping her by the elbows, he points in the direction of the toppled gate. "*Allez!*"

"*Ma fille...*"

A girl-child is huddled against the frame of the door. He lifts her, her little fists pummelling his chest. "Follow me," he says and heads for the gate, the woman's breath catching in her throat as they step over bodies in streets temporarily deserted. When they reach it, he lowers the little girl to the ground. "*Benedicite*," he says.

"*Dieu vous bénisse*," and she's gone.

Back along the alley, him conjuring what he'll say should he bump into Sir Gardrad, and then, Heaven help him, a real knight, a stranger to him, Sir Geoffrey at his side; he ducks out of sight, strips off his borrowed finery, and by using his wits contrives to rejoin the tail end of the army without mishap. His sword is bloodstained. Evidence enough that he's done what he's been ordered to do.

Tis Roye all over again. The fighting done, the church burning, the terrible screams of those caught in the flames, and he cannot save them.

By evening, the army's few remaining cooks have used Lalinde wheat to bake bread, which varlets deliver together with dried herring purloined from a stone warehouse and barrels of French ale; they all eat and drink around their campfires. Now that Haukyn's supply of herbs is gone, he is no longer called upon to tend the wounded, a deliverance he's glad of. Chewing the salty flakes of fish, he watches the flames dance, small flames that are contained by the stones of a makeshift hearth.

Fulk is eyeing Haukyn with suspicion. "You shot as true on foot as on horseback, but I lost you in the thick o' the fighting."

"I was there, sir. I had to clean my sword afterward, did I not?"

He downs more ale, debates if he should drink himself into oblivion, and decides it's not worth the morrow's bust-head. He's one of the first to roll himself in his blanket that night, turning his back on the coals, his appeased hunger a reproach. Despair wraps itself around him, the heaviest of blankets, one not altogether new to him but never before so weighty. Aye, he saved a boy, a mother, and her girl-child, but to what end? Lalinde's scanty stores went to feed the English army, none left for fugitives, no foraging possible in the December woods, and marauders everywhere. From the hope of atonement, he but added to their suffering.

Dieu vous bénisse. Where is blessing to be found?

The army advances to Bergerac, a town in English hands yet with no vittles to spare. They do not linger there but continue south and west toward Bordeaux, and as this final leg of their journey begins, Haukyn retreats into silence, unreachable by either jests or anger. Fulk gives up on him, barely disguising a seasoned soldier's disgust that his best archer should succumb to melancholy. Javyd walks alongside, telling long, meandering stories rich with obscenities, seeming not to mind that Haukyn pays him no heed.

Foot up, foot down, foot up, foot down, each step speaking of futility and death, and distantly he's irked that he cannot brush aside the grind of hunger. The ditch beckons, with its promise of oblivion. The chalice bumps against his ribs. Foot up, foot down. On the second night, bundled in his blanket, shivering and wretched, he tries to recall the psalm that was his father's favourite. He paid too little attention in Flintbourne's church, twas something about a valley in the shadow of death and the comfort of God...*I feel no comfort, for there are too many with me in that valley, a scab-faced little boy, a woman who once was pretty, the fists of her child beating on my chest, and my own heart won't stop beating*...and here his thoughts come to an end and he lies with his eyes wide-held to keep the dead away, and the cold seeps into his bones.

In the morning, Javyd refuses to budge until Haukyn has swallowed the day's bread ration and refilled his waterskin. "Gaunt John, who ain't gaunt like us, him on his big-bollocked horse, he tol' us last night we covered three leagues like we was supposed to clap 'n' cheer. You ignored him like you ignore me, you ain't bothered that he be prince and I be naught. Now get bloody moving, will you."

Foot up, foot down. The bread worsens the hunger. Tis dawn, and for a moment Willem's dour face is in front of him. He stumbles. Javyd grabs his elbow. Foot up, foot down. The short daylight hours pass in a daze of unrelieved misery. And then his boots rattle some loose stones and he's back in Flintbourne where once, years ago, he spent a whole night in his hideaway near the big oak, swaddled in a blanket stolen from the cooper's wife. He can't remember why. Was he fleeing an evening trip to the well? The chickens' empty trough? Or was he hiding from Warty Ivo? After he'd come up with the idea of a hideaway and he'd started tunnelling into the bushes, he sometimes felt as though someone was watching him; Ivo had never bothered him there, so he must have been mistaken. His hideaway, the fierce thorns that kept out trespassers, the hidden entrance, the rim of little flintstones he'd picked from the river, his river, its waters cool and clear, its soft chuckle as it slid between its banks. No one knew where his hideaway was, it was his and his alone, and without fail he felt safe there.

That night when he lies down in the folds of his blanket, he closes his eyes and walks through the lord's woods to the oak tree where acorns lie glossy on the ground. After checking that he's alone, he edges into the bushes. The little stones encircle him. He lies down, tucks his knees to his chest, and drifts into sleep.

For the next three days of marching, he never leaves that circle of small stones, eating his bread ration there, drinking from his waterskin, soothed by the river's gentle flow, so well known, so much a part of him. Javyd's bawdy jokes pass unheard, the chalice is forgotten, he cares not where they're going, because, like that little boy, he's safe.

Bordeaux, a ragged cheer from a ragged army, trumpets out of tune, the drums nattering beneath faded banners waving in a bitter wind.

Tall stone buildings, a mighty cathedral, wide streets through which waft whispers of plague, and a port where there will be ships bound for England. John of Gaunt's starving, unpaid army is permitted no plunder; food and drink are so costly as to be beyond reach; and no one in the city welcomes them. Desertions abound.

Although it has rained for the last few hours, stray bursts of sunlight are now brightening the sky. Haukyn steps over an unruffled puddle, glances down, and sees a face—a skull—Jesu, it cannot be him. The face moves in a fearful grimace. He steps backward. The little rim of flintstones that have kept him safe blur in his vision, the blackthorns thin, and he sees a man at his side, bushy-browed, dirt embedded in his wrinkled skin.

"Ain't we a sight," the man says. "God's gullet, what I wouldn't give for a drink o' strong-brewed ale. The Frenchies here be our friends, so says our mighty leader, 'n' have you ever knowed him to lead us astray?" He sniggers and jabs Haukyn's ribs. "If you forgot m' name, the fog you been in, tis Javyd."

No flesh on Haukyn's ribs—the jab, though brief, was painful. Irritably, he swats Javyd's fingers and looks around, taking his time. He's hungry. A merchant, his back to them, must have heard news of the army and is closing his shopfront. "Javyd," he mutters. "Over there. Knock down the crates and run."

Javyd strolls across the cobbles, Haukyn at his heels. Clatter of wood, Haukyn grabs the loaf resting on the counter, and they both take to the nearest alley, the merchant shouting after them, furiously and incomprehensibly. Another alley, a narrow street, no sounds of pursuit. Javyd says, "You got yer uses when you wakes up. Pass me a chunk o' that bread afore I drops dead on the cobbles."

Weak at the knees, head swimming, Haukyn hands over the loaf. Fresh bread. Two slow-chewed mouthfuls and he's done. Javyd eyes his pack. "If you got summat hid in there, now be the time fer us to pawn it. Else we'll be living off that loaf til kingdom come."

He says vaguely, "Open it."

Javyd takes out a metal chalice set with dull stones. In a flood of grief so intense that he cries out, Haukyn grips Javyd's sleeve. "I stole it. For Piers. Passage to England once we reached Bordeaux."

"Bordeaux is where we be, 'n' I'll come with you so you don't lose yer pizzle in the deal. Down by the waterfront, that's where pawn shops be—Gaunt John won't be hanging round there. Follow me."

At the waterfront, the elusive scent of brine mingles with the ripe odour of a much-used river. "Where's the sea?" Haukyn says stupidly.

Javyd points north. "This here river's the Garonne. It joins up with a bigger one, and you got to sail from here on the outgoing tide—I been here before with the Black Prince's army, now them raids was worth the time o' day." He plays with the hairs in his ear. "I don't like the looks o' that shop, too many scuffs loitering nearby. Let's try the next one." After scrutinizing a second shop, he tows Haukyn inside. Thick layers of dust, dark crannies smelling of mould and sewage, and on a wobbly wooden table, piles of salt-crusted rope and vicious-looking hooks. A rusted ploughshare hangs from the ceiling.

A ploughshare. Even here I can't get away from them.

"The chalice, Haukyn. We ain't got all day."

He takes it from the pack, dull jewels, duller metal…a priest's skull cracked open, and bile rises in his throat. Javyd dickers in a mix of broken English and ill-spoken French until he's satisfied, sweeps the coins off the counter, and dumps them in Haukyn's pouch. "I wouldn't trust this fellow the length of m' tarse. You be a fine archer 'n' a decent thief, Haukyn o' Flintbourne, but can you hold yer end up in a street brawl?"

"Aye," Haukyn says, "I can," and is gripped, fleetingly, by memory. The boys in the vill, led by Warty Ivo, used to mock him for his father's screams and for his own clever speech, ganging up on him until one day, rushing homeward with a split lip and a broke nose, he rounded the byre and ran full tilt into his father. Anger chased sorrow across Edmund's scarred face as he reached for the cloth in his belt and gently stemmed the blood dripping down Haukyn's chin. "I too had a nose broke. Your mother will set it for you and give you something for the pain. On the morrow, I'll teach you how to defend yourself, lessons I learned in the army because there were soldiers who resented my skill with a bow and the dainty way I talked."

Over the next week, Haukyn was tutored in any number of lowdown tricks, and very soon the Cat-Skinner boys and even, once or twice, Warty Ivo were more guarded around him. This should have brought him closer to his father; yet was not Edmund the cause of his troubles?

Javyd says sharply, "Pay attention, this ain't no time for yer head to be in the clouds. If there be trouble, use yer fists. No knives, else we'll dangle at a rope's end."

He heads for the door. The shop owner gives Haukyn an evil glare, and to his own surprise, Haukyn glares back. Outside, he takes a deep breath of river air, letting it fill his ribcage.

Three men are loosely strung across the street, blocking the way to the cogs and carracks moored downriver, and drunk enough to be belligerent. For the first time in days, Haukyn straightens his shoulders. The money in his pouch will pay for him and Javyd to sail home, and no louts in a foreign city are going to rob them of that. "Are they English or French?"

"Do it matter? Only three of 'em, we can take 'em easy."

The men are twenty paces away. To Haukyn's consternation, Javyd breaks into a sprint, bawling, "St. George! St. George!" at the top of his lungs.

Laughing like a lunatic, Haukyn yells, "St. George for England and King Edward!" and heads straight for the largest of the three men, who has a purple-veined face like poor Sir Nigel's and reeks of stale wine. Haukyn flings a punch, feints to the left, then chops brutally at the drunkard's unguarded throat. The man collapses to the cobbles, heaving for breath like a stunned ox.

Javyd, crouched, is baiting the other two when to his horror Haukyn sees the gleam of a dagger and in a moment out of time knows that Javyd must not die, Javyd who kept him moving from Bergerac to Bordeaux, who shoved maggoty bread down his throat and regaled him with lewd stories and has not been thanked for any of it. *Go toward a knife*, his father told him all those years ago. He ducks the swing of the dagger, not quick enough, flash of pain to his arm, and he grabs the man's wrist, bends it til he bays in agony and the knife clangs to the cobbles. Knee to his testicles and he drops too. Javyd has delivered a mean left hook to an unshaven jaw, the third man down. Haukyn reaches for the knife, watching, astonished, the drip of blood to the cobbles through the long slash in his sleeve.

"Now that were a goodly brawl," Javyd says with deep satisfaction, "and who be this lot coming late to our rescue?"

Haukyn is still bent forward. He's half-starved, why wouldn't he be light-headed and him bleeding like a stuck pig in November. He drags in air with its hints of brine, clasps his other hand over his sleeve, and looks up. Four men, one of whom he recognizes, all of them underfed.

Sir Geoffrey says, "Twould seem St. George was on your side, Haukyn of Flintbourne." His eyes sharpen. "Though you bleed. Ansel, would you bind his arm."

One of the archers steps forward. From his pack he takes a strip of linen; efficiently, if heartlessly, he peels back the slit sleeve and ties the cloth tight around Haukyn's forearm. River and houses turn in slow circles. Haukyn sits down hard on the cobbles, head between his knees.

Javyd says in genuine alarm, "Don't go and die on me now, you bonehead. Not this close t' home."

A courteous voice says, "Who is your companion, Haukyn?"

"Javyd." He looks up. "A faithful friend."

Sir Geoffrey nods. A faithful knight, Haukyn thinks muzzily, and doubtless loyal to John of Gaunt, Duke of Lancaster, who does not tolerate deserters.

One of the three archers digs a toe in the largest man's ribs. "Go back to the tavern you come from," he says. Two of the men stagger away; the third is boisterously snoring.

Javyd hauls Haukyn to his feet. "Look lively now. You ain't the dog's dinner, not yet."

Haukyn tries to gather his wits. "Sir, I have money for passage to England…and aye, I am a deserter from the duke's army. You once said I could come to you for help, should I need to…I appeal for your silence until the cog has sailed."

"I sail for England and will take you with me, neither of you in shape for a Spanish campaign. The third cog down, her name *Fair Magda*—poetic licence, as you will discover. But she has provisions enough, and we leave on the morrow's tide. Ansel will lead you there and show you your bunks, and I'll clear your indentures with the duke. My own was up a fortnight ago."

"I ain't going, sir," Javyd says. "I'll finish m' twelve months, in hopes the duke'll dig in his velvet pockets and come up with m' pay."

Sir Geoffrey stifles a smile. "God be with you," he says, and he and two of his archers stride away.

Ansel eyes Haukyn with no degree of brotherhood. "Follow me."

"What's yer hurry?" Javyd says, scowling at him. "Haukyn, I lives in London on Budge Row with m' sister, Petronilla. Ask fer Javyd atte Fermour, which be a fancy name for m' job. You come to the city in March, 'n' I'll be right glad to see you."

Haukyn steadies his voice with an effort. "You helped tip my mare into the ditch, Javyd, and these last days you saved my life— I'd have fallen by the wayside if not for you. I thank you, and in March, I'll come to London." He might take up a trade as a freeman there, he thinks with a quiver of excitement that cuts through pain, exhaustion, and hunger. "God keep you."

"God ain't done so bad so far, nor you ain't half-bad in a brawl." With a yellow-toothed grin, he buffets Haukyn on the shoulder, nearly knocking him down, and marches away.

"Hurry up," Ansel says.

"Are you a cold man by nature, or is there something about me you don't care for?"

Ansel curls his lip. "Sir Geoffrey picks up strays as other knights pick up mugs o' wine, 'n' they been known to suck him dry."

"I brought his cousin's body back from a raid, and he was most grateful that he could give him proper burial. His act is one of reciprocity, not charity."

"Oh," says Ansel, and the smallest of smiles lightens his eyes.

When shown his bunk on the cog, Haukyn is given a pillow and a thick blanket he's not sure he would otherwise have received.

The next morning, *Fair Magda* leaves Bordeaux on the first tide.

PART TWO

1374–1378

Haukyn stands at the top of the narrow track that leads from the Windsor road into Flintbourne. Dusk on a January day, and beneath a sky that presages snow he sees the two stone buildings of his vill, St. Edmund's church with its square bell tower and the lord's manor with its moat. What were his father's thoughts when he arrived home from a different war? Arrived with a purse full of silver, whereas he, to his shame, has but eight coins to his name, remnants of a gift from Sir Geoffrey. He's hungry and tired, as bedraggled as any vagabond.

He scratches the back of his neck. Once proof of bastardy is provided to hallmote, he can go his own way, learn a trade, and live anywhere he likes. He'll be free. Free to make choices, to live in a manner that won't daily drain his will.

Free, as Piers and Willem are not. *Dead*, the very sound of the word is oppressive. His father, over the years, has in all likelihood rhymed it, tidily, with *lead*.

Did he himself not take any possibility of choice from every serf he shot, from every soldier and citizen he killed in field and town? Choices that were limited, aye, rye bread or maslin, sard or swive, laugh or weep. Choices, nevertheless...and the faraway bell that sounds to his ears is a death knell. He shudders, as though the cold has invaded his heart.

He and Edmund are the same, for he, like his father, will never again kill man, woman, or child. Awkwardly he bows his head and crosses himself, marking an oath that must have been brewing for weeks. Strange that he had to reach Flintbourne's tofts and crofts for it to surface.

Enough swithering, Haukyn. Two deep, fortifying breaths and he starts down the track. The village green is deserted where he first shot arrow from bow, the stones of the ford greasy with ice. Along the river path, up the hill—to his relief he meets no one—and there's the house at the edge of the assart, candlelight glowing through a half-open shutter, lazy smudge of smoke against a night-gathering sky. The Yule wreath by the door, the two rain barrels, the swallows' nests under the eaves—the familiarity of it all catches at his throat.

Had he, in some dim recess of his brain, thought he'd find only charred rafters?

Barking, Ranulf races around the corner of the house, skids to a halt in front of him, sniffs the air, and, his whole body wagging, jams his nose into Haukyn's crotch. The spell is broken. Laughing, Haukyn stoops while his face, neck, and hands are slathered, the dog whining in pure joy; would that all welcomes be as simple.

A bucket bangs against wood. Startled, he walks closer, Ranulf nudging his heels. His mother is at the stye, tipping slops into the pigs' trough. Their biggest sow has been called Melicent for as long as he can remember, he doesn't know why.

"Ma," he says in a cracked voice.

Her body goes still. Very slowly she turns her head. The bucket clunks to the ground, then she's running toward him. Arms clinch his waist, her face burrows in his doublet. He holds her close—her waist has thickened, though he will never tell her so—and realizes she's weeping. "Don't cry, Ma, I'm home."

"Haukyn," she says, "Haukyn," as if his name were a prayer. She raises drenched green eyes. "You be thin as a stick, didn't they feed you in the army?"

"I was waiting for the best pottage in France or England."

Through her tears, Hawise snorts like Melicent the sow. He adds huskily, "I haven't washed since Portsmouth, you'll have to toss me in the river with a bar of lye."

"We worried you was dead and here you be... Edmund, see who's come home."

Haukyn looks over his shoulder. Edmund says quietly, "Praise God."

Praise God that I am alive though Willem, Piers, and Modge lie dead and unburied?

Nay, Haukyn, start afresh, the gulf twixt us can be mended, for I will be a freeman with a trade, and we will deal kindly with each other.

"Father," he says and as his mother eases her grasp, he holds out his arms. Edmund walks into them and drops his scarred cheek to Haukyn's shoulder. He's aged, his cropped curls greyer than the winter sky, though his grip is as strong as a much younger man's. His father, gifted with words, and today silent, just as he was the day Haukyn left.

The embrace goes on too long. Haukyn's nerves tense. He says, striving for ease, "Where's Robert? And the twins?"

The silence thickens, Hawise the one to break it. "The twins be sleeping, wore out from picking flint all day."

"And Robert?"

Edmund straightens, still clutching Haukyn's sleeves; the sleeve that was knifed was neatly mended by a Portsmouth seamster. He says, "Robert is dead."

The shock runs through Haukyn's body. "*Robert?* My brother? But—he so young and healthy?"

As though speaking by rote, Edmund says, "Early in December he was given permission to fell an elm on the ridge. The axe slipped, cut into his thigh. The wound got infected and none of Hawise's remedies was of use. His leg swelled. Fever, chills, he couldn't get enough air, he sweated, he raved, then he went quiet, his fingers picking at the covers...and he died."

Hawise says in a broken voice, "Naught I could do. We even searched for a surgeon, worthless though they be, but there weren't one in reach."

Edmund says heavily, "But you are home, Haukyn. Tis a great blessing that I have you, my second son."

The words escape before he can stop them. "You've lost your true son."

Edmund goes rigid in his arms. "Never say that again. Never."

The ground is heaving beneath Haukyn's feet, just as it did the first two days in Portsmouth after he'd disembarked from the cog. His mother says, "Look at you, half-dead yourself. Come inside by the hearth and I'll heat some pottage."

He manages a semblance of a smile. "The privy first, Ma. Army food and my gut were too oft at odds. Then I'll come inside and be glad to."

On the hard seat, he studies the wooden door in the half-dark. Robert the one to fashion it, he, Haukyn, helping him smooth the splinters with sharkskin, sawdust drifting through the air. Robert, always there, calm and easygoing, his big brother. He drops his head to his hands. How can he pray for his brother's soul to a God who takes and takes and gives so little back, to a God who avenged a priest's death by enticing Piers to gobble poison? In early December, though, when Robert died, the priest was still alive. So Robert perished as others have, careless stroke of a sharp blade and the end writ clear.

How old was he when Robert led him to the orchard so he could learn how to prune their apple trees? He liked climbing the ladder to the tall branches and being surrounded by sky, as far from soil and weeds as he could get, and he tried hard to listen. But he'd rather have been playing skittles or trailing Warty Ivo around the vill; he forgot to check the direction of the buds, a branch got in his way and snapped, and even Robert's patience was tested that day. "Haukyn," he said, "listen to me. This is our task, now. This bud, these clippers, this tree, *now* is what we have, and tis more than enough."

Now is gone for Robert, and he'd paid so little attention that day. Ivo rather than Robert? Skittles preferable to his brother? He'd had fewer brains than Wortle Dill, and if he doesn't get off this seat his butt will have a circle engraved on it.

Inside the house, flames are licking the pot on the hearth. His place is set at the table as if he'd never been away. Rich smell of pottage, warmth curling around his cold feet, and he sits down hard on the bench, an ordinary meal an ambush as dangerous as any French peasant. "Not too much, Ma," he says, "I lost my appetite in France."

Edmund says evenly, "Should commissioners or stewards come looking for you, would you go again to war?"

"Never."

He hadn't meant to sound so vehement. His father says, "A goodly choice."

Choice, that word again. Hawise thunks a steaming bowl in front of him and says tartly, "Goodly, aye, ten months too late." She's carved a generous slab of bread, and beside his spoon is a dish of butter with a knife. Butter, how long since he saw butter, and why can't he feel hungry, he who not long ago was starving?

"Once the cog left Bordeaux's estuary, we hit the bay's waves, and I spent the next eight days with my head in a bucket," he says and briefly describes Sir Geoffrey. "He paid for an inn in Portsmouth so I could rest and clean myself up before walking home. His estate is in Essex, so he sailed on to Dover. A kindly man who has my fealty."

Because he knows Edmund will not ask about the war, he adds, "Twas one long *chevauchée* from Calais to the Bourbonnais, but by then it was October, too late for harvests, and food scant. When we reached Bordeaux just before Christ's Mass, we'd lost half the men and nearly all the horses, mostly to hunger and disease." His voice catches. "Willem, Piers, and Modge among them—I'll tell the twins my mare was killed by a crossbow bolt, an untruth, but well meant." He picks up his story. "From Calais south, the French king was too wily to fight a battle, always keeping his army twixt us and Paris. So we won no plunder and no glory." He butters the bread, doggedly chews the first mouthful, and swallows. "I'll gain back what I lost, but it will take time."

Edmund nods, dark blue eyes meeting sea-blue. "Aye, it takes time. Hawise, pour the man a mug of ale…we have happier news, Haukyn. A few weeks after you left, Robert married Johanna atte Water. She was with child, and bore twins late in Advent, a boy and a girl, your mother as midwife. All three do well."

"Took supper to her, didn't I," Hawise says. "I'll do so for the days to come too, 'cause I remember how it were with twins, if one were quiet, t'other were yawping. You'll see our twins soon enough, they wake afore the cockerel."

Edmund says, "Robert and I cleared more land, and with the help of Martin-by-the-Lane, the vill's carpenter, we built a house to the north of our assart, with a shed for brewing her ale—Johanna's the vill's best alewife. You'll see it in the morning."

"That is good news," Haukyn says, and swallows a mouthful of pottage. "I never tasted better in France, Ma."

She cuffs him. "Edmund, bring in water to heat, 'n' I'll find the soap. I wants to be certain this scruff by the hearth be m' son."

After he's eaten as much as he can, Hawise wages war on the lice on his scalp. "Did John o' Gaunt have lice?"

"He rode too high on his warhorse for me to check—ouch!"

"Hold still."

"He was the worst and best of leaders," Haukyn says, "and don't ask me to explain that, because I don't think I can."

"Here be lavender soap, hot water, 'n' a scrub brush. Start with your scalp 'n' work down. Put your clothes in this sack, I'll burn most of 'em at daybreak." With a face screwed in disgust, she flicks his knee with her fingers. "Fleas 'n' lice enough that your hose'd walk out the door by theirselves," she says. "I'm off to bed." She kisses him on the cheek, she who was always chary with her kisses. Even tonight, weary as he is, it amuses Haukyn that although Edmund has successfully tutored his children in proper speech, he's never removed Savernake Forest from his wife's tongue.

Edmund fetches another pot of water and adds more wood to the fire. "Don't spare the soap or Hawise'll have my hide in the morning."

Haukyn dunks his head in gloriously warm water, works up a lather with the soap, and dunks it again. Armpits, shoulders, chest, and Edmund says, "The wound on your arm looks clean, but have your mother look at it on the morrow."

"A brawl in Bordeaux."

The house is quiet save for the fire's chatter and the slop of water, he and his father enclosed by the circle of light from the hearth. Hips, genitals, thighs, he wraps a towel around his waist, sits on the bench, and immerses his feet, closing his eyes. Crack of a spark, soft collapse of coals. Only when the water has cooled does he dry his feet and pull on the clean braies his mother left on the bench. Robert's. They sag around his hips. As he tugs on the cord, a small burst of flame cast shadows over his father's scarred face. Haukyn says, "I told John of Gaunt you fought with his father at Crécy."

Edmund's eyes flick to his, flick back to the neat pile of twigs at his feet. "A fine fighter was our king. Those days long gone."

"Late at night somewhere in the Massif Central I came across two serfs in the woods who were watching their mastiff maul an archer. One of the serfs was laughing. I killed them both, and the mastiff. The archer died." His voice sinks a notch. "I avenged you."

Edmund stands up and rests his hands on Haukyn's bare shoulders, his calluses rough and warm. "So you carried me in your heart in France."

"More strongly than I'd known. I thought I would die over there. Were it not for an archer named Javyd, I might have." He drags in breath. "He stayed in Bordeaux to finish his indenture. I could not."

"I'll add him to my prayers. Go to bed, Haukyn, the twins wake early. I'll cover the fire."

It would be all too easy to lay his head on his father's shoulder and let the slow tears come for Willem, Piers, and Modge, for Robert. "God's blessing," he mumbles and goes to the room he used to share with his elder brother; the twins have their own cubbyhole. A beeswax candle burns on the wooden chest near the wall. He gazes at the blue flame with its curled tip, another luxury, like the lavender soap. Although it takes him a long while to fall asleep and tis a fitful sleep—the bed too soft, the blanket blessedly dry but weighty on his bones—he's grateful for soap, candle, and blanket, for they bespeak that which, in any vill, is too rarely put into words.

He wakes in the morning to two warm bodies pressed to his ribs, which are being energetically tickled. The twins. Gil says, "I can count each rib you got, top to bottom. Did you kill many Frenchies?"

Ralf strokes his cheek, his warm breath in Haukyn's ear. "Your face, tisn't scarred like Da's."

"My arm has my only scar. And aye, I killed many Frenchies. So many I don't sleep at night."

"But they were Frenchies."

Gil's eyes are like Robert's, brown as clay. *Robert*...Haukyn says unsteadily, "They were serfs. Just like you and me."

"Then why did you kill them?"

"If you can answer that question, I'll make you lord of the manor."

Gil jabs him in his skinny ribs. Ralf says, "I don't like it when they kill the pigs at Martinmas. Nor when Ma wrings our hens' necks."

"You eat bacon and you like chicken soup," says his twin.

Ralf looks downcast. "Do we have to kill to get what we want?"

"Nay!" Haukyn says. "You like bean pottage and Ma's oats, don't you?"

"D' you always win arguments?" Gil says, peering into his face, more warm breath, and Haukyn grabs them both and tickles them until they shriek with laughter, and he's more glad than he can say to be holding them, young, safe, and alive.

After Sext, Haukyn makes himself cross the snow to Robert's house, where Johanna tells him to help himself to ale and lets him hold his second set of twins that day, swaddled, solemn-eyed, and fuzzy-headed, the girl, to his eye, indistinguishable from the boy. Terrified he'd drop them, he replaces them in their cradles. With a tired sigh, Johanna sinks onto the bench by the fire.

He'd always liked her, for she had Robert's calm, her features possessing a serenity that came close to beauty. That serenity has fractured since he left; he recognizes the lesions of grief, and as he drinks his ale he talks with great affection about his solid, patient brother. She says, her face turned away as she pokes at the coals, "He didn't love me as I loved him, did you know that?"

His body stiffens. The winter before he left for France, he'd gone with Robert to Swallowbend to purchase a new ploughshare, Jorden Smyth having shown no inclination to supply one. As they'd walked home pulling a cart with their burden, the frozen ground jouncing the wheels, Robert said, "Did you see the smith's wife?"

"Aye," he said. "A pretty wench."

"I asked her to wed me a year ago. But she loved the smith and would have none o' me. Nigh broke my heart." He sighed. "I'll marry Johanna sooner or later, though it might be later, and you'll never mention this."

Now he says, uncomfortably, "Johanna, why would you think that?"

"So you do know." She pushes a faggot into the fire. "He never lifted a hand to me nor lost his temper—did he even know how?" she adds in a burst of anger. "But he weren't ever *with* me, not all of him, not even in the days afore we was wed, us swiving worse 'n the rabbits in the lord's warren—in m' da's byre, in Solomon the Small's loft, hay stuck in our hair 'n' scratching parts you never want scratched." Iron poker to the coals, sparks vaulting the hearthstones. "After we married 'n' he knew I were with child, he'd lie in our bed with his back to me night after night, his duty done. Cuddling ain't prohibited by Holy Church!" Another poke, leap of flames, then something in the quality of Haukyn's silence impels her to look up. "Tis hard to lose what you never had."

"Why did you tell me this? Naught I can do about it, and he was my brother!"

"I ain't breathed a word to your parents, nor will I. I had to tell someone! Patient, loving Robert, perfect Robert, tis all I hear. He stood on the church steps in his new linen shirt for our vows 'n' said in front o' witnesses, *With my body I thee worship*, a lie, naught but a lie, and me fool enough to believe he meant it. Fool enough to love him." Weeping, she kicks at the pile of wood by the hearth. "We argued the morning he went to cut down the elm. Be that why his axe slipped?"

Haukyn loosens his jaw, searching for words. "We often live unknowing of how our deeds play out," he says, and sitting by an English hearth sees a little boy with a scabby face dart down an alley in faraway Lalinde.

"Him well-skilled with an axe, 'n' I'll never know why he were so careless."

"Robert's dead," Haukyn says with brutal truth—*and you to blame?*—"but you have two healthy, well-fed little-uns."

"Oh, aye, m' twins 'n' m' brewing," she says bitterly, "they'll keep me busy enough."

Bitter words hovering over his own tongue—*don't spew them, Haukyn, don't*—he carefully rests his mug, ale still in it, on the bench. "I must go. God's blessing, Johanna," he says and escapes outside, where he heaves cold air into his lungs. His feet carry him through the woods to his hideaway near the river. Blackthorn grows faster than any weed, so the circle of bushes is wider and draped with brambles; through the bare branches and sharp spines he can see the circle of flintstones, disarranged by frost and rain. He can't lay all the blame on Johanna. He was one of those who'd always thought *patient Robert, loving Robert, perfect Robert*...yet in marriage Robert had failed the woman who loved him because he was unable or unwilling to sever himself from another man's wife. How is he, Haukyn, to cope with this new knowledge? No one in the vill he can share it with, not one soul.

He bends and picks up a scattered flintstone, dirt engrained in its rough white edges. There must be couples in Flintbourne other than his parents who have happy enough marriages, although he now knows to his sorrow that Robert and Johanna were not among them. Solomon the Small and his Lucy. Neuton atte Mede and his wife Maud Cat-Skinner, who somehow escaped the Cat-Skinners' pervasive nastiness. But who else?

Not even pretty Margery had caused him to imagine standing on the church steps with Father Mortimer and exchanging vows that must last until the death of one of them. A lucky escape, since she became the worst scold in Swallowbend. Marriage as cage or freedom? Tis a question whose answer he'd better ponder, and ponder hard, before ever he asks Father Mortimer to read the banns at Mass.

On his third day back, fighting the urge to sleep all morning, he visits Solomon the Small, surviving son of a hefty father, a big man with a heart as big, who is pained to hear of Modge's death and who offers him a mug of ale at the hearthside. "We all misses Robert. When he died, he robbed your da's hearth of warmth. Your ma lost two little girls all them years ago, plague 'n' the wasting sickness, but I never seen her so like a ghost of herself. Both of 'em needed you to come home."

Solomon moves to stories of his neighbours' doings, occasionally salacious, but gently so. "You'd remember Wortle Dill? Last autumn he had a fit at Mass in the church's nave, kicked over a bench and died, Father Mortimer much put out by such unseemly doings... Poor bugger, he used to watch me milk m' cows, chortling to hisself, 'n' them the quieter for it."

Sadness for Wortle Dill's passing, shame for his own antics in France, the loss of Modge so closely tied, Haukyn stays silent. Solomon's wife, Lucy, joins them after a trip to the well; she kisses her husband, he pats her bottom, she plies Haukyn with oatcakes and the vill's latest gossip, and his spirits lighten.

As he heads for the river path, near the ford he comes face to face with Warty Ivo. Two years older than he, lean but sinewy, his shirt soiled, his hair a greasy toss of red curls. Red hair, the Devil's mark.

Haukyn tries a smile. Ivo sneers. "I heard you was back. Naught but a skeleton with skin stretched over it. Nor I don't see no plunder."

"An ill-advised campaign, even the Duke of Lancaster gained no plunder. Ivo, I have no wish for enemies in Flintbourne."

"Scairt o' me, ain't you."

"I've killed on horseback and in pitched battles, killed more men than dwell in our valley. I'm not afeard of you." He rubs the scar on his arm, which itches in the cold. "As a boy I used to follow you, learning stealth from you, and in France as a consequence was able to steal horse bread for my mare. I was grateful to you, and so was she."

"Grateful to the likes o' me?"

"She died anyway, of starvation, as did thousands of other horses in southern France...Do you remember the day I offered you apple bread? You as skinny as I am now, me a lad of seven winters wandering the ridge, late autumn and the orchard's yield plentiful that year. You were alone. I held out a piece of cake and said, 'Ma made it from our costards. She has a little stock of spices she adds, tis good.' You reached for it. Then you snatched your hand back. My father had a proverb: *If someone's going to rob you of something, give it to them and save them from sin*...I flung the cake at you and took to my heels, I *was* afeard of you then. Did you eat it?"

"Caught you a se'night after 'n' thrashed you, didn't I. Broke yer nose."

Haukyn's temper outruns him. "Four against one, you full of piss when you were with your gang."

"I didn't need 'em!"

"The next time I came across you, you only had Amos Cat-Skinner for company, and I dealt out bruised shins and a black eye each, you cursing me, Amos wary of me ever after. Does your mother make apple cake?"

"Get out o' my sight."

Ivo pushes past him and plants his worn shoes on the ford's stones. Haukyn watches him go, rubbing the bump in his nose. Of course

Jorden's wife doesn't make apple cake. And now? Once an enemy, always an enemy? Like England and France, with as little prospect of peace?

For the sake of peace, on Sunday Haukyn accompanies his family to Mass in St. Edmund's church. His eyes are still dark-circled, his cheekbones too prominent, but for the rest he's clean and tidy, his face an agreeable mask even when he genuflects to the altar with its chalice and red-hued lamp. They seat themselves on their usual bench, and he amuses himself by putting names to the backs of heads: the Cat-Skinners, including Amos; Waryn atte Water, father of Johanna; bent and withered Bony Mabel, who was old when his father came home from war; Arnulf-from-the-Beeches, laziest reeve in the vill's memory and a long memory it is, he an incomer from a hamlet downriver that was wiped out by plague; beside him, his younger daughter Annabel, sister to pretty Margery.

Before the homily, Father Mortimer says in his shrill voice, "Sir Mauger and I, your humble priest, welcome our valiant warrior home from France. Haukyn of Flintbourne travelled in company with the Duke of Lancaster and gains much glory from that association. We all praise God for the downfall of England's enemies and for the duke's many successes on his campaign."

He beams at Haukyn. Haukyn blushes. Gil elbows him. "Warrior," he whispers in delight. Ralf is half-asleep against his other arm, while he, Haukyn, wishes he could sink through the floor and emerge high on the ridge in the lord's woods. But when the congregation mills about on the dry, wind-swept grass, little whorls of snow rising and falling, plump Sir Mauger smiles on him benevolently and otherwise ignores him; and Haukyn is so heartened by how much pleasure is shown for his return that he allows his mask to slip a little.

At home, Hawise arranges bowls and spoons on the trestle table, Edmund fetches Johanna, and Haukyn carries first one cradle and then the second, Ranulf trotting at his heels. His sister-in-law's serenity is unruffled as they all break their fast together, and there is no mention of elder brothers or warriors.

...defiance...

Four days later, Haukyn sets off at Sext for the manor of Hungerford. He's wearing his Sunday garb, some of it Robert's, his boots have been reshod by the cordwainer and polished with beeswax, there is a light dust of snow on the ground under a pale blue sky, and he has never left Flintbourne with such reluctance.

Reluctance? Dread, more like. What use new hose when he has to face Willem's widow, Heloise, and his old ma, and then Ilotte, whom Piers desired, *desire* a tame word for those ribald descriptions of her charms, and who knows if twas reciprocated and who knows if she married the constable, the man with silver and a face like a pig's arse. New hose? Naked as a newborn and he'd still be clothed in dread. He'll go, he'll fulfill the obligations of fealty to his two friends, and he'll never go back.

He's carrying a staff, his dagger honed; even so, for safety's sake, or is it for the sake of delay, he trails a group of merchants travelling to Bristol with loaded waggons. Before he crosses the bridge to the manor, he eats the bread and green cheese his mother packed for him, chewing each mouthful thoroughly. The fields and woods, church and thatched-roof houses are a peaceful sight, the stables partway up the hillside. He still carries the sawn-off hairs from Modge's mane in his pouch. He'll not go near the stables.

The widow first, for she will be the more onerous.

He and Piers had visited the pretty cottage leased by Heloise and Willem several times in those carefree days of horse archery. Steeling himself, he walks up the path and knocks on the door. Heloise opens it so quickly she must have been watching his approach. "Haukyn, God's blessing," she says. "You be back from France."

She's the same mousy little woman, soft-voiced, her eyes grey as a mouse's fur; hard to believe she was the lusty wife Willem took such pride in, and he says what he knows he must say. "Aye, I am home, Heloise. But your dear Willem will not be returning."

She seems to shrink before his eyes. Slow tears tip down her cheeks. She says quietly, "I thought as much when I seen you coming."

"I wish with all my heart it were not true."

Gurgling and cooing can be heard from inside the cottage. She whispers, "Tis Willem's daughter, born in November, I didn't know I'd conceived when he left in the spring. He'll never know 'bout her... he so wanted a little-un."

She ushers him indoors and wipes her cheeks. After she pours him a mug of ale and gives him bread and cheese he doesn't want, she asks what happened to her husband. He tells her as best as he can. She says, "Willem would've fought til he dropped, there were a stubbornness to him, 'n' he would've thought o' me afore he died."

He describes some, but only some, of the events of Willem's last months, making her smile when he talks of clean nails and sweet breath; and is heartened to learn that after Willem's mother died late in the summer, Heloise inherited her hoard of silver. "Buried, it were, by her bedside. She ne'er spent a cut farthing she didn't have to, ne'er rested her tongue neither—no wonder Willem didn't have much to say for hisself. God rest her soul," she finishes, without much conviction.

So he's been spared passing on news of death to Willem's old mother. He says, "Piers died also, near the end of the campaign. I must find Ilotte and tell her—he was enamoured of her."

"Ilotte?" For a moment an expression not at all mousy crosses Heloise's face. "You'll find her behind the lord's granary. In the stocks."

"The *stocks*?"

"She were sent twice by our steward to clean house for a burgher in Newbury, 'n' twice she run home. So the steward, a righteous man, put her in the stocks. Since the burgher be angered 'n' don't want her back, tis likely she'll stay in Hungerford. Where every man on the manor have his eye on her."

"Willem never did!"

She shakes her head. "Nay, not Willem. But m' two cousins, both of 'em married men. I got no use for Ilotte."

He says faintly, "I'd best go find the stocks. Though tis no place to speak of death. Do you know when she'll be released?"

"Too soon to do any good. Willem's ma's cottage be empty should you not want to set out for home at dusk."

"My thanks. If I need to, I'll knock on your door."

How swiftly the mouse turned into a weasel, and had Willem been, deep down, afraid of his meek little wife? What if you were to marry a mouse and find you'd snared yourself to a sharp-fanged predator?

He starts up the hill toward the granary, which is twice the size of Flintbourne's, and before he sees the stocks hears shouts, jeers, and cursing. Around the corner of the building, he finds a motley crowd confronting a woman whose ankles and wrists are bolted into the rough-edged holes. An urchin no older than the twins flings a rotten apple, which smacks her in the chest; her skirt and tunic are coated in filth, and from the midst of a filthy face eyes black as sloe berries blaze at her attackers. Another apple, a trio of rock-hard pears that makes her wince. She gathers herself, he can see the effort it takes, and calls out through the hubbub, "I tend your beasts, help your ewes to lamb, your cows deliver their calves. I heal your sick hens." She gulps air. "This be how you show your gratitude?"

"Sorceress!" a woman screams.

"Beasts ain't all you tend!"

An outburst of crude laughter. A man as ugly of face as a toad, but smartly dressed in a silver-buckled coat, steps forward and dumps a bucket of slops over her head. Slime and grease slide down her face. She shakes herself, eyes tight shut; she's shuddering in the chill wind, and he sees that her skirts are wet too. How long has she been confined here and does she have to piss where she sits? He doesn't care if she ran from a dozen burghers, she doesn't deserve such humiliation.

Someone, he doesn't see who, throws a stone with diabolical accuracy. It strikes her cheek, a sharp cry escapes her, and her eyes fly open. He shouts, loudly enough to overcome jeers and laughter, "Stop! Where is your priest that he does not condemn such cruelty?"

"Father John? He ain't here."

More laughter. "He be visiting the widow Henshaw, we won't see him afore Vespers."

Haukyn dredges his brain for stories half-heard at Mass. "Then what of your God? Did not Christ say of Mary Magdalene that he without sin was to cast the first stone?"

"Magdalene were a whore. Like this un."

Whore...Benedict the felon ambling past their campfire one evening, his shirt splattered with fresh blood. *"Whores back o' the rearguard,"* he said, *"I picked me one, yellow hair she had. Didn't like what I were doing to her, she cursed me, the bitch. So I cut off her nose 'n' left her in the woods, she won't last the—"* Haukyn on his feet, fist to Benedict's gut, fist to his nose, rage hot as a forge fire, and the shirt now spattered with more than a dying woman's blood.

Another hail of winter-hard pears. Ilotte glares at him. "Go away!"

"I'll not." He strides closer to the rough wooden boards and pivots to face the serfs, one hand resting on the handle of his knife. His voice rings clear in the cold air. "I am but five days returned from France and the king's army. The next man to throw aught will taste my dagger, tis hungry for blood. No Frenchies here, but you'll do."

Silence. The men shuffle uneasily. A hag in a torn skirt bawls, "Will you knife me, laddie?" and throws a brown-skinned apple. It squelches against a post. The urchin thumbs his nose at the hag. The hag shakes her fist at him.

Haukyn pulls in a long breath. He meets the eyes of one villein, then a second's, then those of the man in the buckled coat. "I come from Flintbourne, downriver," he says. "I fought alongside Willem, your manor's champion archer, who was cut down by French soldiers. No shriving, no grave. Piers, who wished to become your bailiff, he was in my retinue, we were friends. He died of starvation, as so many others did, before we reached Bordeaux. Good men, both of them, I was honoured to be in their company." Another breath. "And you, good people, I beg you, go home now and give thanks that you live far from warfare and pillage."

More shuffling. One villein says to another, "Past time to feed m' cow," and walks away. His wife trudges after him. A last leer at Ilotte and two more leave. As the rest drift homeward, the toad-faced man says, "You won't be here the next time she be put in the stocks," and, stiff-backed, stalks out of sight.

The hag lobs her last apple. Ilotte ducks sideways and the apple hits the dirt behind her. The old woman spits copiously, picks up her basket, and totters away. The urchins run down the hill, their arms outspread like the wings of birds.

He takes off his doublet. She flinches from him, a small gesture that says more than he wants to know. "Don't touch me!"

"Tis to keep you warm, it'll cover your shoulders. When are you to be released?"

"Vespers." With a wolfish grin, her teeth very white in her grimy face, she adds, "Your doublet'll be ruined, 'n' they'll be back with cowshit afore long."

"I'll stay until Vespers, and any cowshit will be upended on them."

"So you can have your own fun, once tis dark?"

He gives her a look that would scald hairs from a sow's back. "Don't you want to hear more about Piers? Or did you wed the constable and his silver?" His eyes widen. "He's the man with the silver buckles who dumped slops on you."

"Elyas. Our manor's nose-poking constable."

"A constable who attacks defenceless women? So you didn't wed him. I understand why."

She raises her chin, her eyes bright with defiance. "Wed? Why would I wed any man? Least of all Elyas."

Defiance…how oft as a young-un did he defy his father, and with far less cause? Shame, he feels the heat of it rise in his face, his infernal blushing and she auger-sharp. One hand feels for the reliable crutch of his dagger, the other brushes against the clean cloth his mother insists he carry in case of scrapes or burns. He tugs it free, Stephen Sadlere flashing across his mind as he leans over and begins to wipe her forehead. She pulls back with a gasp of protest. "Be still," he says, "you cannot escape, and I do this for Piers."

Her eyes screwed shut, she suffers his closeness. She's lost her cap, her hair lies wet and stringy down her back, dark as her eyes, and she's still shivering. She stinks.

Christ, Piers, you wouldn't be lusting after her now.

When he's finished, he offers her his waterskin, holding it to her lips. She jerks her head away. "I'll have to piss again if I drink."

"Wouldn't it have been easier to scrub the burgher's floors?"

"Twas me he wanted on the floor, not m' scrub brush. Didn't the army teach you about the worth o' whores?"

"An army calls all women *whore*. But I doubt you are one, Ilotte of Hungerford."

She clamps her mouth shut. From behind him a voice says snappily, "Who are you?"

Had the voice belonged to a French soldier, he, Haukyn, would be dead on the ground. He straightens, feeling the wind wrap cold arms around ribs and shoulders. Tis a man of some consequence, well-dressed, long-nosed as John of Gaunt and as adept at looking down it. "I am Haukyn of Flintbourne," he says, "come to this manor to tell Willem's wife of her husband's death in France. And you?"

"Arthur Bidewell. The steward of this manor."

"Show more mercy than your constable and release Ilotte before Vespers—tis winter and she's soaked through."

"The sentence lasts til Vespers. She suffers from the sin of pride. A good Christian woman would have obeyed my orders and remained a servant in Newbury."

"A good Christian burgher would not have lusted after her."

"She casts her lures before all men." The steward's smile is pinched. "You should beware."

Haukyn says abruptly, "Piers of Hungerford also died before we reached Bordeaux."

Bidewell shrugs. "He harboured too much ambition for a serf."

"He was a fine archer and a valiant soldier for our king!"

"You've done your duty and reported his death." He stretches his neck; he's shorter than Haukyn. "Go back to Flintbourne. Before dark."

"I'll stay until Ilotte is released, to guard her against your manor's cruelties. As any man of conscience would."

An ugly flush stains Bidewell's cheeks. "I am a righteous man and God-fearing! I'll unlock the stocks at Vespers and not before."

Watching him leave, Haukyn says, "I've made another enemy, tis a skill of mine," and sits down on the ground beside the stocks, tilts his waterskin, and drinks, trying not to mind as cold air laves his skin through his shirt; at his side, Ilotte remains stubbornly silent, shoulders back, eyes fixed on the lowering sky. Hungerford's serfs don't stray from their hearths. A pity, since he's spoiling for a fight. Darkness conquers the last grey streaks in the clouds, and they are both shivering by the time the steward returns with a lamp and the key to unlock the boards of the stocks. The locks are well-greased, Haukyn notices with another flare of anger as, knotted muscles complaining, he gets to his feet. Bidewell lifts the top boards and drops them back on their hinges, which are also well-greased.

"You have my undying gratitude, sir," Haukyn says and bows. "May God bless you and keep you."

The steward gives him a most un-Christian look before he and his lamp disappear into the night. Creaking in every joint, Haukyn stretches. Ilotte's heels have dropped to the ground, her legs as stiff as the planks that held her; she's rubbing one wrist with her other hand, her fingers like claws. He steps inside the low wooden walls of the stocks. "Let me help you."

"Nay!" She pushes at the boards, tries to bend her knees, and cries out in pain. Even then she doesn't weep. "I'll manage. I *will*."

The only time he's been known for patience was with Modge; he needs Robert's patience and he needs it now. "Ilotte, you're cold, tired, dirty, and hungry, you're like the English archers who hobbled toward Bordeaux, and for the next hour or more you'll allow an archer to look after you. A stranger, aye, but a friend to two good men from your manor, and I swear by our blessed Mother that you can trust me. Now, I'm going to put my hands under your arms and hold you til you can stand on your own."

When he lifts her, her legs collapse under her. She's taller and lighter than he expected. He tries not to breathe in slops and, Jesu, human feces, not hers but smeared to her tunic, he'd like to kill every one of those bloody serfs. "Easy, take your time."

"Cramps," she gasps, her face contorted.

"I'll hold your weight. Try to move your legs."

Tears of agony are trickling down her cheeks, little runnels in the dirt. He looks away. She mutters, "You...why so kind?"

"I'd do the same for a kitten drowning in a bucket."

A tiny wheeze of...tis laughter. The slow minutes pass with both of them, for different reasons, breathing shallow. She says, uncertainly, "I think I can stand."

His answer is to swing her up in his arms—his shirt is ruined anyway—and step out of the confines of the stocks.

"Put me down!"

"Which way do I go?"

Her face surly beneath its mask of dirt, she says, "Up the hill."

His vision adjusting to a low, fitful moon, he labours up the slope until she says, "The cottage by the trees," and he sees the dull glow of whitewash from a small house set apart from the others, the gate ajar. With his elbow he pushes up the latch on the door, carries her inside, and seats her on a nearby stool. "Stay there. Candles?"

Within moments two small flames reveal hearth and faggots. He touches flint to tinder, builds up the fire, and hangs a pot of water over it. Rooting around on her shelves, he finds towels and soap—lavender soap, like his mother's—and from a hook on the wall takes down a clean cloak, aware the whole time of a silence that screams protest. Pushing a bench closer to the hearth, he takes her arm, rigid in his grasp, and leads her to it. "Sit until the water's hot enough. If you'll take off my doublet, I'll wait outside."

"You'll sit inside with your back to the fire."

"So you do trust me."

"What choice do I got?"

"I said I would wait outside and I meant it!"

Her eyes fall. "Sit."

Shadows dance over the walls; in a while, he hears the splash of water and hiss of steam, the soft rub of soap on flesh, the soft scrub of the towel. As warmth steals back to his limbs, his tarse stirs. His own stink ripens. When requested, keeping his eyes averted, he dumps the dirty water outdoors, fills the pot from the rain barrel, and builds up the fire again so she can rinse her hair.

Her latch is strong, her door and shutters thick. "I'll leave now," he says. "The men won't come back, their wives won't let them."

"Take two torches to light your way. Over there, by the cupboard."

He dons his doublet, discarded on the floor—he won't retch, he won't, it would only amuse her—picks up the rush torches, and looks over at her. She's not beautiful. She's not pretty, like pretty Margery. Yet...

Enfolded in the cloak, she holds his gaze. "My thanks," she says.

"I'll come back in a few days to see how you do."

"No need. You was kind, I be grateful, and there's an end."

Absently he rubs the rough hemp cord that binds the bottom of the rushes. For a few hours, the despair that dogged him at the last in France and that all too readily can return has been ousted along with the Hungerford villeins. He's felt more like himself, like the Haukyn who went to war rather than the Haukyn who returned from it, a lightness that has little to do with fulfilling his duty to Heloise. *Atonement,* he thinks, *could my kindness be another act of atonement for a dead priest? Even more, an act that honours my friend Piers, who would have defended Ilotte to the death from that rowdy mob at the stocks?* Close to tears, touching one of the torches to the flames, he looks into eyes that give nothing away. "Latch the door and buy yourself a dog with teeth."

Across the dirt floor and he's outside. Iron within iron, the door is locked against him.

...the beech leaf clings to its winter twig...

His son arrives home late that evening, dripping river-water, a look on his face that forbids questions. Ranulf noses him. Edmund catches a whiff of the privy from his soaked doublet. What has he been up to in Hungerford that he had to jump in the river in January?

Haukyn walks toward the bay he used to share with Robert and says, over his shoulder, "I've been meaning to ask you, Father, who is Flintbourne's constable now?"

Edmund's skin chills. Wrong-doing of some kind, for doesn't wrong-doing follow Haukyn's every footstep? "The vill voted for Tirrell Wodebyte, our gooseherd. A well-meaning freeman with little training for a role bound to make him disliked. He's also the nephew of our shire's sheriff. Why do you ask?"

An edge to his voice, Haukyn says, "I'm in no trouble."

"I'm glad to hear it."

"I pity the man. Easier to herd a gaggle of geese than Smyths and Cat-Skinners."

The door closes behind him.

"Have he been brawling with someone in Hungerford?" Hawise whispers, and covers the coals.

"It must have been hard, taking news of war and death to Willem's widow and Piers's friend...His knuckles were clean and his face unmarked. I'll ask him on the morrow to do a few chores, keep him closer to home."

On their mattress, the candle blown out, she says into his chest, "*I* ran from my chores at the alehouse whene'er I could, d' you remember? Oft unwisely."

"You were a girl, and beaten. He's always had a good home and food on the table."

"You have not tamed *me*, husband."

"I would never try." Edmund nuzzles her hair, white-threaded now. "How is it you can always make me smile?"

"He ain't been home long. He'll find his path."

"He must, for his path is here." He sighs. "Past time I speak to him about my virgates. I will. After I've fed Melicent in the morning."

Beside the stye at first light, from long habit Edmund scratches his sow's back, contemplating what to say to his son and how to say it, and before he's ready hears Haukyn's voice. "God's blessing."

He's wearing Robert's old doublet. Edmund swallows. "You're no longer grey of face and so desperately thin, Haukyn, and how thankful I am that I didn't lose two sons." A goodly beginning. "Now that you're home, we must decide how best to work my virgates."

"Father, before we talk of thistles and ploughs, I have news, good news for the whole family. You were born bastard, am I right?"

"Bastard? Aye," he says, perplexed. "My father wasn't my mother's husband but a wandering drover."

"If you're born bastard, you're free. Under the law. You and your sons and your sons' children."

"I've never heard of this. Why isn't it common knowledge?"

"No lord of the manor would bruit it abroad, tis against his interests. But I speak true. All we need is proof."

Edmund says dismissively—for this is Haukyn, restless Haukyn, ever seeking disruption, ever in need of change—"I have no proof. My father was killed the day I was conceived, my mother died before plague arrived, and my half-brother, Bart, who knew the truth of the matter, succumbed to the second wave of plague. There are no manorial records to state I'm bastard because I had no knowledge of the need for them." Because Haukyn looks aghast, he gentles his tone. "I regret my ignorance. But ignorant I was, and there's no going backward. What difference, freeman or serf? We have a good living here, two and a half virgates, more than enough to feed us all."

"What difference? Were I free, I could enter the London Bowyers' Guild."

"Swear your life away for seven years? Forbidden to marry?"

"I didn't say I *would* enter, I said I could. Dunstan from up the hill, he used to be the valley's best bowyer. If he were willing—and if you would loan me coin to pay him—I could learn much from him and, in time, set myself up as the vill's bowyer. As you know, we're required by law to practice on the green. Staves, arrows, fletching, I'd find plenty of work. Later, when I'm more skilled, as freeman I could ply my trade throughout the valley, without penalty."

"Dunstan throws stones at any who approach his cot."

"The twins would also be free. How can you say it makes no difference? To you, maybe. But to your family—"

"The twins are content on our acres." Edmund braces himself. "With Robert gone I need you here, my strength is not as it was. Knees, fingers, wrists, shoulders, they fail me at times. The matter's closed."

"You've lived all your life on this manor, you've attended hallmote, you had a priest for a friend who taught you to read and write, how could you not have known about bastardy?"

"I had more important matters to deal with! The loss of our first child, Thomas. A stillborn daughter, after Robert's birth. Then the second plague, the one they called the children's plague, it robbed us of little Margaret, have you forgot her? Your mother slow to recover. Hot summers, cold winters, mildew on the crops, animal murrains that cost me two cows. The parish tax of three years ago, the taxes of fifteenths, the lord's tallage, church tithes, price-fixing by a government that cares for naught as long as it has its fill of wheaten bread—unending the struggle to make a living for my family. And you expect me to worry about the manner of my birth?"

"So I am to be farmer in my brother's stead, is that your plan?"

"You demean all that I have worked for these many years!"

Haukyn drags his hands through his hair. "If I never knew real hunger until I marched the length of France, tis because of you and your acres."

Too angry to be appeased, Edmund says, "If you are to eat at our table, a farmer you must be."

"Labourers roam the countryside. Hire them."

"Despite Parliament's statute, wages are too high and my profits too low to bear them, and the lord took my only ox for heriot after your brother died. Haukyn, is there no fealty, you to me?"

His son forces the words from his throat, Edmund can see the effort it takes. "Fealty, aye. But—"

"I beg you, cannot there be peace betwixt us?"

"Not this day," Haukyn says, dashes aside his father's outstretched hand, and breaks into a run.

Edmund watches him go. He's humbled himself, revealed weaknesses he'd prefer to ignore, sorrows and trials best buried, and might as well have kept his mouth shut.

Robert, he thinks, and bows his head. *Sweet Jesu, how I wish you were still with me.*

His feet, of their own accord, carry him down the hill, over the ford, and into the churchyard, where he kneels beside Robert's grave on the cold ground and tries to pray, searching in his heart for his son's spirit. A grey sky, the soft swish of old yews in the wind, a robin's winter song...how deeply Hawise mourned the loss of two small daughters, and he unable to give her aught but sons. *Why did your axe slip, Robert? Why does Johanna hold herself so aloof? Why do robins sing the year round?*

His nose is running. He wipes it on his sleeve, and words tumble through his brain...*the son untempered by war, buried with his head to the rising sun*...he looks down at his hands, white-boned knuckles, swollen joints, the blue rivers that carry his blood, the many spots, brown as clay, brown as Robert's eyes, brown as the robin's feathers. He turns his hands over, lined palms and the pulse at his wrist, which insists, *I am here, here, here...palm upward in supplication and that small pulse, do not think it gentle...twisted trunks of the old yews from which no bow will be hewn, no arrows fly...a son's lifeblood into the receptive soil, moil of grief, how the beech leaf clings to its winter's twig...*

The deaths unseen, the dead unheard, what if angels are naught but robins, their song piercing to the ear, sung in four seasons... Those long months when Haukyn was in France, words were trapped in his chest. Now they leak, worthless as a pizzle on a ewe.

I would this day were over.

Grunting, he gets to his feet.

Down the baulk past the assart, through the trees to the river, Haukyn keeps running until he sees the great oak tree that no serf can cut down for it belongs to their lord, lazy Sir Mauger, who was enriched by an ox for heriot, his father robbed of it and all according to law; even Sir Mauger bestirs himself for heriot, and aren't all laws for the benefit of manor and church?

His dream has shattered. No trade, no leaving the manor; the chime of a distant bell, the bell of freedom, silenced. His hideaway too small for him, the whole vill too small. He was a fool to harbour such dreams. A fool as great as a father who never bothered to find the rewards of bastardy.

The oak holds to its long-dead leaves. He stares upward into the network of branches. The tree, rooted, dumb, waiting for the lord's axe, has as little freedom as a serf, and tis not the moment to remember *he* wouldn't have known about the freedom bastardy confers had not Piers, in France, told him about it. He flings himself away from the thick trunk and tramps downriver, deep enough into the lord's woods that no one will accost him. The bank is hard-frozen. He sits down and huddles into Robert's doublet. The current burbles around clumps of flint, pulling smooth the long green strands of riverweeds, which sway like a woman's hair, and what would Ilotte's hair have looked like, brushed dry by firelight...

Before he went to war he used to let Modge drink at this very spot. Months ago, a lifetime ago. Are Fulk and Javyd fighting for the duke in Castile, and what of the archer who helped him cover Piers with decaying leaves? Odds are, all three are dead.

I am alive, he thinks, with a wry twist of his mouth at so obvious a thought. No bolt in the back at Moulins's marsh, he wasn't savaged by a mastiff in the woods or hanged for theft of horse bread, he didn't starve or surrender to the squats. He can find no meaning to this, no reason why he is now sitting on the banks of a river as familiar to him as his father's fields, why he wakens to the twins' teasing every morning, to his mother passing him hot oats sweetened with dried apple. Who planted the apple tree but his father? *You demean all that I have worked for...*He winces, watching the ruffle of foam. Robert, a true farmer, is gone; the twins are willing but too young; and his father has aged in the last year, he's not so angered as to miss that. So the work of virgates falls on him, ploughing, harrowing, sowing, and harvesting, and tis up to him whether he does it with some degree of grace or with the ugly mien of Warty Ivo.

His hands are clenched on his knees, hands that from now on will be a farmer's hands, tamed to the tasks that are their fate.

Unaware that he is cold, unnoticing of a pale sun traversing the bare treetops, Haukyn stays by the river for a long time, shoulders taut and mouth set, and could not have pinned the moment when struggle surrendered to...was it acquiescence? Must he abandon the prospect of freedom, or can freedom be found thus?

Slowly he straightens his back. In January, the virgates make few demands, and ploughing doesn't begin til February. He'll visit Dunstan this evening, see if he'd be willing to teach him some of the simplest of a bowyer's skills in the evenings to come.

He must make peace with his father. He'd rather walk from Calais to Bordeaux.

Standing up, he chafes his hands to warm them and heads west along the river path. He feels older than the man who came the other way. Is the giving up of dreams a necessary part of manhood?

Scuffing through dead willow leaves, he sees a brown trout lurking in a pool, lazy flick of tail, no serf permitted to catch it, for the fish are the lord's. On the morrow he'll weave a net and present his mother with a trout for supper, and who's to stop him.

As he walks up the hill along the baulks that edge his father's land, he tries to see the fields in a new light, tries to wed himself to them, although not, pray God, for life. He'll learn what crops are to be sown and how much seed is stored in the byre and how to guide Solomon the Small's oxen. He'll farm with good grace, but with his soul in his own keeping.

His mother is filling a bucket from the rain barrel. When she sees him, she says, her face hostile, "Go to Jorden's for nails. He been paid. Your father needs 'em to repair the north wall o' the byre." Water slops from the bucket as she pulls the door open.

"Ma—"

The door swings shut behind her. Her first and deepest loyalty has always been to her husband, why would he expect anything other? He tramps the fields to the smithy, anger curdling any semblance of grace. Smoke is writhing skyward, blue against grey, and only as he gets closer does he hear—speeding up, he bursts into the forge.

Jorden is snapping a strip of leather through the air, leather entwined with thin chain. Shirt torn and bloody, Warty Ivo is backing up, jerkily, he's being forced past the anvil and ever nearer to the fire. Appalled, Haukyn cries, "Jorden, don't!"

"Stay out o' this! I'll teach the little bastard to talk back."

Another snap of the whip, which winds itself around Ivo's ribs. He screams. Two more steps and the flames will catch the remnants of his shirt. Haukyn charges, fist to Jorden's gut, knee to his crotch, the floor uneven, and though Jorden falls backward, tisn't enough to cripple him. He flings himself on top of the smith, smashes his mouth. Blood and the crunch of teeth, and through a red mist of rage he knees him again, pounds at shoulders, throat, jaw, whatever's closest. Grasping a handful of the smith's greasy hair, he lifts—a deluge of cold water drenches him, head and shoulders.

Hair plastered to his forehead, blinded, he swipes at his eyes. Jorden's wife screeches, "You'll kill 'im!"

Jorden's eyes are shut, his cheekbones grazed and bleeding, and is his nose broke? Haukyn closes his own eyes. He has no memory of hitting eye, cheek, or nose; his last coherent thought was that he mustn't let Jorden wrap brawny arms around his chest and crush his ribs. Christ, he could've killed the man. As he pushes himself up, getting his knees under him, then staggering to his feet, Jorden's bulky chest heaves. "He's not dead," he says, his voice coming from a long way away, and dimly realizes that the oath he made the day he arrived home still holds. He fumbles for his next words, rage still thickening heart, brain, and voice. "Why didn't you throw the water at *him* so he'd quit beating his son?"

"Ivo? That useless scut?"

Ivo takes a single step away from the fire; the sound he makes is like that of an animal tormented beyond endurance. His shirt is past mending, his torso bruised and bloody. Haukyn loops the belt and chain around his own neck, then grasps Ivo by the waist before he joins his father on the floor. "You're coming home with me. My mother will put salve on your wounds, and you'll not return to the smithy, ever."

"I has to!"

"You don't."

"I lives here," Ivo says sullenly.

Shaking his head in disbelief, Haukyn turns to the stone-faced woman clutching her empty bucket. "Attend to your brute of a husband. Ivo, lean on me and we'll walk slow...Where are your brother and sister?"

"Dunno."

Their progress is indeed slow, each step jarring Ivo's injuries; he's barefoot, old burn scars from the forge marring his skin. Haukyn takes as much of his weight as he can, steering him around piles of flint and drainage ditches. "Does your father often beat you and your brother?"

"Sim do what he's told. Usually I sneaks around Da." Ivo takes another shallow gasp of breath; his lip is bleeding, one eye swollen nigh shut. "Dropped a box o' nails, didn't I…got him going."

Haukyn had forgotten about the nails. His own knuckles are split, his blood and Jorden's mingled. Such murderous rage, where does it come from? A French mastiff and a peasant nigh decapitated, four archers whom he fought as a madman fights, but that was in France, that was war. In wartime, *thou shalt kill*, in peacetime, *thou shalt not*, and he'd best be clear about the difference or a hood will be pulled over his head with a noose looped around it.

He hadn't known before today that a man can fear himself.

He'll chain himself as a rabid dog should be chained, he'll embrace farming's tedium and leave rage to men like Jorden Smyth. For certain he'll never go near Ilotte of Hungerford again, with her fierce dark eyes and her truculence; he needs no more fuel added to the fire.

They've reached the top of the slope and the newly whitewashed bulk of his father's house. "Nearly there," he says. "Ma will give you something for the pain."

Edmund hurries to meet them. Haukyn says, "His father was beating him."

"Come inside, Ivo. My wife is home and will look after you. Haukyn, was that the whip he was using? Wise of you to bring it here, in case tis ever needed for hallmote."

"I left Jorden with fewer teeth, sore bollocks, and a black eye, so I'll wait a day or two before I fetch the nails. Why don't we go together, Da?"

The word slipped out; nor, he realizes, does he wish to retract it. Could this be another face of freedom? Or is it a tightening of the bonds around him?

Hawise's touch is gentle. Edmund supplies ale, bread, and cheese, as well as an old shirt of his, with the kindest of smiles. Yet despite the pleas of both of them, Ivo stumbles out of the house clutching his bandaged shoulder. Oafish to the last, thinks Haukyn.

For the next two days, he unobtrusively helps with chores, outdoors and in, repairing the pig stye, spreading rushes, splitting and stacking wood for their house and Johanna's, even scouring Johanna's pots in the river. Watching the current carry away grease and scraps of oats, rubbing his chilled hands against his hose, he wonders if he's trying to make reparation for Robert's negligence toward her, waters not as clear as the river's. He returns the pots and meets pretty Margery's pretty sister Annabel, who's selling candles to Johanna, her artless chatter an antidote to Johanna's restraint.

Ranulf on guard at the house, he and his father leave for the smithy, each carrying a staff, their daggers sharp. Jorden is by the forge in his leather apron when they arrive on his doorstep. He sports a massive black eye, a luridly bruised jaw, and messily scabbed cheeks and smiles at them unpleasantly. "Stay out o' the smithy."

Ivo is working the bellows and doesn't look up. His brother, Slug-Arse Sim, a man who, in Haukyn's opinion, either has had the spine beaten out of him or never had one to start with, is heating a length of iron in the coals. Edmund bares his teeth in a smile so aggressive that Haukyn blinks and Jorden steps back. "If Sir Mauger ever convenes hallmote, I'll have it recorded that you were whipping your son with a chain, beyond the bounds of permissible punishment."

"And Jorden," Haukyn adds, "don't lay a hand on any of my family or yours—you wouldn't want to lose that hand in an unfortunate accident, would you."

Jorden scowls at him. "Time you two moved on. I got work to do."

"The nails," Haukyn says. "The ones my father paid for."

"Yon box on the bench." He transfers the scowl to his son. "Keep them bellows moving, can't you?"

As they walk home across the fields, Haukyn lugging the box of nails, he gathers his courage—not the courage of the battlefield, but courage nevertheless—and says, "I will do my best to work your virgates."

Edmund slows down, his face unreadable. "I thought to transfer the Southwaters' fields to you, Haukyn. Good river soil and a fine orchard. If you wished, I could help you build a small house there. And I'll pay you for your labours on my land."

Aware he's being offered a measure of independence and that his mistakes won't always happen under his father's nose, he says carefully, "I'd rather you kept the acres in your name. But I'll farm them for you and would welcome your help. This evening I'll brave Dunstan's stones and see if he might tutor me in bow-making."

He keeps pace with his father, wondering if their accord is as fragile as it feels, *Da* echoing in the silence between them.

Dunstan's two little-uns died in the children's plague, his wife succumbed birthing a stillborn son, and a bowyer in Newbury gained access to Spanish yew and took over the trade in the valley, a series of calamities that made Dunstan retreat to his house and throw stones at interlopers, his aim particularly accurate when children approached.

Haukyn stands out of range and calls Dunstan's name. The door creaks open, Dunstan's dog, Jackdawe, trots into the open, and, more slowly, Dunstan follows. His hair is a shock of white, his eyes the colour of Moulins's mud, his spine bent. "Go away," he says.

Naught wrong with his voice and no stones crossing the gap. "I am Edmund's son, lately returned from the war. Would you, for coin, one or two evenings a week, teach me the bowyer's trade?"

Jackdawe sniffs his ankles, her tail wagging in welcome. Grey-naped and black-furred, she's a sweet-natured bitch who's borne many a litter of pups; he bends to pat her, and waits for *nay*. When neither *nay* nor *aye* is spoke, he raises his head. Dunstan is staring at him. "I ain't tillered a stave in more years than you been on this earth."

"You'll remember," Haukyn says with more confidence than he feels.

"I ain't got yew."

"I'd be working for serfs, not soldiers."

"C'n you shoot?"

"I can hit the mark on horseback at a gallop. The bows I want to make are for the green on a Sunday afternoon."

"Humph." He points to his shed. "See that ol' cart? Put axe, mallet, 'n' wedge in it. We'll go for a walk."

Dunstan sets off at a good pace up the hill, Jackdawe, Haukyn, and the cart at his heels. The lord's woods enclose them. "Yew trees in the churchyard out o' bounds for staves, so we has to make do with elm or ash. Ash staves get summat called string follow 'n' they lose cast—keeps bowyers in business, don't it? Choose a likely tree."

Haukyn takes his time. "That sapling would yield one stave, while that thick bole...what, eight perhaps?"

"You'll spend hours on a stave. What else?"

"No low branches? No knots?"

"No twist to the bark. Winterside o' the bole be best."

More pacing from tree to tree, looking up, looking down, until Haukyn says, "This ash. Four staves, would you agree, Dunstan?"

"Get to it. Best to cut when the sap be down."

"But—the lord?"

"Sir Mauger wants archers. I don't need no woodbote."

Haukyn puts back and brain to the task. Dunstan, from a distance, watches the tree fall tidily to the ground. "Cut lengths six inch longer than yer stave."

January and he's sweating. The trunk yields two such lengths. Dunstan comes closer. "How many wedges?"

Again Haukyn takes his time. "Four?"

"Too dark to slice 'em now. Bring someone at dawn on the morrow 'n' load the logs on the cart. You handy with a wedge?" Haukyn nods. "We'll split 'em after supper. Tuppence a week, three evenings."

Through the winter, the lessons proceed. After the ash logs are split along the grain, Haukyn roughs out the staves with hatchet and drawknife, and stacks them in layers in an open part of the shed to season. "Til September," Dunstan says. "I got seasoned elm from five year ago, you c'n scrape the bark off it and trim the staves." His grin is gap-toothed. "Then the real work begins."

"Good," says Haukyn and grins back.

He soon discovers that Dunstan, though sparing with praise, has much to teach him, and he eager to learn. He helps the old man through a bout of the gripe, dosing him with Hawise's remedies, and senses that if he has a gift for making enemies, in Dustan he is approaching friendship. After one sharp rebuttal, he does not again ask about the old man's family or his past.

He also repairs Melicent's farrowing pen, chisels new handles for his father's tools, and restrings both Edmund's bows, long and short; while he's replacing the short bow to its perch on the rafters, Edmund says, "My thanks for all you do, Haukyn. You free me to teach the twins how to mend the dead-hedges around the assart."

Praise underlies his father's words. He smiles. "I'll be making you a new bow before you know it."

The days gradually lengthen, the snowfalls of January and February yielding to warm spells, bare patches appearing in field and meadow. When the frost is gone from the ground, Haukyn plants Johanna's garden, she nursing one or the other of her twins and giving precise directions, her eyes never quite meeting his. He also feeds her hens, and how he hates the slime and stench of hen shit; he hopes Robert is looking down from Heaven and applauding him.

Over the last two months, his ribs have gained flesh, his arms strength, and the following Sunday he steels himself to join the men shooting on the green. He hasn't loosed arrow from bow since Lalinde. Memories play havoc with him, French archers tumbling from the ramparts, a scab-faced boy in terror of his life, a little girl's fists pummelling his chest, *Dieu vous bénisse*, and the ghastly stench of burning. His back to the others, he strings his bow, then stations himself next to Solomon and shoots at the mark, accurately enough though his range is so pitiful he has to parry good-natured jests and rude talk of Frenchies. While they're drinking ale afterward, he engages to fletch his neighbours' arrows with feathers from his father's geese and to weave new hemp strings for their bows, a good way to earn much-needed coin.

On the Monday, when Johanna hands him the bowl of scraps for the hens, she says, "I regret that I spoke to you about Robert so soon after you arrived home. Twas wrong of me."

No feeling in her voice and tis a most belated apology. In the bowl, rotten cabbage, burnt porridge, and blackened carrot-tops. "I was one of those who saw him as perfect. Perfection a heavy cloak for a man to wear."

She nods. He carries the bowl to the coop.

The other thing he does is walk the Southwaters' nine acres, which lie between the smithy and the river. The winter rye is dead-hedged. The fallow will need ploughing soon, although he doubts his furrows will be as straight as should be. The apple and pear trees have to be pruned; Robert's careful, long-ago instructions have never been forgot, he realizes with a catch at his heart, and the following morning he returns to the orchard carrying his brother's tools. He starts with damaged and downward-growing branches, with those rubbing each other or growing toward the tree's centre, then, moving the ladder and positioning it with care, he trims last year's growth... *above an outward facing bud*, tis as though Robert holds the ladder and is guiding him. Apples first, then the pears.

In two days, he's done. He lays the ladder on the grass and circles the nearest branch with one hand, roughness of bark and a clean cut where he pruned an upward shoot. *My brother's calm...my brother...* his eyes swimming in tears, he stuffs twigs and branches into a sack he loops over his shoulder. Then he lifts the ladder and takes the river path home.

Three more trips for the rest of the branches, pile them in the wood shed, and that evening as they eat supper by candlelight, Edmund asks if he would go to the market at Hungerford. "I find the walk too long. You could take Ralf for company—Gil went last time."

Haukyn nods soberly, his spirit dancing. A day away from Flintbourne, praise God.

Gil says, "I'm too busy to go anyway 'cause I'm building a new length of dead-hedge."

"Hedges keep things out and hedges keep things in," Ralf says thoughtfully.

"Da never hits me when the branch won't bend like it ought," Gil adds. "Not like some fathers in the vill. When you were little, Haukyn, did he hit you?"

Ralf's spoon stops in midair. Haukyn meets Edmund's eyes. "Once only," he says, "and twas more than warranted."

As though Haukyn were that little boy, Edmund reaches across the table and ruffles his hair.

His staff is lengthwise in Edmund's handcart, sacks in it for his purchases, his father's money and a few coins of his own in a pouch at his waist, and the sun is shining. Because ploughing looms as his next task, Haukyn is determined to extract as much enjoyment from the day as he can. Ralf gives a little skip of excitement. "Ma gave me a silver penny. What will I buy? Will you buy another horse and go back to France?"

"Nay! Never."

"Why don't you like farming?"

"Six winters and already you pose weighty questions…If anyone can make a farmer of me, our dead brother will, and look, there's a chaffinch."

"I miss Robert," Ralf says in a small voice. "D' you think God loves us like Father Mortimer says?"

"Da believes He does."

"I asked you."

"Love should mean kindness, Ralf, should it not? Killing and kindness make poor bedmates, I'm not the one to ask…We're nearly there."

The market is already crowded, a cacophony of bleating, cackling, grunting, and mooing, of vendors crying their wares and buyers bargaining at top voice. "Stay close," Haukyn says. "We'll buy the scythe blades first."

The local smith's prices are fair, as are the potter's for mugs and a bowl. He tucks then in a sack. "Let's find the seamstress for Ma's new cover."

He's paying for a well-sewn cover in a soft shade of green, when Ralf tugs him by the sleeve. "I want to buy some honeycomb for Gil. Over there."

Three stalls down, a woman is selling honeycomb and beeswax. Two strands of black hair lie against her throat, her tunic is clean, and she's smiling as she takes coin from an old woman with a cane. He hasn't seen her smile before. It gives her a fleeting beauty, and Heaven help him, there's a smile on his own face. Ralf says, "How do bees make those little holes with six sides?"

"I don't know."

Ilotte looks up. An emotion he can't decipher crosses her face. Pushing the cart, he walks closer. "Ilotte, this is my brother, Ralf. Ilotte is from Hungerford manor, Ralf, she knew Willem and Piers."

"I want a penny-worth of honeycomb," Ralf says. "Do you keep your own bees? Even in winter?"

"I covers m' hives in the cold." She wraps the comb, takes Ralf's penny, peers at it if she's never seen one before, and says stiffly, "Haukyn. You ain't as skinny as you was."

"Nor you as filthy."

A burgher whose belly threatens to pop his buttons pushes Ralf aside. Haukyn puts a protective arm around the boy's shoulders. Ilotte says, "Fresh honeycomb, sir?"

"A pot of honey." He leers at her. "Though I would sample your sweeter honey and pay well for the privilege."

"Watch your tongue," Haukyn says. "Only the bees' honey is for sale."

The dog hidden behind Ilotte's table, a big, scruffy brown dog, rises to its feet, lips curled. The burgher slaps his coins down, huffs under his breath, and stamps away with the pot of honey. "He won't be back," Ilotte says, "'n' you be interfering in m' life again."

"I'm glad you took my advice—a dog with a large number of teeth and all of them in good repair."

"You be blocking the stall, the pair o' you!"

Out of humour with her—and with himself—he says, "Come on, Ralf, why waste our time with a beekeeper who lacks common courtesy? We need to find the salt merchant."

The bag of salt is heavy; Haukyn tosses it in the cart with scant regard for his mother's new cover. After they pass the green-garlanded alehouse, he buys two pork pies from a vendor, adds them to the load, and on a tall-backed bench beneath a willow grove, they munch on flaky pastry and piping hot minced pork. Ralf breaks the silence. "That fat burgher, he isn't like the bees making their honeycomb."

Baffled, Haukyn says, "What do you mean?"

"You don't know what he'll do next. Jorden Smyth's the same."

"Men who are lustful or violent can be...unpredictable."

"Jorden hit Ivo and you hit Jorden."

"Jorden was pushing Ivo too near the fire. I had to stop him."

"I don't like fighting."

Jorden's battered face, that ghastly hand-to-hand combat in Roye, a dead priest bleeding on a stone floor...Haukyn wipes his mouth, stands up, clasps the handles of the cart, and pushes hard. Ralf says, hesitantly, "Would I have liked you in France?"

"Probably not. Wars are for killing, Ralf. I went there without a thought, anything to get away from my father's virgates and the confines of the vill. I wouldn't want you be as reckless."

The cart creaks and groans through the ruts, and the wheels churn up the dust as they leave the market. He's glad he's seen Ilotte again, she as irritable and ungrateful as she was after the stocks, and he'll forget that moment when her smile lit her face with beauty.

All the way home, Ralf is sunk in thought, although he brightens when Gil shares the honeycomb with him. After they've eaten supper, Edmund says, "Haukyn, let me show you the seed I've put aside for you. And Johanna has requested you weed her garden."

Haukyn pushes back from the table. There is no escaping his nine acres, and why didn't Johanna ask him herself?

Later, down on his knees under his sister-in-law's critical eye, he turfs out the stubborn roots of thistles, bindweed, and buttercups, and wonders how long his own roots will survive, those that anchor the soul to the soul's adventures.

...a pig in a poke...

From the hedge, a wren jingles its improbable song.

Solomon the Small, who always seems to have the time to help others, has supplied his oxen and on Haukyn's nine acres imparts, with no air of teaching, how to plough a straight furrow. If he has to farm, Haukyn thinks, listening to the wren, is he going to do a piss-poor job? Neither Solomon nor Robert would think much of that. But will he end up like an ox, slow and placid, carving straight lines from here to there, there to here, til tis time to lie down and die?

Although his furrows waver a little, within a fortnight there are green shoots on his acres and on his father's, and he cannot deny they give him satisfaction, if rueful.

That same day, Edmund says, "You've done well, Haukyn."

The praise warms him and he seizes the opportunity. "I want to go to London soon, to see Javyd. I told you that he saved my life in the Dordogne. He said he'd be back in the city by March."

"You've earned a rest. Neuton would lend you his grey mare, and the twins can keep birds and weeds from the crops."

So Haukyn leaves for London on Neuton's docile mare almost a year to the day since he left for France on Modge's back. He finds the mare's gait smooth, and oh, how he's missed the smell of mane, the flick of velvet ears, the feel of a road leading him onward. He joins a group of merchants, stays two successive nights in flea-ridden inns, and on the third day enters the city at Ludgate to the chorus of the bells at None.

His nose wrinkles from the stew of sewage, rubbish, and an overused river. He asks for directions to Budge Row, circles the stone bulk of St. Paul's with its tall spire and racket of vendors, then turns east again on Watling. Budge Row parallels the river; in the gutter, a long-tailed rat is rummaging through rotting vegetables. A scrofulous urchin, for coin, tells him Petronilla's house is third from the end of the street on the river side, where the gutters, he notices, are cleaner. The lad rolls his eyes. "Him 'n' his stinking cart should be home by now."

Javyd? Is that who the urchin means?

And then a man appears leading a horse and waggon from a nearby side street, a short man, black-bearded and black-browed, Javyd, unmistakably Javyd, and Haukyn is awash in joy that his friend survived those last weeks in France. "Javyd!" he shouts, spurring the mare. "Javyd, for England and St. George!"

Javyd's head jerks around. "God's bollocks, tis Haukyn! St. George and all the bloody saints, tis good to see you, lad." But as Haukyn dismounts, he holds up a hand. "Not too close—me 'n' m' cart smells ripe."

"Aye, you do…worse than Piers after the marsh at Moulins."

"I tol' you m' last name, atte Fermour. It don't mean naught to you? A gong-fermour? Tis m' trade, and a well-paid one at that—I cleans the cesspools o' the rich 'n' the public privies, loads the shite in barrels, 'n' dumps 'em in the river. Six days a week 'cause we all know no one shits on Sunday."

Haukyn gulps, half-amused, half-appalled. "A useful trade."

"Come to the house. I'll clean up 'n' you can meet m' sister Petronilla. She don't let me in til I've scrubbed m'self head to toes in our shed 'n' changed m' clothes, a right tyrant she be, but I puts up with it for the sake of her pasties. We c'n stable your mare with mine."

"My thanks. And well met, Javyd, you'll have tales to tell."

In the stable, hay, dung, and the scent of horseflesh. For a moment Haukyn rests his face on the grey mare's mane. "I still miss my Modge."

"On the morrow, take yerself to Smithfield. No horse market, but it being an off-day you might get a bargain."

Petronilla is a homely, sturdy woman, taller than her brother, with a kindness to which Haukyn easily responds. She serves chicken pasties and ale around the hearth; Javyd's account of his last weeks in France is unblemished by even a single obscenity, and, in Haukyn's opinion, the duller for it.

"Haukyn, let's take a walk while Nilla clears the dishes. Cut-purses, pimps, 'n' beggars abound in our city, I'll show you where to go and where not." Once they've left the house, he adds, "Now let me tell you how it were in Bordeaux."

The story has exploits and expletives aplenty, further enlivened by Javyd's description of the whore he'd visited last week in one of Southwark's stews. "We c'n cross the bridge 'n' go there, if you wants. Though there be brothels on Cokkes Lane by the church o' St. Pancras, tis closer to home." And he winks.

Haukyn laughs. "Waste my hard-earned coin when I can spend time with you? Let's walk closer to the bridge, I'd like to get my bearings."

"Dowgate, you gets the best o' the bridge from there."

He names the streets as they go: Wallbrook, Old Fish, Candlewick, and Thames. The houses overhang the streets. Cartwheels groan, children shriek, late vendors bellow their goods, dogs bark and snarl—how does anyone live in such an uproar? London Bridge is a mighty spectacle, its huge boat-shaped starlings holding up the stone pillars, the tide rushing and splashing between them. Peaked houses line the bridge from end to end. The chapel to St. Thomas juts over the river; revolted, he sees the dark heads of traitors and criminals mounted on poles, gazing sightlessly at city and river.

Dusk by now, the lights of Southwark gleaming on the water. They walk farther east so Haukyn can see the gate to the bridge, then west along the cobbles of Thames Street. A brindled cat, naught but bones over mangy fur, slinks around the corner. A rat, wet-furred and careless, slithers into the ditch, the cat pounces, the rat squeals, the black waters lap at the pilings, and he smells the river's depth, its dirt, its tides.

Clouds have rolled in from the estuary, no light from a sickled moon, no stars. The street is bordered with houses, many substantial. "Good them upper windows be unshuttered, getting too dark to see yer nose afore yer face," Javyd says. "Cloth merchants lives here, cursed Flemings screwing coin off our English weavers, I got no use fer 'em. This be the Vintry, Queenhithe the wharf where they unloads wine from France."

"You're no cloth merchant, why would you hate Flemings?"

Javyd shrugs. "All Londoners do...Here be a whore 'n' here be your chance."

A woman in a striped hood is sidling up to them; beneath the crudely applied paint on her face Haukyn can see that she's young, as gaunt as a French serf. In France the army was trailed by women like this, who for a scrap of bread would spread their legs; one of them, a woman with yellow hair, maimed by Benedict and left to die.

His tarse shrivels. He scrabbles in his purse and drops a coin into her palm. She says, "I got a place two houses up."

"Nay, tis a gift."

Her red-gashed mouth drops open. Dirty fingers wrap themselves around the coin, and she scurries down the nearest lane. Javyd says, "You got aught in them braies o' yourn?"

"I do, and value it too highly for a dose of the burning sickness."

"Brothels be safer."

"Not tonight, Javyd." He adds, curious, "You never raped in France, did you?"

"I pays coin fer sarding, fair 'n' square. Rape ain't to m' taste."

"Nor mine. I'm weary, let's go back to Budge Row."

Petronilla opens the door to Javyd's low-voiced command. A fire in the hearth, candles against the dark, and she says, "The privy be out back, Haukyn, and a bed for you upstairs."

He says, "I'll have to leave as soon as the gates open on the morrow."

He's had enough of London.

By Terce, Haukyn is riding the mare up Wallbrook to Cheapside. Smithfield is beyond the city walls, stretching as far west as the Fleet River, and tis time he replaced Modge in his heart. A pond in the middle of a trampled field, wooden coops in piles, wooden pens. Moo-ing, baa-ing, hens a-cluck, and as he looks around, above the din he hears cursing and the crack of a whip. A horse neighs in distress. Neuton's grey mare breaks stride. Past a rough outbuilding, he comes upon a man whipping a chestnut mare, she straining against the halter, her flanks bloodied. Haukyn dismounts. "Stop! Or, by God, your blood will join hers."

The man's russet tunic is already blood-spattered; he's red of face and panting. "Good fer naught but the Shambles, and that's where I'll take her once I've beat some sense into her."

"Lower your whip and tell me what's wrong with her."

A look of cunning crosses the man's face. "I be John o' Faringdon, 'n' you, good sir?"

The mare is shivering, head low. "You have no need of my name. Answer the question."

"A mite disobedient, tis all. Women 'n' horses, they both needs a firm hand, wouldn't you agree?"

Ilotte, sentenced to the stocks for disobedience. Ilotte would heal the mare, if he's man enough to ask her, she so unfriendly and sharp of tongue besides. "A shilling for the mare. Which is more than she'll earn at the Shambles."

"A goodly horse with four good shoes? Worth three shillings!"

"Are you deaf as well as cruel?" He reaches in his pouch, extracts the coin by the feel of it, tosses it on the ground well away from the mare, and remounts. "Don't think to rob me of the rest," he says, "I'm a soldier and killing means little to me." Neuton's mare shifts uneasily beneath his weight. "Loose the chestnut's halter and pass it to me."

"You'll soon enough learn her faults. A curse on both o' you."

"The halter."

When he has it secure around his palm, he urges the grey mare forward. The chestnut balks. He thinks of Willem, dismounts, goes to her head, and with a wary eye on the man and his evil grin says softly, "You'll be well cared for, and a whip will never strike you again. Now come, we need to leave London and get on our way."

He steps between the two horses, reins in one hand, halter in the other. Still talking softly, he urges them both forward and forward they go, him checking over his shoulder that he's not being followed. They cross the foul-smelling Fleet Ditch and take the first turn south. The chestnut is favouring one leg.

God help him, he's bought a pig in a poke, a lame pig in a torn poke. But what choice did he have?

...if a distant bell no longer chimes...

Ilotte is sweeping her front step and straightens when she sees Haukyn leading the two horses toward her. Her eyes are dark and unfathomable. Her dog growls a warning. He stands by her fence, which, he notices, has three rotten posts and needs new pickets. "God's blessing, Ilotte, and does your dog have a name?"

"Elf," she says, daring him to laugh.

"An elf with fangs." He sobers. "Will you use your healing powers on the chestnut? She was sore-beaten at Smithfield and hasn't let me touch her wounds, and she's lame in one leg. I'll pay coin for your care of her."

"The wounds be infected. You got great faith in me."

Is she mocking him? He cannot tell. Her hair has slipped free of her cap, black as night—yet, he thinks with a fancifulness rare to him, tis as though the blue gleam of daylight is fugitive within those dark strands. He says, "She needs kindness. And quiet. Such quiet was not possible on the journey home."

"I'll do m' best. Come back after Easter."

His smile breaks through. "My thanks. You look well."

"Better 'n you."

"We had to travel slow because of her lameness. So for three nights I slept twixt two horses, rats running over me and fleas feasting on me."

"I don't want your fleas. Stand away from the mare."

He stays where he is. "Keep my distance, is that what you mean? You trusted me at the stocks last winter, and you can trust me now."

"I trust no man, nor ever will."

She leans her broom against the wall and steps forward, her gaze on the mare, her voice so soft a murmur he can't distinguish what she's saying; the chestnut stands very still. Taking the halter, her fingers brush his. Ignoring him as if he didn't exist, she rests one hand just above the mare's muzzle. "You'll come with me 'n' I'll salve your hurts til you be whole again." Then she looks up at Haukyn, all gentleness banished. "Barnaby-up-the-Hill will sell you hay 'n' deliver it here for a fee. Go there now."

He does so. Then he mounts Neuton's grey mare and rides home to Flintbourne.

Her face when she touched the mare. So intent. So tender.

I trust no man, nor ever will.

At Dunstan's, the real work has begun. Under the old man's tutelage, Haukyn has stripped elm bark, drawn lines for the limbs of a bow, removed excess wood with hatchet and drawknife, and filed the nock grooves. Though tillering requires great patience, he soon realizes he possesses that patience, as well as the steady hands needed to slice painstakingly thin layers of wood from the belly of the bow so the limbs will draw evenly: the arc at full compass must never be less than perfection, no stiffness, no weakness. Bow as a living thing, bow with memory, bow taught to be steadfast.

He's found his true craft.

On Sunday, he gives his usual lesson on the green. More often than he cares for, he ponders Ilotte and her lack of trust. Now and again, stealthy as Warty Ivo, he nets a fat trout, which Hawise cooks to perfection. Edmund raises his brows and says nothing, while to Haukyn, the pink flesh tastes doubly good for being forbidden. It can now can be washed down with Johanna's ale, because to the gratification of all the customers at the alehouse, and with the help of pretty Annabel, Johanna is back in her brew shed, Ralf and Gil watching over her twins.

Palm Sunday and Easter Sunday pass with due pageantry. On Hocktide Tuesday, incautiously, Haukyn walks to the well, and there is surrounded by young women, giddy because tis the day they can choose the men they have their eyes on, trip them, tie them, and demand coin of them for freedom. Annabel, blushing, is the one who knots the cord around his wrists. His cheeks as red, his elbow colliding with her breast, he pays his ransom and manages not to lose his bucket down the well.

The next morning, he takes his father aside. "The day I left London, I bought a mare at Smithfield that was being mercilessly beaten. Paid a shilling for her and took her to Hungerford to a woman called Ilotte, who heals hens and horses and all creatures in between. I'll fetch the mare today. Solomon the Small will rent his byre for a small sum, and I've coin for hay. And when I say she will never go to war, this time I mean it."

"The mare will make your acres the more bearable."

Taken aback by such understanding, he says awkwardly, "I do my best, though tis not always a very good best."

"You are not supposed to be Robert. Haukyn is well enough."

His wretched blush again stains his face. "Over the summer I'll begin my house, with your help and the vill's."

Edmund claps him on the back. Staff to hand, waterskin sloshing at his waist, Haukyn leaves Flintbourne. Although he could have gone on Easter Monday, he'd decided to wait a day or two before he walked to Hungerford, either to prove something to himself or to Ilotte, a distinction he doesn't examine. Keeping a vigilant eye for strangers, he strides along. Weeks of a mattock wedded to fists and back, of the hard tug of plough handles, the swing of hammer and careful sharpening of saw—his body the better for it, and if his soul chafes at the confines of his hands' work, if a distant bell no longer chimes to his ears, at least he's breathing God's good air, as Willem and Piers are not. As Robert is not.

Within the hour he's reached Ilotte's little white-washed house. The fence is still in need of repair. The mare, tethered to a stake in the small patch of grass to one side of the house, is peaceably grazing. He lays his staff on the ground and walks closer. Her head swings around, grass and slobber drooping from her lips. "You'll sleep in another byre tonight," he says. "Will you let me mount you in the weeks to come?"

She tugs at the halter. Her flanks are healed, though she is still scarred, long, thin lines where the hair has not grown back. "Never again," he says, "I swear it."

Behind him, Ilotte says, "I done what I could. Rest be up to you."

He turns around. "Her coat is glossy and I can no longer count her ribs. Is she still lame?"

"Fluid from a bruise and easy mended."

"My thanks, Ilotte."

"You owes me coin."

"I never thought otherwise."

Her eyes, they're black as river stones, polished by currents he cannot imagine. She's tall and gawky, small-breasted, a woman so unlike pretty, rounded Annabel, yet...aye, he thinks, *yet...*

She says irritably, "You gawk at me like I be a goose at the market."

"I'm happy to see you," he says with complete truth. Her hair, bundled under her cap, he can feel the weight of it, the way it would slip and slide through his fingers, and adds hastily, "How much do I owe you?"

She charges too little and will take no more. As he drops the coins into her palm, he says, "I shall call her Trefoil. We grow it for fodder, its buds almost chestnut in hue, its leaves in threes. One for the Smithfield merchant, one for your care of her, and one for myself...I never told Willem or Piers, but before I went to war I used to dream of breeding horses for my living, selling them at the market...a dream long-abandoned. Ilotte, have you dreams?"

She flinches. He says, "I trespassed, I'm sorry," and impelled by he knows not what, steps closer, drops his forehead to her shoulder, and inhales her scent.

Her fist ploughs into his belly. He doubles over and backs off, rubbing his gut yet on the verge of laughter. "You smell as I imagine a wolf would smell that's slept in bracken."

"Stay away from me!"

"It seems I don't want to."

"I'll lie down for no man."

He allows a puzzled frown to crease his forehead. "Have I asked you to?"

As she bares her teeth, much as a wolf might, he adds, "I've never entered any woman. Nor will I, til she and I burn in the same flame." The former a secret he's never told anyone, the latter a truth he hadn't known was his, and both spouted to a woman who looks not one whit impressed.

"You be virgin? You expects me to believe that?"

"I am and I do. What if I came courting you, Ilotte of Hungerford?"

"I'd call you fool."

The words burst from him. "Piers spoke of you often, yet you've never asked how he fared in France, nor the manner of his death. Did he mean so little to you?"

"He were good to look upon, and he ne'er did aught I didn't want him to."

What did *you want from him?* Jealousy a hot sin, new to him, and more words escape. "When I left France I was nigh-dead in body and full-dead in soul. You waken me, your spirit calls to mine—I can't explain it and it makes no sense."

"I ain't here to waken no man. Take your Trefoil 'n' don't come back."

"You're like the mare you've healed, unwilling to be mounted. Or are you like an anchorite, walled in so none may touch you?"

"Walled in? I couldn't bear it."

"I'd never confine you. The distant bell of freedom, I hear it when I'm with you."

"Go home!" she cries, whirls, and runs for her house.

The mare whinnies. He's a fool right enough, a man who doesn't think before he spouts words that can't be stuffed back down his throat. He breathes deep, trying to calm himself. Trefoil needs calm, and he needs Trefoil. After a long drink from his waterskin, he walks closer to the mare, murmuring her name so she will grow used to it, his empty hands outstretched. She stands still, her muzzle whiffling, he in hopes she remembers him from the long walk here and those nights in the inns' stables. With the patience Willem called up in him so long ago, he waits until he thinks she's ready before he unties the halter from its peg in the ground. He picks up his staff, keeping it to one side and down low, and after a single tug backward, she follows him through the gate and down the hill. Why would he even think of wooing Ilotte, a mare who kicks and bites and is afeared of fire, a she-cat hissing at a tom?

He stops dead. Trefoil swings her head; her eyes are a deep brown. He wants a loving marriage, a marriage of devotion like that between his mother and father. The depth of understanding, the fond brush of hand to hand, the swiving in the dark and its remembrance the next morning; he's seen that remembrance, its tenderness. He's never had the courage to ask how his parents met, how they became friends as well as lovers.

He didn't seek out pretty Margery before she married the bailiff's son; he now understands why. Ilotte as friend seems distantly possible, but as anything more?

He'll end up a crotchety old man like Dunstan, firing stones at his neighbours.

At first Trefoil cowers from the bulk of Solomon the Small. But she grows used to him, as she is now accustomed to Haukyn's daily grooming of her coat, his untangling of mane and tail, his lifting of her hoofs to muck them out; she'll poke her head out of the stall when he sneaks her a wizened carrot from last year's crop. Although she quivers when he lays an old saddle of Solomon's on her back, she soon ignores its weight, and a few days later accepts harness and reins. Three days in a row he leads her into the woods on the ridge, and on the fourth, having checked that they are alone, he mounts her. She stands still, ears pricked. She's no Modge, tossing him groundward. His chest tight with an old grief, he risks pressing knees and heels to her, and obediently, as if all along she's been waiting for this, she weaves through the coppiced hazels. He laughs out loud. She swishes her tail. *So I can still be a happy man, this is all it takes. Why would I need Ilotte, and the Smithfield merchant was right, this horse was worth more than a shilling, for someone has trained her well.*

Of a sudden she shies, almost unseating him: Warty Ivo, also weaving through the trees, a dead rabbit dangling from one hand. Haukyn says, "That'll be tasty in your mother's stew pot."

"If you don't blab to the constable."

"I'll not. The burn on your cheek, how did you get it?"

"How d' you think?"

With passionate intensity, Haukyn says, "Why stay here, Ivo? You could run away to Newbury, or better still, Windsor, live there for a year and a day and you'd be free...*free.* You have many of a smith's skills, you'd find work, you could make something of yourself."

Ivo spits on the duff, grinds the spittle into the dirt. "'N' then I'd be out o' yer face? I ain't stupid, I c'n see the game you be playing."

"You can leave here as I cannot, don't you understand?" Raw anguish in his voice now—God's bones, he's pathetic.

"Yer mare wouldn't be so pretty were she hamstrung."

For a flash in time he's back in a rain-sodden forest, the haunt of French serfs with blackened faces and sharp knives, English horses and English soldiers hamstrung, crippled beyond repair, a cut throat the only cure. "Touch her and I'll feed your tripes to the sow."

"Have to catch me first, wouldn't you."

In a blur of motion Haukyn dismounts and grabs a handful of Ivo's tunic, his other hand clamping Ivo's knife-arm to his side. "You don't understand," he says softly. "I spent five months in France, I killed more men than you'll see in your lifetime, shot them from horseback, stabbed them, slit their throats, decapitated them. War breaks you or it hardens you. It didn't break me, I don't scream in the night like my father. Stay away from me and mine, Ivo, or one day you'll disappear and no one in the vill will ever find you because I'll have buried you deep. Then the rumour will spread that you fled to London to work a city forge and you'll be forgot as if you never existed—aye, you're wise to look affrighted."

He shoves Ivo hard against the nearest tree and remounts. A rustle of undergrowth, a sway of new-leafed branches, and Ivo is gone. He'd dropped the rabbit to the ground. Haukyn leaves it where it lies, bloodstained fur and blank, dark eyes. Had he really hoped to befriend a man who's long been his enemy? Pathetic indeed. Haunted by images he'd rather forget, his enjoyment in the ride gone, Haukyn nudges Trefoil down the hill. That same afternoon he moves her from Solomon's byre to his father's, into a narrow stall with a cow on either side; when she objects to the change, he feeds her another of their dried-up carrots and rests his face on her mane's coarse hair.

Edmund watches his second son as the days pass, his heart aching for his elder son. Haukyn never lifts to his nostrils the earth's crumbs and inhales the richness of generations of decay and dung and digging; for him, soil is a place to plant his feet. Yet—and Edmund's heart aches the harder—he's doing his best to look after his own nine acres and Edmund's virgates. No joy in it, though. He'd heard how pretty, blue-eyed Annabel, abetted by other women in the vill, had captured Haukyn at Hocktide. She could have saved herself the trouble. Ever since, his son has buried himself in the byre, stacking wood, cleaning the cows' stalls, shovelling dung as if his life depended on it. Praise God for Dunstan, Trefoil, and the twins, they're the saving of him.

Never again has he called me Da.

Haukyn wakes before dawn and lies still under the angled roof, his spirit troubled. He should never have prated to Ivo about freedom. Today he has to milk the cow that birthed a heifer last week, dodging her hoofs and the switch of her dung-wet tail. After he's trod his own acres pulling young thistles and early poppies, he'll do the same on his father's virgates, then he'll start clearing the area where he wants his house to stand, overlooking the river. A house. Another cord binding him to the land. Soon enough he'll be joining the men in the meadows to dig out ragwort and burn it. Haying, weeding, hedging, harvest, the orchard to tend, and what if his father should die before the twins are grown? It doesn't bear thinking about.

That evening at dusk—and aye, the cow planted her hoof square on his toes—he meets the vill's new constable, Tirrell Wodebyte, near the well. Bow-legged, fresh of face, the freeman calls a cheerful greeting and into Haukyn's ear, indiscreetly, pours his manifold troubles with Amos Cat-Skinner and Jorden Smyth.

Haukyn nods at him, picks up Johanna's buckets, and takes the river path, limping a little on his sore foot. A serf can't be constable, you have to be freeman. No wonder Tirrell looks so cheerful. Freeman, a bowyer roaming the valley with his wares, living wherever he chooses, a dream as impossible as any he's had.

When he delivers the buckets, Johanna invites him in to sample her brew. "I'd be happy to, though I'm no ale-taster," he says, stepping over her threshold.

"Our reeve's taken that on, in his spare time." She snorts. "Spare time, him lazy as a winter trout. Lucky for me that Annabel, though his daughter, puts her back into the work…she captured you at Hocktide."

"A game. Yet the whole vill knows of it."

She laughs at his irritation, pours ale into a mazer, and passes it to him. She looks well in the candlelight, her cheeks flushed, her heaviness of spirit seemingly lessened; savouring the amber liquid, he says, "Good ale, the grout distinct. Your secret, am I right?"

Topping up his mazer, she says, "Of course," and adds a faggot to the fire, her movements graceful. "I be glad of your company, Haukyn, I miss a man about the house."

"I would he hadn't died."

She puts her ale down on the bench and steps closer. He holds his ground, aware of a stirring of unease. "Haukyn," she says, "I always been a woman o' heat, I knowed that and thought marriage'd be the saving of me. But Robert didn't want me that way. Tis spring, you must yearn for a woman in your bed, 'n' it says in the Bible a man can take his brother's widow to himself." Closer still, she raises her face, her lips soft and inviting.

He lowers his mazer to the bench. Ale slops over the edges. "Johanna, I'm not—"

She's pressing her body to his, and that too is soft, breast and belly and thigh, and he can't think, the candle is flickering, her hand finds his crotch and he feels himself harden, hears her small sigh of pleasure as her fingers, her clever fingers, knead his flesh, heat engulfing him as never before. Instinctively, his hips thrust forward, his whole body craving whatever will come next, and then she lifts his hand to her breast, nipple a small flintstone, and she smells biscuity, like malt, and milky from the twins, and somehow he's brought to his senses. With a gasp he pulls back. "We mustn't!"

"I'll not conceive."

The thought hadn't occurred to him; the possibility makes his blood run cold. "That isn't why I naysay."

"I beg you—"

He blurts the only words that will save him. "I cannot think of you as other than Robert's wife."

"Your body says different."

"The message false."

She recoils, as if the blow were physical. He says with true desperation, "Johanna, I'm sorry. If I'd known, I'd not have—we'll never speak of this, and I pray you will forgive me."

He's out the door and as it slaps shut he hears a terrible keening. His hair lifts on his nape. He can't go home, not yet. Dark, and a thin moon, the stars as distant in the sky and as close among the treetops as the brother he could so easily have betrayed. He staggers down the baulk. Where was reckless Haukyn, devil-may-care Haukyn, him running from Johanna like a hare with the pack baying at its heels, and he's furious with Robert for she deserved better of him than cold duty, and now his memory of his brother is so tarnished that there's no mending it and were he a woman he too would be keening at the moon. What could he do but run?

Hasn't he always run from the demands and buffets of family, from Robert's love of soil, Edmund's unspoken disappointment, and his mother's ire?

He doesn't run from the twins, from Ralf's unending curiosity and Gil's mischief.

He runs toward Ilotte, foolish though it be, she a woman whose only softness is toward horses, cows, and hens. He'd best learn to crow like a cockerel, bellow like a bull.

He stumbles over a clump of grass. How will he face Johanna on the morrow when she brings the twins over and eats supper at his father's table, as happens most days?

How will he keep his hands off himself in his bed tonight?

His close-guarded virginity, he prays Johanna hasn't divined it. Piers, quite possibly, did, but was friend enough not to taunt him.

Willem too wrapped up in Heloise to care about anyone else's tarse. Annabel would have him, he's seen her eyeing him since Hocktide, before and after Mass, and he's tired of his ignorance, he wants to feed his body's hungers, he wants to lie with a woman, skin to skin in the dark.

Piers could sard someone and leave her laughing as he wended his way toward the next bed. But himself? Sard pretty Annabel and walk away?

On May Day, a fool on a fool's errand, he mounts Trefoil and rides to Hungerford, the sun warm on his back, a bundle of wood tied to the back of his saddle, his saddlebag containing saw, nails, and hammer; his pouch holds a small bouquet of sweet violets and primroses plucked from the riverbank, an impulse he hopes he won't regret. On the other side of Ilotte's gate, Elf barks at him as if heralding the Second Coming. He tethers Trefoil to the farthest gatepost, takes out his tools, checks the fence for the worst pickets, and knocks two of them clear of the rails.

"What are you *doing*?"

Her skirts are in a flurry, her hands dirty, and her cap crooked. "God's blessing, Ilotte. Tis May Day and I've brought you flowers." He stoops and picks them up. "They need water."

"You be knocking down m' fence!"

"Tis in need of it, wouldn't you agree? Put the flowers in water before they perish."

She looks from him to the flowers and back again. "But—"

"Has no man ever given you flowers?" He smiles as he passes her the bunch of wilting purple and cream petals. "I was up at dawn to pick them. Were you weeding? Why don't you get back to it, you and Elf, and leave me in peace to mend your fence."

Were she to hold him as Johanna did…He bends for his hammer and turns his back on her, and within two hours, hot and thirsty, he's used up his small stock of wood and measured the rails that need replacing. He finds Ilotte and Elf behind the house, the dog vigilant, she on her knees with a trowel, bees humming in lazy circles around the blooms on her apple and pear trees. A bench beneath a rowan tree beckons with its shade. "If you've whitewash, I'll paint the new pickets," he says.

She scrambles to her feet, avoiding his eyes. "A task for me once I'm done here. I'll bring pottage 'n' fill your waterskin. Sit on the bench."

A bee hovers in front of his nose, then buzzes away. He hauls his tunic over his head and wipes his face on his shirt-sleeve. Contentment, tis less fleet of foot than joy, more like a foundation than a high-pitched roof, yet not to be disparaged.

When she returns, the bowl held in her apron, he cajoles her to sit beside him and tell him what she has planted in her garden, watching her hands gesture as she talks, long-fingered hands, and strong. "Good pottage, my thanks, Ilotte. Now I must ride home. Paint the pickets before it rains."

An impartial smile, his own hands firmly at his sides, and he leaves her in the garden. The flowers beguiled her, and he, hasty Haukyn, apparently has a strategy. But to what end? To bed her? Wed her? Or, perhaps more difficult, gain her trust?

During the next week, he and Martin, the vill's carpenter, mark out the foundations of his house. Martin fashions beams and roof trusses; Haukyn's hoarded coin dwindles fast. In a concerted effort he, Edmund, Neuton, Solomon, Martin, and Martin's brother Simon raise beams and trusses, he discovering muscles he didn't know he owned. He's had the foresight to provide plenty of Johanna's ale, and when they're done, there's laughter and back-slapping, a comradeship similar to that in the army, he thinks, but without the army's miseries. As he reaches for the last jug of ale, he sees someone standing between here and the smithy, looking down at them, utterly still. Ivo. Warty Ivo, the outsider, who roves the fields and lanes, thieving, and finds little welcome anywhere in the vill. Warty Ivo. Time he dropped that name. He turns his back and when he looks again, Ivo is gone.

What though, if in the night, Ivo took an axe to the beams? That evening, he carries a blanket from his bed at home and lies down on the bare ground, the roof trusses cutting into the stars, and when he wakes at first light the beams are intact. His house, he thinks, the newly chiselled wood straight and tall against the orchard's shadows and the last stars. His house and Ilotte's, could that ever come about or is he the world's biggest fool even to imagine it?

During May's longer hours of light, he works harder than he's ever worked in his life. Edmund insists on paying for the thatcher, the twins take great delight in mixing daub, his own fingers are scraped and sore from weaving wattle, and slowly two walls take shape. His visits to Dunstan are fewer.

On a Sunday after Mass, when he rides to Hungerford with more boards, Heloise hails him on his way up the hill. "You seek Ilotte? She be helping with sheep-shearing. She likes to be with the men."

"Tis the sheep she likes," he says, and does his best to hide disappointment from Willem's widow. No mouse, she. Watchful as a weasel. "I'm mending her fence," he says. "For Piers's sake. God's blessing, Heloise." *And forgive me the untruth, Piers. It would seem I lust after Ilotte as you did, though I doubt you bedded her and I doubt I ever will either, and if tis more than lust...*and here his thoughts come to a halt.

Heloise walks away, her back rigid with disapproval. At the white cottage, he unloads the wood and starts on the new railings, taking pleasure in the ring of his hammer and scrape of his saw, a far cry from the delicate and painfully slow work of tempering. He's nearly done, gulping from his waterskin, his shirt sticky with sweat, when he sees a woman running down the hill toward him, skirts flapping, black hair falling loose from her cap. Running as if she can't wait to see him. Joy like a burst of sunlight in his chest, he hurries to meet her.

No matching joy in her face, only distress. He grasps her by the waist; she's panting, and sags in his hold. "What's the matter? Has someone laid hands on you?"

"I knowed you was here, you must go, you must leave, summat's wrong, but I can't see further—"

"What do you mean? What's wrong?"

She's gripping his arms, the first time she's so freely touched him. "I don't know!"

"I'm here, I'm holding you, Ilotte, and look around, there's naught wrong. Save I bashed my thumb with the hammer."

"Haukyn, you must leave, you must go to your vill—how I hates these fits, what they does to me, but always they tell me true. Tis the only thing m' mother ever give me, this curse of knowing 'n' not knowing, 'n' a curse it is. I beg you, get on your mare, ride for home."

"I've never seen you act like this."

"Tis why they call me sorceress," she says.

Trust, he thinks, must it not go two ways? His heart cold, one small part of his brain noticing she smells strongly of sheep, he says, "Is it my father? My mother?"

She pounds his chest with her fists. "I can't tell, why ain't you listening. Just *go!*"

Shaken, he releases her to rub his breastbone. "I'll return as soon as I can."

He looses Trefoil and fastens his saddlebag, swiftly kisses Ilotte on the cheek, her hair silken, smelling not of sheep but of lavender, then mounts. "God be with you," he says, and canters down the hill. Why does he believe a woman so obviously deranged and why was a curse her mother's only gift?

The journey goes fast. At his father's house, from his frantic mother, he learns that Ralf disappeared after Mass. "Didn't come home for soup." Her voice quavers. "Gil off with Edmund searching the woods. Solomon, Tirrell, Neuton too. The river, Ralf loves watching water bugs, what if he fell in and the current—"

"I'll search the riverbank."

"Find Ralf, Haukyn, find him."

So Ilotte saw true.

The river path first, he thinks, and scours the banks on both sides, calling Ralf's name. The river deepens. No shoes on the bank, no sign of a small boy's passing. A kingfisher flits past him, swift as an arrow's flight. Fern fronds brush his knees. "Ralf!" he shouts. "Ralf!"

Something caught in the watercress, a little furry body. A kitten. A few feet farther, a second body. His brow furrows. Farther and farther he goes, til he sees the big oak—his hideaway, why didn't he think of that? He leaves the path, his feet crushing bracken, branches catching his shirt, and there in front of him is the circle of blackthorn and bramble, in full leaf. "Ralf," he says, "are you in there?"

The faintest of whispers. "Haukyn?"

"Aye. Come out now, Da and Gil have been searching for you since Sext."

"Don't want to."

He hunkers down. "What's the matter?"

Even through the thick blanket of leaves, he can hear snuffles. "Boys were drowning kittens in the river, but not drowning them, lifting them out and then holding them under, over and over, and I ran at them and they hit me and laughed at me and why are people cruel, the kittens were mewling..."

Sobbing now, not snuffling.

Haukyn says, "You tried, Ralf, you did your best, tis all we can do."

"M-maybe Da'll hit me, like he hit you."

"He won't. I promise. Can you back out of the tunnel? Feet first?"

The leaves quiver and shake. Yelps of pain, for the spines are sharp. Kneeling at the entrance, Haukyn eases the boy free, then takes him in his arms, pressing his blood-streaked face to his chest. "Let's go home."

"Ma'll be cross."

"She'll be too happy to see you. And I'll tell her and Da how brave you were to take on a gang of nasty lads."

Because he doesn't want Ralf seeing those two sodden little bodies, they walk home through the woods, hand in hand. His mother clasps

Ralf close, Haukyn sounds the hue to let the men know the boy is found, and he tells Edmund and Gil what happened. "Ralf trusts people to be good," he says, "and I sorrow to witness him learning differently."

Weeding his crops and his father's—how many times has he already done so?—back-breaking work even when helped by the twins' quick fingers. Ralf stays close. Ralf must never go to war, it would break him as it would not break Gil. Annabel joins them, smiling artlessly at Haukyn. "The barley be soaking two more days, so Johanna sent me to help you." He nods his thanks, aware of how pretty she is, the hair peeping from her cap the hue of ripe barley, her eyes as guileless a blue as her chatter, her incessant chatter, while her body...With overdone care he digs out the deep roots of burdock, saving leaves and roots for his mother. Ilotte's strangeness—can she read too much of men's thoughts when the sap rises in spring and the birds mate in the hedgerows, and hence her lack of trust? That moment of joy when he saw her running toward him, what meaning can he put to that? Is she, like Solomon's red-eyed bull, a challenge he cannot resist?

He should see thistles as the challenge, he thinks, not a sloe-eyed woman.

On a day of mizzle Haukyn rides to Hungerford with more boards. Ilotte is not home, shearing again in all likelihood. He finishes what he left undone the day of her spell—is that what he'd call it?—and as he starts nailing the last of the pickets to the new railing, Trefoil neighs. Ilotte pushes the gate open and trudges through it; he can't tell if she's pleased to see him. He smiles at her. "You look weary."

"It earns m' keep."

"I'll be done shortly."

When he's finished, the day too damp to whitewash the new boards, he walks, soft-footed, around the corner of her house. She's seated on the bench under the rowan tree, leaning against the trunk, eyes shut, her tunic misted. Why is he drawn to this woman, so unapproachable, so full of secrets? Quietly he says her name.

She jerks upright, her cheeks rain-damp. "You makes yourself needed in toft 'n' croft."

"My brother Ralf, the boy you met at the market, he was lost the other day, the men searching the woods. I found him near the river. I thank you for your warning."

Getting to her feet, she rubs her back. "So m' fears tol' true. Do the whole o' Flintbourne now know what I sees and don't see?"

"I've told no one, nor will."

Her lips soften—not quite a smile, but he's beginning to know how to read her. He says, "You feel it as a curse, why would I share it with anyone? Ilotte, you spoke of your mother. Is she dead?"

She shrugs. "How would I know? She left when I were a little-un. Ain't seen nor heard from her since."

"I'm sorry…your father?"

"I'll feed you, afore you rides home."

He looks around the garden, droplets hanging from every branch, the apples needing the moisture, her bees quiescent. "I desire only your well-being."

"I c'n look after m'self. Spinach 'n' pea soup."

He follows her into the same room where he'd sat with his back to her as she washed off the filth of the stocks; it feels like yesterday, it feels like a lifetime ago, and while she heats the soup and then places a bowl before him, he tells her about Ralf and the kittens.

She digs her nails into the grain of the table. "We all has to lose our innocence."

"Who harmed you so grievously?"

"Haukyn, stop."

A man. It had to be a man. Elyas? Bidewell? Swallowing frustration along with delicately herbed peas, he says, "Tis fine soup and there now, you can smile. Do you have other chores I can do?"

"Ain't there women in Flintbourne after you to do their chores? Be they blind? You be comely enough…the more so when your cheeks goes red as bergamot."

He stands up with as much dignity as he can muster. "I must ride home before dark."

Birds to scare from his crops, Gil using a sling, Ralf a clap-board, more weeding in the company of Annabel, then the men of the vill gather to uproot ragwort from the lord's hayfields. "A cow'll sicken 'n' die if ragwort be in her hay," says Solomon the Small. "The root seeks the underworld 'n' sprouts new roots if but a fragment be left in the soil."

"A root longer than a horse's pizzle," Haukyn says, "and why the lord's hayfield before our own?"

"Ancient custom."

"So we revere what is ancient though it serves us ill? God's nails, I've broke the end off the cursed root."

"Thrice now you've called on God's nails."

Viciously he digs deeper. "Are they not farthest from His heart? Should He have one."

"Good thing Father Mortimer ain't here listening to such blasphemy. Be you crossed in love, so testy you be?"

Triumphantly Haukyn brandishes the pointed end of the root. "Why would I need a woman when I have a farmer's tasks to beguile me?"

"Tis spring, more 'n sap's rising."

In a swift change of mood, Haukyn says, "Solomon, did you love your Lucy when you stood with her on the church steps?"

Solomon pauses to consider. "Aye. More now, though, since the little-uns 'n' the daily rub o' the two of us." He scrubs dirt off his fingers. "Annabel'd have you."

"I seem to want what I can't have," he says, "and the next root will come out whole or I'll curse God's nether parts."

"A task takes its appointed time. Tis like love, it ain't to be rushed."

Patience with tillering at Dunstan's, patience with ragwort in the fields, and patience with an intractable woman? Whose fleeces, he's certain, are unbloodied, for she would guard from the ewes' flesh her shears' sharp edges.

Two days on and the ragwort is now being uprooted from the common fields, Haukyn's temper short and his nails dark-rimmed. As he's plodding his way homeward from the fields, Johanna comes out of the brewing shed. "I hear you visits a woman on Hungerford's manor," she says. "Do you care for her more 'n Robert cared for me?"

So much venom and he's bone-weary. "I need the rain barrel and my supper."

"Your father 'n' mother, you know he risked death for her, 'n' her vagrant?"

His body goes still. "What do you mean?"

"Hanging from the scaffold she were, for theft of a loaf. Your father shot through the rope. The lord—Sir Roger it were back then—tossed 'em both in gaol, marry or a double hanging, that were your father's choice, no choice at all. So they married the next morning b'neath the scaffold." Johanna smiles at the shock on his face. "*She* weren't no virgin. Claimed she'd been raped afore she come to the vill, but who knows the truth o' that?" Her smile widens. "You didn't know the story?"

"How do you know?"

"Robert."

Another layer of hurt. "He never told me."

"Clever Hawise with her pretty herbal, kind Hawise with her midwifery. Naught but a common whore."

"Clever enough to help birth your twins, kind enough to feed you ever since. When will you winnow your rage and toss it to the four winds, Johanna?"

If eyes were daggers he'd be twice dead. He stamps toward Edmund's rain barrel, douses head and hands, and shakes himself like a dog. Indoors, the hearth, the smoke, his father's cheerful greeting, his mother's smile. He grabs for the towel Hawise keeps by the door and scrubs at his face. He can't speak of what he's learned, not now, not yet. Not ever? But by the hearthside, he sneaks glances at his mother's face, so familiar, a face he's always taken for granted, and the words are out before he can prevent them. "Ma, why did you leave Savernake Forest?"

The ladle in her hands stays poised over the bowl. Edmund says, "Her parents had both died. She had naught to keep her there. You'll be done the ragwort in another day."

Neither of them asks why, of a sudden, he needs to know.

More ragwort from the common meadows of hay, then poppies, thistles, and cornflowers from the wheat fields, and although Haukyn tries to shake off Johanna's words, he cannot. In the long June evenings, he works on his house, he weaving wattle, the twins helping with the daub; the byre is now enclosed and has two entrances, one inside, one out. Martin has framed the windows and when the last two walls are done, hangs shutters and a door with a stout latch. Whitewashing, furniture, rushes for the floor must wait until the hay is mowed, but otherwise his house is finished.

His house. Is it only his, when Ilotte has hovered at his side with every nail he's driven, every board he's planed? In Flintbourne, she'd be away from Elyas, the ugly constable with his silver and his bucket of slops, and from righteous Bidewell; she'd have an archer's protection.

If he pays court to her with more than fence-mending, he'll have to take his time, the prize too great for hurry.

On a rainy Sunday when no hay can be cut, he saddles Trefoil and rides to Hungerford, mud splashing her hoofs. He pushes open Ilotte's gate and knocks on her door, vain enough to take off his felt hat and shake out his crop of curls.

Elf barks on the other side of the stout boards. "Ilotte, tis Haukyn."

The door opens, the dog at her side. She looks him up and down. "An exceeding wet Haukyn."

"You wouldn't see me drown, would you?"

"You left the family hearth on such a day?"

The hearth at which Johanna will eat a meal cooked by his mother. "Family. You might be luckier than you think to have none."

A fat drip from the roof lands on his forehead and dribbles down his nose. He flicks it off, wondering why he bothered riding through the rain when the woman won't even let him in the door.

"You be troubled," she says, bites her lip, gives Elf a low-voiced command, and stands aside so he can enter.

A small fire plays in the hearth against the day's dampness. He passes her his hat and canvas cloak and brushes off his hose. Stooping, he holds out his hands to the flames, saying meekly, "Would you offer a mug of hot water to warm body and heart?"

"I should banish you to the shed," she says as she hooks a small pot over the fire and takes a mug from the shelf. "I'll put honey in it 'n' fennel, though why I bothers I don't know."

"Because the day is long and you're bored with your own company and I am, after all, comely."

Her quick chuckle takes them both by surprise. Elf yawns and stretches out by the hearth, a blue flame leaps upward and vanishes. Ilotte says, "Tell me why you come here this wet day."

Troubled…*is* that why he came, to share the burden? Taking his time, he sketches what he knows of Johanna's marriage to a beloved brother who was everything he, Haukyn, is not: patient, calm, and a lover of soil, but also desirous of another man's wife. He repeats Johanna's disclosure about Edmund and Hawise, rape, theft, and a noose, an arrow, gaol, and a forced wedding. "Now, when I look at them, I no longer know—"

"Her raped 'n' you scorn her?"

Through a veil of smoke, her black eyes condemn him. "Nay! You're wide of the mark. If you'd seen what I witnessed in France, you'd loathe the very word." He waves the smoke aside, unable to bear its stinging, and should she not know the worst about him, before…before what? In a low voice, he says, "Not far from Bordeaux, when I was half-starved, I stole a chalice from a French chapel and killed the priest."

"A chalice? You can't eat a chalice."

"I stole it for Piers. So I'd have money in Bordeaux to buy passage for us to England. But he died before we got there." And then it all pours out, deadwarts, Piers in agony, Sir Gardrad and the four archers, John of Gaunt on his destrier. "God avenged that priest's death and Piers paid the price, and why would you sit at hearth with a man like me?"

"Why'd you kill the priest?"

"He was about to raise the hue, the peasants would have ripped me to shreds. So I struck him, not intending to kill him, and his head hit the stones by the altar."

"So it were an accident, 'n' didn't war teach you that God don't bother 'bout us?"

A soldier trampled into the mud by his own army, a mastiff's teeth sunk in an archer's thigh, and where then was God? Fennel and honey slide down his throat. "I'd have died too had it not been for a soldier named Javyd."

"That priest knew what'd happen to you if he shouted for help. He were no different from his flock save he didn't want blood on his hands."

"The man who harmed you, was God absent then too?"

"Darkness have always walked the land," she says and for a moment her eyes become as smoke, become...other.

His hands grip the heat of the mug. "I wish I could put into words—my father could, but not I—what it is about you that pulls me in. Tis a mystery and one it might take me a lifetime to fathom."

"No need to fathom aught!"

Temper, to his relief, has replaced strangeness. "My parents told Robert about the manner of their marriage, but they never told me, the younger son, the wayward son, who if he has to pick one more tick off his father's dim-witted cows will be clapping it to his own skin...I came today because it sits heavy on my shoulders that I had to find out from Johanna. Who does indeed scorn my mother." He swishes the last of the liquid in his mug and adds in a rush, "You listen well, and all I have to do is ask them what happened. Simple. Yet I'd rather face the French army with my bowstring frayed... Ilotte, I want you to meet them both. Ma would ask about your healing of beasts, she'd share her herb-garden with you, and a fine one it is. And Ralf would pester you about your bees. Not today, tis too wet. But another Sunday, after Mass, I could ride here and we'd go together, I wouldn't have you walk alone on the roads."

He seems to have run out of words and a good thing too. He's as dim-witted as the cows. One of whom Gil named, of all things, Ragwort.

"You'd lure me to Flintbourne with talk of family?"

"I would."

"Though I hated Newbury, there be times I longs to be beyond the bounds of Hungerford."

"You and I alike in that need for wider skies."

"You a man 'n' able to go."

"To war," he says sharply. "Not a true choice."

A charred twig collapses into ash. "First Sunday there be sun, I'll walk to your vill."

He tries, unsuccessfully, to smother a grin; he hadn't expected her to give in so easily. "I'll come and get you. On a Sunday twixt Mass and Sext, and before the Feast of St. John the Baptist."

Not giving her the chance to change her mind, he drains his mug, throws his cloak around his shoulders, and rides home, very soon wet and, most oddly, given the manner of their talk, altogether happy.

After a day of sunshine, the whole vill is summoned to the lord's meadows to scythe and rake his crop of hay. Haukyn has an ash bow to rough out. With ill grace he swings his scythe, skillfully, aye, he has too many of a farmer's skills, and the grasses and field flowers topple, the lord's rabbits run for cover, the lord's doves whicker upward. "These cursed rabbits," he mutters to his father. "Blunt-nosed arrows and the cooking pot, had I my way."

"And a fine at hallmote."

"To further fatten Sir Mauger's coffers."

"Haukyn, the sun shines and tis honest labour."

"Honest, how can you say so? His rights before ours, his fields before ours, and if it rains on our own hay and our beasts starve and we alongside them, tis a pity but there are always more of us."

On his other side, one of the atte Mede lads swats at the midges, then picks up his swing. "Working our arses off, that be the only right we got."

"We have the lord's protection and the use of his land," Edmund says.

The lad's name is Walter atte Mede. Haukyn stores it away. "Protection? The only man Sir Mauger would stir himself to protect is his cook. Can you think of no other justifications for the lowly estate of serfdom?"

"Serfdom is serfdom and talk such as yours does damage."

"Serfdom from this day forward, world without end, amen? I think not," Haukyn says and takes out his anger on the lord's hay. The day warms. Their lazy reeve, Arnulf-from-the-Beeches, father of Annabel, saunters the bounds of the field with his white wand of authority, smiling amiably at men and women alike. They genuflect for the Terce bell, the bell for Mass, then the Sext bell, which frees them to sit in the shade under the trees, where Sir Mauger has provided plentiful bread, cheese, and ale to sate hunger and thirst.

Jorden has set himself up beneath an oak to sharpen the blades of scythes. Haukyn sits with his father and Walter, tips back his head and swigs ale. Did a drink ever taste better? Johanna's grout, he recognizes it. Edmund squawks a warning, something bangs his shoulder, and the ale goes down his windpipe. Choking and sputtering, he hears Ivo say, "Sorry, Haukyn, weren't watching where I were going."

Twas Ivo's scythe that struck him. He's on his feet, his face thrust into the other man's, and one of the Cat-Skinners shouts, "Fight!"

"There'll be no fight, Ivo," Haukyn says, "because you know who'd win."

"Pity the blade missed you. Fresh-sharpened by m' da."

Ivo's shirt is part unlaced, glimpse of—of what? Haukyn grips the cloth, pulls it aside. A burn, oddly shaped, Jesu, tis the shape of an oxshoe, inward curve, squared-off holes for the nails. He stares at it, sickened. Ivo drags his shirt to cover it. Shame, fury, hatred, which is uppermost in Ivo's face, and as clear as if it were yesterday Haukyn remembers him sobbing against a beech tree, the burn that day horsehoe-shaped. He says, "Ivo, fathers beat sons, tis the way of it, but this—"

"Get away from me!"

Ivo swings around, the tip of the scythe blade narrowly missing Haukyn's ankle, and dashes down the slope. "Pair o' cowards," a Cat-Skinner bawls.

Naught changes in the world, Haukyn thinks, wiping ale from his chin with the back of his hand. Cruelty seeds itself, hatred is as deep-rooted as ragwort, while kindness is left to struggle toward the light, too thin-stemmed to hold its own weight and next thing he'll be a maker of verses like his father.

His appetite has fled.

The good weather holds, the lord's hay stored, the villagers' hay cut, raked, and stooked, Haukyn's share stacked in his byre. Rather to his disgust and only because it will feed Trefoil, he eyes it with pleasure.

It rains on Sunday, prayers of gratitude at Mass that the hay is garnered. As he steps outside with his holy bread, rain pelts his face and soaks his hair, the gargoyles on the church roof spew rain, the trees drip rain. He cannot expect Ilotte to come from Hungerford in this.

The keenness of his disappointment shocks him, and not even the prospect of putting the last touches at Dunstan's to a bow ordered by Tirrell can alleviate it.

The rain stops, two days later. Gradually the ripening grain stands tall again. In the long evenings, Haukyn builds a privy and with Solomon's help a trestle table and bench; he cuts rushes and lays them to dry. His house begins to feel like home. From the miller's son he barters for a rangy, long-eared dog whom he calls Rust for the colour of his fur and whom he teaches to guard house and byre. With the coin Tirrell paid him, he buys boards for a bed. His bed and Ilotte's? His loins tighten. The next day he asks Hawise for enough down from their geese for two pillows. "Two?" she says.

He swallows. "There is a woman from Hungerford. Should the sun shine on Sunday, I will bring her to meet you."

"Ah," she says, "so that be why you been to Hungerford so oft. Be she Willem's widow?"

"Heloise? Nay! Her name is Ilotte, she is a healer of beasts and keeps bees."

"I will be happy to meet her," Hawise says, with rare formality and even rarer discretion.

His father will be happy too, because a wife will tie a malcontent son tighter to serfdom and soil.

The sun rises in gilt splendour on Sunday, two days before the Feast of St. John. After Mass and after breaking his fast, he rides to Hungerford on Trefoil. Birds chirp and chatter, rather like Annabel, aspen leaves jig on their branches, and white clouds scud from west to east. He finds Ilotte kneeling in her garden, Elf at her side, a small cluster of uprooted herbs beside her on the ground. "God's blessing," he says, sounding quite normal, though his heart is a rollick in his chest.

"These herbs be good for horses," she says. "Your ma might want to plant them herself, or p'rhaps you. If you have a garden."

"I've dug a small plot. Clover and piss-a-beds in it. Will you show me how to plant the herbs and succour them?"

"Naught to it. We're bringing Elf, she don't like being left alone."

They leave the manor, he leading Trefoil, the dog patrolling the ditches, Ilotte with a long-legged stride that fits his own. She tells him the names of birds whose calls he doesn't recognize and of weeds for which hens wage barnyard squabbles; she lifts her face to the sun and breathes in the warmth of summer. "I don't understand why air that ain't on the manor feel different. But it do, it do."

"Because we are betwixt manors, in limbo—we belong to no one but ourselves."

She snorts. "Then why don't every serf take to the roads?"

A chill travels his spine. "The roads in Normandy and Artois were clogged with the dispossessed, and I undo my own argument."

"No midges'll land on your nose, Haukyn o' Flintbourne." The war is eclipsed by laughter; he doesn't think he's ever known such happiness.

Flintbourne's track arrives too soon. As they cross the ford, Trefoil lowers her muzzle to suck at the river, then they take the baulks to

Edmund's house. Haukyn falls silent in another switch of mood: he's as nervous as if he were indeed going into battle with his bowstring frayed.

Ranulf, known for barking, sniffs Elf when they arrive, then lies down, head on his paws, amber eyes fastened to the woman at Haukyn's side. Gil says, "You be nigh as tall as Haukyn," and Ralf says, head tilted, "Your eyes be like the night sky when the moon's resting." Edmund welcomes her with genuine cordiality. Hawise, so often rough of tongue, accepts with gratitude the pot of honey Ilotte has brought and leads her through the gate into her garden, Ranulf close on Ilotte's heels, Elf trotting behind. Haukyn places the herbs carefully on the shelf by the door, then plays a rowdy game of football with the twins, his kicks going awry because his attention keeps wandering to his mother's garden.

They eat an early supper of vegetable soup with maslin bread, then he picks up his herbs and he, Ilotte, Elf, and Trefoil leave to cross the vill's fields to his house.

He's as nervous as if he were on *chevauchée* with no bow at all.

...a bed of bluebells...

When his son and Ilotte are out of earshot, Edmund says, "It wouldn't be a peaceable marriage...but then, have we had a peaceable marriage, wife?"

"Once you understood you wasn't master o' the house, twas smooth as the cow's cream."

In the corner, Ralf smiles and Gil rolls his eyes. Ralf says, "Our cockerel pecks me, but twas like he was bowing to Ilotte, his wattles a-waggle."

"Haukyn kept missing kicks while we were playing football 'cause he was watching her," Gil says. "D' you think her bees sting her?"

"They wouldn't dare," his mother says. "Take the pots to the river to scour them, both o' you."

"You don't want us listening," Gil says.

She tucks his hair behind his ear. "You got your da's brains. Off with you."

Once they are gone, she says, "Ilotte be a woman with secrets."

"And eyes that can go right through you. Haukyn and she, they're too much alike, I doubt she'd settle him down." He rolls his shoulders to loosen them. "Do you think she loves him?"

Not sounding altogether sure, Hawise says, "She come here, didn't she."

"He hasn't the look of a man who's been well-swived."

Last night, he and Hawise had come together, slow and in silence, the way of it often in their years of sharing a mattress. Although—memory carrying him backward once again—there was that morning near the chicken coop, a miracle they didn't smash the eggs. And the time in the lord's woods on a bed of bluebells under a heaven-blue sky, and young Robert, after they'd ambled home, plucking half a dozen crushed flowers off the back of his tunic. A verse or two came from those bluebells, he thinks, grinning, although when he'd recited them to Hawise after the boys were in bed, she'd threatened to dose him with hemlock should he include them in his book.

Holy Church would say it was sinful to so deeply love a woman.

He refuses to believe that Almighty God measures love in careful ounces, and he doesn't always have to agree with Holy Church.

For months after the death of little Margaret, Hawise couldn't bear to be touched, he unable to comfort her in any way that counted, her white-faced grief so unnerving him that never had he pulled so many weeds from his fields or picked so much flint. And then one April morning, when he was in the byre milking their cow, she'd walked up behind him, rested her hands on his shoulders and her cheek to his ruined ear, and said, "Let's to bed when you're done?" and his tears had plopped into the milk, his hands so hesitant on her flesh that she'd straddled him in a manner forbidden by every priest in the land, and only afterward was there a storm of weeping...*sorry, I be so sorry, I knew I'd break in pieces like dropped pottery had you swived me...sorry* and again *sorry*, and he'd prayed a daughter would come from their coupling.

He says, as though there'd been no gap in their talk, "Gil is right, Haukyn watches her every move."

"Worse 'n you watch me?" she says and dodges his reach, laughing.

"I would wish for him a marriage like ours."

"He got to make his own, Edmund, it ain't up to you."

He draws her into his embrace. "When we're too old to hobble from bench to bed, will we still worry about our sons?"

"Our sons and their little-uns. Now get out o' my way, I got work to do."

Haukyn and Ilotte are crossing the headland toward his house when she says, "You rub against your da."

"You see too much."

"He be a kind man. Yet you call him *Father*."

He wants to show off his house, not argue about his father. "He accepts a serf's bounds while I push against them. Against any bounds, if I speak true. It's been that way since I learned to walk." Too late he regrets his tone, caustic as lye. "Look, you can see my house from here, tis nigh ready for me to move in, and the distance twixt him and me will be good for both of us."

As overeager as Rust, who, like Ranulf, pays instant obeisance to the woman at his side, he shows her his garden plot and orchard, promises to plant his herbs that evening, and unlocks his door. "Your hinges better behaved than mine," she says and crosses the threshold.

The two of them are inside his house, he and Ilotte of the gleaming black hair; through an open shutter, the sun catches her profile, her straight nose, her decided chin, and he is flooded with such love as he has never felt before. How can this be? Where does it come from? Might God be like this, he wonders, wonder-struck. Does Ilotte gift him with a glimpse of Heaven?

She runs her palm down the wall, then fingers a smooth-bevelled shutter, and brushing against her skirts is the pile of boards intended for the frame of his bed. Their bed and the words rise up, unstoppable as a river breaching its banks. "Ilotte, you must have guessed, for you have eyes that see far and deep—I want to stand with you before our priest and pledge to you my undying fealty."

She freezes. Like rabbit to stoat, he thinks and banishes the thought before it goes further. Turning to face him, moving so slowly he almost expects to hear her bones creak, she says, "I did guess. I trusted you to heed what I tol' you before. I belongs to no man, nor ever will."

"Elyas and Bidewell, the burgher in Newbury, the burgher at the market, I understand why you would say that. But I'm not like them. I've proven to you that you can trust me, you've laughed with me and eaten at my mother and father's table, and Ilotte, you would be safer living here in Flintbourne. Aye, we have our measure of men who abide by no law but their own, Smyths and Cat-Skinners. But I'd be your husband, I'd protect you with my last breath. My father also would defend you, as would Solomon the Small and the atte Medes. No threat of stocks, no accusations of sorcery or whoredom, your bees happy in my orchard."

"I'm villein. I belongs to the manor of Hungerford."

"I would gladly pay chevage to your lord." He breathes deep, for this next is a vow as serious as any he could make on the church steps. "I'd work hard and well in the common fields and on our own acres to feed us both, I'd chop wood to warm our hearth, I'd barter for our own sow, hens, and geese…I'd have no need of a distant bell that chimes freedom, for I would have you in recompense, and wouldn't each of us gain a new freedom? Of a kind we've never known before? As for the marriage vows, Father Mortimer always charges the man to repeat to the woman, *with my body, I thee worship*, and don't we humble ourselves when we worship?" His voice thickens. "Twould humble me were you to entrust me not only with your body but with your daily life, your bees and healing herbs, your laughter and your tears, your spirit that at times sees more than it wishes to see."

It seems he's run out of things to say. He rests his hand on her wrist, where her fingers are now grasping the shutter's edge, her nails white from the pressure. She brings her other hand up and all too fleetingly it covers his, skin lying on skin, his blood a torrent in his veins. Then, with some care, she lifts his hand from her wrist and passes it back to him, her eyes trained on his. "You be a good man, Haukyn, and were I to trust anyone it'd be you. But I won't marry you—I pray you, don't argue with me, *don't*." She straightens her shoulders, bracing herself, he thinks in a wash of fear. "Walk back to Hungerford with me 'n' I'll tell you why. I has to be moving to speak of it, the walls o' your house too close, they press on me."

Outside, he untethers Trefoil. His hands are trembling; he wills them to stillness. Trefoil bumps him with her muzzle. Elf following, they leave the house, cross the ford, walk up the track to the road, Trefoil's hoofs crunching the stones, and turn toward the west and a slow-lowering sun.

Ilotte says, "I've never tol' a living soul about—swear you'll never speak of it to family or friend."

Dread clenches his belly. "I'll not."

"We be serious folk, you 'n' me, Haukyn, so I be honoured that you'd marry me. But I won't ever lie willingly with any man, nor marry." When her steps speed up, jerky and uneven, he paces himself to stay at her side. "I tol' you m' mother left when I were a little-un. Nine winters, I had. Da took up drinking, shamed by the vill's gossips, them mocking him that he couldn't keep hold of a wife. P'raps in the dark he thought I were her. He were rough 'n' stank of ale, his tarse too big, 'n' I cried out but he didn't stop—then, or in the nights that come after. I used to hide but he'd find me 'n' drag me home, so I tol' the priest. He piled penances on me for calumny—I didn't know that word so I asked him what it meant. He spat a big gobbet at m' feet, stuck his face in mine, called me a foul daughter of Eve." She adds fiercely, "I ain't no temptress, tis the last thing I'd be."

"Ilotte," he says helplessly, "Ilotte," and what is left of that little girl but her name?

"The years passed til I were turning twelve, near as I could guess. From talk in the fields at reaping I knew something called m' monthlies would start 'n' that babies was tied to the moon—twas a mystery 'n' I were scared. One morning I woke with blood on m' thighs, so I reckoned I could get with child by m' da." Her breath hitches. "Bear a daughter who'd be m' sister or a son who'd be m' brother. I waited til he'd left for the alehouse afore I packed a bag, stole a blanket, a waterskin, grub, a length o' canvas. Ran for the woods, watched for vagabonds by day, by night, made it to Hungerford's town, too far for Da to look for me, he'd forget me soon enough. I begged on the streets, stole when I were hungered, found I had a gift with watchdogs 'n' starving cats, healed a woman's gander, poor bird only needed purging. She were kind, she had a sister named Bess on Hungerford manor who took me in. Bess died four years after, but by then I had m' bees 'n' moved into m' cot. The rest you know."

"Ilotte—" Can he say naught but her name? His fingers, clamped around the reins, are cramping. He rubs them down his side, remembering Benedict's casual cruelty to a yellow-haired camp follower, remembering the young woman who ran for the woods outside Lalinde with her little girl, and feeling the same useless rage, the same inability to be of true aid. "May your father burn in Hell for all eternity. The worst of sins, I cannot bear to think of it...I marvel at what you've made of yourself."

"He called me his little whore. *I* marvel how men call a woman *whore* after they've used her up."

Two burghers on roan palfreys trot past; Trefoil whinnies. The aspen leaves hang still and the light warms to gold. He dare not touch her. "You are no whore and never have been," he says. "I pray your Bess sings with the angels."

"I prayed for help when he were a'top o' me, didn't do no good." She walks faster. "He were angered by a wife fey as a swallowtail, t'ain't that I blames Ma for leaving. But I got no forgiveness that she left me behind, as if I were worth naught. She knew what he were like."

On the hillside ahead of them cluster the houses and byres, fields and gardens of her manor. She says, "Ride home to Flintbourne, Haukyn. Don't come, ever again, to see me."

"You mean I am to leave you here? Nay, I—"

"Don't you understand?" she says in sudden fury. "Us villeins own naught. Cot, bees, garden, orchard, they all belongs to the lord. M' sole possession be m' body, tis all I owns that be mine. I can't share it. I won't."

She whirls and runs up the slope, Elf at her heels, and a little girl with tangled black hair runs beside them.

He plants the herbs in his garden, first loosening the soil and adding a little of Trefoil's dung. He waters them so they'll take root and flourish.

For each of three evenings, he drinks enough ale that he passes out on the floor of his new house. The boards for the bed are still stacked by the wall. His dog slinks around him, nostrils twitching to the reek of an unwashed, ale-pickled serf.

On the fourth morning, knowing he can no longer shun his family, he upends a bucket of cold water over his head, sputters and spits, and trudges up the hill to his father's.

Gil says, alarmed, "Be you sick?"

Ralf pats his arm. "We missed you."

Edmund looks him up and down. "Woodbote has been granted, so we'll gather fuel from the lord's trees. I'll sharpen the axes, you'd be likely to cut your fingers off. We'll start on the ridge."

Hawise brings bread, cheese, and ale at Sext. "Eat, Haukyn, 'n' I'll brew a tonic for you."

He gazes at the hunk of bread in his hand. "I would have had with Ilotte what you and my father share. She won't marry me."

"She's a fool."

"Her reasons are sound. I'll drink your tonic but I'll not talk about it."

Two fine days then a day of drizzle and Martin arrives at his house. "Your father sent me. We'll put a bed together so you ain't sleeping on the floor. Your ma'll stuff the mattress."

After the bed frame is built, his father and mother deliver the mattress and one pillow. He lays the mattress on the bed and arranges his blanket over it: bed, mattress, and cover wide enough for two. At dusk, before he starts drinking, Ralf arrives. Haukyn says, "Did Ma send you?"

"Nay. I came 'cause I wanted to."

"Do you snore?"

No snoring, but enough wriggling to keep Haukyn, sober, wide awake.

The next night Gil, not be outdone, arrives at dusk. He does snore.

The Matins bell sounds in the night. Haukyn gets up and goes outdoors. Dark of the moon and a cold dazzle of stars. *Tis why we need God,* he thinks, *yet why is He as distant as His stars?*

His hideaway, blackthorn hunched over a ruptured circle of stones.

Annabel smiles at him at Mass. She waves whenever she sees him, in Edmund's fields, or near the well, or passing Johanna's shed. To be polite, he waves back.

Johanna's smile at Mass is full of mockery. He's behaving like a fool, a love-struck fool, and he knows it and he can't fill the emptiness with work or food or—he admits this on a morning when he wakes with his own vomit crusted to his shirt—with ale.

A day or so later, Rust's barking sends him outdoors, to find Samuel Cat-Skinner's cow trampling his crop of vetch. At the alehouse it takes three men to pull him off hapless Samuel. Violence not the cure either, he thinks, as he walks home nursing bloody knuckles.

Gorging on the stars, the moon fattens.

Edmund arrives after Vespers the next day. Haukyn is watering the garden, Ilotte's herbs along with rows of carrot, turnip, and parsnip seedlings; Ralf had cozened the seeds from Hawise and insisted on planting them, late in the season but no mind, and Haukyn knows he must tend them, for Ralf has a heart too easy bruised.

"I heard about the brawl," his father says. "You're lucky the whole scurvy crew of Cat-Skinners weren't in the alehouse. Let's sit on your bench in the orchard awhile, I have a story to tell you."

"You aren't come to lecture me?"

"That the trespass of a cow might not warrant the slaughter of its owner? Nay, you're past the age for lectures," Edmund says. His smile fades. "Tis a true story, as not all stories are. Before I left for war and after I came home I was deep in love with the daughter of our reeve, Juliana, elder sister of Martin. I ignored all the signs, confident my pretty words would win her—until one evening in an orchard much like this, she told me she didn't love me and, worse, couldn't abide the scars on my face."

With a pang of compassion, Haukyn sees that those long-ago words still have the power to hurt. "Thirteen months in France followed by months in Dover's hospice, and all that time I'd carried her image in my heart. She married a steward from the downs, a good man, I knew she'd be happy with him." He picks at mud stuck to his hose. "Later, Sir Roger forced me to wed your mother, neither of us wanting marriage but neither of us wanting to be hanged either. We came slow to love, Haukyn, your mother and I, a second love for me, for her a husband after a tinker's brutal rape. It wasn't easy, yet our feelings for each other have been strong for many years. I can only pray you'll be as fortunate, and that is the end of my story. It has no moral attached."

"Johanna told me of rape and the gallows, how you shot through the rope."

"She shouldn't have! It was not her story to tell…Hawise half-strangled and struggling, it took two arrows before she thudded to the ground. I was no champion archer that day. Solomon the Small's father loosened the noose around her throat, then she and I were tossed in the lord's gaol. The longest night of my life."

"You told Robert all this. Why didn't you tell me?"

"You were in France, and afterward…I should have told you, twas wrong of me not to." He puts an arm around Haukyn's shoulders, weight and warmth. "I liked Ilotte. Though you would not have had a peaceable marriage."

A flash of temper cuts through the heaviness that accompanies him everywhere. "Is that all we ask of life, that it be peaceable?"

"We cannot tame that which will not be tamed, and despite my good intentions, I've just foisted a moral on you. Haukyn, I can't lessen your suffering, and as your father that pains me."

"She'll never marry. I don't have to be jealous of a husband." He links his fingers, unlinks them. "But I'm jealous of every moment she spends without me."

A chaffinch flits through the nearby pear tree. "This has gone deep with you. Leave Flintbourne for a few days, go to London and see your friend Javyd and his sister."

He says huskily, and he is not referring to a visit to London, "My thanks, Da."

Javyd's rough humour, so Haukyn discovers in London, is no salve. Nor is spilling his seed at moonrise in his pitch-dark orchard, for it fills him with a loneliness beyond any he's ever known. Could Hell be endless night, in which he will meet no other living soul and, should he speak, should he pray, there would be no sound?

Stop this, Haukyn! Stop it! She's but a woman.

On his heap of dung and old leaves, a forget-me-not is blooming; the seed must have been blown there by the wind. The petals are the hue of Annabel's eyes.

There are no black flowers.

Love, such a small, soft word. Shouldn't it creak and squeal like the wheels of his cart?

Summer passes. Haukyn resumes his visits to Dunstan, who asks no questions and insists on perfection. Harvest begins. In the lord's fields, he wields sickle and scythe between Amos and Ivo, something in his stance daring them to give him trouble; they work in silence and keep to their swaths. After Sir Mauger's crops are stored in the granary, he and his father reap their own crops, the twins and Hawise stooking and tying the sheaves. Arnulf-from-the-Beeches, their easy-going reeve, wanders the baulks and rarely chides a soul. Apples and pears ripen, are picked and dried, nuts are garnered, blackberries, mushrooms, and cherries, grain is ground and butter churned. Geese graze the stubble, ploughs roll the soil. All the able-bodied of the vill, with their hooks and crooks, scavenge the lord's trees for dead wood.

On his several trips to Hungerford market over summer and autumn for the purchase of salt herring and the sale of their own excess, Haukyn has kept well away from Ilotte and her pots of honey. But on a Saturday late in October, when the leaves are already shading to yellow and rust, Hawise sends him for two ells of linen. The cloth merchant has set himself up two stalls down from Ilotte. She hasn't noticed him. Without bargaining, he pays for the linen and bundles it into a sack, his pulse throbbing in his throat. When he swivels the cart to go back the way he came, the wheels grate against the stones.

She glances over. Shock, swiftly masked. She jerks her head away, her profile so well remembered that he almost cries out. Three months and he'd thought the wound had scabbed—and now he bleeds afresh, his need of her as ferocious as ever it was.

Somehow he's turned the cart and hauled it away; he's trembling like Ralf when he was bit by a black-fanged spider. Salt, a new knife blade, an iron trestle, he pays too much for all three, and, encumbered by the cart, hurries home. Will he ask the twins to stay the night so he won't get drunk?

He takes the jug of Johanna's ale sitting on his table and pours it on the ground near the rain barrel, watching it soak into the soil. That night he dreams Ilotte has loosed a swarm of bees, which circle him, their humming closer and closer, the first sting like a touch of fire.

The seasons march by in their inexorable manner, each with its toil, its particular weariness, and, as Haukyn can now more easily admit, its sometime rewards. As he works, he's found himself pondering courage, a word his father says stems from the French for heart but in which he can only see four letters that spell rage, the same rage that caused him to kill a mastiff and attack a smith. He refuses to claim courage for either of these acts. Is there, though, a quieter courage, requiring him daily to pace the paths of duty, however muddy they be and however heavy his pattens are to lift, and therein find the occasional gift of grace? A courage with no flash of steel to it, no coat of arms. And then he cuffs himself for a pomposity akin to that of Father Mortimer's at Sunday Mass.

In the spring at Hocktide, he steals dead branches from the lord's woods, poaches two trout, and wonders if any of the vill's girls would have encircled his wrists with twine had he ventured forth. Not, in all likelihood, Annabel, though he's noticed she still smiles at him at Mass every Sunday, and waves should she pass him in the vill.

Ploughing, weeding, haying, more weeding, and on the Feast of St. John the Baptist tis just over a year since he walked at Ilotte's side to Hungerford and was told never to return. Two days afterward he visits London, where he eats chicken pasties at Javyd and Petronilla's hearth and declines to visit the stews. He doesn't know whether to be glad or sorry that he only rarely dreams about Ilotte; instead, faithfully, he bears the dull ache where once she lived in all her vitality.

The distant bell of freedom never chimes, but he has food aplenty, family nearby, and an acreage to which he is bound by more than duty. Naught to rebel against, serfdom the least of his worries. That time in his life has passed.

After the briefest of courtships, Martin's younger brother Simon, known as a lusty man who cowers before no one, marries Johanna in July, moves into her house, and becomes father to her twins. Simon is no Robert: Johanna has met her match. Haukyn, in turn, is glad to have a man of weight as his parents' nearest neighbour.

Harvest rolls around again, an abundant harvest. The lord's fields first, he thinks, noticing to his surprise that he's angered by this, although not enough to act. At least this year he's between Walter atte Mede and Solomon the Small, who with minimal effort cuts the widest swaths. Arnulf-from-the-Beeches smiles at all and sundry, his white wand of office tucked into his belt. A hot day; Haukyn gulps ale when they all pause for breath. Behind them, the women stook the cut grain: Solomon's Lucy, Neuton's Maud, the cooper's Catherine, and Annabel. As the Sext bell peals, they all head for the shade and Sir Mauger's bountiful supply of food and ale.

To Haukyn's bemusement, for he's tended to avoid her the last year or more, Annabel plumps herself down on the grass beside him. Her breasts bounce beneath her tunic. She chatters to him about this and that until, on her other side, John Cat-Skinner says loudly, "Though daughters be all he begat, tis a miracle to me how Arnulf our lazy reeve got it up at all."

Annabel flushes, flicking at the crumbs in her lap. Haukyn says with equal loudness, "Better two pretty daughters than a pack of thieving, drip-nosed layabouts."

John glares at him. Haukyn glugs his ale.

The sun eventually sets and they all troop homeward. The second day, the heat has intensified. The river glitters in the light. Haukyn is between Walter and Ivo, keeps his mouth shut, and scythes with grim focus.

Annabel shares her chunk of cheese with him at Sext, she rosy-cheeked, her eyes rivalling the sky's blue. A nuthatch *chi-chis* as it busily works its way down the trunk of a beech, and Annabel's father meanders up the hill toward them, mug of ale in one hand, white wand in the other; he's red-faced, nodding at everyone from the woodward to the Cat-Skinners, inured, it seems, to any derision. His smile broadens when he sights his daughter, and his steps speed up—Arnulf's version of a canter, Haukyn thinks, amused. The reeve says, "Annabel, God's—"

A sound, uncouth, between gasp and groan, cuts off the blessing. He drops the wand, clutches his chest, and with a look on his face as though his worst nightmare has confronted him in the heat of day, he drops like a stone to the ground. Annabel gives a sharp cry of distress, springs to her feet, then sinks to her knees beside him, all the colour drained from her cheeks. "Da! Da, look at me...blessed Mother, come to his aid."

Hawise, who had been sitting farther up the hill, hurries toward them. She searches for his pulse at wrist and throat, waits, checks again, then smooths his eyelids over his stark, blank stare. Annabel bites her knuckles. "Nay, not Da! So quick, how can it be?"

"His heart quit its beating and no longer powers his spirit," Hawise says, patting the girl's arm. "To my sorrow, naught I or anyone can do."

Others gather around. Haukyn says, "Four of us will carry him home, Annabel, and the women will wash and shroud him for you."

"Died of overwork," John Cat-Skinner says. Ivo laughs and others join him.

Haukyn stands up, one hand, not to his surprise, on the haft of his knife. "You'll show respect for the dead in his daughter's hearing," he says and the noise subsides. He, Solomon, Edmund, and Waryn atte Water awkwardly lift the dead man to their shoulders and trudge across the mown hay toward Arnulf's croft. So sudden a death, like an arrow to the heart, yet merciful in its way. In the heat, Haukyn shivers.

At Arnulf's funeral, as at all funerals, Bony Mabel sits quiet and avid, rejoicing that it is not her own, or so Haukyn has decided. He feels true compassion for Annabel, left without parents, her only sister living in Swallowbend. Not long before she'll wed though, pretty as she is, and then she'll have a husband's protection.

Late one October evening when Haukyn is sitting by the coals of his fire fletching an arrow, Rust sits up, ears pricked, and barks. A tap on the door. *Ilotte*, he thinks and springs to his feet, the thin cord falling to the rushes.

The flame on his tallow candle wavers, then steadies. Furious with himself, he picks up the cord, places it on the bench, and opens the door. Annabel is standing on his step, wearing a cloak against the evening's chill; dead leaves are caught in the cloth. "You're alone?" he says in surprise. "Come in."

He latches the door behind her and drags his bench nearer the fire. "Sit and warm yourself. I could mull you some cider?" Her hood falls back. Her chin is trembling and she's on the verge of tears. "What's wrong?"

When he sits down beside her, she wraps her hands around her knees. "Samuel Cat-Skinner, he been bothering me off 'n' on since Da died, he come late last night to m' cottage, banged on the door, tol' me to let him in or he'd come back with John 'n' Amos. I tol' him to go away, 'n' in the end he did. I knows you beat on Samuel once, last year weren't it, so I come here." Her voice falters. "M' name be Annabel-from-the-Beeches, but Samuel, he calls me Annabel-of-the-Bitches 'cause m' sister be a scold...I be so afeard of him 'n' his kin."

"Those scuts. I'll take you to my father's house, you can stay—"

"Nay! What if they be out there? You can't fight three of 'em at once."

The dog is noisily lapping water from his bowl in the corner. The corner by the bed. "You want to stay here? But Annabel, you a maiden, the gossips will—"

"I'll leave at dawn, go home by the woods." She reaches out a hand, snatches it back, and chews on a fingernail, her cheeks flushed from more than a scanty fire. "Haukyn, I captured you at Hocktide a year past, 'n' since then you must've seen me smile at you 'n' wave, what else were I to do short o' tripping over you at the well. You spoke up for me 'gainst John at harvest, you helped carry Da to be shrouded. I knows you brought a woman here from Hungerford last summer, but I ain't heard of her since, would you think o' marrying me?"

He gapes at her. What a fool he is, why didn't he see this coming?

She jams her fists to the bench and pushes herself upright. "I shouldn't have spoke. I'll sleep in your byre tonight, 'n' I won't bother you never again."

More slowly, he too gets to his feet. "Wait, Annabel, wait. You took me by surprise, no hiding that, is there. And aye, there was a woman from Hungerford I wanted to marry. But she wouldn't have me, nor ever will, and it still causes me grief."

"You never thought o' me that way, then?"

He risks letting his hand rest on her sleeve. "The forget-me-not blooming on my dung hill last summer reminded me of your eyes, and you must have had better compliments than that."

Agitated, she says, "I wants to be married, I wants little-uns round m' hearth. Da always said I could burn pottage by sneezing on it, but I makes candles, I weaves baskets, Johanna pays me coin for working on the ale, nor I ain't stupid like m' sister Margery always said I were."

"Are you a scold like her, Annabel-from-the-Beeches?"

"There ain't no verjuice in me. She got it all."

"Honey only?" he says without thinking, and winces. His fingers grip her arm. "Why me? There are other men in the vill with more land than I, good men who'd be happy to marry you."

"Hocktide Tuesday twas you I chose. I been lonely since Da died. When I sees you round the vill, m' heart cheers up—you ain't hard to look upon neither," she adds with a sly smile.

"Nor you, pretty Annabel. But...should two lonelinesses mate?"

She steps closer and puts her arms around his waist, a bold move, he thinks, and notes the shyness underlying it. She says, "We could try."

One more truth must be spoken, the same truth he once spoke to Ilotte. "I've never lain with a woman, here or in France, as perhaps you think I have."

"Nor me with a man, 'cause tis you I wanted. We seen cows 'n' bulls, we'll manage."

Her smile isn't as confident as her words. He cups her face in his hands, nerves tight, heart bumping. *Decide, Haukyn, decide. Ilotte is gone from you. Do you want to be alone for the rest of your life, no warmth in your bed, no children around your hearth? You're tied to the vill, for even if Edmund were to die, you couldn't leave your mother and the twins with the work of virgates...and Annabel is very pretty.* He takes a deep breath. "I won't deflower you unless I promise marriage. Will you stand on the church steps with me, Annabel?"

"I–I will."

She stammers from happiness, he realizes, humbled. "So," he says. "I'll let the dog out and cover the fire, why don't you get into bed," and does he already sound like a husband? He hopes to God he can give her more than Robert gave Johanna.

A night of clouds that shroud most of the stars. Rust lifts his leg to the elderberry near the door, Haukyn goes to the privy, then both of them go inside. He locks the door and covers the coals. In his bay, Annabel's clothes are tidily folded on the bench. She's lying on her back on his mattress, her eyes tight shut. He undresses, blows out the candle, and slides into bed beside her.

Each of them is nervous, clumsy, and seemingly most willing to learn. Haukyn, privately, is astonished by the feel of a body so gratifyingly different. They muddle their way through it, and though he causes her pain near the end, he knows from her determined grasp of his hips that she wishes it so. They lie still, each perhaps with too much to say, and in the greater silence of the night they fall asleep.

Haukyn wakes at first light to find an arm over his ribs and huffs of breath against his shoulder. His eyes jerk open. Her fair hair, thicker than he'd expected, drapes his chest.

She wakes with a little snort. Wide-eyed, she says, "Oh! I ain't dreaming."

"Tis no dream, Annabel, and next time I'll know better how to please you," he says, rubbing against her and hearing her breathless giggle. "If I'm to walk you to my father's, we must do so before the vill wakes. But I'd rather stay here. Would you also?"

"Aye," she says, "I would, 'n' Haukyn, here's me nigh to crying 'cause I be so happy."

"Will we go and see Father Mortimer today and ask to have the banns read?"

"Aye," she says, "we will. Your dog be staring at me."

He looks over his shoulder. Rust wags his tail, head cocked. "We have his blessing," Haukyn says, and the day begins in laughter.

The next time, after they are married on the church steps on a windy day in November in view of all the vill except Smyths and Cat-Skinners, is indeed better, the third better still.

The seasons race past, spring of the following year edged out by summer, summer by autumn and the beginning of winter. The weather has been kind to them; the barrels, larders, and rafters of Flintbourne's crofts, Haukyn's among them, are well-stocked. Annabel has been nagging him to buy salt herring for Advent, so on a Saturday in November he and Trefoil leave, later than should be, for the market. As a small crowd of serfs impedes them, he almost drops the reins: Ilotte is walking toward him down the aisle between the stalls, empty-handed, pouch at her waist, Elf at her side, and nowhere to hide. He nods at her. She slows down. "I heard you was married." He nods again. "Tis better that way," she says.

From fealty to Annabel, he stays silent. But fealty requires fidelity at its heart, and how can it be fealty when his own heart is a racket in his chest? Trefoil nudges her, she giving the horse the smile she's withheld from him. He tugs hard on the reins and walks past her. An old wound, reopened, copiously bleeding. It will scab, he knows this, yet not for the first time wonders if it wouldn't be easier were she dead, God forgive him for such a thought.

He tells no one of this meeting, for he's a married man and his feelings shame him. How is he any better than Robert, wed yet pining for another woman?

A few days later, on the feast day of St. Cecilia, Annabel leaves to deliver goat cheese to the atte Medes and Solomon's Lucy and wag her tongue in both houses, while Haukyn sits at home, rubbing salt into their two hams, a task he dislikes for the salt enters every cut and scrape on his hands and stings like a swarm of bees…Ilotte's bees? That brief sight of her at the market a torment ever since.

He's glad to have a few hours alone.

Married a year now, and he's discovered Annabel often burns the pottage, and if he wants a dinner fit to eat he has to take an interest in it himself. She has a softness for spiders, a blind eye for cobwebs, her apple butter tastes better than his mother's, and the two goats she persuaded him to buy more than earn their keep. She helps Johanna brew ale, she makes cheese, she darns his hose. None of this stills her tongue. She can tell Haukyn he's about to belch before the gas rises in his belly; she recites whose hens aren't laying and whose cockerel is due for the pot, whose gardens go unweeded and whose children are unwashed; she mimics Father Mortimer's declaiming of scripture and Ivo's curses; and to all of this and more he's learned to listen with half an ear—or, like his father, with one deaf ear. Yet when he describes to her a serf's bounds and how he sometimes chafes against them, or when he muses out loud whether Holy Church concocted Hell to terrify tithes out of them and Heaven so they wouldn't bemoan their lowly lot on earth, she turns on him a look of incomprehension and asks him to empty the slop bucket.

He's stupid to think this matters, and pushes away the ache of loneliness it causes.

Another kind of loneliness: Annabel used to love what they did together on their mattress, and he could always still her chatter with kisses and fondling; but once her monthlies cease, puking in the privy replacing them, she turns her back on him, slapping at his hands should he reach for her. He buys a bowl so she doesn't have to rush outside, and although he's patient, on the whole, toward complaints of sore breasts and sore back, leg-cramps, and aprons that won't reach around her middle, sometimes he's reminded of her elder sister, Margery the scold. But then, twixt haying and Michaelmas, thrice she launches herself at him and they swive with a wild abandon that leaves him breathless, grateful, and nail-raked.

Is the man born who can comprehend womankind?

Over the next few months, with the help of Martin, Walter, and Solomon, he builds another bay on the back of his house, which pleases Annabel. She'll soon be brought to bed with their child, a son to be called Thomas after Edmund's long-dead friend Father Thomas, a daughter Alyce after his mother's mother. Secretly, he'd like a girl-child. It thrills him when, all too rarely, his wife lets him press his palm to her hard, swollen belly so he can feel the kicks of the child they've made. "Keeps me awake half the night, you snoring t' other half."

A few months ago, he'd have been the one to keep her awake half the night.

Besides, he doesn't snore.

He escapes from all this to Dunstan's and his own ever-increasing skills as a bowyer.

The salt's running low, praise God, and then Rust leaps up, barking. Haukyn opens the door to find Ralf panting on the step. "Tis Annabel, the baby on the way, she's at Ma's."

Haukyn's jaw drops. "Jesu," he says, covers the ham, washes his hands, and leaves Rust on guard.

His father meets him halfway. "Hawise says Annabel does well, but it will take time. Lucy is with them. Naught you and I can do."

"There must be something."

"Her distress will bother you."

As they approach, he hears someone shriek, as though being torn limb from limb. Annabel? His pretty Annabel, who for all her chatter and complaining rarely raises her voice?

His father says, "Why don't you help me bring faggots from the back of the assart?"

Armload after armload, then an axe to split those too thick for the hearth, no reckoning how long it is before Lucy emerges on the step and throws a bowl of water to the ground, water cloudy with blood. Haukyn stands frozen, axe poised. She calls his name. "You can come in now."

He drops the axe and grips his father's arm. "Does that mean I'm a father?"

Edmund cuffs him on the shoulder, laughing. "Go indoors and find out."

The air too close, smelling of blood and travail. His mother's face, how lined it is. She presses his hand and says, "She were the best o' pushers, 'n' there weren't much bleeding."

Someone has combed Annabel's sweaty hair back from her forehead and washed her face. "Haukyn," she says, "you'd best enjoy your daughter, 'cause I swear there won't be a son."

"My daughter?"

A bundle rests on her belly, fine strands of reddish hair sticking up like little thorns. The bundle mewls. "Can I hold her?"

"Watch her head."

He sits on the bench near the fire, the bundle arranged with immense gentleness across his thighs, and loosens the blanket. A scrunched red face with fingers pawing at it, the neatly tied cord, two fat little thighs, and his daughter's mewling turns to wailing until her fist finds her mouth and she slurps at it.

I would kill for her, this pink squall with ten perfect fingers and ten perfect toes and the tiny crease twixt her legs, and I've lost the last vestige of my freedom. Propping the head, his hands never so large, he lifts his naked daughter and holds her to his chest. A wet trickle soaks through his shirt. He laughs in pure joy. "Annabel, dear Annabel, how can I thank you? And already she's hungered."

"Cover her, Haukyn, let's see if she'll latch on."

He marvels at his wife, so naturally does she put the child to breast. Then he crosses the room to where his mother is standing by the wall and embraces her. "My thanks to you and Lucy, Ma…Has Gil gone for Father Mortimer? Our daughter will be baptized Alyce, in remembrance of your mother."

Firelight on the tears in his mother's eyes. Haukyn pulls the bench closer to Annabel and sits down. For once, she has naught to say, and has she not gone beyond prettiness to a place he can never go?

Whimpers and gurgles, and through them, Annabel's quiet breathing. He sits very still, his palm resting on her bare elbow, nor does she slap him away. The fondness he feels for her has without his volition become more primitive, more possessive; both words shock him. *Love, a word not always soft, and my wife and I, together, within its mysteries?*

For a week Annabel stays with his parents so that Hawise can watch over her, Haukyn back and forth between his house and theirs. When, early one morning, he takes the river path to fill his mother's buckets at the well, a dark shadow is hunched against the old beech that overhangs the water. Watchful, he walks closer, the leather buckets swishing against the dead bracken.

Ivo looks up. Welts on his face, new-dealt. "Did your father do that, Ivo? I would to God you'd leave him! Come with me up the hill, my mother will put salve on your face and my father give you enough money for an inn or two on the way to Windsor or London."

"Then who'd keep Da's tarse off m' sister?"

The empty buckets clump to the path. "Blessed Mary…is that the way of it?" Ilotte fleeing her father, a young girl with a striped hood roaming London's streets, what hope for Jorden's daughter, and why has it never occurred to him that women are serfs twice over?

"You think I be too bone-headed to leave the forge, you with yer snugged-up family 'n' yer pretty wife. God's arse, I can't bear the sight o' you."

The old animosity is there. But despair has dulled it, and Haukyn knows the power of despair. Wondering if Annabel will murder him, he says, "Your sister could sleep in my byre, she'd be warm there and out of harm's way."

"He'd burn house and byre to the ground."

Such leaden conviction in Ivo's voice. "Stay here, I'll come back as quick as I can with salve."

Ivo's smile is twisted. "I might come to like you, did I not hate you."

Although Haukyn runs home and back, Ivo is gone, the buckets lying at the foot of the beech. He tucks the salve in his pouch and goes to the well. Ivo wishes he'd been born in Edmund's household rather than that of Jorden the smith, and for all his own lofty talk of freedom, perhaps he simply envies those born into households with the power and money to allow them untrammelled lives.

I am lord to Ivo's serf. A clever thought and no help whatsoever.

He tramps up the hill with the full buckets and rests them near the hearth. Edmund gives him a keen look. "Is aught wrong?"

"Jorden whipped Ivo. A brother trying to keep his sister from his father's bed."

"God in Heaven, why should that shock me? Haukyn, go to Sir Mauger and ask him to take the girl into his household as a servant."

"So our lord can lure her to *his* bed?"

"Sir Mauger lusts after vension, spiced sauces, and sweetmeats. Ivo's sister will be safe in the manor."

"A wiser solution than acquainting Jorden's head with his anvil?"

"A safer one."

So Haukyn traipses to the manor, where he is admitted to the lord's presence; on the table, dishes of marzipan, dates, and figs, and a glass of red wine. After he excuses his intrusion, he explains its cause. Sir Mauger waves his plump fingers. "Betsy could do with more help. The usual pay and she can sleep with the other girls. Bring her here."

"Perhaps you could send two or three of your larger menservants to fetch her, m'lord? As soon as they are able?"

Sir Mauger nibbles a date. "My men will bear the message that should aught untoward occur, the smith will be summoned to hallmote, the verdict outlawry. You may go."

"Permit me to trespass a little longer on your time. Jorden's son Ivo is whipped for protecting his sister. Would you allow him to leave our manor?"

"Upon receipt of chevage. Three shillings fourpence the usual fee." Sir Mauger plops the date into his mouth and speaks around it. "Sixpence."

Haukyn bows, something he rarely does. "You have my true fealty, m'lord."

"I should hope so."

Haukyn lingers within sight of the manor, and very soon three brawny men troop toward the smith's house and disappear inside. When they reappear, they are accompanied by Ivo and his sister, Jorden's wife screeching at any who will listen, Jorden glowering in the doorway. Haukyn waits until rescuers and rescued are level with him before he joins them. The girl looks dazed, Ivo belligerent. "Ivo, your sister will be safe in the manor," he says, "with other girls for company and coin in her purse...and for only sixpence in chevage you may leave Flintbourne. All this at my father's suggestion."

Ivo is holding himself so rigidly he could snap at the lightest breath. "I wants to see where she be lodged in the manor. I'll come by later."

Haukyn runs to his mother's, tells them of the outcome, begs some pottage, kisses Annabel, hurries home, and lights a fire to heat the pottage. Rust barks. He lets Ivo in. "You'll eat with me," he says.

Ivo sits down hard on the bench and buries his face in his hands. Haukyn turns his back and makes much of lighting candles, pouring Johanna's ale, and ladling pottage into two bowls. He says grace. Ivo rubs his face on his sleeve. "She be well placed, m' sister, 'n' outlawry a dread threat."

"You can stay here or at my father's until you leave the manor."

Ivo stares at his spoon as if he's not sure what it is. "I thrashed you when you was a young-un."

"I thrashed you back after Da taught me how. Ivo, I learned in France how much water can pass under a bridge—now eat your pottage, you must be hungered."

"I ain't leaving m' sister. Her name be Jenet. I been thinking. At first light, I'll go to Dunstan's, a few stones ain't naught to me. I could weed his garden, patch up his house 'n' shed in return for roof 'n' food. Even though you be there in the evenings, he be lonely, tis why he has that fool of a dog he calls Jackdawe so he has summat to talk to."

"He's a good bowyer and a good teacher, and deserves your respect."

"He ain't m' da. We'll rub along. Let's drink to it."

They drink to it rather too much. Haukyn wakes in the morning to the door closing behind Ivo—who, away from Jorden, might be a different man—to Rust whining to go outside, and to a headache the rain barrel doesn't cure.

Annabel and Alyce come home that same day, and no sooner is she in the door than she tears linen into strips and binds her infant in them. "Your ma don't believe in swaddling," she says, "but without it, limbs grow evil-shaped."

Alyce's cheeks redden. Her whimper turns into the full-throated roar that bespeaks a born rebel; Haukyn feels the stirrings of sympathy for his father. "Nay," he says, "remember how she kicked in the womb, she was free there to move, and her limbs are perfect."

"Ma tol' me 'bout swaddling. Swaddled she'll be."

He knows that look on her face. "For a week only, then we'll try it my mother's way."

"Tis custom, to swaddle."

"Custom becomes swaddling bands in itself, tight around body and soul!"

In seven days, he is the one to unbind their daughter, whose first movements are so timid it cuts him to the heart. "We must give her freedom, Annabel, we must. Could *you* bear to be tied at ankle and wrist? I couldn't."

For another three days they argue, Alyce unswaddled when Haukyn leaves the house, swaddled when he returns. Finally, in cold anger, he says, "You vowed obedience and even you must see she cries less when she can move in her cradle."

Annabel chews her lip. "Aye…but Ma were always right 'n' me the stupid one."

He's won. He folds her in his arms. "Your ma was wrong on both counts."

Alyce remains unswaddled and does cry less. Haukyn becomes an expert with loaded clouts, and from another length of linen he makes slings so he and Annabel can carry Alyce wherever they go, the small weight of her a delight. Over the last months, he's learned to take what contentment he can from his marriage, a contentment his father might compare to the little scarlet pimpernels that bloom by the river. The happiness his daughter brings though—ah, tis like a field-poppy, brazenly red in the sunlight.

...justiciable by thee in body and chattels...

The riverbanks crust with snow and ice. A few days after Annabel's churching, Sir Mauger bestirs himself for a stroll around his moat, slips on the ice, and falls in. "Landed on his arse," says Amos Cat-Skinner, who pulled him out in hopes of a reward. The water only waist-deep, but the lord catches a cold that moves to his chest. No bleeding or purges administered by the surgeon from Newbury, and no herbs of Hawise's after the surgeon departed with his fee, can cure him; he's dead before the Feast of St. Sebastian. Neighbouring landowners arrive for the funeral, the bishop presiding, Father Mortimer much fussed by the whole affair. The vill mourns benevolent Sir Mauger to a more than acceptable degree and goes about its business.

Irascible Dunstan sharing his hoarded grain and beans with Ivo has amply fed the gossips. Haukyn helps Ivo build a new roof for Dunstan's shed, in the company of Jackdawe, and after Christ's Mass, Jenet starts attending St. Edmund's church, for tis well known that Jorden refuses to worship a Father more imposing than himself.

Soon after, Haukyn delivers a small bow to Solomon for his eldest son. "Our lord were a childless widower," Solomon says, passing Haukyn coin. "M' cousin in Hungerford, he were at the market this week and heard that a nephew o' Sir Mauger's will inherit Flintbourne. What were his name? Sir Gardrad, that be it."

Silver coins clatter on the table and roll to the floor. "Are you certain?"

"Aye. M' cousin says he be known for squeezing every penny from his tenants."

"I met him in France. I hate his guts. And he mine."

Solomon blinks. "Likely Flintbourne be too small for him to bother overmuch, he got bigger manors in our shire. He'll send a bailiff to manage us."

Haukyn stoops to pick up his earnings. "I pray the bailiff be a better man than his master."

He has no new commissions and needs bodily comfort, so while Alyce sleeps through a windswept afternoon, he entices Annabel to bed. "M' breasts 'n' belly sag like an ol' hag's," she says tearfully, and, "you be hurting me," she cries when he enters her. "Pull out, Haukyn, I beg you, I don't want another little-un, not so soon."

"I'm sorry I hurt you," he says, forehead to her shoulder, and is he to beat out his seed in the byre for the rest of his days?

He, a priest-killer—knowledge that always lurks at the back of his brain—how dare he expect happiness, in bed or out?

And beneath it all, Ilotte, a bond that will be, he's beginning to realize, constant til death.

Soon after, on the feast day of St. Valentine, a stranger trots down the track to Flintbourne on a dainty white palfrey. A dainty-looking man altogether until you looked into his eyes. Three men march behind him, bulky men, each bearing a stout staff. He installs himself in the manor as Sir Gardrad's bailiff, harries the housemaids to whapping tapestries and sweeping cobwebs, the menservants to cleaning hearths and carrying wood, the cook to produce meals fit for his consumption, and expresses no gratitude toward those who do his bidding. He's seen entering Father Mortimer's house and leaving shortly afterward, and on Sunday, visibly nervous, the priest makes an announcement. "Master Osmond, our new bailiff, has called hallmote for tomorrow at None, in the manor hall. All the able-bodied in the vill, men and women, must attend."

Bony Mabel cackles. Father Mortimer shakes an admonishing finger at her. Osmond sits alone in the pew that used to be occupied by Sir Mauger, he, like Sir Mauger, wearing a velvet doublet. His greying hair lies wispy over a pink scalp, the back of his neck scrawny as a plucked hen's; gossip on the green after Mass tends to discount him. Two of his henchmen, word goes around, are brothers, Saul and Mauld, the third man named Oakum.

Annabel and Haukyn walk together to the manor, Haukyn carrying Alyce and chucking her under the chin, rewarded by fat bubbles. Inside the hall, Sir Mauger's favourite tapestry, a gift from his wife, is gone from the wall. No benches have been provided for freemen or villeins, nor is there a fire in the hearth; the chatter is subdued, feet shuffle among the rushes, and those carrying babies, or with little-uns clinging to them, try to hush them, not always with success. Osmond has stationed himself above them all on a dais, flanked by his three burly henchmen, each holding a thick staff. The bailiff says, "Can anyone here read and write?"

Samuel Cat-Skinner shouts, "Haukyn."

"Then Haukyn will scribe the proceedings."

"I knew Sir Gardrad in the war. I'll not write one word for him."

Edmund says hurriedly, "I will act as scribe," and seats himself at the table, which bears ink, quills, and a scroll.

"You will address me as Master Osmond," the bailiff says, his empty eyes travelling from face to face. "It seems Sir Mauger bothered himself neither with amercements nor taxes. This laxity is at an end. Oakum will collect tallage on the morrow, and I will go from house to house counting families, chattels, poultry, and beasts."

The men and women adjacent to Haukyn stiffen in apprehension, though Annabel is too busy jigging Alyce up and down to pay much attention. Haukyn stands still, anger no longer dormant as it has been for so long. *You won't have it all your way, Master Osmond,* he thinks, *for we also have thick staffs and won't be cowed by an upstart bailiff.*

Osmond waits with visible impatience for Edmund's quill to catch up. "I also expect the constable to make himself known. Because other offices have fallen vacant, you've had no supervision from reeve, hayward, or woodward, and that too is at an end."

A baby wails, a little girl cries, "If you hits me agin, I'll hit you back," and laughter ripples through the crowd. Osmond flushes. *So you have blood in you,* Haukyn thinks, *and your dignity is easy-disrupted.*

"I will summon another hallmote a week from today for the collection of entry fines, heriot, merchet, leyrwite, and childwyte. All males from the age of twelve will attend, but only those women who are in mercy." His smile is thin. "In addition, the byelaws will be read, in case you have forgot them. The following week, you will swear fealty to me, in Sir Gardrad's stead." He pauses. "Do not hide aught, it will go ill for you. Have you questions?"

Haukyn says clearly, above the mutterings of his neighbours, "It might go ill for you, Master Osmond, should you push us too hard and too fast."

The mutterings now are of assent. "I think not," the bailiff says. "Sir Gardrad's armed retainers are at my beck, and you would not want them to descend upon your vill. Hallmote is dismissed. God bless King Edward."

Walter atte Mede shouts, "Bastard," and there are many who nod.

Annabel grabs Haukyn's sleeve. "Keep your gob shut 'n' take me home."

"I want to stay awhile and talk to our neighbours."

"Alyce too heavy for me to carry her the whole way."

"You sound like your sister Margery."

She pushes through those already outside. "I got cause, she didn't need none. Haukyn, you be a fool, making an enemy of our new bailiff. He'll spy on you day 'n' night now, him 'n' his three churls, be *that* what you want? Me your wife, them men hanging around our croft—you got no more sense than a whirligig in the goose pond."

"I won't be spoken to by any man as if I'm the dirt beneath his feet! Ancient custom has rights as well as duties, and tis up to us to guard those rights. Hallmotes and records languished under Sir Mauger, and how will Osmond know who owes fines and who's fornicated or left the vill other than setting villager against villager, encouraging one to betray the other?"

She thrusts his daughter at him, a downy head bumping his chin, clouts soggy against his bare hands, and crosses the ford in three nimble steps. "I wants m' house to m'self 'n' Alyce left in peace."

"You think I won't protect my daughter? Annabel, don't you see—if we don't stand up for ourselves, under Osmond we'll be little more than slaves."

"You'll teach Alyce to read 'n' write, she won't be no slave." In a flurry of skirts, Annabel crosses the meadow and rushes up the hill, he trying to keep up with her. When they reach their house, she unlatches the door with an angry snap. "Give me Alyce 'n' bring in wood from the byre."

He does so, armloads of wood that he dumps in an untidy heap on the floor. "I'll be back once I've talked to those outside the manor," he says and slams the door behind him. Rust woofs and Alyce starts to cry. More angry voices, he thinks with a twinge of guilt. Yet how else can he make Annabel see sense?

The light is fast fading. The only men near the lord's moat are the two brothers, staffs upright as they parade up and down in front of the manor's stout oak door. Sir Saul and Sir Mauld, he thinks sourly, his eyes searching the shadowed fields and baulks—in the distance the cooper and his family, up the hill Solomon the Small, no sign of Jorden, the atte Medes, or his father and the rest of his family. He has no wish to visit Edmund, the vill's new scribe. He trudges up the hill, and when Solomon opens the door, says bluntly, "What happened?"

"We was tol' to go home. After Walter were bashed on the shoulder 'n' Neuton in the ribs, twas home we went."

"There's no law against villagers talking on the green."

"There be now. Come in, Lucy's heating soup."

"Nay, I've left an angered wife, I'd best go home."

So Osmond has no qualms against using force, he thinks, *regardless of custom or law.*

The moon is rising over the bare-limbed trees, the first scatter of stars, stars content to stay hid through the hours of daylight. As he has been hid for too long?

Closer to Prime than Terce, Rust starts barking. A staff raps hard against their door. "Open it, Haukyn," Annabel says. "Else they'll wake Alyce."

Haukyn does so, Rust snarling at his side, his own face in a smile as sweet as Ilotte's honey. Osmond and Saul, the latter's staff already raised to knock again. "Good day, Master Osmond," he says, "come in, both of you."

"Stay outside, Saul," and Osmond shuts the door in his henchman's face.

"As you can see," Haukyn says, "I have one wife, named Annabel, one daughter, named Alyce—her clouts, as usual, full—and one dog, Rust, our good watchdog."

"How many beasts?"

"Come through to the byre. Can Annabel offer you ale, Master?"

"Nay. The byre."

The bailiff is already heading toward the door that leads into the byre. Haukyn winks at Annabel and follows him into the warm, straw-scented byre. Trefoil whickers, the goats butt their stall, and from their winter coop the hens squawk and cluck. "Six hens and an early-crowing cockerel," Haukyn says smoothly. "My orchard has three apple trees, two pear, and an elderberry. The nine acres around this house belong to my father, Edmund. Will you remember all this?"

"I'll sit at your table and record it."

Sit he does, inscribes the scroll that was tucked in his pouch, then stands. "I go to the smithy next."

"Ah...I trust you are able to discern truth from lie, Master Osmond. God's blessing."

"I am able to discern more than you might think."

The door swings shut behind him. Annabel gives Haukyn her first proper smile since hallmote. "You were most amiable."

He picks her up, whirls her around, and plants a kiss on her mouth. "So I was."

Ilotte would have seen through the honey to the barbs within, but he is not married to Ilotte.

Restless, he sharpens his blades and carries his ladder outdoors. Robert's instructions clear in his head, he begins pruning the largest of his apple trees. Twixt Terce and Sext, Oakum, who is heavier around the girth than Saul or Mauld, labours up the slope. "Hills in this cursed place whichever way you look," he says. "Tallage. Eight pence."

More than should be, but not so much as to cause rebellion. Shrewdly done, Master Osmond. Haukyn climbs down the ladder, extracts the coins from his pouch, and passes them over. "Come to the house," he says. "On my slate, I've written that Haukyn of Flintbourne has this day paid tallage. I'll add the amount and you'll add your mark."

Oakum scratches his head. "Master said naught 'bout slate."

"It'll take but a moment."

The deed done, he watches the man head for the smithy. Brawn equal to that of Jorden, but fewer brains.

That evening, Alyce asleep in her cradle, he puts an arm around Annabel as they sit by the fire and—knowing he should have told her sooner—describes how he, Piers, and Javyd saved Sir Gardrad from drowning in one of France's many rivers. Then, trying to keep any feeling from his voice, he tells of the knight's role in Piers's terrible death and of John of Gaunt's censure. "So twice I saw Sir Gardrad humiliated. He was leader of our retinue by the end, he won't have forgot me and has every reason to detest me."

Gazing into the coals' flickering, she says, "War don't end when it ends, do it."

Grateful for understanding, he kisses her. He hasn't told her everything, and the following morning says he's off to London to see Javyd, she to stay at his father's, Rust to guard their croft. She says crossly, "You ain't never learned to sit still."

"A farmer's life leaves scant opportunity for practice. The weather looks to hold, I'll finish the pruning when I get back, and once ploughing starts, I'll have no time for sitting or for London."

Edmund raises an eyebrow at such a hastily planned visit, Hawise pleased to have a cradle in their house again. He leaves at Terce.

Javyd and Petronilla are happy to see him, and his other errand, his reason for being in the city, goes better than he'd dared hope.

He arrives home in time for the next hallmote, a seethe of anger because Master Osmond has ferreted out too many of the vill's misdemeanours, and his fines, levied on prosperous and poor, are higher than need be. Bony Mabel is rebuked for causing disturbances in church and Father Mortimer for delinquency in collecting tithes; the dairy maid is amerced for fornication that was forced upon her by Wulstan, the cowherd; trespasses, fist fights that drew blood, fallen-down fences, rickety byres, the list is endless and the bailiff's coffers much enriched. Once again, the three henchmen prevent any gatherings outside the manor.

That evening Haukyn says he's going to the alehouse, a place he rarely visits. "I want to determine the vill's mood. I'll take a torch and Rust will stay with you."

"Fines has gloom in their wake, no need of alehouse to tell you that."

"Osmond is a dangerous man, and I'd as well keep a step ahead of him. I'll take a torch and I'll drink only one mug." He drops a kiss on their sleeping daughter's forehead and leaves.

The alehouse is busy. With his jug of ale, he wanders from bench to bench. There are those, the arthritic and grizzled, who claim that Osmond's arrival is God's will, "naught to be done." Others say, "Tis penance for having it too soft under good Sir Mauger, naught to be done." A goodly group—atte Medes, Blundred the cooper and his three sons, Tirrell the constable, Ivo, and a clutch of Cat-Skinners— are outright hostile, the degree depending upon the amount of ale guzzled. Much hot air is expelled, unburdened with thought or strategy.

Haukyn leaves before last call.

Another week, another hallmote. He stands to one side, his waterskin at his waist, for fealty under oath will take time. One by one, the men kneel before Master Osmond, place their hands between his and repeat the words, *faithful and loyal to thee…the tenement that I hold of thee in villeinage...justiciable by thee in body and chattels...so help me God,* an oath sworn to Sir Gardrad, Osmond merely his representative. When his father's name is called, Edmund dutifully kneels, one more villein swearing that the court has due power over his body and goods. Edmund stands and meets his son's eyes; Haukyn would have to be blindfolded not to see the pleading in them.

Osmond calls, "Haukyn, second son of Edmund, come forward."

Haukyn crosses the floor toward the bailiff. Instead of kneeling, he turns so the crowd can hear him. "I'll not swear fealty to our new lord, Sir Gardrad. I met him in France, he is a knight without honour, charity, or mercy, and twice I beheld John of Gaunt, Duke of Lancaster, chastise him. I owe Sir Gardrad neither fidelity nor loyalty. I owe him naught."

The silence is absolute. Then Osmond says, clipping each word, "I have the power of distraint, invested in me as Sir Gardrad's bailiff. I will confiscate your land and your chattels, even your body, should you persist in going against me."

"I think not, Master Osmond." All his movements unhurried, he extracts a parchment from his pouch and unfolds it. "I visited London a fortnight ago, and in his Sauvoye Palace John of Gaunt, son of our king, was gracious enough to grant me an audience. This parchment was dictated by him to his scribe. 'I, John of Gaunt, Duke of Lancaster, absolve Haukyn of Flintbourne from present and future fealty to Sir Gardrad of Faircross and all his heirs and successors.' The parchment is dated and signed and bears the duke's seal. I will give the court this copy, all in this room being witnesses. A second copy is housed with the duke's scribe in the Sauvoye."

The bailiff's face is as red as if he were standing on the brink of Hellfire. When Haukyn passes him the parchment, Osmond's eyes bore into his, impotent with fury. Heels of his boots clicking against the stone floor, Haukyn walks out of the hall, nods at Oakum, who is guarding the oak door, and then he's outside, breathing God's chill air.

He's in no hurry to go home, for Annabel, rightly so, will be as furious with him as was the bailiff. How can he explain to her that every nerve, every muscle, every drop of blood in his body would have screamed betrayal had he sworn fealty to a man so unworthy?

Even if he could, he doubts she'd listen.

He'll also have to behave himself—or at least appear to—in the manor's fields and woods every hour of every day. Irksome, but foolish to do otherwise.

As he ambles up the hill past the alehouse, the moon casts his shadow slant on the winter grass. He gives Solomon's a wide berth so their dog won't bark, and skirts Dunstan's, although Jackdawe is more apt to wag her tail in greeting than bark, and wonders what Ivo thought of a public refusal to bow to authority. In London, he had bowed to John of Gaunt and bowed deep.

It had taken courage of a kind new to him that day to approach the Sauvoye Palace with its elegant gardens and well-kept outbuildings on land that stretched to the river; if Javyd hadn't told him of Parliament's public humiliation of the duke the year before—"not one cut farthing o' taxes would they grant him"—he might simply have gone home. He hadn't gone home. He'd spoken to the guards outside the Sauvoye, rattling off words like *known to the duke, horse archer, rescuer of knights*. Though they looked dubious, they let him in, two of them accompanying him across the great hall, past rich tapestries, paintings, and the glitter of gold, braziers warming the air in empty rooms, he dazzled and as nervous as the day of his first *chevauchée*. One of the guards made him wait outside a door intricately carved with images of a hunt, and now that he was actually inside the Sauvoye, he couldn't imagine why the son of a king would deign to receive him.

The door opened. He walked in and bowed. "So, Haukyn of Flintbourne," that well-remembered, cultured voice said, "you look somewhat better than the last time we spoke."

The same aura of power, the same long nose, face not as thin though, and Haukyn began to laugh. "You also, Your Highness."

"Most supplicants grovel before me."

"More valuable than grovelling, you have my respect. You rode at our side through those ghastly woods and valleys, that ceaseless rain, encouraging us, urging us onward, day after endless day—would I be here now were it not for you and your destrier?"

"You did not request an audience to tell me that."

"Perhaps, strangely, I did." He swallowed, then did his best to describe Osmond, the bailiff whose lord was Sir Gardrad, to whom he must swear fealty. "I beg you for absolution from such an oath."

John of Gaunt closed the book on the table before him, his face darkening, a face more careworn than in Dordogne's valley, Haukyn realized, his heart sinking. "Fealty is the glue that holds this country together, from villein to king."

Again, Haukyn took courage into his hands. "I've not heard much talk of fealty in London."

"Londoners despise me." The duke's fist clenched on the table. "They question my legitimacy, calling me the son of a Ghent butcher. They doubt my loyalty to my father and his heir, my nephew Richard. Worse, last year's Good Parliament—from which no good came—refused taxation because of that *chevauchée* I led, and other equally unfruitful campaigns." With a visible effort, he loosened his fist. "I am curious. Would you again go to war with me?"

"I am of more value to you as an archer who teaches others the art of bowmanship, and as a farmer who, however distantly, feeds your troops."

"For a villein, you always had a clever tongue. I'll dictate an absolution to my scribe. Wait outside til he's done."

"May I request two copies, one to be stored here?"

"You do not trust this Osmond."

"No more than you the king of France."

A short laugh. "Begone."

Haukyn bowed again. "War tests our mettle, Your Highness, and yours stood most firm."

Though it was indeed an unfruitful campaign, a thought he does not share.

And then he was outside the door, the guard impassive at his side. He made the king's son laugh, and he will never have to swear fealty to Sir Gardrad of Faircross.

A branch slaps his sleeve. He's in the lord's woods, a copse of birch, trunks white as bone in the moonlight. He has to go home and confess to his wife what he's done.

"Oath o' fealty 'n' you did *what*? Too high 'n' mighty to bend your knee to a bailiff 'n' now we'll lose house 'n' land, we'll be vagabond the rest of our lives."

"We won't! If only you'd listen—we have John of Gaunt's protection."

"I were a fool at Hocktide, more 'n a fool to come to you for safety from Samuel Cat-Skinner. *You* never asked me to marry you, did you? Nay, me the one what had to ask, me who got you into bed, you too busy sorrowing after that skinny black-eyed bitch from Hungerford. I rue the day I thought you comely 'n' a man o' sense!"

She rushes into their bedroom. The door, slammed, shivers on its hinges. Alyce wakes with a start, wide-eyed. He picks her up and rocks her; with her, at least, love comes easy and deep. Such wild accusations, such long-brewed resentments, he never even suspected their existence. How can a marriage abide after the vat has boiled over?

Wedlock. Holy Church holds the only key, and holds it tight.

When, on the morrow, tired before the day begins, he takes himself to his father's orchard to prune the pear trees, Edmund's anger is ice rather than scald. "You are never content, Haukyn—what is it in you that seeks out conflict and hostility? You now have Osmond for a sworn enemy, which could redound on me, your mother, and your brothers. Or had you even considered that possibility?"

"Tis me he resents, not you."

"And what of your wife and child? You are a fool, your pride such that you'll not bow to anyone."

The words stab sharp; too closely, they echo Annabel's. "I bowed to John of Gaunt. I have trees to prune—if you trust me that far?"

The pear trees are ruthlessly docked. He goes home to burnt pottage and Alyce's toothless smiles.

Haukyn cannot always evade his father; for those mutual tasks that are unavoidable, he works in silence and leaves as soon as he's done.

The vill's humour, like his, like his wife's, remains dark. The constant surveillance by Osmond or one of his three henchmen, who roam the vill by daylight and torchlight, wears on everyone. A hallmote three weeks later presents a litany of offences, including Johanna's breaking of the assize for bread and ale; this last does not improve Annabel's temper, although at least now tis directed more at Osmond than her husband.

The days lengthen and warm, robins, sparrows, and chaffinches chorus in the hedgerows, and blackbirds warble to the heavens. The small purple violets are blooming by the river, Haukyn never able to see them without remembering the bunch he delivered to Ilotte and how it charmed her.

By way of penance, he breaks off a few and gives them to Annabel. The smallest of smiles, then she turns away.

That evening he strolls over to Dunstan's for a length of seasoned elm. Past Solomon's byre, angry voices: Dunstan, Ivo, and is it Mauld? He speeds up. Mauld has his face stuck in Ivo's, Dunstan is stooping to pick up stones, while Jackdawe sniffs Mauld's heavy boots, her long black tail, for once, still.

Mauld yells, "You started a brawl on the last afternoon o' the lord's harrowing, 'n' your stupid cur been hanging round the lord's kitchen."

Ivo pushes him in the chest. Mauld stumbles, recovers, and kicks Jackdawe in the ribs so hard the dog goes flying, landing with a thud on the ground. She cries out, her paws scrabbling for purchase in the grass. Dunstan fires two good-sized stones at Mauld. One hits his nose. Blood spurts. Ivo laughs, Jackdawe wheezes for breath, and Haukyn shouts, "Stop this nonsense! If Ivo brawled in the fields, tis a matter for hallmote, you know that, Mauld, as does every soul in Flintbourne by now. Go back to the manor and stay there."

"Who be you, giving me orders?"

"I'm the man protected by the Duke of Lancaster. Get the cook to put yarrow to your nose."

Ivo says, "Choke on your own blood, why don't you," plugs his own nose with two fingers, and rolls his eyes in a mock faint.

Murder in Mauld's eyes. "I'll make your blood flow, Ivo Smyth, til there ain't a drop left in you," he says, and stomps away across the grass.

In true distress, Dunstan says, "Jackdawe can't get up, he busted her ribs, bone sticking out her skin."

"God's balls, I'll kill the bastard," Ivo says.

Haukyn kneels down. Jackdawe is groaning horribly, and he too can see the split bones and the blood seeping through her black fur. "Dunstan, she's in agony. I'll have to cut her throat."

Dunstan gives a loud, uncouth sob. "Aye—do it fast."

"Talk to her," he says, takes out his knife, and slices through fur and muscle with the skill and precision he learned in France. Blood pulses into the grass. Jackdawe's legs convulse and her eyes go blank with death.

"I'm sorry, Dunstan." Awkwardly he pats his mentor's bony shoulder.

"Best bitch I ever had. Kept me company many a winter's night."

"Ivo and I can bury her, if you like. Near your shed."

"Say a prayer for her, you got a way with words."

The hole is dug and the dog lifted into it. Dunstan tucks a bone she'd been chewing under her chin, then they shovel dirt over her and tramp it down hard. Ivo gives him a sly grin and bows his head. "Jackdawe," Haukyn says, "I commend your soul to our blessed Lady, and may She be with your master in his grief...*in nomine Spiritus Sancti.*"

"Should've kept one o' her pups," Dunstan says, sniffling. "Drowned most of 'em, sold the rest to whoever'd take 'em. I be off to alehouse."

He slouches down the hill. Ivo looks at Haukyn, who looks back. "Mauld's not worth the noose, Ivo."

"He'd be dead though, wouldn't he."

"Dunstan needs you here."

"You got a quick hand with a knife."

"You'd remember Modge, my first mare. I had to slit her throat. Nigh broke my heart, and let's for the love of God follow Dunstan to the alehouse."

The alehouse breeds unrest that night, for Jackdawe was well-liked.

The well is surrounded by women. Muttering women. Cursing women. Warily, Haukyn approaches. The cooper's wife calls, "You the one what cut Jackdawe's throat?"

"Mauld's boot drove the dog's ribs into her chest, twas the only thing to do."

"She were Dunstan's bitch, but she were ours too...every dog in the valley had his way with her, her dugs a-droop, were she ever without a pup snapping at her heels?"

"Pups she could've done without," a Cat-Skinner's wife cries.

"Holy Church don't care if you drown pups, do it."

"Holy Church says us got to bear *our* litters."

"Year in. Year out."

Bony Mabel snorts. "Til we be too old to bear aught and we ain't worth a turnip's arse."

Haukyn edges through them and lowers his bucket into the well. Little chance of Annabel bringing another pup into the world.

When it comes time for the next hallmote, the vill's men can only enter the manor by pushing through an orderly crowd of the vill's women, Annabel among them, Alyce in a sling against her chest; she had not mentioned this venture to Haukyn. Oakum, whose staff is leaning against the manor door, is striving, ineffectually, to send them home where they belong. Oakum, Haukyn has decided, had a heart before he unravelled into what he is now, a man of bulk in the service of a man without a heart, and he is not surprised that before proceedings begin with Father Mortimer's prayer, these same women enter the hall, again in orderly fashion. Osmond gawps at them. Mauld and Saul move forward, staffs at the ready. Catherine, the cooper's wife, stands firm. "Master Osmond, all us women be here to accuse Mauld your servant o' murder, the unwarranted murder o' Dunstan's bitch Jackdawe. He did bust her ribs without cause when he were trespassing on Dunstan's croft, 'n' we hereby calls him to account."

"Aye!" Ivo shouts. "Trespass and murder."

Osmond bangs his gavel on the table. "Only women accused of misdemeanours are permitted to attend hallmote."

Solomon's Lucy says, "We be here and here we stays til you passes judgement."

"You'll leave immediately or I'll—"

"Mauld's staff ain't long enough to reach all of us."

"What be beneath his hose ain't, neither."

Laughter ripples through the women. Mauld's face darkens. Walter's mother calls, "What about you, Saul, how long be your staff?"

A Cat-Skinner's wife, voice like a drill. "Ain't it enough we can't light our fires without you count the faggots, Master? You tell your men to leave the vill's dogs alone."

"Or it won't be a dog's ribs broke."

Osmond sputters, "Silence! You dare issue threats in hallmote?"

"Put all us women in gaol 'n' our men wouldn't get no pottage."

"Nor no sarding."

"Tell Mauld to keep his boots to hisself."

"Else he finds them stuffed up his—"

"Clouts," says Annabel with overdone primness.

More laughter. Then, as though a silent signal had passed among them, the women say in unison, "God bless King Edward," and in as orderly a fashion as they entered, start filing out of the hall.

Samuel Cat-Skinner shouts, "You be the bitches, go home where you belongs!"

Haukyn, full of admiration for a wife who'd condensed her chatter into one perfect word, shouts, as loudly, "You were brave to do this, and your words spoke true."

Samuel pushes Haukyn. He pushes back. Mauld raises his staff and the gavel bangs the table so hard that the men nearest it jump. Father Mortimer says hastily, "Let us pray," and bows his head. From habit, if not reverence, the men in the hall follow suit.

On the *Amen*, Ivo yells, "How much be Mauld amerced?"

Osmond says coldly, "Hallmote has more pressing matters than a dead bitch, and all of you will keep your women in order—I will not tolerate such interruptions. For the trespass of his ox on Waryn atte Mede's fallow..." and the business of hallmote proceeds.

Alyce is fussy when Haukyn arrives home, perhaps having caught the women's mood—women, he realizes, who did not behave like serfs twice over but as the equal of every man in hallmote. Annabel's smile is demure as she puts her daughter to breast. "I doubt Mauld will kick anyone else's dog."

"You did well, Annabel, to speak as you did." She blushes with pleasure, looking very pretty by the light of their candle. He smiles at her. "I thought to buy a grandson of Jackdawe's from Reginald-of-the-wandering-eye and give it to Dunstan, would you agree to that?"

"I would," she says.

When he delivers the pup, Dunstan stretches out his hand, pulls it back, stretches it out again, and the wriggling pup licks it.

Shoots push up on the new-sown fields, the ash trees flower, bluebells carpet the woods, and the blackthorns over Haukyn's hideaway are blooming in a froth of white. Craving a trout for dinner on a rainy morning, he watches one lazily swim upriver through the dappled shadows, glances up, and sees Mauld on the other bank. "A pretty fish, Mauld, is it not?"

Mauld shakes his fist. Haukyn walks up the hill and engages the twins to scare birds from his nine acres. Weeding, that infernal task, begins, and one night, sleepless against Annabel's back, he eases out of bed, throws on his tunic, and goes outside, Rust with him, tail wagging at an unexpected outing. The dog pisses against the nearest tree trunk, a clear night, the sky as full of stars as weeds in the fields. Rust stiffens beside him, barks once.

"Hush, we don't want to wake Alyce."

Rust whines, straining forward. A figure is wavering up the hill from the ford. A woman? A girl? She falls, lies still, then struggles to sit up. "Go home, Rust," Haukyn says softly, "guard the house."

He hurries down the hillside. She sees him, a man looming out of the darkness, her cry of despair stopping him in his tracks. "No cause for fear," he says, "'tis Haukyn, I live nearby. I'll not harm you...let me come closer."

As he does so, he recognizes her. "You're Jenet, Ivo's sister. What happened?"

Dark splotches on her face, bruises and blood, her clothing torn, and when his hand brushes hers as he stoops beside her, she cries out in pain. "M' wrist, he broke it," she says and starts to weep, almost silently.

This girl he can help as he couldn't help those in France. "If you'll let me, I'll carry you to my mother's, she'll look to your hurts." As gently as he can, he picks her up. She's too thin, trembling in his arms. "Who did this to you?"

"Mauld. He know I be Ivo's sister."

A beating, or worse? "You'll be safe at my mother's. We'll take the river path."

He steers his way between the willows, the river rippling past, chill and uncaring, her voice a whisper in the darkness. "T'ain't the first time he been at me, but someone always come along afore... hand over m' mouth tonight so no one heard me scream. He be like m' father. I been so scared. Didn't dare tell Ivo, he'd kill him."

Worse than a beating, then. He swallows bile. "I'll speak to Ivo, Jenet, there'll be no killing. How did you escape from the manor?"

"Scullery door. We all be scared o' Mauld, save Master Osmond."

"I'm not," Haukyn says, and knows it for truth. "We're nearly there."

Ranulf barks. Haukyn knocks on his father's door, shuffle of footsteps. "Tis Haukyn, we're in need of my mother."

The door opens to the flare of a new-lit candle, Jenet flinching from the light. Edmund rouses his wife, uncovers the fire, and coaxes the coals to flame. "Why don't you take her into your old room, Haukyn," he says, "she can rest there in privacy."

A pity, Haukyn thinks, that his father's kindness doesn't extend to his second son. "Her name is Jenet, she's Ivo's sister. Mauld did this to her. I'll fetch Ivo, she'll want to see him, then I must go home in case Annabel wakes."

His mother has lit another candle and thrown a shawl over her chemise. With great care, he lays the girl on his bed. "Her wrist is broke, but worse than that...she'll tell you."

He lights a torch before he tramps the grass between the fields of grain. Dunstan's pup yaps a happy welcome, and Ivo opens to his knock, scrubbing at his eyes, red hair tousled in the torchlight. "Haukyn?"

"Your sister Jenet—Mauld attacked her, she's at my mother's and wants to see you."

Ivo's body goes rigid. "Mauld?"

"Leave your knife on the shelf. Before we take one step, you'll swear in the name of our Saviour that you won't kill the man. Now or ever."

"I'll not—"

Haukyn takes a step forward and blocks the doorway, a show of belligerence somewhat marred by the puppy lavishly licking his ankles. "Your sister needs solace," he says, "not a brother throttled on Newbury's scaffold. We're not moving from here til you swear."

Sulkily, hunching into his tunic, Ivo repeats the vow. "I don't go nowheres without m' knife."

"Take it then."

Edmund opens the door to them. "Ivo, come in, warm yourself by the fire. Jenet will stay here until she's recovered."

Haukyn starts for home. He needs go no farther than the boundary stones of Flintbourne to find all the cruelties of war, and of what use any atonement he can offer?

Before yet another hallmote can convene, a tax collector arrives from Newbury, the same man who came for the parish tax some years earlier, and as unpopular now as then. A poll tax, he explains, a mere fourpence per head, those under fourteen exempt, his teeth in a fixed grin as though he wishes to be congratulated for Parliament's generosity.

"An unjust tax for a useless war," Haukyn says, resting his hand on the haft of his dagger. "The lord of the manor, the dukes and earls of the realm assessed for the same amount as I, a serf, and where's the justice in that? I'll not pay a single penny."

There are those in the vill who pass over their groats, and those who do not.

Hallmote, to the surprise of none, dismisses the charge of rape against Mauld. "No witnesses, and we are to take the word of a scullery maid against my chief henchman?" The gavel bangs and Osmond moves on to other matters.

Afterward, Ivo takes him aside. "Your ma saw to it there'd be no child from what Mauld done. But Jenet be soiled now, she'll not find a husband the length o' the valley."

"After Mauld, she might not want a husband. You made a vow before God, Ivo. Keep it."

Ralf has pledged to help Haukyn scare birds away and weed his crops, his young fingers nimble among the shoots. He arrives early, distraught and white-faced. "Haukyn, Haukyn, I heard a ghost!"

"A *ghost*? Where?"

"In the bracken near the river path. It cried pitiful 'n' I ran."

"You'd best show me. Rust, stay."

Knife at his belt and he takes his staff. Ghosts, he thinks stoutly, they're more oft flesh than not. Ralf leads him along the path, he with a hand on the boy's shoulder, and Haukyn hears it, a faint moaning, more a wail than a moan. His heart speeds up. He pushes into bracken that is tall and spring-green, sees broken stems (ghosts would pass through bracken, would they not?), and then sees, on his back among crushed fronds, a man. Mauld. His face battered, both wrists bent at impossible angles, and someone has stripped his braies down to his knees, his member lying small and shrivelled in the dawn light. If ever he were to feel compassion for the man, it would be now. He searches his heart and finds none. "I'll go to the manor and fetch Saul and Oakum to aid you."

"Four men," Mauld mumbles through broken teeth. "Hooded, cloths over their faces. Boots on 'n' gloves. I'll kill 'em."

"You'll have to find them first. Ralf, run home and tell your mother she'll be needed at the manor shortly, I'll come for her. Off you go."

He runs the opposite way, over the ford and across the green. When he bangs on the manor door, Oakum answers and Haukyn relays his message, suggesting they bring a stretcher. Osmond accompanies them across the ford. More bracken is crushed by the two men and the stretcher; Mauld cries out when they move him onto it. Haukyn watches, declining to help. Osmond says, "Do you know who did this?"

"Ask Mauld. Not me."

"Do you know?"

"I do not. Though if I did, I wouldn't say." As Oakum and Saul brush past them with their moaning burden—they've covered his nakedness with a blanket—he adds, "The punishment fits the crime, Osmond, and our women would call it justice."

"I'll root out the culprits if I have to upend the vill. Send your mother to the manor. Now."

With Jenet skulking in the background, Haukyn tells his father what happened, sees to his fury the unspoken question in Edmund's eyes, and says in a clipped voice, "I had no part in it, Father. But I won't condemn it either."

"They took the law into their own hands."

"Only because the law failed them. Are you ready, Ma?"

Hawise has bundled salves and herbs into her basket and strides down the hill ahead of him. At the manor, they cross the great hall into the private quarters, where Mauld is laid out on a bed, a fire already sending warmth from the hearth, Osmond and Saul on the bed's far side. Hawise slaps the contents of her basket on the trestle table. "Comfrey for the healing o' bone, yarrow 'n' marigold for the open wounds, set the wrists with lathes 'n' sit on him when he screams."

"You will apply the salves and do the setting," Osmond says.

"I'll not lay a bent finger on the man what inflicted on a young girl wounds that won't never heal."

"It was not proven in court!"

"Your court. I got my own, Master Osmond."

Haukyn follows her out of the room, not bothering to hide his smile; he comes by his rebellious nature honestly. After Oakum lets them out, she stomps up the hill, her empty basket swinging at her side.

That evening, moving stealthily and without a torch, he waits outside Dunstan's until Ivo comes out to use the privy. "Show me your hands."

Not a mark on them. "Did you bury the gloves and clean off your boots?"

"What gloves?" Ivo sniggers. "If the men was silent 'n' masked 'n' did their work in darkness, not even Osmond can haul anyone to court."

A court under Sir Gardrad's jurisdiction. "Be careful, Ivo. Osmond is out for blood."

But Osmond, although he calls in three of Sir Gardrad's armed retainers and disregards weeding, bird-scaring, and the Feast of St. James the Less to interrogate every man in the vill, even men like Edmund and Solomon, cannot find anyone to accuse for the assault on Mauld. Jorden accuses Ivo, but there is no proof. The Cat-Skinners maintain a sullen silence. Haukyn, seated on the riverbank after the retainers left, muses on a vill united in common hatred of its oppressors.

Mauld's nose sets crookedly and his wrists may never wield a staff again.

Marsh marigolds bloom golden along the riverbanks, cuckoos send out their two notes the day long, crabapple blossoms scent the air, and the tassels on the oaks sway in the breeze. One morning when Alyce wakes early, Haukyn takes her outdoors, puts his fingers to his lips, and as the sky lightens to the east, they listen: robin, blackbird, wren, chiffchaff and chaffinch, bullfinch and dunnock. Alyce, eyes wide, smiles in wonderment. Haukyn whispers, "May the birds always sing for you," and together they watch the first glint of sunlight touch the river.

He has his Alyce and he lived without swiving for twenty winters.

The chickens are laying, the cows are milked, crops and weeds flourish, and in June the hay is cut, Osmond with his white wand and Saul with his scowl arousing resentment from one end of Flintbourne to the other. News comes to the village that the old king is dead, Richard II their new king, a ten-year-old whose powerful uncle is John of Gaunt.

Strawberries are picked, then raspberries, the apples fatten and the damsons. July, too much hot sun, too little rain, St. Swithin's feast day without a drop falling from high white clouds; the fields of wheat, barley, and rye suffer, and the men are short of temper.

Haukyn rides to the Hungerford market for nails, as always planning his route among the wares so he avoids the bee-woman selling her honey. Another man is talking to the smith, so Haukyn waits, listening idly...*ancient demesne, writ, exemplification*... words that mean nothing to him until *freeman* is repeated, twice. He says awkwardly, "I couldn't help hearing...is this to do with manumission?"

"Nay." The man looks him over, a solid-built man, level of eye, who reminds Haukyn of Solomon the Small. "Daniel o' Chisledon, in the shire west o' here."

"Haukyn of Flintbourne, to the east."

Taking his time, Daniel explains that manors belonging to the Crown at the time of Domesday Book are exempt from customs and services, their tenants in effect freemen. "Many vills in our shire be sending writs to London to gain copies o' Domesday, *exemplifications* we calls 'em. There be cost in coin to the vill. Worth it, though, to end serfdom."

"Lawyers must be involved?"

"We got a counsellor, aye, he'll travel to London on our behalf since he know his way round Chancery 'n' the Exchequer. The men o' Warfield in your shire sent writs. I heard rumours Chertsey Abbey lands might also. Men from Surrey 'n' Sussex done it, the shire south o' you too. One o' my tasks be to spread the word, for there be power in numbers—when your business be done here, we could talk more over a jug of ale."

Haukyn rides home in a state of high excitement, succeeds in hiding it from Annabel, and that night in the alehouse lays what he has gleaned in front of Solomon, Neuton, Walter, Waryn, Tirrell, and Blundred. "I'll ride to Daniel's vill on the morrow to talk to the counsellor and find out more. We'd have to provide the necessary coin."

Neuton says, "If it ended Osmond's hold on our vill? Coin a cheap price."

He has to tell Annabel where he is going, suggesting he might find a possible curb to Osmond's tyranny. She tasted power at what Haukyn privately calls The Women's Hallmote; she looks at him thoughtfully and says she'll stay with his parents should he not be back by dark.

He rides through a mizzle that cannot damp his spirits. Finally, something he can do.

The counsellor is with Daniel, his name James of Liddington, a man lathe-thin, his eyes the twin fires of a zealot; Haukyn takes careful note of everything he says and knows the emotion flooding him as hope. He arrives home at dusk. Annabel is full of news: Alyce started to crawl that very day. "You must make a leather harness for her, Haukyn—she'll be across the rushes afore we knows it, didn't she already pick one up, cooing to it, then try to stuff it in her gob. The pottage be overcooked, I were that excited."

The pottage is burnt. He eats it without complaint and lies awake, his arm draped over his wife's waist, cudgelling his brains how to gain the necessary money. By Lauds, he has a plan: he and his six compatriots will divide up the vill's houses among them, he collecting from those north of him. He alerts the six at first light, and they set off. Because he needs it over with, he visits his father first, with a carefully worded explanation. Edmund listens with equal care, then says, "Osmond will find out—his ears can pierce daub. He'll discover you as ringleader, and what then?"

"There are manors west of us where the villeins are refusing boon works. I only collect coin."

"I wish you'd be content with what you have, as Robert was."

He stretches the truth. "I have a wife who is content, which is more than Robert had."

"Will she be content to take food to you in gaol?"

Why does his father fill him with such a desperate need to be understood? "Surely we should strive to end wrongs!"

Edmund pushes up from the table. "You saved Jenet, isn't that enough?"

"Must we always disagree?"

"It seems so."

"Will you give coin?"

"I will not."

Sore of heart, Haukyn goes to the next house and the next, and the money accumulates, a measure of how deeply Osmond is loathed. When he's done, the coin in a purse under his tunic, he walks along the river path to meet those who collected across the ford. Bracken skims his thighs, a kingfisher rattles from the sallows. Someone coughs, startling him. He looks up. The path is blocked by Osmond and Saul, the latter armed with knife and staff. Osmond says, "Where is the money?"

"Money? What money? No laws have been broke, Master Osmond. Let me pass."

Saul raises his staff. Haukyn laughs. "Do you think to leave me beaten in the bracken, as Mauld was left? Assault does break the law, and our constable has the sheriff's ear."

He sees the intent in the man's eyes before the staff strikes out, and like the little boy he once was, pivots and races back the way he came, then dodges between the trees, nimble of foot, Saul panting behind him, for Saul stuffs his face with too much rich food. In a burst of speed, he swerves into the open and up the baulk. Saul has fallen back. Haukyn keeps running and in short order Annabel and Alyce are with his mother, the men meet at his empty house, and he and Neuton, on horseback, are treading through the woods to the west, each armed, each with a pouch of coin.

He's doing what he's meant to do, and by the Virgin, it makes him happy.

In Chisledon, after the money is handed over and a receipt given, James says, "I leave in three days for London. I will find you in Flintbourne on my way home with the exemplifications."

"Come through the woods." Haukyn sketches a little map. "Our bailiff spies on us."

James nods. "It will take time, for there are other writs besides your own. God's blessing and may freedom reign."

The summer heat and dryness continue, day after slow day, Haukyn watering their garden every evening, the twins taking on the same chore at his father's. Poppies are tugged from the fields, their petals bruised and torn. Alyce objects to her harness and her fat-bottomed perch in the rushes, as anxious to explore the world as Haukyn is anxious for the counsellor's return.

He's lugged buckets of water from the river for his beans and cabbage on a day in mid-August when a horse whiffles and James of Liddington emerges from the trees level with the orchard. He dismounts; his eyes are tired, their fires damped. Haukyn lowers one of the buckets so James's gelding can drink. "I've well-water indoors, and ale, sir. Tether your mount in the shade and come indoors. My wife is at the ale shed, my daughter with my younger brothers, we can talk freely."

"A mug of ale would go down well. My thanks."

The coals are covered because of the heat. Haukyn pours the ale and puts bread and goat cheese on the table. James lowers himself to the bench. "I feel my years," he says wearily. "Not one of the exemplifications I paid for is in our favour. Flintbourne, Liddington, Chisledon, Badbury, Pewsey, even Chilmark and Wylye to the south. None in ancient demesne, the chancellors quick to blame me for malicious counsel, for spreading lies that exemplifications would grant personal freedom." He tips back the mug, swallows, and wipes his mouth. "You are the first to hear this from me. Perhaps by the time I say it for the dozenth time, I will not care so deep."

Haukyn's ale sits untasted. "Were you expecting this?"

"I always hope. Yet hope shrinks with each rebuttal. They would say to you, Haukyn, those London lawyers, that your station in life is God-given, nor will they countenance you striving to better it." He picks up a piece of bread, looks at it, and puts it down again.

Crumbs on the table. Haukyn counts them, his disappointment so strong that it forces revelation upon him: what had been, in part, a game—the merry jingle of coin, the outwitting of Osmond, the race up the hill from Saul and his staff—is a game no longer. He feels, physically, the shift in his chest. "I am prone to rage," he says slowly, "I know I am. Can rage harden to purpose?"

"At times you'll have to bang fists—or head—on the nearest oak."

"Hornbeam's wood the harder."

The faintest of smiles. "I used to pray. But my prayers have gone silent as cuckoos in summer." James bites off a chunk of cheese and chews it. "No one loves the bearer of bad news, your neighbours will be no exception. A word of advice to you and your vill—beware too much violence. Our lords and masters are adept at punishment."

Needing the contact, Haukyn clasps the counsellor by the wrist. "I thank you for your efforts on our behalf. Villeinage will end, it will."

"You have lifted my melancholy, and tis good cheese."

"My wife looks after the goats."

"Tis better than aught I ate in London." After talk of city markets and Londoners' hatred of John of Gaunt, James mounts his mare with renewed energy. "Perhaps we will meet again."

"We will. God's blessing on you, sir."

"My name is James. Rebuttal or nay, we are equal, serf, counsellor, and duke, remember?"

"Godspeed, James."

Haukyn goes back inside to put the food away. Then he tells Solomon and Neuton that their money was wasted and their serfdom confirmed; these words, he knows, will fly around the vill, and he braces himself for censure. He's weeding Edmund's lowermost field in the company of the twins when Osmond calls his name. He wends his way through the wheat, the ripening kernels brushing his knees. Osmond says, "You do a serf's labour and you wasted serfs' coin to fatten city officers." He leans forward, his malice palpable. "There will be no freedom in my lifetime or yours."

"The lure of freedom made our attempt worthwhile, Osmond."

"Master Osmond."

"The days are done when I'll call you Master."

"I'll not tolerate sedition on this manor!"

"Then perhaps I should return to weeding wheat." He turns his back and swishes through the pale stems.

Gil says, "I don't like our bailiff."

Ralf says, "His eyes be like a dead trout's."

"Both of you, be careful in his vicinity. He's a man with power and a small soul."

"Small as a dung beetle's," Ralf says.

Annabel is angered by the rebuttal and hugs him before he walks to the alehouse that evening, her body soft against his. At the long tables, the men are disgruntled with Osmond, lawyers, and Londoners, but not, to his considerable relief, with him; the crowning surprise comes when John Cat-Skinner slaps down ha'pence for Haukyn's mug of ale. "That arse-wipe Osmond. Drink up 'n' drink deep."

Haukyn wends his way home not altogether sober.

The heat persists. On a Sunday in September, Father Mortimer announces that harvesting the lord's wheat will commence at first light. But when Haukyn goes outside with whetstone and scythe, the lord's field is nigh empty of harvesters, the distance too far and the light too dim to tell who they are. His neighbours' fields are being reaped instead. He props his scythe against the wall and runs from here to there. Solomon, Blundred, Tirrell, and the atte Medes give him a cheerful *God's blessing* as their stems fall in tidy rows. His father, his mother, and the twins, them he cannot find. A knot in his gut. The lord's field, he'd find them there, he knows it.

By the time Osmond seeks him out, he has his own swaths falling, Annabel stooking, Alyce harnessed to one of their apple trees with Rust nearby. The bailiff says, "You instigated this."

"The vill instigated it."

"You are their leader."

The knot in his gut tightens. "I've neither been elected to the post nor chosen it."

"I've sent Saul for Sir Gardrad's armed retainers. Five o' them. The lord's fields will be harvested by force if need be."

"Then I'd better get on with my work til they arrive," Haukyn says and watches Osmond stalk down the hill, stiff-legged as Rust when Jorden's dog pisses against Rust's apple trees. Does the vill consider him their leader, he who started the collection of coin and who spread the news of rebuttal? *Leader,* a weight to it and not the time to remember James's stooped shoulders.

Annabel calls, "I be caught up to you, Haukyn."

"I must go from field to field to warn of the retainers."

And there he learns that the vill does indeed want him as leader... *you talks like Master Osmond, you ain't afeard o' him, you be the one what started us on this road...*none of which, he thinks wryly, he can rebut.

Afterward, he crosses the ford to St. Edmund's church. Alone inside, he genuflects, walks closer to the altar, and kneels on the rushes. Silence presses on his ears. No words come, and what good is a leader without words? *I will do my best,* he thinks, small words, unadorned, yet a binding oath just the same. Moving as an older man might move, he leaves the church and heads for the lord's wheat field.

Edmund, Hawise, and the twins, and a few villagers from across the river walked to the lord's field at dawn. No one else has joined them. No rows of harvesters, no jesting back and forth, no grumbling. Even the skylarks are silent. Is this lack of obedience toward Osmond and Sir Gardrad Haukyn's work?

He believes Haukyn had no part in beating Mauld; he suspects he refused to pay the poll tax; he knows he headed that wasteful collection of coin that disappeared into London's coffers.

Swish, *swish* and the wheat falls, Hawise swinging her scythe beside him, as slow and steady as himself, Ralf's stooks tilted and wispy, Gil's as straight as soldiers. How many more harvests will he see?

That orderly bevy of women at hallmote, Haukyn's delight in Annabel's intervention; yet Edmund would have sworn all was not well between husband and wife, for Haukyn looks as drawn some days as Robert used to, married to Johanna.

He sighs. Poll taxes, rebuttals, women disobeying the rules of hallmote, a vill disobeying ancient custom, times are changing whether he wants them to or not, and is he become just another old man—another Dunstan, God forbid—who doesn't want the winds of change to ruffle the hair on his head or the wheat at his knees?

He has yet to fire stones at his neighbours.

"Look, Edmund, others be coming," Hawise says.

He glances up. A steady stream of villagers armed with scythes are congregating in the fields; they arrange themselves and begin to reap. Haukyn is one of the last to arrive, but arrive he does, smiles at his father, and cuts his first swath. "It seems I'm still the vill's leader despite lost coin."

I would it were otherwise, Edmund thinks, *I who taught you to read, write, and speak in a manner above your station*. He says, "The vill looks up to you." His voice sharpens. "Who are they, coming down the track?"

"Sir Gardrad's retainers. Did you not guess? Tis why our vill is so peaceably at work."

Five men on horseback, each wearing a padded leather doublet, each armed with dagger, sword, and staff. Osmond, his white wand clutched to his chest, approaches them for a brief colloquy before they dismount at the edge of the field. Haukyn says, "Scurvy bastards. A scythe to the knees and they'd jump. I'd best go meet them."

"I pray you, guard your tongue," Edmund says, and finds himself following Haukyn down the baulk, scythe still gripped in one hand.

Haukyn nods at the captain, a man swarthy of face with a wrestler's build. "We want no bloodshed," he says, "and we'll finish the lord's fields before we reap our own."

"Why did you not begin in Sir Gardrad's fields?"

"There must have been a misunderstanding. We regret you and your company have come this way for naught."

"Master Osmond says you incite rebellion, Haukyn of Flintbourne."

"Does this look like rebellion?"

"You incited Domesday writs and rumours."

"Incite? A strong word for a rumour without a rebellious bone to it."

Tirrell has strolled down the baulk. "I be the vill's constable, a freeman who reports to the sheriff. Be there trouble here?"

The captain says, "I am to deliver a message from Sir Gardrad, your lord. Any seditious acts in Flintbourne will be punished to the fullest extent of the law and their instigators gaoled. You, Haukyn, will pass on this warning to every villager."

"I will," he says with a mock salute, and watches the captain swing himself back in the saddle.

"Be you ready to gaol the whole vill?" Walter shouts and laughter rises from the field.

Osmond brandishes his white wand. "Be silent! Get back to work."

John Cat-Skinner cries, "We expects ale with bread 'n' cheese at Sext. Plentiful ale."

"If we ain't allowed to go 'gainst ancient custom, neither be our lord."

"We got a goodly start on our own fields this morning, didn't we."

More laughter, then a slash of scythes as the five men wheel their horses and cross the green to the road.

At Sext everyone trails toward the trees, where tables of bread, cheese, and ale have been set up, less of each than was supplied by generous Sir Mauger. Edmund has been watching Haukyn, who, under the trees, is sitting apart from the others. The cost of being a leader, he thinks, and passes in front of a gang of Cat-Skinners to sit beside him. "The cheese was stored overlong, watch your teeth," he says. "Haukyn, I see a change in you."

"Aye?"

The caution in his son's voice, it hurts, although deserved. "When you spoke to the captain, you were a hedgehog curled in the duff, all your bristles flat."

"I didn't ask to be the vill's leader."

"They chose well, for already you grow to fit the task."

"I do?" Haukyn's face softens. "A task you oppose, though."

Edmund says with some care, "I came home from war craving peace, and still do. Freedom...although I understand its pull, I don't believe it will happen in my time on earth. Or in yours." He adds abruptly, "Power never relinquishes its hold without a struggle. Tis a jealous sin, greedy for its own gain, deep-rooted in fear. And always, violence begets violence."

"You've given this thought."

"You sound surprised."

"I shouldn't. You are a man of thought." He draws in a breath. "I only wish thought and verses could have rid you of war's nightmares—I can't banish them either. The slaughter of little-uns, the women...so often I turned away."

"You and I were but two men in armies of thousands, atrocity unstoppable."

Haukyn bends his head; the shade darkens his curls. "I killed a priest," he says in a low voice. "Near the end of our march." Then he spills the story of the chalice, the red light over an altar, the priest's head hitting stone. "How can I confess this to Father Mortimer?"

"Father Mortimer has never been to war. He will load your penitent heart with penances, and if they would bring ease, then by all means confess." He hesitates. "Kings begin wars and we are induced to fight them. War is a place of extremity—terror, boredom, fire, blood—our souls left to a terrible confusion and a lifelong search for forgiveness. My verses? A leaf of plantain on a mortal wound, and I am of no help to you, Haukyn."

His son looks up. "You understand."

"As only those who've been through it can...War is a soup with too many herbs and most of them poisonous. Should you drink it, you never fully recover."

A faint smile on Haukyn's face. "Annabel would burn the soup."

"And Hawise throw it on the midden. Women have more sense than we wooden-heads."

The bell chimes, once, twice, for them to resume work. Edmund stands up, reaches down a hand, and pulls his son to his feet. Of a sudden, he wraps his arms around him. "You did not intend the death of a priest, Haukyn. And I pray you remember, as the vill's leader, that Gardrad is the worst of lords. Be careful."

"I will. I do this, in part, for my child, Da...Yesterday I found her in the garden squinting at the worm in her fist, it wriggling to be free."

"Gil ate a worm once, it didn't seem to harm him." Edmund bends to pick up his scythe, trying to loosen his shoulders. Fear as the bedrock of power, fear entwined in the roots of love.

Uneasy peace lies over the vill. Harvest is not as bountiful as last summer's, nor the meadows as good for grazing; one of Haukyn's cows will have to be slaughtered as soon as she dries up. Although some scanty rain falls as autumn proceeds, the apples are smaller than should be, the damsons harder, even the ripening blackberries have less juice. Rose hips, elderberries, sloes, hazelnuts, sweet chestnuts, and rowan berries, the time of gathering and preserving is upon them. In the midst of this, Mauld resumes his rounds with Osmond and Saul, staff to hand, temper foul.

Late October, the feast day of St. Jude, brings Haukyn a letter from Javyd, ill-writ by a paid scribe. He stands outside his house, reading it in growing dismay. In response to the many Domesday exemplifications, and alarmed there might be an uprising of serfs as happened in France twenty years ago, Parliament has set up special commissions to travel to the affected areas, commissions that have the power to try the rebels and their counsellors and imprison them without bail. The scribe, who must have written all this by rote, finishes by saying Javyd knows of Haukyn's part in the rebellion and wishes to warn him.

He folds the parchment, thinking fast. He must ride to Wiltshire to alert Daniel and James. But first he must tell Annabel where he is going, and why. But when he goes indoors, she's bent over by the table, one hand pressed to her belly, her face contorted. "Annabel, what's wrong?"

Hurriedly, she straightens. "The last two days…too much turnip in the pottage, I ain't never been one for turnips."

"Are you certain tis the turnips?" She has a hand to her right side, and low—blessed Mary, may it be burnt turnips and naught else.

"Aye…did you get a letter?"

He'd forgotten about it. "Bad news, I have to—why is Rust barking?"

A curse. A yelp. He runs for the door and pulls it open. "Stay away from my dog!"

Saul, Mauld, and Osmond, with Oakum half-heartedly swiping his staff at the snarling dog. Osmond says with cold formality, "I received a letter from Sir Gardrad. I have the power to gaol you as a rebel against our Parliament. No bail is permitted. When the commissioners arrive, they will try you. Secure him, Mauld."

Mauld advances on him, grinning, small black squares where his teeth were knocked out. As Saul takes out his knife, Haukyn says, "I'll gut the man who lays a hand on me."

"Oakum, seize his wife," Osmond says. "Put hand to dagger, Haukyn, and she'll go with you to the manor gaol."

"Nay! She's not well. Leave me free and I swear I won't go beyond the vill's boundaries."

Mauld grabs one arm, Saul the other. Annabel cries, "He did naught!"

"He is the vill's leader in seditious acts against King and Country."

Pompous scut. "Annabel," Haukyn says, "you and Alyce must stay at my father's. Gil and Ralf will feed Rust. Go now, and God be with you."

Saul stamps on his foot, Mauld cuffs him on the side of the head, and as he staggers in their grip, Annabel flies at them, nails poised to rake bare skin. Rust, teeth bared, is at her heels. "Annabel, don't! Put Rust indoors and go to my father. Now."

"Four o' you for one man, cowardly arses."

Osmond says sharply, "Take him away before we have more trouble."

Haukyn's last glimpse is of Annabel dragging Rust by the collar toward the house. Another cuff to the head, it ringing like a chorus of Terce bells, and he's hauled down the hill and across the ford, and despite a fear as keen as he's ever felt, he's warmed by his wife's defence of him. Across the green, Father Mortimer on the church steps, mouth agape, atte Medes emerging from their houses, then the bridge over the moat, the solid oak doors, into the hall and down a flight of stairs he's never noticed before, ten stairs, he with difficulty keeping both feet under him...was this the way his father and mother were dragged the night before their wedding? A dank corridor, another oak door, iron-studded, key to the lock, hinges that need oiling, and he's rammed so hard in the back that he falls to his knees on the hard dirt floor. The door bangs shut, the key grates, and he's alone in a darkness as thick as night.

Alone, and on his knees. He bows his head and speaks the words aloud. "Not the right-side sickness, not Annabel. Mary, Mother of us all, hear my prayer, for she is the best of mothers and Alyce needs her. As do I."

Into a silence as thick as the darkness, he lets his *Amen* fall.

If the right-side sickness, they'll let him out.

Better him here than Annabel in pain.

He pushes himself upright, rubs his knees, then looks over his shoulder. High in the wall is a narrow slit. Light comes through it from the corridor, a faint light but light nevertheless. He waits for his eyes to adjust, then turns in a slow circle. In the far corner a bucket for him to relieve himself; judging by the stench, some of those confined here didn't bother with it. A hand to the wall, he walks the bounds of the gaol.

No food. No water.

Panic closes his throat. His father had his mother for company, and their sentence was but one night. How long before a commission arrives in Flintbourne? Days, weeks, months? He stamps his feet, one after the other, the soreness in his knees and the twin thuds somehow reassuring. Osmond won't let him starve. Osmond wants him condemned for sedition.

Javyd's letter is still stuck in his belt. So there was a statute of Parliament because the serfs in two-score vills in ten different shires sent for exemplifications. Parliament must have panicked. Parliament, the seat of power. Although the exemplifications were denied, even ridiculed, they were not without effect: they frightened knights and merchants, they rattled wealth and pomp. And he, Haukyn of Flintbourne, played a small part in that.

He sits down and hugs his knees to his chest, for the air is clammy and he without cloak or blanket. He pictures Annabel with his mother, Hawise administering purges against too many turnips—burnt turnips at that, he remembers them well. His wife is in good hands, the twins will be laughing at Alyce's efforts to cover ground, and his father will watch over everyone.

He and his father, reconciled, and he smiles to himself.

Eventually, night falls; he can no longer discern the slit. Although he's thirsty, hungry, and cold, he's also confident his mother's herbs will have brought Annabel's sufferings to an end, for not even Osmond would keep him from a dying wife.

He'll plant fewer turnips next spring.

The floor is rock-hard, his sleep broken by dreams in which a forest drips water into his open mouth and he gorges on his mother's bread. The narrow slit brings light but nothing else; again, he has to fight down panic. He pisses in the bucket. He walks the length of his prison, back and forth, back and forth. His thoughts darken. He, a nameless serf in a nameless vill in one of many shires, how dare he think that anything he did would bring change in its wake to church or state? They can gaol him, distrain him, starve him, and who's to protest?

He remembers a snapped bow, neglected chores, a spring day's ride to a distant war. Did he always rebut authority, his reckless nature blinding him to custom and limit? Has he led his neighbours astray, endangering them also? *I did not choose to be leader*, so he'd said to his father. But was that the truth?

Twas the feast day of St. Jude when he was imprisoned. St. Jude, the apostle of desperate predicaments. His mouth is so dry tis hard to swallow; he mustn't think of rain barrels, buckets dripping with well-water, new-brewed ale in mugs and jugs. Johanna's ale, she with child by Simon now, yet still no ease twixt himself and her. There'd be no ease were he to meet Ilotte at the market either. The thought of her still pains him, such constancy to a woman who only once laid her hand on his, and what would she think were she to see him now?

The hours of light, faint though it be, are passing. His stomach growls and grumbles in the stifling air; he's light-headed from lack of water, his lips cracking. And then he hears another sound. Scuff of feet in the corridor. A key turns in the lock. An angle of light spills over the floor, he blinking at its brightness. Mauld. A bowl of gruel lowered to the dirt, the contents slopping over the edge. A waterskin dropped beside it and Haukyn finds his tongue. "My wife," he says hoarsely, "has she recovered?"

"How would I know 'bout your wife?"

"I pray you, you for charity's sake, find out."

"When you be one of 'em what dumped me in the bracken like a sack o' mouldy rye?"

"I was not one of those men!"

"The Devil watch your wife die in agony."

The door bangs shut, the key rasps, and as the footsteps sink to silence, Haukyn beats on the rough wood with his fists til his knuckles bleed and his sobs have died away. He sucks on skin and bone, resting his forehead against the door. For the love of God, not the right-side sickness.

Driven by hunger, he hunkers down. The thinnest of gruels, and cold, a few bits of cabbage and—he winces—turnip swimming in it. What was he expecting, lamb stew? He drinks it slowly, chewing the vegetables to a pulp, knowing he should save some but unable to do so. He does save the water, placing the skin against the wall to the right of the door. The narrow slit of light eventually vanishes.

Another day goes by. He keeps track of it, knowing he must. Mauld delivers gruel and water, deaf to his plea for news.

Fear and boredom, fitful sleep and endless hours robbed of light, and through it all Haukyn paces his prison, talks to himself, prays for Annabel's well-being. He lists all the soldiers in his retinue, Javyd's colourful curses and Fulk's more stringent ones, matches coats of arms with knights, and is astonished by how many of the towns and villages he can name between Calais and Bordeaux. Tis All Hallowes Eve and he imagines bonfires, drunken laughter, and doors bolted against evil and the night. He dreads falling asleep...*he's locked in a black-walled house in Puy de Dôme, he gropes for his bow, his dagger, but they are gone, and in each corner the gleam of eyes. A low snarling, the eyes come closer, he sees bare fangs and flails his arms, teeth clamp his wrist, spurt of blood, hot breath at his throat and he wakes screaming...*

His own hand around his wrist, and he enveloped in darkness. "I am in Flintbourne," he says as strongly as he can. "My neighbours, my wife, my little Alyce are nearby, I won't start gibbering like Wortle Dill, whom I mocked in France and who died in St. Edmund's church."

A slit of light ushers in the Feast of All Saints and still he's here, sweet Jesu he'll farm with a glad heart and eat burnt pottage for the rest of his days should he ever breathe the valley's clean air again. Freedom, how it wavers in meaning. The small freedoms of his day-to-day life, has he not taken them for granted? Pruning his orchard, walking to the alehouse, talking to his father, listening to Annabel's chatter—when he's released, he'll abandon leadership.

How many miscreants have been jammed in this space at one time? How long has a solitary prisoner been held? The bucket stinks. He stinks. Lice crawl his scalp. His flea bites itch. Has Alyce taken her first steps, his daughter who is so determined to explore the world around her? If so, how his wife's smile would mingle pride with love. He closes his eyes, the better to picture them both.

Two more days. He develops a dry cough that keeps him awake, a cough his mother will dose with coltsfoot once he's let out. At night, he fears the ceiling will fall on him, he feels it pressing on his chest, the stones of the manor slowly crushing him; when he stands tall, though, and lifts his arms, naught within reach but stale, fetid air. One by one, out loud, he names the herbs growing in his mother's garden, rearranges them by colour, by the letters that begin their names. He stumbles through such verses of his father's that he can remember; he lingers over Ralf and Gil as little-uns, each from birth so different from the other; he stamps his feet, he marches back and forth, twenty steps by twenty-three. And then, on the afternoon of the sixth day, a few hours after he was fed, he hears footsteps along the corridor.

He stands transfixed, his heart battering his chest. The key, the angled light. Recoiling, he recognizes the two men outside his prison: Tirrell and a stone-faced Osmond.

Tirrell says, "No commissions appointed by Parliament has sat in our shire. You be released on orders from the sheriff, your imprisonment recorded as unjust."

Osmond says nothing.

"You mean...I am free? Free to leave here?"

"Aye."

"My wife?" Haukyn says urgently. "How is she?"

"Your family be waiting for you outside."

He moves from darkness into light; for all his marching up and down, his legs feel brittle as sticks. Tirrell takes him by the arm. "Osmond, have your henchmen clean that stinking gaol, 'n' do it soon."

The light broadens with each of the ten steps. The hall is empty. As Osmond puts his shoulder to one of the manor doors, sunlight streams in. Haukyn scrunches his eyes against the stab of pain and says foolishly, "I thought it later in the day."

"Over the bridge," Tirrell says. "Though I should push you in the moat, you smells so ripe."

He opens his eyes, closes them, opens them again, and through a bright haze sees his father at the end of the bridge. Behind him, a solid mass of villagers. Is this another dream and he'll wake to malodorous darkness?

Edmund's arms go around him, hard. "Come home. Your mother is waiting for you, and the twins."

"*Annabel*, how is she?"

"Ah, Haukyn, your wife was buried yesterday."

He pushes his father away, muttering, "I'll be passing my lice to you. Was it the right-side sickness? Did she suffer greatly?"

"As little as Hawise could manage. Alyce is with her, come home now."

He looks around, wavering on his feet. "The villagers?"

"They've prevented Osmond from leaving the manor since All Hallowes—although, it would seem, they were unable to prevent trespass on the lord's fields or theft from the lord's granary. Father Mortimer begged Osmond to release you, both at Sunday Mass and on the feast day, I didn't think he had it in him. Osmond refused. The sheriff's courts were being held at Hormer, Ock, and Ganfield, so it took all this time for Tirrell to track him down. He didn't return from the north til this afternoon, his horse in a lather, he with the sheriff's writ."

Haukyn looks around, and it is only now that his voice breaks. "I thank you, friends. As I thank our good priest and our constable."

His neighbours shuffle and nod. Ivo yells, "Osmond be a rat's arse." A chorus of *ayes*, of obscenities and hexes echoes across the valley.

Edmund leads Haukyn away, across the ford, along the river path, and up the baulk to the house. At the door, Haukyn halts, his throat clogged. "Alyce will be frightened of me, looking—and smelling—as I do."

"Hawise put her in Ralf's bed for a sleep, and the twins will keep her busy should she wake."

Inside, Hawise takes one look at him. "Water by the hearth, fresh clothes on the bench. I'll not touch you til you rid yourself o' lice 'n' fleas. You ain't as skinny as when you come back from war, summat to be grateful for, I s'pose." She swishes into the room she shares with Edmund.

"She's angry with me."

"She had the care of Annabel, who called for you in her ravings. And Alyce cries for her mother."

"I'll never forgive Osmond."

"Forgiving yourself the harder task."

Forgiveness follows wrongdoing. So not only Hawise is angry with him. "Water, soap, and a clean shirt," he says glibly, "can forgiveness be a greater luxury than those?"

By the time he's washed and dressed, Alyce is awake. Steeling himself, he walks to the bedroom and opens the door. Ralf is smiling, Gil narrow-eyed. Alyce gapes at him, then to his infinite relief opens her arms and throws herself forward. Haukyn picks her up and buries his face in her soft belly. "Alyce, Alyce, I must be mother and father to you now."

But Alyce is straining toward the door, hope, or is it joy, written clear as she babbles, "Ma...Ma...Ma."

If he can come back, so too, of course, can Annabel. "I wish to God we could bring her home. But you have me, I'll not leave you as your mother had to leave."

Joy dissolves into disconsolate crying. Tears on his own cheeks, Haukyn mumbles such comfort as he can; within the hour, against the wishes of his father and mother, he's carrying Alyce toward their own house, the twins trailing behind bearing food and clean clouts. After they've left, he covers the coals and pulls his mattress to the floor; his daughter burrows into him, and he falls into a dead sleep.

The knock on the door at first light startles the two of them awake. Patting Alyce on the back in an attempt to quieten her wails, Haukyn opens the latch.

Ivo and his sister Jenet, strands of fair hair drooping from her cap. She smiles at him and relieves him of Alyce, who stops crying, blinks at her, and tugs on her hair. Ivo says, "Jenet got a plan. You needs help in the day, you could hire her, she be good at making pottage out o' naught. You ain't heard 'bout m' father?"

"Jorden?" Haukyn rubs his eyes. "Come in. I must uncover the fire, tis cold in here."

"Sit down afore you falls flat." Ivo adds twigs to the coals and puts water on to heat, the flames a cheerful crackle. "While you was locked up, Ma caught a fever. Da arrives at Dunstan's, banging on the door, shouting that Ma needs help, Jenet's coming home if he has to drag her there. M' dagger point to his gut, Dunstan's stones to his mug, 'n' he were persuaded to leave, cursing like the Devil hisself—too many year I were scared o' him, but no more. Where be the oats?"

Haukyn watches like a man in a daze as Ivo tips some into the pot. "Didn't he go home to the forge, start raving at m' brother, 'n' then didn't he drop to the floor like he'd had a hammer to his skull. Apoplexy, so said your ma, naught to be done. He got no speech, drools like your little-un, can't move off the bed. Ma left to change his clouts and spoon pottage into him."

Haukyn finally finds his tongue. "So there is justice in this world."

"M' brother wants me to work with him at the forge. Without Da bashing him for every move, Slug-Arse Sim now be neat-fingered as any smith from Hungerford to Newbury. 'The name's Sim if you wants new nails,' he says, and with jaws a-drop the villagers don't make no mention o' slugs nor arses. As for m' sister, like I said, she could look after the little-un."

Jenet has put Alyce on the floor and is playing pat-a-cakes with her, Alyce's giggles easing the ache in Haukyn's heart. "Jenet, would you like to do that?"

She smiles again. "I trusts you."

Ivo's jaw juts. "Nor you won't betray that trust."

He clears his throat. "I won't. You are hired, Jenet, and my warm thanks to you and your brother. Now, let us eat oats together."

That night, Alyce asleep beside him, the little whuffles of her breath, and harsh truths facing him: if he'd sworn fealty to Sir Gardrad, as a serf should, the vengeance of gaol might not have been inflicted on him. Tis his fault that Annabel died without her husband at her side, and guilt the cruelest of scourges, drowning grief, rendering it impotent. How can he grieve a wife whom he betrayed?

Worse, below guilt, lurks a serpent-slither of relief, small, sinful, unbearable. He has been released from a marriage that was too often a door locked against him.

Annabel, flying to his defence with her nails outstretched. He feels like a bow drawn to full compass and held taut, no arrow, no loose. A bow, its limbs bent thus, will snap.

A routine imposes itself. As the days go by, Alyce starts to look for Jenet rather than her mother. Although she usually fills her clouts the moment Jenet leaves, she sleeps the night through. Her first steps are, for all three of them, a delight; Annabel hovers nearby. Mass is better attended since Father Mortimer twice urged Osmond to clemency, and after Mass every Sunday, Haukyn goes to the churchyard with his daughter, crouches beside Annabel's grave, tells her of the week's doings, and tells Alyce stories about her mother's fondness of spiders and cobwebs, and how she was butted by their billy goat Pyke.

He doesn't share everything with Annabel. The cruelty of his confinement, Osmond's adamance, the hatred that has invaded him, a hatred inseparable from rage. Were it not for Tirrell, a freeman with access to the sheriff, he'd still be in gaol waiting for a commission that might never have sat in judgement.

Freeman. The word urges rebellion.

He'll never forget how the village, men and women, came together to blockade the manor's thresholds, a silent resistance, an unexpected union. He wishes he'd known it at the time. *There be power in numbers*, so Daniel had said. He'll harness that power. He already understands, from the manner in which the villagers nod at him, that he is still their leader. Hatred and rage are not enough for a true leader; he'll need his wits, and must ensure his neighbours use theirs.

At the woodpile one day, Edmund says, "Your daughter needs a father. Not a leader."

She needs a father she can be proud of, who thinks beyond ragwort, dung, and harrow. Haukyn says, "You learned how to read and write, then passed on this skill, together with the skill of good speech, to your family. I would call that rebellion, and tis one reason the vill looks to me as leader."

Edmund grimaces. "Tell them to choose someone else."

"So far, I've done naught to arouse them." *Enough*, he thinks, *enough*. "Da, it hurts me to see Alyce run to Jenet as if she is her mother."

"Alyce will soon forget her mother, she too young when Annabel died. You have the skills of a leader, deflection being one of them."

His fists clench. "I'll never forgive myself for being locked up while my dying wife called for me."

Edmund thwacks his axe into the nearest log. "I'm too hard on you, I know I am! Time and again I push you away. It comes—it has always come—from fear for your welfare."

"I'd shoot an arrow to my own heart before I'd end up in gaol again. We'll finish stacking the logs later."

Restraining him with a hand on his sleeve, his father says, "You think I don't notice that you split the biggest stumps and lift the heaviest flint, that you plough that wretched headland I inherited from my brother?"

"You've earned the right to lie fallow."

"The fate of an old man? Verses don't come to me as oft as they used to, and I doubt them when they do come."

"Dunstan is older than you, Da, and throws stones with great accuracy."

Edmund's smile is rueful. "You won't allow me to feel sorry for myself. So there is peace betwixt us?"

"You and I, we are as unlike as Ralf and Gil, and isn't their love for each other a fixture in the heavens? I must go home and relieve Jenet."

Osmond lost face over Haukyn's imprisonment; Osmond knows it and so does every villager. Although the bailiff resumes his patrols of field and croft in the company of Saul or Mauld, small rebellions begin to break out, here and there, nor can he discern their source.

"M' cows on the lord's fallow? Nay, they was with Blundred's bull that day."

"The fire what broke out in the kitchen 'n' ruined your supper, Master Osmond? Mauld ordered us to shovel out the byre, weren't no one's fault but his."

"Shoot the lord's rabbits? Me with no bow?"

Misdemeanours cease as sudden as they arise, peace again reigning in the vill. Then coulters crack the day the lord's fields are to be ploughed, Ivo unable to mend them for his hand is bandaged and Sim is locked in the privy, his shite like water. Osmond's cook curdles the sauces, "Eggs must've been old." The millwheel comes off its axle, "How that happened, tis a mystery. No flour for the kitchen today, Master." And behind it all, Haukyn counsels, watches, and waits.

Jenet plays a role here, because her devoted care of Alyce frees Alyce's father. She never speaks of it, but he knows she is gratified by these small acts of revenge.

At least once during every cycle of the moon, he wakes from a dream of a stone ceiling slowly crushing him, a dream threaded with the screams of a woman dying in agony.

Early in spring, he rides to Newbury to buy a brass pot for his mother, the Hungerford merchant having moved there in search of bigger profits. Trefoil curvets like a youngster. Violets are blooming in the ditches, he remembering the small bouquets he gave two very different women. He's a widower now, would that matter to Ilotte? He lacks the courage to put it to the test, or has he at last learned common sense?

A cock pheasant dashes across the road. Skylarks circle high above, their slow wingbeats and their endless singing, those drab brown birds, drab as any villein. Over the bridge and into the town, the square with its scaffold, the close-packed houses, the bustle of market stalls. He dismounts, leading his mare through them, finds the merchant, buys a pot, inserts it into his saddlebag, and turns back toward the bridge. A sumptuously dressed man with a crooked nose is haggling at a stall that displays velvets and silks. A respectful distance behind him, two servants carry loaded sacks.

Sir Gardrad. Here in Newbury. Haukyn's skin chills; his free hand flies to his dagger, the urge to plunge it into the knight's back so strong that his spine goes rigid.

Alyce needs her father and he'd vowed not to kill. But, oh, how he wishes he'd held Javyd back and let Sir Gardrad drown in the muddy torrent of a French river.

PART THREE
1380–1382

...underfoot...

Winter has come early this year, yesterday a snowfall, today's dawn dull and unconvincing. Winter will bring, as it always does, death for the unprepared and the landless with empty larders, their little-uns grizzling, their bird traps gaping. For the prepared, as Edmund and Haukyn are, a tightening of belts.

Haukyn lies on his back on his mattress, tugging the covers up to his chin. Alyce is asleep, chestnut curls tousled, on the smaller mattress beside him, a mattress made by Hawise. He scrubs his face with both hands; his mother's death, four months ago, is an ache to his heart. His father had woken one morning to find her lying cold and still beside him in their bed, she who was so rarely still. The vill, who had lost a sharp-tongued herb-woman and compassionate midwife, turned out in force for her funeral. Edmund not the same since, the spirit gone from him, his forehead lined, his hands not always steady. "I cannot write a lament for her, nor could I for Robert, words as dead in me as she is dead...Ah, what's the good of me, why am I still here, and she not beside me?" Haukyn has no answer to these ramblings, other than to hold his father close and pick up the extra chores Edmund no longer bothers with.

His mother...For twenty-four winters he was a trial to her, he too much like her to be otherwise, yet he never doubted her love for him. The twins, at twelve winters, are bereft. Ralf, often red-eyed, is never far from his father's side and tends house and garden. Gil minds the fields, kicks fences and flint, yells at rook and crow, and has storms of weeping where his fists fly should you try to comfort him.

Haukyn is grateful to both of them for their help. Faithfully, Jenet still arrives for Alyce.

He sits up, moving quietly, and goes outside. Ice on the rain barrel. After breaking it with his fist and tossing the shards to one side, he braces himself and dunks his head. Wide awake, hair and beard streaming, he listens to the silence. Mass this morning. He should trim his beard, and Alyce is never pleased by fasting. Sighing, he goes indoors.

On his bench in church, Alyce in the circle of his arm, he seizes a rare time for reflection. To the pleasing jingle of coin, he now fashions bows from elm and ash, and fletches arrows with feathers plucked from his own geese, to their distinct annoyance; his name is becoming known the length of the valley. With due care, he steals wood from Sir Gardrad's trees. Greater mischief is afoot, though, than a few stolen faggots. Over the last three years, Master Osmond has been worn to the point of lunacy by small, carefully planned rebellions, the culprits elusive as ghosts. Often he's to be found wandering the vill, bawling accusations, kicking woodpiles, and screaming at dogs, the target of pranks and laughter in which Haukyn joins—he's discovered, to his discomfiture, how hatred feeds on itself.

Yet what changes have been wrought by these rebellions?

None. Lord is still lord and serf is still serf.

He shifts Alyce to his other side. Four years since Annabel was churched, his daughter now a dreamy, grey-eyed little girl who, if not watched, will trot into the woods to lay leaves in patterns on the ground, stones in swirls from large to small; dreamy or no, she can cover the ground with the speed of a hare and has a will of iron, which she exerts not by confrontation but by evasion. Slippery as an eel in mud, so Haukyn has thought more than once. Ralf has taught her words like *buttercup, sunrise, poppy,* and *hedgehog,* lately adding *hoarfrost, snowflake, icicle.* To Gil goes the blame for *fisticuffs* and *arsewisp*. Should he himself have taught her *manumission*, *exemplification*, and *Domesday*?

Why bother? The words as meaningless as rebellion.

After Mass, he and Alyce eat at Edmund's, salt herring for Advent, season of penitence, his father largely silent. The twins offer to keep his daughter til the morrow, an offer he accepts because sometimes her antics can rouse Edmund from gloom. He works all day as if driven by an ox goad, falls asleep as if the goad hit him on his skull, and wakes in confusion to Rust barking, the loud whining of another dog, and the press of night.

He fumbles for the latch, Rust at his heels. The dog...tis Elf, he recognizes her instantly. Elf, Ilotte's dog. He rubs his eyes. He's dreaming. Elf takes his bare hand in her teeth and tugs, and the dents in his skin are no dream. "What is it? Why are you here?" He stands very still, listening. "Is Ilotte in trouble? *Where?*"

Elf drops his hand, trots five or six steps from the threshold, then looks back over her shoulder, her whines more insistent. "Wait for me," he says, and inside dresses quickly and lights a torch. After ordering Rust to guard the house, he follows Elf through the orchard and into the woods. Snow squalls, a crescent moon scudding between the clouds, Elf's tracks already half-filled with blown snow; he holds the torch low to shield it from the wind. The dog trots ahead, two oak trunks loom in front of them, then a clearing surrounded by beech and willow. Elf yelps. Haukyn rushes forward and in the torchlight sees Ilotte, curled into herself at the base of an old beech tree, cloak and hood masked in white. He digs the torch into the snow and drops to his knees. Her face is bruised and cut, her hands bare, blue with cold, her fingernails bloody. "Haukyn," she whispers.

To hear his name on her lips, Christ, he's in trouble.

"Twisted an ankle. Couldn't walk no more."

"You're safe now. I'll carry you home."

"Twas Bidewell."

Her eyes black as night and the words are out before he can stop them. "Did he—"

"Me 'n' Elf got him off," she says, her voice breaking on a sob.

He douses the torch and leaves it where it is, gathers her into his arms, and pushes himself upright. "I'll follow Elf, the snow'll give us enough light."

Elf bumping against his knee, he stumbles through the woods; she's shivering and he can hear, over the wind, the chatter of her teeth. He says, "You smell better than the last time I lifted you, those many years ago. We'll save what happened til we're indoors and you're warm again."

She's heavy, his steps lurching over buried roots. Then Rust barks, Elf whines, and he's fumbling with the latch. Rust scents Ilotte and ignores the other dog. Haukyn sits her on the bench, lights candles, drags his mattress from his bay to the floor near the hearth, and with care lays her on it. Her face is a mask of dried blood, though when he gently tests her nose, tisn't broke as he'd thought it might be. One cheek nail-ripped, her hair a tangle over a nasty bump on her scalp, her tunic torn to the waist. He carries wood from the stacks by the wall and feeds the coals. Elf collapses with a sigh on the other side of the fire.

Crouched beside the mattress, he lifts Ilotte's head and inserts his soft down pillow under it, then covers her legs and feet with thick-woven wool. After washing the blood from her face, hands, and shoulder, he brings over his small stock of herbs and, neat-fingered and without fuss, ministers to her wounds and binds her ankle. The whole time she gazes at the rafters. He says, "You put up a goodly fight. Drink this, tis steeped from willow bark and will help you sleep."

She does so, and her eyes soon drift shut.

He brings out another blanket along with Alyce's pillow and mattress, blows out the candles, and lies on the floor. The mattress is too short. He can hear Ilotte's breathing. Six years since she sent him away, and as she whimpers in her sleep, he stoking the fire to keep her warm, his feelings are in a turmoil he doesn't wish to explore.

In the dim light of dawn, muffling a groan, he sits up. Ilotte is awake too, her eyes pools of darkness. He says with an abruptness he deplores, "I'll build up the fire. I must go to my father's, ask if they'll keep my daughter another day, and tell Jenet she's not needed. Go back to sleep."

Her lashes flicker at the mention of a daughter. When the fire is leaping in the hearth and her eyes have closed again, he gets himself and his muddled brain out the door. Gil is feeding Melicent the sow, Ralf the chickens, accompanied by Alyce with a fistful of discarded feathers. Haukyn goes inside and says to his father with something of the same abruptness, "Ilotte arrived in the night, Hungerford's steward beat her. I can't let her return there."

"I'm glad she came to you."

"I doubt I was her first choice. She'd twisted her ankle, her dog led me to her in the woods."

"She can stay here if that is her preference. There are clothes of Hawise's in the chest, the skirts too short for Ilotte, but clean."

"Da…"

"Take them, Haukyn. Your mother would want it so. A spare mattress cover there too, if you have straw enough?"

"I do." He lifts the lid of the chest, mingling of rosemary and lavender and he listening for his mother's voice. The bundle tucked under his arm, he goes home across the fields. Ilotte is sitting up. She says, "I needs the privy."

"These clothes were my mother's. You'll be short-skirted, but we can mend your own clothes in the meantime. I'll stuff another mattress too. Up with you."

Her closeness so painful he can scarce breathe, he carries her outdoors and leaves her at the privy door. "I'll put water on to heat and come back."

Intimate tasks, the laying out of towels and soap, his mother's clothes. He lifts Ilotte from privy door back to the bench and leaves her there so he can look after his sow, geese, cows, and chickens. When he goes inside, she's wearing the borrowed tunic and skirt. She says, "Your ma died?"

"In September. Has Bidewell attacked you before?"

"Every Saturday he beats Agnys his wife, his barren wife, to cleanse her for Mass. Late Friday, she fled to Newbury. He went after her, but her brothers put the run on him. Him back only a day afore he come after me." She pleats Hawise's skirt in her fingers. "I got out o' the house, Elf trapped inside, but he caught me, threw me down, me kicking 'n' screaming. Elf clawed her way out, tore into his leg, I jabbed his eye 'n' we both ran, the snow hiding us."

Truth being malleable, he says, "You did well to come here."

Two days pass. Jenet and Alyce are both back with Haukyn, Alyce cautious around this strange woman who sleeps on a new mattress beside her and the rest of the time treats her as if she were naught but a stick of wood. Ilotte is wearing her own clothes by now, the tunic neatly stitched and a cap fashioned out of his mother's wimple; her hair is stuffed beneath it. In the midst of all the coming and going, she takes as little notice of Haukyn as is possible. On the evening of the second day, Alyce asleep, Haukyn can no longer bear the silence. "Did you know I'd been widowed?"

She nods. "I heard talk at the market."

"Yet you made no move to visit me, or my parents—your bees know how to sting."

"You tol' me never to walk alone on the road."

"So you remember that much. Had you not one friend on your manor who would have walked with you?"

More pleating of Hawise's skirt. "I can't stay here. With you."

He grits his teeth. "My father would welcome you."

"M' sore ankle'll bear m' weight by the morrow."

She'd rather hobble from west to east of the vill than stay one hour longer in his company, he thinks in a combination of fury and— God's nails—is it misery? "I'll help you," he says with pardonable coldness.

On the morrow, Ilotte is forced to lean her weight on his arm across the fields. He suffers this the whole way to Edmund's and eats dinner there, cooked by Ralf, who has a talent with peas and herbs. Ranulf drapes himself over Ilotte's feet. Alyce tickles Ranulf's belly.

Ilotte pays no heed to either of them. Haukyn says he'll come back for Alyce later, saddles Trefoil, and rides to Hungerford, where he asks directions of the first serf he meets for Bidewell's house. "Didn't his Agnys run from his good Christian sticks, one wood, t'other flesh," the man says with a malicious grin. "He be in alehouse. Watch him, touchy as a chained boar."

The alehouse, like Flintbourne's, is pungent with stale ale, unwashed men, and smoke. Arthur Bidewell is sitting alone, staring morosely into what is clearly not his first mug. Haukyn marches up to him and tosses coin on the table. He says loudly, in a mix of truth and invention, "Chevage for Ilotte of Hungerford, whom you tried to rape before she fled. Flintbourne's constable attests to her injuries. Do not, on threat of death, attempt to bring her back."

"That bitch? She ain't worth the bother."

"Watch your tongue or I'll tear it from your head." He looks around. "Do you all stand witness, that I, Haukyn of Flintbourne, paid two shillings for her absence?"

A chorus of *ayes* and jocular laughter from the men, some of whom, odds are, threw rotten fruit when she was in the stocks. Well satisfied with his afternoon's work, he rides home and brings Alyce back to share his otherwise empty house.

The days of Advent drag past, Haukyn staying away from his father's as much as he can, yet always aware that Ilotte is to be found across the width of a few fields. Mass of the Angels, Shepherd's Mass, Christ's Mass, he attends them all, for did not the holiest of births take place in a stable, not in castle or palace, and is that not, every year, a sign of hope? Ilotte comes to none of these services; she in all likelihood declines to worship a deity who was deaf to the pleas of a little girl. Late on the day of Christ's birth, at Edmund's, where Ralf has cooked a feast of which he is justifiably proud, Haukyn keeps his distance from her in the confusion of visits from Lucy, Solomon, and their family, Johanna, Simon, the twins, and their own two little-uns. The Feast of St. Stephen is followed by the Feast of the Holy Innocents, and that afternoon he's outside chopping wood, Alyce weaving a little basket from brush, Jenet at Dunstan's tending his cough, when a voice he'd know anywhere says behind him, "I needs to talk to you."

The log is near-split. He turns and takes his time looking her over, head to toe. "Elf looks well-fed and you've added a length of russet to my mother's skirts."

"Father Mortimer don't want to see a woman's ankles." A gust of wind flattens her hood. "C'n we go inside?" she says. "Tis bitter cold."

"Tis winter," he says, smiling a little, a smile she doesn't return. Wondering what's on her mind, he orders Rust to watch Alyce, ushers Ilotte indoors, and drops his gloves on the bench.

She steps closer, so tight-wound he thinks she might snap. "I wants to live here. Your orchard would support a hive or two, 'n' by the looks o' your garden now the snow's blown off, it sore needs my touch."

"Live here? With *me*? With me and Alyce?"

"I'll sleep in her bay."

Through a flick of pure rage, he says, "What of my father?"

"He be too close to the alehouse, drunken men coming and going. Too close to Ivo at Dunstan's. Your father a good man who wants to teach me to make m' letters 'n' read so I could use your ma's herbal, but there always be folk, in the door and out the door, Ralf, Gil, the cooper's sons, Solomon and his lot, Johanna 'n' hers, you can't get one moment's peace, talk talk talk, no end to the talk, 'n' I ain't like that." She adds doubtfully, "I don't think he'd mind."

"My daughter lives here too, nor is she always quiet, and Jenet here most days as well."

"Cooking, sweeping, m' bees, m' letters, I wouldn't be underfoot. Likely I'd get used to her."

Rage burgeons, his voice cold as the wind. "She must be kept away from hearth, ditches, and river. Can you bestir yourself that much?"

She says sulkily, "I never had no use for little-uns."

"She's my daughter, Ilotte!" He rubs his fingers up and down his hose. "The priest will think we share more than table and hearth, and Osmond will charge us leyrwite."

"Gossip don't bother me none 'n' I'll pay you back once the market opens."

Tipping her chin up so she has to meet his eyes—tis evident she suffers his touch—he says, "Do you trust me never to do what Bidewell did?"

"Be I a fool to do so?"

He drops his hand. "So you still doubt me. You'd best go back to my father's and think about all this."

Her cheeks are flushed with matching anger. "I tol' you six year ago I trust no man!"

"Go!"

Elf slinks after her. Ilotte underfoot day after day? He'd be as big a fool as Wortle Dill.

Edmund had managed all too easily to fill his house with friends and their noisy little-uns and had watched Ilotte's ill-hid dismay at each new arrival. Ralf fed them all, bowls and spoons a-clatter, wood tossed on the fire, pots stirred, dogs barking, clouts filled, talk and laughter, jokes and tales of woe, his house busier than any bee hive. After a mere three days of this conviviality he was worn out, though he kept that to himself. The next morning she announced she was a burden on him, that Haukyn could use help in house and garden, and that she was most grateful to him for his hospitality. A lie, doubtless, but a well-meant one. "Are you certain?" he said.

A most vehement nod.

She leaves, he sends the twins outdoors, and he has the house blessedly to himself. He pours a mug of ale and sits by the fire, gazing into the ever-changing flames.

Within too short a time, his door snaps open and she's back. She looks around. "The house be *empty*?"

Her cheeks are red from more than cold, and anyone who lived with Hawise can recognize a woman in a temper. "Solomon and Lucy may come," he says. "Does Haukyn not want you?'

"He be angered. 'Bout his daughter. I got no use for little-uns."

"She's my granddaughter, Ilotte."

His tone is mild. Her flush deepens. "You raised little-uns 'cause you wanted 'em."

"We both did, my wife and I."

She's pacing the room like a wild creature, her feet kicking the rushes. "I won't marry him!"

"He told me six years ago that he'd asked you. He's been married and widowed since then, it's changed him."

"Aye, but can I trust him?"

"Though my son can be hot-headed and rash, his word is solid as the floor you're tramping. You and I will have a short lesson in letters, then you'll go back to him."

"You don't want me to live here," she says, visibly hurt.

"Haukyn has less company than I. He'd be good to you, Ilotte… and maybe good for you."

Her frown is prodigious. "You be a strange man."

"Hawise would have agreed with you."

"So, like Elf, I must tuck tail twixt m' legs and crawl back on m' belly?"

He laughs. "Take off your cloak and sit down. We'll start with the alphabet."

Once she's absorbed her fill, he leads her over to the shelves of Hawise's woven bags, he reading the name of each herb on the top shelf, its preparation and its uses, she sniffing the contents. "As you learn them, you could move them to Haukyn's, he'd build you a shelf or two."

"I ain't no wise-woman."

"Your mind is as restless as my wife's, and Lucy, though she does her best as midwife, has no aptitude for tinctures and concoctions."

"You would tie me to your vill."

"I'd need but a short cord." *And with luck*, he thinks, *you will deflect my son from rebellions small and large.* "Perhaps I shouldn't say this…Annabel was a good woman and a hard worker, but not his match."

Low-voiced, she says, "I be afeard. If Haukyn give you his loyalty, you got it for life, 'n' why do I feel like summat passed over m' grave?"

Haukyn is trimming hair and beard into the bowl his pregnant Annabel used for her sickness, Alyce in bed, Rust dozing by the fire. When he's done, he tosses the clippings into the fire, where they sizzle, flicker, and die. No one in good conscience could send Ilotte back to Hungerford, and where else can she go? He'll get used to her being across the fields at his father's.

He'd rather have the pox.

Rust woofs. Ilotte pushes the door open, Elf at her heels, closes it behind her, and shakes back her hood. He says, "Have you come for your clothes? I'd have brought them on the morrow."

"Your da says I belong here. With you."

"Does he?" He gets up and puts the bowl back on the shelf. "And what do you say?"

"I can't go back to Hungerford! It weren't just the stocks 'n' Bidewell. Heloise's cousins was after me, I were called sorceress, too oft I lived in fear. You don't want me here, but I knows you'd keep me safe from them in the vill that ain't good men, 'n' your da says you'd be good for me." She pulls off her cloak and looks down at the folds of wool as though not sure what they are. "What do he mean by that?"

"I cannot imagine. There's a hook to hang your cloak."

Firelight plays over her face. "So I can stay?"

"Aye," he says, "you can stay." To his huge alarm, he sees she's near tears. "You'll sleep in Alyce's bay and we'll rub along."

"I be grateful," she says, scrubs at her eyes, and tosses her head with some of the defiance he remembers so well. "I won't be no bother to you."

"Why would you be? And now I have a bow to tiller."

"If you can spare a crust o' bread, I'll take m'self to bed."

"You know where tis kept."

When the door closes to Alyce's bay, he lowers his head to his hands. He can't, in good conscience or bad, curse his father.

Ilotte is at Edmund's for her second lesson, Haukyn glad of her absence. Jenet didn't arrive this morning, so Alyce, well-bundled under the apple tree, is playing with her skittles and Haukyn splitting wood he's poached, when Rust barks. Ivo is tramping toward him. He grabs a handful of Haukyn's tunic, face too close, greasy red curls under a greasy grey hood, sourness of rotting teeth. "So m' sister ain't good enough for you."

Haukyn drops the axe, clips Ivo's hand away, and shoves him backward. "I don't know what you mean. Rust, down."

"Jenet hoped you'd marry her—'n' don't tell me you don't know what I mean!"

"*What?* Not once did I think of Jenet that way. She never spoke of it, nor did I behave in a manner that might have encouraged her."

"She wouldn't speak up for herself, now would she. This morning I hears her weeping enough to flood the valley, and didn't she burn her hand yesterday on a hot trivet 'cause she were upset you got that black-eyed slut living with you again. Taking yer father's leavings, ain't you."

"Keep your tongue off my father. I'm fond of Jenet, of course I am, she's been unfailingly kind to Alyce. But fondness is all."

"She'll not be looking after yer little-un no more."

"Her choice or yours?"

"She don't get no choice."

"So we're enemies again—perhaps we were never other than that and I was a fool to think of you as friend. Get off my land and don't come back, or I'll set the dog on you."

Ivo drills a dirty fingernail into Haukyn's chest. "A dose o' poison'll fix yer dog."

"Harm my dog and I'll beat you senseless."

"You'd best remember Mauld. Made a right mess o' him, didn't we." An obscenity hurled at the dog and Ivo is gone.

Haukyn picks up his axe and waits for his blood to quieten. *Full circle*, he thinks. *Seven years since I came home from war and met my old enemy Ivo by the ford, and despite a rescued sister and shared ale, naught has changed.* He leans down to rubs Rust's ears. "How to teach you not to eat carrion? But teach you I must."

A dead crow alive with maggots, a heap of rabbit bones and ripped fur, a puzzled dog who yet wishes to please him—the lessons make Haukyn's stomach heave, lessons he only carries out when Ilotte is across the fields at Edmund's.

Alyce misses Jenet for days, calls for her when she slips on the ice and bangs her elbow, weeps in fury when Haukyn won't allow her to go up the hill to Dunstan's. Such explanations as he can come up with—Jenet's burnt hand, Dunstan so old he's in need of more help—fall on deaf ears. Of what use a father when Alyce's mother is in Heaven's far-distant reaches and her beloved Jenet out of bounds?

He tells Ilotte there is no need of Jenet now that she's living with them.

Mass on Sunday, he's filing into the church with Alyce in his arms, when she flings herself backward, shrieking, "Jenet, Jenet!"

Haukyn's head swivels. Jenet is tucked among a group of atte Medes, her cheeks scarlet, and tis obvious she wishes the ground would swallow her. What can he say to her? *I'm sorry?*

"Be quiet, Alyce, Jenet is going to Mass like us and cannot sit with you."

But Alyce is now sobbing in a manner Haukyn knows from experience is not easily quelled, and his own cheeks redden. He slips out of the crowd, hurries home, and rocks his daughter to sleep, Ilotte not best pleased to see him back so soon, and does he care?

Ilotte and Edmund have bonded over words traced on slate, over herbs and herbals; she and Lucy are becoming friends, the more so after she helps Lucy deliver Walter atte Mede's sluggish-from-the-womb second daughter; Alyce follows her as Rust does, and while Ilotte accepts hens, sows, and cows doing likewise, she brushes off a small girl. Alyce, who has, it seems, inherited her father's stubbornness, trudges after her from here to there and back again, to Ilotte's obvious annoyance. On an afternoon of unrelenting sleet, when Ilotte is weaving, Haukyn smoothing a hornbeam stave with sharkskin, and Alyce fractious, the child plumps down by Ilotte's skirts, curls herself around her ankles with her head on one foot, and falls asleep. Ilotte eyes her askance, the warp around fingers that have gone still. Haukyn scoops Alyce up. "I'll put her on her bed, she'll rest better."

"Aye," she says and bends to her weaving.

Fealty to his daughter, fealty to a sloe-eyed woman, and he caught in the middle.

Sloes are a bitter fruit, borne by blackthorns.

Word comes to the vill of a third poll tax, a shilling a head, an unheard-of amount. On Haukyn's visit to Javyd last autumn, Parliament was in session in the Midlands, and though it had promised no taxation for eighteen months, rumours of a third poll tax were rumbling over London's cobbles and through its lanes. "Arseholes," said Javyd, "Londoners'll kill the lot of 'em, taxes the last three year 'n' now more? Taxes for what? So John o' Gaunt can call hisself King o' Castile 'n' Thomas Woodstock ponce around Brittany? By God, King Richard might be a young-un, but he'd best snag his braies to his hose 'n' govern."

Haukyn took a heel of bread still warm from Petronilla's oven. "Fifteenths collected last April, a poor harvest in September, no tax officer would dare show his face in Flintbourne."

And now Tirrell as constable is charged with the unenviable task of amassing Flintbourne's contribution to that poll tax; worse, he is to keep a record of all the villagers, those who pay their twelve-pence and those who do not. No villager wants to be a name on a list, for lists lead to fines, and Tirrell knows this. Haukyn makes a point of following him around the vill, amused by how much noise the constable makes as he approaches each house, poor relatives and the mutinous leaving by the back door as he bangs on the front. There are some who surrender their coin without argument; there are many who tell Tirrell in lurid detail what he can do with list and tax; and there are others who pay for the indigent and aged: Haukyn for Dunstan, Solomon for Bony Mabel, Edmund for Amos Cat-Skinner's destitute old father. He himself refuses to pay, not to anyone's surprise, nor does he allow Ilotte's name to appear on the scroll. Tirrell takes himself off to London to deliver such money as he's accrued, and the vill huddles around its hearths to keep warm as January passes into a February that grips winter harder than it has in living memory.

Haukyn has shovelled a bucket of snow to melt by the fire and with the handle is knocking icicles off the eaves when Rust, who prefers the warmth inside, whines to be let out. "Around the back of the house, you know where to go, and don't linger else your pizzle'll freeze. Ilotte will be home from Edmund's soon, with Alyce."

Icicles thicker than a giant's pizzle, he thinks, and hits two more, which plunge, dagger-like, and splinter on the frozen ground. Rust is still whining, now from behind the house, then as a third icicle shatters, breaks into a howl. Keeping hold of his shovel, Haukyn marches around the corner. Rust, slavering, is hanging over a chunk of ham, fatty and thick. "Nay," he shouts, "leave it," and walks closer, poking at the ham with the point of the shovel. A knife cut on its underside, long enough to lace the meat with poison. Ivo's work.

What if Alyce had come across it, before Rust? Why didn't Ilotte's strangeness warn him of this peril, and why won't he ask her?

He can't bury the ham in frozen ground. He can't throw it in the woods. He edges it onto the blade and carries it indoors, lays the shovel on the table, takes an end of bread from its box, and tosses it in the air. Rust gulps it down. "You obeyed the lessons," he says, rubbing the dog on the chest, "even though we're all hungered these days. Stay and guard the house."

In the forge, the heat is atrocious. Sim is pounding red-hot iron on the anvil while Ivo, his back turned, is sorting nails. The brothers' shirts, belts, and daggers are lying over a bench against the far wall. Soft-footed, Haukyn comes up behind Ivo. "Well met," he says.

Ivo's shoulders stiffen. He drops a handful of nails in the box and whips around, his eyes darting to the bench. "Out of reach," Haukyn says. "But you won't need your dagger. I have a gift for you, and such a gift in these meagre times. A chunk of ham, fatty, not a maggot in sight. Open your mouth and let me feed it to you, for the sake of our one-time friendship."

"I ain't hungered!"

"You'll eat it anyway." Dimly aware that the hammer blows to the anvil have halted, he pushes Ivo so hard the man falls back against the wall. He thrusts the ham at him. "Did it occur to you that my daughter might pick this up and eat it? Or didn't you think beyond poisoning my dog?"

Ivo's eyes bulge in abject terror. "Nay," he gasps, "nay."

The same terror twisted Ivo's features that long-ago day when Jorden whipped a chain through the air. The scars still mar Ivo's chest. In sudden disgust, Haukyn steps back.

He looks down at the piece of poisoned meat in his hand. The forge fire like an inferno. He steps closer to it and drops the ham. The fat sputters, the meat blackens, and from the flames a coil of green smoke rises.

Not until March does the sun, grudgingly, send warmth to melt the last of the snow and ice. Ploughing, by unspoken consent, begins in the tenants' fields before the lord's, Osmond's furious shrieks to no avail. Ash Wednesday ushers in Lent, another season of penitence and fasting. Haukyn scarcely notices because his larder has been scant and his nerves frayed for weeks on end. The ash scarce off his forehead when two fist fights break out because of taunts about his black-haired whore: the first with Ivo and Amos, the second Samuel and John, him coming home bloodied each time, his set face a warning against questions.

A woman who won't touch his hand or acknowledge the existence of his daughter, who cringes if he walks too close to her, who measures out smiles and speech like the rarest of gems, a woman who, on occasion and disconcertingly, he catches watching him, and he too pig-headed to ask her why. Pain, lust, frustration, rage—what matter the name he gives to this stew of emotion, he must do something, send her back to Edmund's, anywhere where he doesn't have to eat with her, bump into her in his garden, watch her go to bed in Alyce's bay.

Day after day and night after night go by and he does naught.

Alyce has decided Ilotte is but a piece of furniture in her father's house and treats her as such, lying against her, clambering over her to reach something she wants, and, unless Ilotte takes her to visit her grandfather, otherwise ignoring her. A skill Haukyn sorely lacks.

Late March and he's tucked inside, gutting two fine trout poached from the lord's river. Tis Friday, a day for fish, and a fine feast it will be, cooked over an applewood fire. Alyce is with Ralf for the day. Ilotte is cutting reeds below the meadow, he not missing her one whit. When Rust pricks his ears, barking, he rinses his hands, tucks the fish under some fresh rushes, and goes to the door.

A man is standing there, holding a black mare by the reins. Astounded, he says, "Sir Geoffrey? Sir Geoffrey Stratton?"

"Haukyn, God's blessing."

"Sir, tis good to see you. You can tether your horse in the byre. Or in the orchard, to eat the early grass."

"The orchard will do well."

This done, Sir Geoffrey enters the house and sits by the fire, hands to the warmth. Haukyn gives him a mug of Johanna's ale and sits across from him. "Bordeaux and your cog, tis as yesterday. Yet more than seven years have passed."

"Despite a bad harvest, we are better fed now than we were that day. Haukyn, in London I met by chance, at the conduit, your friend Javyd, who invited me to sup with him and told me of your rebellions against lordship and taxation. Are you still of that mind?"

"I refused to pay the last poll tax."

"Evasion and fraud everywhere. John of Gaunt has made peace with Scotland, Thomas of Woodstock's campaign in Brittany is ingloriously over, yet the government, which could abort a tax intended for war in Scotland and Brittany, is pushing ahead with it instead, in utter stupidity and most punitively. New commissions have been appointed in nine counties, including my home county, Essex, commissions that will be countrywide. They are to travel to each county, make lists of all who are subject to the tax and of those who have evaded it, and extract the money on threat of immediate arrest and imprisonment. Rebellion quickens in Essex, and resistance in shire after shire. I left parchment with Javyd inscribed with your name and Flintbourne's, to be delivered should rebellion boil over... and before I forget, Sir Gardrad assiduously attends Thomas of Woodstock—son of a king—so you'll not see your enemy in these fields for a while."

"Good."

"Both his sons died this year, we should spare him some compassion."

"You may do so, Sir Geoffrey. I will not."

They talk strategy, the power of numbers and of passivity, talk as equals, Haukyn realizes, and as they eat the tender fillets of herbed trout, speak about their families: in Flintbourne, a dead wife, a daughter, and a difficult woman; nephews and nieces in Essex, the children of Stephen Sadlere. The visit over, as Sir Geoffrey readies to ride back to Windsor, Ilotte approaches them, her cart loaded with fresh-cut rushes, her cheeks flushed from her exertions. She halts when she sees the well-dressed man holding the reins of a black mare. Sir Geoffrey says calmly, "Ah, Haukyn, this must be your wife?"

"I be no man's wife."

Sir Geoffrey bows. "I should learn not to jump to conclusions, should I not?" He eyes the heaped reeds. "You aid a good man by taking on an onerous task, mistress."

She blurts, "I wouldn't do it were he not a good man."

"A good man, whom I name as friend." Sir Geoffrey turns to Haukyn and clasps him by the hand. "Watch for a letter from London, Haukyn. God's blessing on you and your household."

"I too have gained a friend, sir," Haukyn says, and as horse and rider trot toward the ford, pivots to face the woman with the cart. "You call me a good man? Yet you talk to my hens and my horse more than you talk to me!"

With a violence that shocks him, she says, "You mending m' fence so long ago, bringing me violets, I wanted *you* for friend. But nay, you wanted all o' me and I gained naught."

"I made no secret of what I wanted—to give you of the best in me." He drags his fingers through his hair. "I'm making an arse of myself. I'll be in the byre."

"I didn't have no friends back then."

"You do now. Da and Lucy. Ralf, Gil. You won't let *me* near enough."

"There be such darkness in you, Haukyn, m' strangeness, it feels it!"

"Aye, there's darkness in me. Am I to slough off five months of killing, rape, and starvation as though they never were? Then here, at home, Annabel, my wife, suffering from the right-side sickness and I in the manor's gaol for inciting rebellion—she called for me, my mother said, she cried out my name in her death throes, but they wouldn't let me out. Then, or for her funeral. I loathe Osmond and Sir Gardrad and always will."

She wraps her arms around herself. "You loved your wife."

"My bed empty ever since and so it will remain. Unless you join me there." His smile is ferocious. "You'd as soon bed a slug."

"Have you forgot what m' father done?"

"Never."

Her frown draws sharp lines in her forehead. "But you haven't tol' another soul 'bout him…do that mean I can trust you?"

"Tisn't my story to tell."

She says slowly, "Over three months, 'n' you ain't touched me."

He should run for the byre and take his temper with him. "What of *my* trust in *you,* Ilotte? I love Alyce with all my heart and you act as if she doesn't exist. We'd all be better off if you went back to my father's."

"He won't have me and I got no coin for my own place." She comes closer, lays a hesitant hand on his sleeve. "I know you been in fights 'cause o' me."

He looks down at her fingers, skin to cloth, and jerks his arm free. "I've got work to do," he says and flees to the byre.

Ilotte does not move back to his father's. She cuts wattle for a hive, goes to her reading lessons, visits Lucy, and, more and more often, busies herself healing the vill's sick beasts. She has no time for him, Haukyn thinks irritably, leaning on his shovel; the garden is much bigger and free of weeds, ready for her to plant what she will. Another yard or two and he'll be done. He needs to scythe the grass around his apple and pear trees next and rake it for Trefoil and his cows. Stretching his back, he sees Ilotte and Alyce close by on the headland, Ilotte carrying the hive she and Edmund must have woven from the wattle, Alyce toiling to pull a little cart that used to be the twins', now bearing a load of small boards, and Ilotte not helping her. Haukyn stifles an all-too familiar anger and heels his spade into the dirt.

Ilotte surveys the fresh-turned soil. "A goodly garden. Your father has given us extra turnip and parsnip seed."

He wants no talk of turnips. "That cart's too heavy for a little girl."

He strides past her and lifts the wood from the cart, his daughter red-faced and puffing. "You did well, Alyce. I'll build a stand for the hive with these boards, and there'll be honeycomb for you as reward."

"Now?"

Haukyn laughs and ruffles her curls. "The hive needs bees to make the honey."

After he carries the boards to the orchard, Alyce trailing behind him, he piles them on the ground, then picks up his shovel again and turns back to the garden. Tossing flint to one side, breaking up clods, he sweating and Ilotte shrieks, "Alyce, *nay!*"

His head jerks around. She's racing toward his daughter and to his horror he hears hissing, sees a snake rear its head. Alyce too close, dark arrowhead on the scaled neck, dark zigzags down the body, *Christ*, an adder and he's running, spade held high. Ilotte whips the child into her arms and leaps backward and the adder, alarmed, slithers from the rock where it was sunning itself and into the new-leafed bushes. He turns to the woman clutching Alyce. "Did it bite either of you?"

"Nay, nay, neither of us—I weren't watching her, Haukyn," and as she buries her face in Alyce's neck, his daughter, in belated terror, starts to cry. The spade clunks to the ground; Haukyn throws his arms around the two of them and strains them to his body. Ilotte mumbles, "She be so solid, so warm, I ain't never touched her before. Why didn't I, were it fear 'cause of how I were touched by m' da?"

"You wouldn't do to a little-un what was done to you!"

"Nor I would." She lifts her head, her eyes swimming with tears. "Haukyn, I never tol' you...I had a sister. Emma were her name. When Ma left, she took her with her, she were the age of Alyce. I loved her 'n' Ma took her in the night, she weren't there when I got up in the morning nor any morning after..."

Tears are now streaming down her face, this woman who shuns tears. Alyce, held close, has abandoned crying for listening; she reaches up a finger and strokes Ilotte's cheek. "Wet," she says.

Ilotte draws in a breath, seemingly oblivious of Haukyn's embrace. "Alyce, I ain't been kind to you. But from now on I'll do m' best for you. If you'll let me."

"Honey?" she says hopefully.

Ilotte's smile wobbles. "I has to find bees first to live in our hives. You'll like watching 'em, and I'll show you what to do so they don't sting you…Let's go inside now and start our supper."

All these years Ilotte has grieved, alone, for her little sister. Haukyn lets his arms fall and watches them go indoors, Alyce patting Ilotte's cheeks; he could learn a lesson or two in forgiveness from his daughter. After sharpening his scythe so he can cut the grass in the orchard, he picks up the rock, warm from the sun, and throws it as far as he can into the bushes.

Supper eaten, Alyce falls asleep on the mattress in her bay, worn out from cart and adder. Haukyn has too much to say and no clear way to begin; he settles on the bench to weave a bowstring, hoping it will shed light on his thoughts. In a high-pitched voice, Ilotte says, "Will you take me to your bed?"

The hemp drops in a tangle to the floor. "What? You mean… *now?*"

"You'd have to light candles. M' father always done it in the dark."

In this same room, years ago, Annabel had offered herself, he virginal and the bed in darkness. He stands up, bowstring forgot. "My body is made the same way as your father's. As Bidewell's, also. Are you forgetting that?"

She bites her lip. "You don't want to swive me?"

"I want it more than I can say."

"We be tangled together, you 'n' me. Like the hemp."

"Why don't you light the candles? I'll cover the fire."

In his bay, it takes her several tries to light the three wicks, and he as nervous as if he were, once again, virginal. He rubs his work-roughened hands down his hose and leads her to his mattress, not quite able to believe this is happening, after so many years, on a spring evening the same as any other, a few birds still chirping in the orchard. She's standing rigid as a soldier on duty, determination to the fore, underlaid with emotions he might call courage or desperation and still miss the mark.

He tugs off his shirt and hose, loosens her skirt, lets it drop to the floor, and pulls her tunic over her head, she nervously laughing at his awkwardness. Once they lie down, he does his best to couple her courage—for courage it is—with restraint, striving to give only what is wanted and never what is not. When they are done, she lies quiet in his arms. Unsure she found any release, he says, and again there is that echo of his former self, "Next time we'll do better."

"You wants to do it to me again? Why?"

"Not *to* you. With you." He runs a finger down the long line of her throat, then up again to her most decided chin. "Your skin, tis smooth as the river, yet warm. Could I heal, even in part, what so long ago was broken in you..."

"No man can do that."

"Or should?" he says, fumbling into ideas new to him, stroking her shoulder as once he stroked Modge's when flames whipped through a field of barley. "No more, perhaps, than you can take from me the death of Piers, the killings, the hunger?"

"Our darknesses be our own."

"Yet I would give you a man different from those you have known."

"Would I be here..." she gives an incredulous laugh, "had you not already done so, at the stocks all them years ago, 'n' ever since you found me in the snow?"

He drops his forehead to her breast, moved to tears. "Would you now marry me?"

"Haukyn, nay."

"Not ever?"

"I can't, I can't. When I run from Da and our vill, I stumbled onto an ol' track where I come across a statue, a woman, worn by weather, blackthorn twigs criss-crossed at her feet. The Virgin? Or were she older, a goddess of the earth? Didn't matter, she were holy. I swore an oath in her presence that I'd never marry, 'n' it give me comfort."

"Did I not vow never to kill again? Yet were Alyce to be threatened—or you, my father, or my brothers—that oath would blow on the wind."

"Will you be satisfied with what I c'n give?"

"I'll not ask you to break an oath."

"Past time to blow out them candles."

She gets up and he waits to see if she'll return to his bed or to her mattress in Alyce's bay. One by one the candles are blown out. Darkness, and swiftly she lifts the covers and lies on the very edge of his bed with her back to him.

He says, "We'd best get some sleep," keeps his hands by his sides, and closes his eyes.

...on opposite sides of the wall...

Half a dozen armed men arrive in Flintbourne, ride to the manor, dismount, and disappear. Rumours whip from house to house, *Sir Gardrad, his retainers, poll tax.* By the time the men emerge with Osmond trit-trotting in front of the horses and a reluctant Tirrell in their wake, those who refused to part with their twelve-pence, including Haukyn, have converged at the ford, some with staffs and pitchforks, others with drawn bows, all with knives, their women in the background. Water ripples between the stones. A fitful wind blows from the east and, lifting on it from the church tower, a jackdaw *chak-chaks*. The retainers are burly men with skin as tough as leather; at a sharp command from their leader, they unsheathe their swords. Osmond brandishes a scroll and in his scratchy voice cries, "This document has been sent to every sheriff in the kingdom. We are authorized by the Commons to use whatever means necessary to collect all arrears without delay or dispute. You will pay in full what you owe our good King Richard, or force will be used."

"We'll show you force," Blundred says.

"Come closer, Osmond," Amos bawls, "so I c'n rip yer scroll to shreds."

"Or stuff it up yer hole."

Ivo's contribution. Sharply, Haukyn is reminded of Annabel, who'd be telling Osmond to stuff it up his clouts. He feels as if he's standing in an open field in a lightning storm, the very air charged.

Although the horses look ill-fed and ill-groomed, six mounted men with swords could do significant damage. James of Liddington and his father, both warned against force. He says calmly, "No violence."

The six retainers urge their mounts closer, closer still, sword-points glinting. Raising his voice, he says, "Neighbours, stand shoulder to shoulder. Together we make a wall they cannot break through."

Ivo: "You afeard of a brawl, Haukyn?"

Amos, with relish: "Yellow-bellied as a wagtail."

Samuel: "Did you kill Frenchies, Haukyn, or did you show 'em yer backside?"

Wulstan the cowherd, not the brightest of men: "Kill the bastards!"

Osmond grabs the nearest set of reins; the horse shies. "Scatter these rebels!"

Giles the hayward: "Aim your horse at me 'n' I'll shoot. Ample flesh twixt its bones for an arrow to lodge."

Giles's father: "Aye…me eyes ain't as good as they used t' be, but a nag be a decent target."

Giles: "Six arrows in m' quiver should you miss, Da."

Haukyn has taught both men on the green, their accuracy admirable. The captain of the retainers, the same swarthy-faced brute he remembers from the lord's wheat fields, shouts, "You think we be daunted by a gabble of ignorant serfs? Ride forward."

A bowstring twangs. An arrow lodges itself in the dirt a foot in front of a rough-coated gelding. Osmond chitters with rage. Tirrell stands, helpless, to one side.

Thunderous barks from the hillside behind them. Heads turns, Haukyn's included. A dog is charging down the slope past the alehouse, a hefty, unkempt dog. Tis Jackdawe's pup, who's never outgrown puppyhood, named Jack-for-Short by Dunstan, and joyfully he gallops into the crowd, women and men parting to let him through. He heads for the nearest horse, a scrawny chestnut, and leaps at its throat. The horse skitters sideways and bumps into the next horse, which rears, its pock-marked rider tumbling backward.

Amos goes fist to fist with the man on the ground. The riderless horse tries to bolt, another horse kicks it, the rest scatter, neighing, in a clomp of hoofs. John and Ivo haul another retainer from his saddle, his bald pate shining in the April sun, John's knife unsheathed. A line of blood springs from the man's arm, he cries out, his own knife flashes, and Ivo kicks the legs from under him. *A bloodbath, nay!* and Haukyn charges, flanked by peaceable Solomon and fiery Walter. He grabs Ivo by the back of his tunic, flings him to one side, kicks John in the ribs, and follows it with a boot to the bald man's gut. "No killing! Stand back, sheathe your knives."

Jack-for-Short barks maniacally, dancing around John and Haukyn, then slurps his wet pink tongue over the retainer's bald skull. Swearing, the man swipes at him; the dog, long-practiced, dodges, knocking Wulstan into Amos and Amos into a panicked horse, which bites him in the arm. He howls in pain. Laughter breaks out and Haukyn releases a long breath. Why try to prevent murder when Jack-for-Short can do it for him?

Solomon pats his knife in its leather casing and says in his mild voice, "I ain't paying one cracked farthing, but I ain't ending up in the manor's gaol neither."

Tirrell steps forward. "If any wish to pay their twelve-pence, let 'em do so. Osmond, record your gains 'n' put an end to this. And you, sir," he looks at the captain of the retainers, whose face is red with suppressed fury, "I suggest you leave without causing more trouble."

Walter says, "You tell them knights 'n' lords in Parliament to pay for war with their own coin. They got plenty."

Abashed, one of the miller's sons pays the tax, as does his scraggly wife; two of the manor's house-servants do likewise. Osmond scratches an X next to each name and rolls up his parchment, his pride salvaged, Haukyn thinks sardonically. Swords are sheathed. The captain herds men and horses together and spurs his own mount into a canter across the green. Turf flies. Osmond hurries after them, coin clinking in his purse.

Haukyn says to anyone who's listening, "Jack-for-Short the only hero of that cock-up," and heads homeward.

Violence begets violence, isn't that what his father said? It could have been worse.

Ilotte has made soup from nettle leaves, burdock, chickweed, wild garlic, and the stems and roots of horse parsley. They eat, Alyce is put to bed, and she says, "What happened at the ford?"

Ilotte will listen to talk of rebellion, as Annabel rarely would; she's also a better cook by far than Annabel. Briefly he describes how Jack-for-Short saved the day. "I doubt we've seen the last of them. Osmond will order them back."

"Bidewell 'n' Osmond, cuckoos both, pushing hatchlings out o' the nest."

"The last few years, rebellion has bubbled in the vill's cauldrons with every now and then a fart of steam. Osmond's white wand naught but a white-washed stick." He smiles. "Dark of the moon last October, a lewd painting on the manor's oak door, and not a villager with a brush in shed or byre. December, after a dry night, a sheen of ice on the bridge over the manor moat, half the vill watching through chinks in their shutters as Mauld lands on his arse. When he goes looking for salt to sprinkle on the bridge, the salt barrel is perched on the seat of Osmond's latrine." Basking in the glimmer of amusement in her dark eyes, he adds, "Three mysteries and none, as yet, solved."

"A game what could be dangerous?"

"We're careful, not once has he caught any of us. Too careful." An edge to his voice, he adds, "You use the right word, Ilotte—tis a game. We gain naught, we're still serfs, necessary and worthless."

She says drily, "Gains c'n be small…I found an early swarm o' bees low on a birch tree in the lord's woods. Could you make me a box with a hole in it for air?"

A soothing task, after which they lie separate on the bed.

He and Alyce follow her to the swarm, he watching in trepidation as Ilotte lowers it into the box. "They be docile," she says, kneeling beside the box, "no brood to protect and their bellies too full o' honey for 'em to sting. We'll leave the box til sundown, then on the morrow I'll move the swarm to m' hive." She smiles at Alyce. "Honey, come late summer."

Haukyn curls his hand around her elbow to help her stand. Her muscles tense; she brushes his hand away. No use complaining, naught he can do or say to bring about change, much as he wishes it were otherwise. They swive rarely and tis constrained, and although he hides his hurt, she divines it, and in his better moments he wonders if she hurts for him.

Her father hovers over their mattress, and it is beyond his power to exorcise him.

A week later, before Mass, there is low-voiced talk on the green. Earlier that morning Osmond was seen on his dainty white palfrey riding up the track that leaves the vill and turning toward Bristol, Oakum in his wake on one of the manor's cobs and leading another cob bearing laden saddlebags; soon after, a stranger on a handsome white stallion trotted down the track followed by a manservant, both of them headed for the manor's stables, the stranger the same man who entered the church not five minutes ago. "Nodded to us friendly enough," Tirrell says. "We best go inside and find out who he be."

In the church, Father Mortimer takes his stance by the altar. "Our new bailiff wishes to address you."

The man sitting on the front bench stands up and turns to face them. "My thanks to your priest for this opportunity. My name is Bertran of Faircross. Because Master Osmond wished to relinquish the post of bailiff for reasons of ill health, Sir Gardrad has appointed me to replace him. I will be pleased to make the acquaintance of each one of you. God's blessing on all in this vill."

He is a man of perhaps forty winters, solid of build and even-featured, his manner straightforward, his smile easy. Haukyn sits quietly with Alyce, astonished that such a man could have been selected by a knight he abhors, a feeling that persists over the next few days as Bertran does his rounds. Unaccompanied by Mauld or

Saul, he wanders from house to house, all with the same easy smile, and does not record names, chattels, virgates, or beasts. When it comes time to weed the lord's fields, most of the villagers obediently arrive; only Blundred, Solomon, Walter, Waryn, Neuton, and Haukyn absent themselves. Bertran finds Solomon and Haukyn in Solomon's north field, where in separate furrows they're tugging out bindweed, cornflowers, and thistles. He speaks to Solomon before crossing to Haukyn. "You understand that I must fine you at hallmote."

"We'll be done our own weeding two days hence, and will then have no objection to working in the lord's fields."

"You go against ancient custom."

"Old age does not warrant wisdom."

"Nor youth good sense. Serfdom is divinely appointed and upheld by law and church. To run against a stone wall guarantees a sore head."

"To chip away the mortar guarantees a lower wall."

"A pity you inherited your father's clever tongue without his fealty to the lord."

"My reasons for that lack of fealty would not agree with Sir Gardrad's," Haukyn says, feeling his nerves tighten, for this man is intelligent as Osmond was not, and it would be unwise to underestimate him.

Bertran says easily, "When I met with Osmond on my way here, he told me of rebellions in this placid little vill, more recently the refusal of many to pay the poll tax, along with molestation of our lord's retainers—a dog's attack, blood drawn. Had I been here, I would have seen the vill's leader, would I not?"

"Jack-for-Short?"

Bertran laughs. "We both know I don't mean that ill-trained beast."

Such a friendly laugh, such an open face. "A man called *yellow-bellied* by his neighbours? You jest."

"I rarely jest about matters I consider of importance."

"You exaggerate my importance. I am but a villein, a humble serf."

"I'm glad you know your place. The stone walls in our kingdom are essential for good governance."

"Stone walls can be heaved, both by God's frosts and by the strength of men."

"The wall I speak of is immovable."

Bertran's smile has vanished. Haukyn says recklessly, "In France, we heard talk of the Jacquerie, an uprising of peasants in that country, who broke through the stone walls of castles and châteaux."

"That uprising was brutally repressed."

"Yet it is remembered to this day, there and in London, where it played a part in the repression of our Domesday claims."

"If I can trust Osmond's word, you were the leader of that too."

"And proud to be so."

"Then we know where we stand," Bertran says softly. "On opposite sides of the wall. Westminster will not let go of this poll tax until every man and woman in the country has paid. Royal punishments can be extreme."

Haukyn gives one last tug to a lusty thistle. "Watch the spikes," he says and tosses the weed over the furrows to lie splayed on the grass.

I've made another enemy. Tis a gift I have, and I must learn to dodge like Jack-for-Short.

As though speaking of Domesday conjured him up, James of Liddington appears in Flintbourne the next day. Haukyn is trying to teach Alyce how to remove eggs from beneath the hens, a lesson neither she nor the hens is appreciating. Over affronted clucks and Alyce's wails because her thumb got pecked, he hears the sound of hoofs and clink of harness. He packs his daughter under his arm and exits the coop arse first.

James, dismounted and chuckling, says, "How many eggs?"

"Horse," Alyce says.

"None," says Alyce's father.

"A mug of your admirable ale would go down well."

"Come inside, I'm glad to see you, and this missie needs hen-shite wiped from behind her ears."

When they're settled, Alyce curled in her father's arms, James says, "I've been travelling my shire from manor to manor, talking but mostly listening. In Flintbourne I believe you still owe your lord boon works and labour services, but on many manors villeins have changed those services to cash payments to the lord, who then can hire labourers for the work. Commutation, tis called, and tis widespread."

"Exemplifications, commutations, how you counsellors love long words. Sir Mauger was so generous and lazy a lord that we didn't, overmuch, mind mowing his hay and harvesting his grain. Master Osmond was of no mind to commute anything. As for Bertran, our new bailiff, though he and I clashed yesterday over the poll tax, I could raise the matter at the hallmote he's called for the morrow. Tell me more."

They discuss technicalities over ale. "In effect, no more servile works, those works that label us as underlings," Haukyn says eagerly. "Wouldn't all lords prefer cash in hand to a group of grumbling villeins?"

After Haukyn relates Sir Geoffrey's news of resistance and rebellion throughout Essex, their talk meanders to wives and children, harvests and weather. That evening, Alyce in bed, a fire dancing in the hearth, he describes commutation to Ilotte. She says, "You sounds so excited, like Alyce when she sees Ralf coming."

"You don't think it worth raising at hallmote?"

"You be the upward flight of a lark, Haukyn, I be its plunge. Raise it 'n' be ready for *nay*."

"What do you think of Bertran?"

She busies herself with her spindle. "When I were alone with m' da, he were always smiling."

Talk of her father renders him speechless. He adds wood to the fire and picks up the next goose feather, and that night, in their bed, is once again presented with her back.

At hallmote, after Father Mortimer's prayer, Bertran says, "Haukyn, I hear you are literate."

He makes it sound, subtly, like an insult. Haukyn says, "I regret that my letters desert me when it comes to Sir Gardrad."

"I see. Then your father as scribe?"

Edmund says, "My eyes now fail me for close lettering, Master."

As Haukyn smothers both surprise and a smile, Bertran says, "Tis as well I brought my house-servant then, who holds loyally to such skills as he has."

The usual trespasses and broken byelaws are listed, Haukyn pays leyrwite for Ilotte's fornication, wondering what Bertran would think were he to know how rarely it transpired, and pays his own fine for untimely weeding. John Cat-Skinner is amerced for drawing the blood of a retainer, Ivo and Wulstan for inciting a brawl, and Haukyn waits to see if he himself will be further amerced. Bertran's eyes come to rest on him. "Although I have been but a short time in your vill," he says, "I recognize Haukyn as the man who is leading many of you into dangerous waters. I counsel you to choose another leader, someone of moderation who understands that the old ways have worked well for generations and need no—"

"Worked well for whom?" Haukyn says. "Lord, bishop, and knight?"

"Parliament will brook no rebellion."

"Parliament should remember how vastly we outnumber Commons and Lords, and how a serf's arrows can pierce a knight's armour and a bishop's chasuble."

A chorus of *ayes* surrounds him, and to his great satisfaction he sees Bertran's cheeks are flushed. "I would bring another matter before the court," Haukyn says and describes how commutation, widespread in their neighbouring shire and also occurring in their own, puts coin in the lord's purse and frees his tenants to be more productive. The men present are listening, many of them nodding and exchanging low-voiced comments. "What say you, Master? I imagine your lord would be of an open and progressive mind for a change that could do naught but benefit him?"

"Sir Gardrad has been most explicit. He wishes no change on this manor for at least a year. Is there other business?"

"Shame!" Walter cries, and others echo him.

Haukyn says, "I would raise another issue. Manumission. A freed villein is a happier man and hence a better worker. What is your lord's stance on manumission?"

"Any villein on Sir Gardrad's manors can purchase his freedom."

"For how much?"

"A mere seven pounds," Bertran says, and now he is smiling.

A concerted gasp from those present. Haukyn says, "Such a sum is out of reach for every serf in the kingdom. On Judgement Day, Sir Gardrad's greed will cost him dear."

Bertran snaps at his scribe, "Strike that last remark. I hereby end hallmote and may God bless our good King Richard. Father Mortimer."

The priest mutters a prayer that might have reached Heaven's ears but was inaudible in the great hall. Saul and Mauld, using their staffs, push them all outdoors, where Haukyn raises his voice to be heard over the shouting and grumbling. "We now know that Master Bertran, for all his smiles, differs little from Master Osmond. Will we weed the ragwort from the lord's hay, poppies from his grain, the same lord who would free each of us for the princely sum of seven pounds?"

Shouts and obscenities his answer. Haukyn circles the crowd so as not to meet his father and heads for the alehouse to further foment fealty's rupture.

The last day of April is unseasonably hot; drenched in sweat, Haukyn has been weeding his father's fields side by side with the twins, his daughter heaping bindweed happily enough. He and she drag themselves home, where Ilotte is tending her bees. "What say we all go to the river," he says. "There's a pool at the east end of the lord's woods, Ilotte, deep enough for wallowing. We could take soap and I'll come home a new man."

"I has to finish here."

He hadn't really expected her to join them. "Follow the river path should you change your mind," he says, and soon he and Alyce are dropping their clothes by the riverbank. Haukyn scrubs the garments with soap, she slaps them back and forth in the water and chases the bubbles downstream. Once the clothes are spread on the bushes, Haukyn lifts his daughter into the pool. "I can't swim," he says, "but I'll hold you. Try kicking your legs and paddling with your arms and we'll see what happens."

What happens is a great deal of splashing. Alyce cries, "More!" and this time, going with the current, she floats, they both feel it, so they try again and it works even better. Haukyn lifts her from the water and holds her high, dripping, both of them laughing and bare as the day they were born. "Lotte, Lotte," Alyce calls.

Haukyn's head swings around. He grins at Ilotte. "My sweat's travelling downstream to London. Take off your shoes and dabble your feet."

"Only m' feet? Tis all a woman's allowed on a hot day?"

She kicks off her shoes, drops her skirts, and hauls her tunic over her head. Her cap falls to the ground, her hair tumbling to her shoulders. Cautious, she steps into the river. "Tis cold!"

He lowers Alyce so she can splash Ilotte. Ilotte shrieks. Chuckling, Haukyn hits the water hard with the edge of his palm. Vengeful, she splashes him back, her chemise clinging to the curves of breasts and flanks, and hurriedly he dunks his groin into the river. Instead of retreating, she advances on him, tossing handfuls of water that trickle down his chest, then lets herself fall forward, the ripples like cold caresses to his ribs. Alyce wriggles to be let down. "I can swim, Lotte," she cries and as Haukyn supports her, she pants and gasps her way toward Ilotte.

"Try this," Ilotte says and lies on her back in the water, kicking hard and finning her arms until she bumps into the bank.

"You can swim," Haukyn says in delight.

"Taught m'self in the pond when I were a little-un…it cleansed me. Lie back, Alyce, I won't let go o' you, now kick hard as you can 'n' stroke with your arms."

Alyce, trusting, does so, once, twice, thrice, thrilled when again she floats. Haukyn falls backward, butt, shoulders, and head sink, and he rises sputtering and coughing; when he shakes his head, drops fly outward in a jagged halo. Ilotte has Alyce tucked into her waist, both of them giggling. "Not as easy as it looks," he says and wades hip-deep toward them. "The birch leaves are shaking in the wind and we're all cold, let's go home. For a treat we'll add the last of our bacon to the soup. Alyce, you're never to go swimming by yourself— you must have me with you, or Ilotte."

When he looks back at the pool, it has quietened, its surface green-shadowed.

They spread their damp garments by the hearth in favour of dry clothes, and eat warm soup, Alyce's head drooping to her chest. Haukyn puts her to bed, kissing her forehead, her lashes already fallen to her cheeks, and now he should spend an hour scything the grass in the orchard, though he has never again seen the adder.

"Haukyn."

Ilotte, from the other bay, and he finds her standing beside their mattress in her dry chemise. "Let's to bed," she says.

She's not quite as sure of herself as she sounds. "Aye," he says, as though this happens every day. His clothes fall to the rushes and they're lying face to face; he can scarce breathe through the tumult in his chest and she the one who reaches for him, he remembering her little-girl giggle as she clasped his wet daughter in the river.

Play, parity, and pleasure, this new Ilotte, this woman who has the power to shake him to his soul; her dark eyes hold him captive, her hands seek him out, and when, eventually, she guides him into her, he feels the throb of her release, and in passionate gratitude finds his own. In a voice he scarce recognizes, he says, "With my body I thee worship," and only then realizes she's weeping, and in an instant he's back to the stocks, her tears of agony as she tried to stand. "Did I hurt you?"

"Nay...nay." Lifting her head, she whispers, "I be free. Free of m' da, and you the one what's given me freedom...all along, not just this night. Remember that, Haukyn. Remember it always."

The next day, she trims his clean hair, teasing his scalp, trims his beard, fingertip lightly tracing his lips. He nuzzles her breast. She leans into him. He pulls her into his lap, laughing. "I will be the happiest man ever to pay leyrwite to the lord."

"Tis my task to pay that."

"There...we're as good as married, already we are arguing."

Has there ever been such a May-month, a month of love-making, of swimming lessons in the river, such a lightness in Ilotte, he marvels at it. He can talk to her about anything, for she listens with care and concentration and asks questions that he cannot always answer; as the days pass, she begins to offer tales of her flight to Newbury, of her friend Bess, of her spells of dread, obscure and fickle. One wet morning Alyce calls her *Ma*, and although Ilotte's busy fingers pause on the spindle, she answers as though naught were unusual, nor does Haukyn look up as he glues a horn tip to a bowstave.

Until now, has he ever known real happiness? When Alyce was born, aye, but otherwise?

He has enough hard-earned wisdom that he doesn't again ask Ilotte to marry him.

On an evening when he's peacefully fletching arrows by candlelight, a skill Dunstan taught him years ago, and she spinning wool given her in gratitude by Walter, he says, "These arrows are for Samuel Cat-Skinner—pity the lord's rabbits."

"He passed me yesterday on m' way to Lucy's. Afore he come to this life, he were a carrion crow. Haukyn, did you have a place to run to when them like Samuel 'n' Ivo crowded you?"

He's never told her about his hideaway, partly, he supposes, from shame that he needed it. Frowning, he winds hemp around trimmed feathers and the ash shaft. "I have a place. I'll show you on the morrow after I finish weeding Da's south field. For every Samuel and Ivo, there's a Solomon and a Walter."

"A Haukyn also," she says a touch smugly, and whirls her spindle.

They walk through the woods to the oak tree the next day, having left Alyce with Edmund and the twins. "I had a tunnel into the midst of this clump of blackthorn," he says. "Hawthorn used to grow here, tis mostly smothered now. When I came home from the war, I cut my way into the tunnel again and bellied through it to the room I'd made, a small room, rimmed with flintstone. As a boy, I was in terror of Ivo, and this my place of safety."

"Blackthorns...remember m' vow to her o' the criss-crossed blackthorns that never would I marry?" She grips his sleeve. "Can we cut into it now? I needs a place I can run to."

"You have me, Ilotte, do you not feel safe with me?"

"Tis Ma's strangeness come upon me...please, Haukyn."

"Warn me if you see anyone...when I first found this place, I used to feel someone watching me." He takes out his knife. "Blackthorn suckers overnight. It would have been a froth of bloom a while ago, and in autumn the berries will be the blue-black of your eyes."

He walks back and forth until he thinks he's found the place, pulls his hood up, and lies belly to the ground, his hands soon bleeding, a litter of spiked twigs and bramble marking his passage. Then the space opens up, high enough that by cutting more branches he can crouch. "Can you follow me in?"

She wriggles through the tunnel, muttering as her skirt catches, then she's kneeling beside him and looking around. She whispers, "Them stones, did you put 'em there?"

"Aye."

"Hold me, Haukyn."

He lies on his side and draws her down beside him. "Keep your knees bent," and he too is whispering.

"You were wise to have this place."

The strangeness has gone from her eyes. He smiles into them. "If we wouldn't be impaled by blackthorns, I'd swive you."

She giggles, the little-girl giggle he first heard in the river's pool. "You be a right coward."

"Oh? A coward am I, me and my tarse?" He twitches her skirt up, his braies are undone, and he's slipped inside her. "If I thrust, dear Ilotte, that branch by your shoulder will snag you worse than I have you snagged."

She giggles again and pushes her hips against his. "I got you snagged too."

"Forever and always."

"There's times you steals the breath from m' body, Haukyn," she says unsteadily, "'n' this be one of 'em."

"My hideway a true sanctuary now."

She lies still in his arms. Then, cramped and cold, they crawl face forward into the light of day.

...green of May's leaves...

Edmund can tell when a man and woman are in accord, in bed and out; it was thus with him and Hawise for many years. Hawise... his grief unassuaged, its emptiness and heaviness immovable, and any attempts to marshal words that might bring consolation come to naught. She haunts his daytime hours, yet he never, to his sorrow, dreams of her, even though he keeps her chemise under his pillow. Her scent gone from it...*green of May's leaves, green of her eyes.* He chides himself for self-pity. He tries to eat for Ralf's sake, to be cheerful for Gil's.

Haukyn's newfound happiness is a like distant beacon, one he helped set afire, and what better proof than Haukyn whistling as he digs for the roots of ragwort in Edmund's fields? Ilotte now laughs at her mistakes on her slate; when she leaves to go home, she kisses him on his scarred cheek. Yet she has not succeeded, and he dare not ask her if she's tried, in ridding the vill of rebellion, Haukyn, he's certain, its leader. On a clear night with a thin moon, Saul and Mauld busy with a brawl between Coopers and Haywards—a brawl raucous with threats but, as it happens, bloodless—someone scythes in the lord's meadow an over-sized representation of tarse and balls, considerable trampling of the hay the regrettable result; two dawns later, the cook finds the barn's latest litter of kittens strangled and afloat in the manor's well. Bertran's smile, according to the cook, deserts him when he fails to attach Haukyn to either occurrence.

He, Edmund, was naive to think that harmony on Haukyn's mattress would quell his restless spirit...*fervid for freedom, rabid for rebellion.* He won't inscribe those palsied comparisons on his slate, a waste of good chalk.

As Haukyn douses head and shoulders in his father's rain barrel the next day after weeding the south field, Edmund says against his better judgement, "When will the banns be announced for you and Ilotte?"

Haukyn peers at him through the water sluicing his face. "Never."

His tone doesn't encourage questions. "Why not?"

"You'll have to ask her."

"Tis clear there is great affection betwixt you, and Alyce happy to have a mother. Leyrwite a waste of good coin when vows on the church steps would put an end to it."

His son's wet face hardens. "The three of us are happy, Father, isn't that enough?"

Father... A demon in Edmund compels him to continue. "Yet you still spread rebellion against manor and lord, Haukyn, and naught but grief will come of it. I beg you, be content with what you have. Happiness comes to us too rarely and is to be treasured."

"You are as deaf to me as Annabel was, God rest her soul."

Haukyn strides away, anger in every line of his body. *What verse would you put to that exchange, Edmund, you old fool?*

When Ilotte arrives for her lesson the next afternoon, he teaches her a number of new words, *leyrwite*, *banns*, and *marriage*, and waits for her reaction. Her voice stilted, she says, "You wonder why I won't marry Haukyn. Your son have my undying fealty, you must be content with that. Now, why be there an *i* in *marriage*?"

Under cover of darkness that same night, a dead rabbit from the lord's warren is delivered, skinned, to each of the indigent in Flintbourne, and by the time the news leaks to the manor after Sunday Mass, not a rabbit's paw is to be found in any pot in the vill.

...pride, that mortal sin...

Ilotte curled into him, Haukyn wakens light of heart morning after morning, rain on the thatch or sun chinking through the shutters, weeding or scything to be done, a bowstave to be shaped, no matter, happiness is his, *to hold and to have until my life's end*, a vow he's heard from more than one man on the church steps. Ilotte had told him about the *i* in *marriage*, he humbled to realize he is the only one to whom she's revealed the horrors of her childhood.

Once again he must make peace with his father.

Rain is dripping from the eaves, there'll be no mowing of hay today. He coaxes her awake, and after they have coupled with the lazy sensuality that befits a grey day, she says, "M' monthlies've stopped, you didn't notice?"

"Nay." He clutches her, chest to breast. "Are you with child?"

"'Tis early to tell, but aye. Twill be a boy, I knows that, though how I knows, don't ask, t'ain't m' strangeness." With a shyness rare to her, she drops her eyes. "Be you happy?"

"I could not be happier. But you?"

"A brother for Alyce, a son for you 'n' me, never did I think I would be so blessed."

Alyce wanders in, sleepy-eyed, and curls up on the covers between them. "Can a man die of happiness?" Haukyn says to no one in particular, and closes his eyes.

Rust barking, a banging on the door, a harsh voice overriding the dog's snarls, "Open up!"

His mood shattered, Haukyn grabs for braies, hose, and shirt, Ilotte for chemise and skirt. "Wait," he shouts, "and tell me your business."

"Poll tax. Two shillings owed by this household."

Through the nearest shutter he sees seven men, Tirrell to one side looking grim: this must be the royal commission against which Sir Geoffrey had warned him. The man who banged on the door is unknown to him, his face brutish as a boar's.

He opens the door and, yawning, walks toward the rain barrel.

"Hold!"

Haukyn smiles amiably. "'Tis now against common law for a man to wash his face in the morning?"

"'Tis agin the law to incite rebellion. As you done in this vill."

Another wide yawn before Haukyn splashes copious water over his head and combs his fingers through his hair. "You make an early start," he says to a man who has just dismounted from a chestnut mare, a man unknown to him who wears his undoubted authority easily. "Today is the day in June, so we are told, that the birds cease their singing. Did you notice how our reed warblers below the meadow disobey that dictum?"

"I am the sheriff of your shire, John James, and he who roused you is our serjeant-at-arms. You speak well for a serf."

"You do not bellow to prove your office."

A half-smile flashes across the man's features. "We are here to list all lay persons in the vill above the age of fifteen and gather the tax from any who have evaded payment."

"John of Gaunt has made peace with Scotland. Thomas of Woodstock's campaign in Brittany is over. Why would Parliament pursue a tax intended for two campaigns that no longer exist?"

"You do not decide government policy, Haukyn of Flintbourne."

"Policy should take into account the effect of heavy taxation on those who, unjustly, bear the brunt of it."

"I am not here to debate but to collect."

Alyce sidles through the door. "Da, a shiny red horse! Like Trefoil."

Haukyn scoops her up. "My daughter, as you see, Master Sheriff, is under fifteen. I'll pay for Ilotte, who lives with me. But why should *I* pay?"

The serjeant-at-arms says, "We are to seize any who oppose us or rebel against us and imprison them until we make provision for their punishment." He sneers at Haukyn; his nose is hairy as a sow's snout. "Newbury's gaol be the nearest. Underground. Shackles at ankles and wrists. Farthing a day food allowance, not enough enough to feed a rat."

Underground...what if something happened to Ilotte, she pregnant with their son, while he was confined—shackled, even—in total darkness, he couldn't bear it. His knees turn to water and the serjeant's sneer widens.

Alyce, her voice quavering. "Da?"

Groping for his pride, that mortal sin, Haukyn speaks only to the sheriff. "The lord of our manor, Sir Gardrad by name, imprisoned me unlawfully years ago, my wife dying and no release til after her funeral. I cannot risk such calamity again. So you have won, sir, and will have your shilling. Do you gain pleasure from this victory?"

"Fetch the money and we will leave you in peace."

Inside, Ilotte has built up the fire and is cooking oats. Haukyn lowers Alyce to the rushes, stalks to his purse, and extracts the coins. One by one, he drops them into the sheriff's palm. "For Haukyn of Flintbourne and for Ilotte, formerly of Hungerford. Your clerk will record our names and full payment."

As the inoffensive little man beside Tirrell leans his parchment on the dry bench under the eaves and writes, the sheriff regards the meadows, the rushes, and the river. "You have a most pleasant prospect here."

He's not ready to relent to an official, a royal official, despite the man's commendable patience. "If I can afford to keep it."

"Forge next," the serjeant says. "Ivo and Sim in arrears."

"I wish you Godspeed," Haukyn says with more than a touch of sarcasm.

His the first house and the serjeant will make it known to everyone in the vill that their leader in rebellion has meekly passed over his coin. He strides around the byre, through the orchard, and dives into the woods. A terror of the dark and he's become traitor to all he believes, he's paid a tax that has no justification other than the exercise of power, he's humiliated himself in front of a loutish serjeant and an admirable sheriff. He pounds his fists against the wet trunk of a hornbeam, wishing it were the serjeant's bulbous nose; he kicks it, grunting, and the sole accomplishment of this fit of rage is to leave blood slithering down the bark. Do all men have a weak link in the chain of their manhood?

By the time he goes back to the house, the rain has ended. Rust is watching Alyce as she carefully places pieces of flint around her little garden, where parsley, onions, and feathery-topped carrots are growing. *Just so did I outline my hideaway with flint from the river,* Haukyn thinks, *and may she never need a place to hide, as I did.*

Indoors, his oats are over-cooked. He shovels them in. Ilotte eyes his knuckles and says in a voice far from friendly, "You paid that tax today 'cause of Annabel."

"In part."

"She still be your wife."

His spoon stops halfway to his mouth. "She's long dead."

"That don't make no difference."

The Terce bell not yet rung and already too much crammed into the day. "I'd take you for wife. As you know."

"Second wife."

Contempt is it, or bitterness? "Annabel married only those parts of me that fitted comfortably in her life and her bed, Ilotte. You encompass all of me."

Her sloe-black eyes fasten on his face. "You didn't give in to that sheriff 'cause of her?"

He rubs his sore finger joints. "The manor gaol had but a slit of light, each day and night endless, and you heard what the serjeant said about Newbury's gaol—underground, shackles, that same endless night, and how could I leave you and Alyce, it could have been for weeks, for months. So I gave in, I surrendered, I paid the tax. The mere thought of gaol made of me less than a man." He gazes at the splits in his flesh. "And there you have it. A rebel? Nay. A coward? Aye."

Her hand covers his. "The oath I made 'gainst marriage, it were rooted in fear. You ain't done with rebellion, Haukyn, 'n' never would I call you coward." Her voice wavers. "Took me on, didn't you?"

"A brave man indeed," he says, his own voice none too steady.

It takes a certain bravery to pick up his buckets and walk to the well. Catherine the cooper's wife is there before him. "Shame on you, Haukyn, for paying that cursed tax."

"I'm of no use to the vill if I'm mouldering in Newbury's gaol," he says and lowers the first bucket into the well's dark circle.

"Blundred, Neuton, Giles, the look on their gobs when they heard you passed over your shillings without clouting serjeant nor sheriff."

He hauls the bucket upward and lowers the second one. "The vill is free to choose a new leader."

She sighs, for she is in essence a fair woman. "It'd be worse 'n electing a new reeve, a task no man wants."

"I can fight bailiff and lord, Catherine, but not the king's sheriff. His the power of the Crown, unalterable by any serf."

"Move over, I got to fill me own buckets."

Because his are overfilled, water sloshes shoes and hose.

Once Ilotte falls asleep that night, Haukyn leaves the house under cover of a drumming rain and crosses the ford to the manor. Ladder to the granary wall, climb up, haul the ladder up behind him, lay it against the tiles, clamber up the roof, hook the ladder to the other side, slide down, and if he breaks arms, legs, or skull, the vill will know him as a fool but not a coward.

The drag on his back when he lowers the ladder to the cobbled yard, the hard grip of his sore fingers as, rung by rung, he climbs down. In the granary he lifts the lids from two barrels of wheat and rolls both barrels outside. Panting, he tips them over. Within the manor, a dog half-heartedly barks. He freezes. Rain pelts his face and body. Up the ladder, heart thrumming, and by a miracle of recklessness and God's own luck he finds himself back on the ground outside the walls. He takes the first baulk up the hill; his footprints won't show on the grass.

With the door propped open, he carries the ladder indoors. Stealthily he closes the door, builds up the fire, rubs the ladder with a dry cloth, and Ilotte sleeps through all this, another miracle. After he wrings out his wet clothes, he lays them over the bench near the fire and feeds it generously.

At dawn she joins him. "I woke in the night," she says, "where was you?"

He grins. "You'll find out. Shake my hose over the fire, would you, they're not quite dry, while I turn the ladder."

"Ah," she says, "I must've been mistook, you was in bed with me the night through."

By the time Bertran and Mauld arrive, the dry ladder is back in the byre and his dry clothes are on his back. Questions are hurled, accusations are thrown, and he as innocent as a hatchling.

Later that day, he walks up the hill to his father's. "I ask you to forgive my loss of temper the last time we talked," he says stiffly.

"I should not have said what I did. You and I are like the river, Haukyn, its current smooth, its breakage into foam when it meets flint. But the current? Why, tis love, from father to son and son to father."

"So we are in amity?"

"Til we hit the next flint, aye."

He chuckles. "I bring you good news, Da. Ilotte is with child, you will be grandfather again...I only wish Ma knew."

Edmund's smile is as wide as if Hawise were standing beside him. "Good news indeed! And I doubt that Heaven can keep your mother's nose out of the vill's affairs."

"She'll know that I paid the poll tax then."

"You were wise to part with your shillings. Royal power was grossly misused in this case, against serfs most of all."

And then it hits him. "Da," he says, dazed, "Da, Ilotte says she'll bear a son. She'll never marry me. Our son will be born bastard, he'll be born freeman!"

"So he will…a freeman you will teach to read and write. Maybe he'll bring about the changes you long for that I fear are beyond the two of us."

"Would you decry it if he did?"

"Nay, Haukyn, I would not."

Haukyn says huskily, "The flint in the river's current would have to be bigger than this hill for it to part you and me."

Well into June, a letter is delivered to Haukyn's door by Walter atte Mede. "A passing merchant from London," he says. "Tol' me it had your name on it."

Haukyn unfolds the creased parchment. "Tis from Sir Geoffrey, in Essex. If there's news of rebellion, I'll come to the alehouse later."

The letter is long and written in haste, he struggling to make sense of it. Men from sixteen Essex vills turned violent toward a poll tax commissioner in Brentwood; many more rebels have sworn oaths of loyalty; in neighbouring Kent, the same story, riots in Dartford on the fourth day of June, assemblies, and uprisings. "London is next," wrote Sir Geoffrey, "from both north and south of the Thames. I am to spread the word in Essex, but if I go to London, I will leave news of my whereabouts with Javyd. Godspeed."

He reads it again, the parchment shaking a little in his grip. Here is his chance. He can gain courage from other rebels, talk strategy— men from sixteen vills acting together, how can that be? Ilotte will understand and look after Alyce in his absence. He won't stay long, he can't, for within the next fortnight his hay will need cutting. His. He'll not cut one stem of grass that belongs to Sir Gardrad.

Ilotte is thinning seedlings in the garden. He reads the letter to her, hearing the excitement in his voice. "I could leave early on the morrow, be in London in two days."

She's holding two small leaves on the thinnest of stems. Her words come slow, her head bent. "Once there be honey in m' hive, I must guard against robber bees who'd attack the hive to steal the honey 'n' kill m' bees. Wasps 'n' hornets too, them the more vicious." Only then does she look up. "Don't go, Haukyn, don't go."

"Is this the strangeness again, your mother's legacy?"

"Tis a heaviness in m' chest. I can't explain it, only feel it."

"Ilotte, I need to go, you the one who said I'd be rebel again. We must protect our vill, our hives, from the real robbers—tax collectors and the Commons."

"Then go," she says and drops the seedling.

The next morning, early, her mood unaltered, he holds her hard against his body. Resistance, aye, he recognizes her resistance. "I'll stay out of harm's way," he says, "for naught will keep me from you and our unborn son."

"I can't see the outcome," she says in true anguish. "Nor you won't let me keep m' hive safe."

Trefoil stamps her hoof. He kisses Ilotte, swings his leg over the saddle, and trots toward the ford.

Hour by hour, Haukyn's journey passes without mishap and Ilotte's warning retreats to the back of his mind. By None on the second day, the Feast of Corpus Christi, he's ridden past Temple Bar along the brown, tide-turgid Thames, across the filthy Fleet River, saddled by a prison, and arrives at Ludgate with its statues of ancient English kings. The gatekeeper says genially, "You be in luck, city gates open again. Vermin from Kent come across the bridge, vermin from Essex through Aldgate. Good King Richard with his court safe in the Tower."

"I come from Windsor's shire."

"Ain't heard o' no rebels that way."

The bells of None are chiming city-wide. The bells of freedom, Haukyn thinks, and no longer distant. He rides along Bowyers Row, past the guild to which he'll never be admitted, and through the vast courtyard of St. Paul's, with its noisy vendors and its tall spire reaching to Heaven, then takes Watling Street to Budge Row. Petronilla welcomes him warmly, providing oats for Trefoil and a chicken pie for him. "Javyd asleep. Gossip says the rebels be orderly. No looting, no plunder, 'n' they'll pay the going rate for their provisions."

"I need to see them for myself. I'll go on foot, Petronilla."

She pats his sleeve. "Be watchful, I beg you."

On Thames Street, slop of water against the wharves, and to the west the flag-tipped tower of Baynard's Castle and the close-packed houses where many of London's Flemings live. Smoke hangs over the river's south bank. He meets a wherryman, Crop-Ear by name, who says with gusto, "Kentishmen broke into all three Southwark prisons, released every soul in 'em. Destroyed the house o' the warden, wrecked the Clink, oh, they had themselves a time, nor it ain't over yet. That smoke to the sou'west, that be Lambeth Palace, him what owns it be our chancellor Sudbury, Archbishop o' bloody Canterbury, up to his neck in that bollocks of a poll tax. Scurried to the Tower, didn't he, to hide b'hind the king's skirts. Kent running loose in the city? There'll be trouble a-plenty."

Up to Cheapside, the clock on St. Pancras chiming four bells, the street a jostle of men, most of them russet-clad like himself, armed with pitchforks and swords. Londoners lean out of their windows, yelling greetings, mangy curs slink down the alleyways. Jubilation in Haukyn's heart, and on the faces of the invaders. When a peasant stops to piss in the gutter, he asks, "Are you from Kent or Essex?"

"Essex. Black Notley. Kent have gone ahead of us."

"Are you here to bring the king down?"

"Nay! Essex 'n' Kent, we holds with King Richard 'n' the true commons—us serfs. Parliament, bishops, lords, more 'n enough to take on, wouldn't you say?"

A good-natured salute and he rejoins the crowd, a crowd as orderly as Petronilla had suggested, though Haukyn smells smoke drifting from the north. He searches the faces for Sir Geoffrey, but to his disappointment, doesn't find him. Hawkers are shouting, hens squawking, a donkey braying, the sounds of every day; yet beneath the bustle, he's aware of a silence, a waiting for no one knows what.

He makes his way to the taps at the conduit and fills his waterskin, Londoners mingling with rebels, then aims for the Fleet River through the stench and entrails of the Shambles. From the prison on the Fleet's banks, roisterous shouting, crack and clatter of stone; he keeps to the shadows and waits. Hammers, mauls, mallets—did the rebels bring them or Londoners supply them?—and then to yells of triumph he sees a group of prisoners shuffle into the sunlight, their faces furtive, disbelieving, fearful, or lit with joy, all ghost-pale. Cheers, fists raised, pitchforks waved, as felons, murderers, and debtors are greeted as though dukes of the realm, such a celebration of freedom that, notwithstanding their crimes, he wishes he could raise a jug of ale. Prisoners freed from Southwark and now from London, and did he look as bad when he was freed from the manor gaol?

His nose wrinkles. Smoke, and closer. He leaves his post to follow Fleet Street to the Strand, that wide street lined by the houses of the rich, the street that leads to Westminster, seat of power and of the Church. Shops burning, their roofs torn off, a splendid house in mid-street on fire—is this Kent's work? He hurries past the Bishops' Inns because he sees more smoke, this rising from the Sauvoye, palace of the king's uncle, Gaunt John, a duke loathed by Londoners and rebels alike, the palace he visited before Annabel died. High stone walls, the gates askew on their hinges. He edges through them, and an uprising that, until now, has seemed tidily contained, is wrenched apart.

The lawns are littered with the corpses of keepers and guards, beheaded or axed to death, one body draped over a clipped hedge, the head perched atop. He stares at the head in repugnance, unable to drag his eyes away. Were he man enough he'd lift it, with due reverence, to the ground—and knows he cannot. He steps backward. His boot slips in a dark pool of blood, bodies strewn around him… *uncounted, uncountable the bodies*…one of the nearest but a lad, the others men who were doing their duty, guarding their lord's property just as French serfs tried to guard their crops…*a field of charred barley, a horse who wants to run for her life*…and his hands cold as icicles in winter.

He has to move, he can't just stand here. Close to the river, smoke and flames billow from some of the palace's smashed windows, objects large and small flying through other windows, while outside, luridly lit rebels batter furniture and gold vessels: clamour inside and out. He skirts the blood-soaked grass, the byres, stables, and fishpond, and walks past the men with their mallets, walks into the great hall, down a corridor, up a wide, elegant staircase, its newel posts and balustrades splintered, its tapestries torn from the wall, smouldering. He cannot prevent this destruction, and why would he try?

A man grizzled of beard, broad of chest, surges into sight carrying an armload of gold goblets, bejewelled and softly gleaming. Over his shoulder, menace in his voice, he says, "Throw 'em in the river, toss 'em out the window or down the sewers. No robbery, no plunder. Any guilty o' theft we hangs from the rafters."

Farther down a lofty hallway a bedchamber, the windows overlooking the river, rebels firing the last of the carved benches and silver plate through their shattered panes. A voice cries, "The wine cellar, tis full!" and some twenty men shove past Haukyn. He enters the room, empty now, deciding from the toss of rich velvet garments that it must be the duke's chamber. A doublet embroidered with gold leopards has been anchored to the wall by a dagger, the haft where the duke's heart would be. A ruby, in smithereens, glitters on the floorboards. The gouged, wood-panelled walls have caught fire, flames licking at the ceiling, the heraldry on the headboard also afire, and when he runs a finger over the handle of a ceremonial sword plunged through the mattress, he springs back, so hot is the metal. Chairs, benches, and chests axed, sheets slashed, and if John of Gaunt himself were here, he too would have been torn to shreds, burned alive, no fate too foul.

On the other side of a vast bed and all too close to a lit torch, a book has been flung to the floor. He picks it up and leafs through it. Never has he seen such a book, the colours leap out at him, jewels of another kind, leaves and flowers interwoven, little figures on horseback, all of them gold-bedecked. Such beauty shouldn't burn. He looks over his shoulder, thrusts the book under his belt, tugs his tunic down, and scurries from the room, hood over his mouth against smoke and heat.

To his right, like a great sunburst, flames burst through the floor. From another doorway a man screeches, "I weren't stealing, I were going to—"

"Toss him in the fire."

Frantic pleas for mercy, boots scrabbling on the floor, four rebels dragging the man toward that inferno. "Nay," Haukyn cries, too late, one hard push and a horrible, prolonged shrieking. There isn't a serf who hasn't scorched fingers at the hearth, but to be clad in flame, smell the stench of your own burning...*Roye, flames rising to the heavens, the screams of the trapped, the smoke of human flesh... You're in London, Haukyn, and you'd best get out of here unless you want to die like that other poor sod.* He races for the stairs, they too ablaze. Throat and eyes smarting, he keeps to the bannister that has not yet caught, takes the stairs two by two, and in a leap he couldn't have made in cold blood, lands on the charred flooring beyond the greedy lick of fire. Down the corridor, it thick with smoke, hood over his mouth, and he's back in the great hall where the smoke is thinner, the wide doorway blessedly open. He staggers outside and leans against a pear tree, its sap oozing from deep blows of an axe. Bent double, he gasps for air.

The duke's book digs into his belly.

He eases upright. His chest hurts. Waterskin, nigh empty, against his hip. He drains it. The water cools his throat, and only then does he look around. Outbuildings afire, a pretty orchard chopped to the ground, gardens trampled, much of this, he'd swear, the work of Londoners.

From his left, beyond a thicker hedge, a sudden boil of smoke laced with flame and a screaming—tisn't human, that sound, and he runs around the hedge, a stable, *Jesu*, horses. Not a soul in sight, the bar on the door bent outward, the lock smashed. He rushes inside, eight stalls, thrash of hoofs and terrified neighing.

Racing from stall to stall, he unbars the chest-high doors, unclips the tooled leather harnesses. Two horses charge through the door, six too fear-struck to move. He searches for Ilotte's patience when there is no time for it, speaks softly, urges another horse out. The fourth kicks him against the wall, teeth bared, the whites of its eyes reflecting fire. He escapes, limping, circles the fifth, a chestnut mare, whacks her rump, and with a snort of terror she runs for the opening. The flames are nearer, the great stack of hay in the far corner has ignited, the waste of it, the terrible waste. Into the next stall, a black gelding, shivering, head down, its coat streaked with sweat. Trying to subdue panic, he says, "Come with me, come now, all will be well," and it follows him out of the stall. Palm to its backside and it bolts through the door. Three more left, the heat intense, a roil of smoke, again he jams his hood across his mouth, drum of hoofs from the frenzied horse that kicked him, so he runs to the end stall through a haze of sparks. "Come now, come along!" As one of the rafters collapses, he hauls on the harness, his whole weight behind it, by some instinct lets go before he's trampled underfoot, and they're both outside and the roof falls and he blocks his ears to the screams of death.

He saved six of eight. Six against thousands starved, oh Modge... He stumbles over the grass and collapses on the ground. When, eventually, he looks up, the stable is engulfed, its end beams wreathed in fire. The six horses have herded themselves against the highest of the hedges, the one that marks the boundary of Gaunt John's estate. He can do nothing more for them.

Sparks have burned holes through his tunic. A constellation of black-edged holes in his hose. His hands are blistered, the skin split open. Quietly, insistently, pain burgeons in his palms, in the thigh that was kicked by a horse mad with fear.

He's done with rebellion.

Time passes before Haukyn is able to get to his feet. Swaying like a cog on the open sea, he makes his way through the duke's gate onto the Strand. Eyes straight ahead, he tries to block his ears to the crackle of flames and the shouts of the mob. He's in England, not France. This is rebellion, not war. Though, he wonders, is there a difference? Englishman against Englishman, he never thought he'd witness such cruelty and destruction on his own soil. The true price of freedom, and he an ignorant villager with his head in the clouds?

Although Ludgate is wide open, his passage is blocked by two half-starved men dressed in rags. One holds out wrists scarred by manacles. "Left m' chains on Greyfriars altar. Rebels got us out o' Newgate. If you be one of 'em, God's blessing on you, sir."

"I'm but a serf seeking freedom."

"Freedom be bread and a hand unshackled to lift it to yer mouth."

Freedom is your harness unclipped and an open doorway through which you can gallop.

"Don't let them catch you again," he says and keeps going. A rabble on Cheapside, the baying that means blood, then Watling. On impulse, he turns north on Soper Lane and pushes open the door of St. Pancras Church, the interior dimly lit, red light over the altar, flicker of votive candles. He kneels at the back, his spirit, more so than usual, questing for some sense that the Almighty knows of his existence...and, as usual, returning to him empty. His thoughts crowd in on him. He knows what men are capable of in wartime, yet he'd never pictured rebellion's violence, its dark side, he'd been too busy scaling the granary roof, pouring water on the manor's bridge, cajoling the cook to move the salt barrel to Osmond's latrine—a lad's tricks, a boy's. His oath as the vill's leader in Flintbourne's church, *I will do my best*...over and again, he had negated his own words. What do those words mean now, on London's bloodstained streets?

His burns are stinging.

On Budge Row, Javyd, scrubbed and clean, opens to Haukyn's knock. It takes a lot to shock Javyd, he must look ghastly. Petronilla says, with a bleat of distress, "I'll heat water for you, Haukyn, and I got goose grease for them burns."

"Man called Tydd, one street over, he sells garments," Javyd says, "I'll be back," and Haukyn, without the will to argue, is very soon washed and newly clad, his burns salved, Petronilla stirring eggs over the fire. The book has been laid with care on the bench.

Javyd says, "Tydd tol' me 'bout the goings-on all day, bloodshed, fires, beheadings on Cheapside. Our merchants, lawyers, 'n' councillors must be shitting themselves, the mayor too. All the more work for me." He wipes eggs from his chin. "Gaunt John be in Scotland 'n' best stay there if he don't want his head separate from his body."

"The two armies of Essex and Kent arriving outside London on the same day, one to the north of the city, one to the south, that took planning and discipline, Javyd. Gaunt John could learn from them."

"He ain't into learning. Now, where'd you get them burns?"

Haukyn describes, as briefly as he can, the destruction of the Sauvoye and the escape of the stabled horses. Petronilla gasps. "You could've been killed, us not knowing where or how."

"I was careful."

"That book weren't in no stables," Javyd says.

"The duke's bedchamber. I couldn't leave it to burn."

"Tis pretty," Petronilla says. "I got clean hands, c'n I pick it up?"

He watches as, with great care—nay, with reverence—she studies it. "See these pictures where the women be on their knees with angels watching 'em? Tis a book o' prayer," she whispers and crosses herself.

He'd seen it merely as an object of beauty. "Don't show it to anyone, or speak of it."

Insulted, she says, "Course not."

Javyd says with a touch of impatience, "Esssexmen amassed at St. Katherine's, near the Tower. We could walk there, Haukyn, see if the king'll parley with 'em. I'll not be working this night, the city like tinder. A bit o' piled-up shite might stop it catching."

Is he, Haukyn, to cower indoors the rest of the day? "We could," he says.

The city is quiet as they trudge toward Aldgate, pass beneath the rooms that arch overhead, and walk ever closer to the Tower's turrets and the noisy, restive crowd outside its moat. The Tower, so says Javyd, is a fortress so stout, so strong, it cannot be breached—wide moat, crenellated walls, watchtowers, the solid bulk of the White

Tower rising above it all—and somewhere therein King Richard is hiding from an army of rebels, many of whom, Haukyn knows, are serfs like himself. A heartening thought.

Behind the rebels stands the hospital of St. Katherine's, whose mandate is to feed the poor. In a flash of anger, Haukyn wonders if a boy-king who lives in luxury gains merit from its closeness.

Javyd says, "From atop the White Tower, our good king'll have seen the flames o' Sauvoye 'n' the priory, heard the screaming 'n' screeching from Cheapside, he'll be afeard o' Londoners as much as rebels, he'll—"

A great roar of anger erupts from the throng. Javyd grabs the sleeve of a man clutching a pennon. "What be happening?"

"King hisself come out on the ramparts, we tol' him we wants the traitors in the Tower who levied that tax 'n' we wants charters o' manumission for every last one of us. We jus' got his answer." His voice fills with contempt. "Write down our grievances, send 'em to him, 'n' he'll remedy what profits him, his lords, his councillors, and his kingdom. Pardon fer our felonies 'n' now go home."

"To the city, find the traitors!" a rebel shouts, and the shouts rise to the heavens: "To London, to London! Behead the lawyers! Us'll make our own justice!"

Essexmen storm up the road that leads to Aldgate. Bloodthirsty Essex has left, Haukyn thinks, and stubborn Essex is staying, because the real traitors, Sudbury and Hales, archbishop and treasurer, are sequestered in the Tower. "I've heard enough," he says.

"Naught we c'n do here. M' neighbour be an alewife, and last Tuesday I wheeled a barrel home. We wouldn't want it to go sour, would we, 'n' m' sister don't like me frequenting taverns."

"A mug of ale would go down well."

"Three'd go down better," Javyd says, and five mugs later, Haukyn tumbles into bed.

When Haukyn surfaces the next morning, unthinkingly he flexes his hands; the pain cuts through the fog of too much ale and his brain jerks to wakefulness. The law with its long words wouldn't help serfs, and coin, of which serfs have too little, could not. So rebellion has shifted to destruction and destruction to brutality; freedom becomes the freedom to kill.

Is this why Ilotte warned him against riding to London? Did she foresee what could happen—the violence, the cruelty—she who had known both since her ninth winter? He pulls the down pillow over his head. Cling of her wet chemise in the Kennet's pool, the lavender scent of her skin and hair, sloe eyes that have seen too much in her short life and he can't spill his seed on a mattress not his own. He turns over, daylight seeping through the shutters, clomp of footsteps on the stairs, and the door flies open. "Move yer lazy bones, Haukyn. Six bells and word's out from our alderman that every man twixt fifteen 'n' sixty must go to Mile End—on pain o' life 'n' limb, if you please—to meet with the king. Nilla's putting eggs 'n' sourdough together 'n' filling our waterskins."

Meet the king? Why? He stumbles down the stairs, tucking his shirt into his braies, uses the latrine copiously and cold water sparingly. Petronilla insists on wrapping his hands with freshly greased cloths; the sourdough goes in his pouch, the waterskin to his belt, and he manages to get his shoes on the right feet. "Powerful ale," he mutters.

"Best alewife in London. I made a study of it. Don't fuss, Nilla, I'll look after him."

Up Soper Lane to Cheapside and east toward Aldgate. Commotion ahead. Javyd wriggles and pushes his way, and of necessity Haukyn also uses elbows and knees, blocking his ears to curses, his belly queasy from the press of rebels who've been sleeping rough and, like himself, drinking too much.

Closer now, he sights the colourful banners of the king's knights on their caparisoned horses. Astride a magnificent black destrier, a slim, erect figure, as long-nosed as his uncle, John of Gaunt: Richard, England's king, arrayed in purple cloth embroidered with gold leopards, a narrow gold crown circling his fair hair, and Haukyn feels the pull of fealty, the age-old veneration for a ruler who is sacred, anointed by God.

Richard and his attendants are struggling to work their way through the crowd. Short of using the flats of their swords they're as stuck as he is. Javyd squeezes between two corpulent monks, Haukyn following suit, until he's as close to a king as he'll ever be, aware now of a disturbing mix of reverence and rage. Reverence, when Gaunt John led an army into ambushes and starvation? Rage for a young king's inconceivable wealth?

Richard's black destrier jerks its head. A rebel has grabbed its reins; he's shouting, his words almost indistinguishable in the hubbub, though Haukyn catches *revenge* and *traitor*. His own words rise above the din. "Stop! Tis our king you assault," and fleetingly— so fleetingly he might have imagined it—the king's eyes meet his. Richard's lips move, nor does he look frightened, although he should. His assailant shakes his fist and bludgeons his way through the mob.

They inch forward. Under Aldgate again and a leisurely tramp to Mile End, he and Javyd still close to the king's party and stepping in horse shit; Trefoil will be chafing at her second day in a stall, tis as well she can't see him in these open fields under a clear sky. More men than he's ever seen in one place, more than in John of Gaunt's army that left Calais on a day of pale sunshine.

They've come to a halt. A banner snaps in the breeze. He's near enough to see the three men at the forefront of the rebels; then they must have knelt for they are out of view, although still, he hopes, within hearing. In the silence that falls, he can hear the punch of his heart.

The king signals that the men may rise, his words, their words, his again, the demands simple and enormous. Freedom forever, for all tenants, their heirs, and their land. Freedom to work when and for whom they wish. Rents and commutation fixed at four pence an acre. An end to serfdom, Haukyn thinks, dazed, and the king says, he hears him say it, "I am well agreed thereto."

Five words that will change lives from west to east, from north to south.

At the king's request, the rebels arrange themselves in two long rows. Haukyn pushes to the very front, listens as Richard states that clerks have been summoned to write letters patent with the Great Seal affixed, letters that will guarantee these freedoms; two or three men from each vill should wait to receive them. The rest of the rebels are to return home bearing the king's banners, and by so doing will be fully pardoned for any offences against the realm.

I will be a freeman, Haukyn thinks. *Alyce will be free. Everyone in our vill will be free, their children and their children's children, their land and their work. No longer can a lord—not even Sir Gardrad— demand fealty.*

He wants to cheer and shout and dance. Instead he stands decorously in line, for again the king is speaking, this time about traitors, granting the rebels the right to seize all traitors in the kingdom and bring them to him, where they will be tried according to the laws of the land.

With a gracious signal he dismisses them, wheels his destrier, and, accompanied by his party, rides away. Only then does Haukyn become aware that Javyd is tugging at his sleeve. "To the Tower, where the traitors abide, you heard what the king said. C'mon, Haukyn, hurry!"

"I must stay here to get a letter for our vill. I have to do this, Javyd, I have to, for the sake of my family and my neighbours. You go to the Tower. We'll meet at your sister's."

"You don't want the seizure o' Sudbury 'n' Hales?"

"I want freedom."

"A choice twixt parchment or blood? Scarce be a choice."

Haukyn says slowly, "I begin to think all parchments are written in blood."

"There be times I wonders 'bout you. Keep your knife sharp and your wits too, you hear me?"

Javyd barges into the horde marching to Aldgate behind the king. Others of the rebels are already heading east toward home, the king's banners flapping above their heads. The rest, like himself, are waiting while servants set up tables and tonsured scribes lay out quills, ink, and parchment, then start writing, line by line. As the rebels push forward, the scribe's leader says, "Wait! Until the king rides to Baynard's Castle, the Earl of Arundel cannot deliver the Great Seal to us."

Haukyn reins in his impatience. Tis the most worthwhile of waits, for no man the length and breadth of England can deny the Great Seal and the freedom it will confer.

On the flattened grass, Haukyn takes out his sourdough and egg. Did the violence, the killings, change the king's mind, or did he disregard the lure of his own power and listen, heart and mind, to his downtrod countrymen? He'll never know the answer. The letter answer enough, he thinks, realizes he's finished eating, and stands up. He's brushing the crumbs from his tunic when a familiar voice says, "Well met, Haukyn! Our young king has proven himself worthy of sacred anointment, has he not?"

"Sir Geoffrey!"

They clasp hands, as equals do. The knight says, "I'm glad I found you. I've no mind to see more beheadings, so I'm riding back to my manor once I have my letter. And you, what will you do?"

"I too wish for home."

"Has she married you?"

"She has not. After today, though, no more leyrwite."

Sir Geoffrey laughs. "Godspeed, Haukyn. May you father many children and fashion many bows."

"Your kindness in Bordeaux saved my life, sir. God's blessing on you and yours," Haukyn says. He watches the knight stride away to his place farther down the line and understands that not all fealty will end on this day.

The small rolls of parchment gradually accumulate until, well before the sun is at its zenith, a nobleman on a bay stallion canters up the slope surrounded by eight armoured guards. Wax is melted. The line of rebels shuffles forward until, finally, Haukyn is at its head. He says, "I am from the vill of Flintbourne in the shire of Berks. If possible, although I am not from Wiltshire, might I have a letter for Liddington too?"

Empty spaces have been left in letters already written. The scribe, whose scalp is turning red in the sun and who looks altogether bored, fills them in, rolls up the two parchments, pushes back from the table, and waits outside the circle of guards for the signal. When he returns, a wax impression of the Great Seal is fixed to each roll by a cord. He passes them over. "Next."

Haukyn walks away. On the seal, a slender-waisted king is seated on his throne, flanked by two adoring dogs and a pair of shields, King Richard himself, guarantor of an end to villeinage, a marvel beyond reckoning. The seal is indented, the king sunken in the red wax. Sunken, yet today his virtue and honour have been fully evident. With great care, Haukyn tucks the rolls in his pouch. He'll go straight to Budge Row, then leave the city.

He whistles ballads to a flock of lapwings, to a sky without a cloud in it, and at the fork in the road he bears south. Smoke drifts to his nostrils, a man darts down an alley, four others pound after him yelling *traitor*, their axes bloodstained, and worse is to come; as he approaches Grace Church, the fading shouts are surpassed by a sound like no other he's ever heard. He backs into the nook between two shopfronts, the caterwauling closer now, strident, triumphant, loathsome to the ears, and down the street comes a procession bearing on lifted poles—blessed Saviour, tis human heads. Aghast, he counts them. Nine in all, a red mitre teetering atop the one in the forefront, Sudbury, it has to be Sudbury, Archbishop of Canterbury, England's chancellor. So the Tower was not impregnable, and the head jammed on its pole behind the archbishop's must be that of Robert Hales, the country's infamous treasurer.

Urchins, beggars, rebels, Londoners, women among them, prance alongside, gleeful, ever closer, close enough now for Haukyn to see that the mitre is held in place by a single nail hammered into the archbishop's brain. His gorge rises and he fights it down, he'll not puke on a London street, yet he can't pull his eyes away, the image burns into his own brain. Sudbury's neck and face so hacked and gashed—years ago, his first attempt at cutting down a tree, sap leaking from multiple wounds, the tree still standing—and this a man. He cannot imagine the terror of it, the agony, and involuntarily crosses himself, only to pray that no one saw him.

The leaders of the procession turn down the street toward the bridge, where, by custom, the heads of traitors are mounted. Will the archbishop face the Chapel of St. Thomas Becket, also hacked to death? Was Javyd part of this hideous procession? And did it pass Baynard's Castle so the king could witness a revenge that mocked royal justice?

Must rebellion feed on hatred?

Hood over his face, he runs along the street of candlemakers, and the city surrounds him, aroused, dangerous as a pack of hounds in search of prey, and who decides what makes a traitor—gangs of Londoners, felons, and Kentish rebels crazed with bloodlust? The chiming he used to hear, of a distant bell, the chime of freedom, it was a pure sound, and beautiful, and he'd believed in it. He now knows that although he'd understood the wrongs of serfdom, he'd been woefully ignorant of the cost of righting them; he'd left as lightheartedly for London's revolt as he'd left for France's war, the disenchantment of each as shattering. What he's witnessed today is the true payment exacted for freedom, and he lacking the proper coin.

He has his two letters. He needs space, he needs the fields of home, he needs Ilotte and Alyce, and he's reached Javyd's door. He taps on it. "Tis I, Haukyn."

Petronilla opens the door, pulls him in, and closes it so fast it raps his heels. "Did you see m' brother?"

"He went to the Tower while I stayed at Mile End."

"He were here since then, but out he went again, though I railed at him, the stupid scut." Her breath catches on a sob. "Every Londoner with a grudge be out there with axe t' hand, 'n' there be merchants what owes Javyd good coin for cleaning their cesspits, that's where he'll be. Cornhill or north o' Cheapside or along Thames."

East, north, or south. He manages not to roll his eyes. Home and Ilotte will have to wait, he can't abandon Javyd. "Petronilla, I need to hide these letters, they promise manumission. Then I'll search for him."

"I got a chest with a lock, I keeps it under m' bed."

When she comes back, he fills his waterskin and accepts with gratitude more bread and a hunk of cheese. "Javyd knows the city as few others do, try not to worry," he says and leaves the house.

Cornhill is too close to the bridge and he has no appetite to cross Cheapside. He'll go south to Thames Street. He dodges down a malodorous alley toward the river. Baynard's Castle first, then back to the Vintry and Dowgate. A good plan until—tis like the sound of battle, screaming and shouting, weapons gouging flesh and bone. He rounds the corner. Londoners, Kentishmen, what matter, they've found the Flemings, they're hauling merchants from sanctuary, the door of the church hanging on its hinges. St. Martin Vintry, he thinks numbly, though why he should remember its name he doesn't know. An axe swings, a man's head severed from his body in one clean blow, coarse laughter, panting, curses. "Thieves, aliens, kill the bastards!"

Three Flemings slash out with their daggers before succumbing to axe-wielding louts. Haukyn eases backward until he's hidden from sight and jams his fists to his ears, but that makes it worse, and is this not more horrible than any war, this massacre, this abomination in the eyes of God, and naught he can do unless he wishes to add his own headless body to those already splayed on the cobbles…*his boots slithering in a mess of bowels and severed limbs, an archer's face sliced from his body, screams cut off, blood, so much blood and he drowning in it…*With an effort that makes him sweat, he drags himself back to a London street, and is his face his father's gone-back-to-the-war face? More shouting, "Flemish up at Austin Friars... too far...not if we run, we're done here...don't slip in the blood...we showed 'em, didn't we."

He lowers his fists. A rush of footsteps toward Dowgate, the lap of the river, and then, blessed Mary, someone moaning.

He'd been helpless to prevent the killing. But suffering he can end, and he's catapulted into the past, when as a little boy he'd complained to his mother about his father's screams in the night, and she'd sat him down, not gently, and listed Edmund's deeds of mercy in France, seven deliberate killings to end incurable, unbearable pain.

One man still alive in that heap of dead men and the moaning has not ceased. Christ, it comes from underneath two—how can you say bodies when the heads are gone?—two sprawled carcasses, a butcher's word. His stomach heaves. He closes his mind, hauls the bodies to one side. Beneath—tis a young Fleming, his neck gashed, his face distorted and blood-spattered. Haukyn says, his eyes holding to pain-glazed brown eyes, "You're safe, I'll look after you," the last word scarce out when the man's breath rattles and his soul leaves his body. With two fingertips, very gently, Haukyn brushes his eyelids closed. He crosses himself, and, his voice strong, says to the man, to all of the dead, "*In nomine Patris, et Filii, et Spiritus Sancti. Amen.*"

What more can he do? Knock on each Flemish door, help the families find husband, father, son in this terrible heap? Slipping on blood, he falls to the bare cobbles, banging his knees, and his bandages are stained with blood and then he's running past the wharves as if the Devil were after him.

He did enough.

Is enough ever enough?

Baynard's Castle with its tower and small windows, guards in leather and chain mail surrounding it. He feels their eyes watching him. The king, the most powerful figure in the land, is holed up inside, like badger to sett.

He's supposed to be searching for Javyd, who, praise be, was not among those murderers. Past the cathedral, he crosses Cheapside, which holds no terrors for him now, and one after another traverses the northerly streets of rich merchants and aldermen. His burns hurt, as does the pressure in his chest. South again, and before he can duck down another alley he's accosted by a drunken group of rebels. Their leader grabs Haukyn by the tunic; his breath is vile, his garments smeared with soot and blood, an axe swinging at his hip. "Sh-swear fealty to our cause," he says and hiccups. "Else we beheads you as traitor."

He's outnumbered and one more beheading would mean naught to a deranged Kentishman; he swallows any tendency to a matching brutality. "I swears fealty to good King Richard," he says. "Ain't us serfs better 'n any archbishop, nor all them scurvy lawyers?"

The leader spits with enthusiasm, punches him on the shoulder, and reels away, his band weaving after him. Haukyn lets out his breath in an angry *whoosh*. Fealty to those ruffians? *He* chooses to whom he owes fealty.

Back to Budge Row and there's Javyd strolling toward him, not a worry in the world. Furious, Haukyn says, "I'm come from a massacre of Flemings in Vintry, two score of them. By Londoners like you, who hate their guts."

"Nigh the same number at Austin Friars. Fewer at another church, don't know where."

"Do you even care?"

"You got a spider up yer arse? I ain't never in favour o' ten men with axes 'gainst two with knives, 'n' you looks like the shite I shovels into m' barrels." More moderately, he adds, "Riots 'n' slaughter the width o' the city. Proclamations out for the rebels to go home. But they ain't listening."

Haukyn's shoulders slump with exhaustion. "They heard *traitor* from the king's lips and were deaf to *laws of the land*."

"Come into the house, Nilla got pottage 'n' you needs ale."

Once they've eaten and have drained their mugs, Petronilla puts fresh salve and bandages on Haukyn's hands. Javyd says, "Met up with the Kentish leader today, man called Wat Tyghler, he led Kent across the bridge. Cock o' the walk, he be, the king in hiding, the city his, or so he think—his men'd follow him to the Devil's doorway. But there be more to London than a boy-king, there be rich merchants 'n' nobles with swords. I knows this city, the Commons'll rally, they got to, 'n' our mayor be a doughty fellow, he'll cry vengeance on Kent 'n' Essex. On London too. You could be mistook for a rebel, Haukyn. If you got a drip o' sense, you'll leave now, even if you only gets as far as Staines this night."

Javyd, his mind made up, his black brows bristling, is a force not easily gainsayed. And Haukyn longs for home and its simplicities. "What have we started, Javyd, and where will it end?"

Javyd shrugs. "With more blood on the cobbles. I'll saddle yer mare."

So Haukyn stores his precious letters under his shirt, the book of prayer in his pouch, says his farewells to Petronilla and Javyd, and two days later, as dusk deepens to darkness, he and his tired mare arrive in Flintbourne. He dismounts at the ford so Trefoil can drink. From his house near the trees, light gleams through the shutters. They approach together, he on foot, the reins trailing. Rust's barking changes to frantic whines. "Ilotte," he calls, "tis I, Haukyn."

The door opens. Rust bolts out and sniffs his ankles, tail batting Trefoil's knee, and Ilotte is standing in the doorway, holding a tallow candle, her cap off, black hair past her shoulders. Haukyn says unsteadily, "I am come home...Trefoil needs oats and I need soap and water. Will you let us in?"

"I'll unlock the byre."

Rust nosing him, he tethers his mare in her stall with hay, fresh-cut, and a small measure of oats. In the shadows, Ilotte watches. He says, "Is Alyce well?"

"She been a right imp with you gone."

"And you, are you well?"

"Aye. No sickness day or night."

"Did you miss me?"

"I might've. A bit."

"I was too pushed on the journey to be fussy about inns. Is it the river for me, or warm water by the hearth?"

"Last two evenings I been heating water. M' strangeness, it don't work for happy."

His smile breaks out. After he strips, she bundles his dirty clothes together, just as his mother did the day he came home from war. "Rebellion is war of a different kind," he says and starts scrubbing himself, head to foot. "Both, it would seem, bring out the worst in men."

"Them hands o' yourn?"

"Later," he says, rinses himself, bends his neck as she towels water from his hair, looks up, and asks the question whose answer he can never quite predict. "Will you lie with me, Ilotte?" She nods. "You are my heart's rest," he says roughly and draws her close.

In the morning, Alyce pushes open their door, sees him, runs for the bed, and lands on top of him. "Had you a tail, twould be wagging," Haukyn murmurs and hugs her. Alyce, Ilotte, and his unborn child, the deepest of bonds yet a freedom beyond imagining.

While Alyce plays outside with Rust, Ilotte says, "There be news from the vill. Jorden Smyth died the day after you left, a relief to all. But Haukyn, Dunstan died too. He were firing stones at Amos Cat-Skinner's dog, 'n' it seems like his heart were tired and give out, no fuss save for Jack-for-Short's howling. The funeral were Saturday."

He crosses himself, slowly, with his burned fingers. "He taught me much...a crotchety old man who loved his craft." Crotchety or nay, Dunstan would have smiled to hear that his pupil, a freeman, can now ply his trade the length of the valley.

"I'll visit the churchyard," he says, "and light a candle for him in the church." Then, knowing he must, he tells Ilotte about the destruction of the Sauvoye and the saving of six horses, and shows her the book with its vibrant, miniature paintings, she delighted to find a hive surrounded by tiny bees. Picking at a knot in the table, he describes the procession of heads, the massacre of the Flemings, and his own awakening to the cost of freedom. "You were right to warn me and I slow to listen—yet, despite the cost, or because of it, freedom is ours," he says, and tries to paint a picture of Mile End and a young king who put his seal to manumission and pardon. "Manumission, Ilotte, a lawyer's word for *free*. I can still scarce believe it, but here is the evidence," and he spreads his vill's parchment flat on the table and they read it together, he in awe of how much she has learned from his father. "I must spread word in the vill today that we are all freemen, and I must ride to James in Wiltshire with his letter."

"Bertran won't welcome this news."

"The letter bears the king's Great Seal." He grins. "Bertran'll have to pay us for cutting the lord's hay."

"Tisn't a game, Haukyn!"

"Tis freedom," he says, gripping her hands. "To go where we will, work for whom we wish, demand commutation, appeal to the royal courts."

"We ain't going to leave here, and the lords won't like it."

He buries the doubts Javyd raised about rich merchants, armed nobles, the king at their beck. "The lords must bow to the king, *he* rules the land. How I wish you could have seen him ride though the mob on the way to Mile End, a stripling lad, royal to the core. Ilotte, for once I'm not being reckless. This freedom was pledged, tis a covenant before God."

She's biting her lip. He says, "I must share the news with my father before I go to the alehouse. I fear he will be as wary as you."

When he smooths her hair back from her face and bends his head to kiss her, she clasps him around the waist with all her strength, then, as fast, releases him.

Twill take a lifetime to learn her ways, he thinks, and heads across the fields.

...two gifts...

Edmund sees Haukyn coming across the headland. His son, safely home. He grasps him with his old man's arms, arms that could once draw a bow longer than his height. "You've heard about Dunstan?"

"Aye, a sorrow to me. Such skill as I have comes from him."

"The funeral was well-attended. Ivo his heir." He scrutinizes Haukyn's face. "London was not easy?"

"While I'd miss Javyd, I wouldn't care if I never saw London again."

"Come in, I have some of Johanna's ale."

"I have a gift for you, Da. Two gifts."

Intrigued, Edmund pours the ale into mugs and they sit down. Haukyn passes over the small book he's been holding. "I rescued this from the Sauvoye. Its owner, John of Gaunt, is still in the north and disinclined to come south, so greatly is he hated."

Edmund strokes the smooth leather cover with a work-rough hand. "So tis on loan?"

"You can return it to him should you feel the need, though he doesn't know it still exists. Everything in his palace was burned or smashed or tossed into the river."

His eyes dwell on one of the paintings, its exquisitely small figures, its garlands and gargoyles, carmine, sapphire, and verdigris, delineated in gold leaf. He says in a hushed voice, "Tis a Book of

Hours. I've never seen a book such as this. Father Thomas had books, but plain script only. You must have wished to salvage more than one."

"The penalty was death were you caught doing so."

Edmund grimaces. "How can I blame you for recklessness when this is the prize?"

Haukyn spreads the king's letter on the table. "This the other gift, a prize for the whole vill."

With a visible effort, Edmund pulls his attention away from an angel with indigo wings and an expression haughtier than any duke's. He reads the letter, fingers the seal, reads it again. "The Great Seal? So this is meant, it must be…but how can it be? It would turn our world withershins."

"We're freemen, Da. All of us. Freemen, freewomen, and the little-uns growing up free."

Edmund shakes his head. "You saw him, our king?" and gives his full attention to the story of Mile End. "So you heard him agree to these changes?"

"'*I am well agreed thereto*,' his exact words, and I not ten feet from him. Richard is God's anointed and his word is law. This letter, these words, they are his and his alone."

He wants to believe, for his son's sake, for the sake of every serf in the kingdom. "What will you do with the letter?"

"Call a meeting and read it to all in the vill, in Bertran's presence."

"Sir Gardrad will hear of it."

"Sir Gardrad is in Wales, fawning on Thomas Woodstock, Earl of Buckingham."

Sir Gardrad will not stay in Wales forever; but he is only a knight, not a king, no reason for dread. Edmund hears himself say, "Do not think to plumb the depths of freedom nor reach its heights too quickly, Haukyn. The manor's moat wasn't dug in a day nor its dovecote raised in a day, and the foundations of all manors are deep. And aye, let me say it before you do, I'm a cautious old man."

He rests his hand on the book, a book of prayer, and opens to a page near the end, where an ochre lion with pointed ears is bowing to a squirrel armed with blue acorns—acorns, not stones. He points it out to Haukyn. "You gave pleasure and stature to Dunstan by valuing his knowledge. Ilotte continues our lessons and learns faster than I can teach her."

"Will you come to the meeting, Da?"

"I will," he says and is rewarded by his son's smile.

A t the alehouse, with new authority in his voice, for he is, once again, the leader in the vill, Haukyn calls for a meeting on the green after the Vespers bell; in the meantime, he scythes the grass around house and orchard and makes a start on his share of the common meadow, the weather clement, and he'll do more on the morrow. Then he walks up the hill to Dunstan's because he still can't quite believe the old man is dead. Or is it to console Jenet and Ivo? As he nears it a dog barks, a chain rattles then snaps, the dog yelps in pain, and a woman screams. He runs toward the clearing. Ivo is swinging a thin length of chain at Jack-for-Short, Jenet trying to grab her brother's arm, the dog tethered and cowering.

"*Ivo!*" he shouts.

Ivo whirls and the chain whirls with him, wrapping itself around Haukyn's ribs, the pain acute, and have they not always been chained together, he and Ivo? Infuriated, he twists his body enough to loosen its grip, grabs the end, and hauls on it. Ivo, taken by surprise and without the wit to let go, is pulled to his knees. Rage and humiliation stain his cheeks. Jenet gasps and fumbles to untie Jack-for-Short.

Ivo blunders upright. "You! Back from London. Cock o' the walk."

"And you, beating a dog that took on armed retainers!"

"Useless cur, whining 'n' moping like it were Dunstan what fed him all these months, not me."

"To think I came here to commiserate with you."

"Living with the ol' bugger, it got me a house 'n' land, didn't it. I ain't stupid."

"Did you encourage him to throw the stones that killed him?" Another gasp from Jenet. Haukyn lets out his pent-up breath. "If I see a mark on that dog—or on your sister—I'll take both from you and you'll never get them back."

"I wouldn't beat m' sister."

"Nay, just reduce her to tears while you beat a dog for mourning an old man who gave you a roof over your head."

Her hand on the dog's collar, Jenet says, "Ivo, Johanna tol' me if I ever wanted to, I could live in her shed, take Jack with me."

"You cooks fer me!"

"I don't have to. I got friends in the vill."

Haukyn says, "I always wanted a sister, Ivo. We must take love where we find it and be glad," and why is he preaching to a man deaf as a tree trunk? He turns on his heel and walks away; he's still grasping the length of chain.

After Vespers, he reads the king's letter to the crowd on the green, explains its consequences, and answers questions, all the while striving to keep his exultation swaddled. Ivo stands on the outskirts, sneer well in place, Bertran, Mauld, and Saul close by. Edmund is also at the edge of the crowd, could he not have planted himself at the front? Haukyn says loudly, "Master Bertran, the king's letter changes everything. Should you wish the lord's hay cut, you must not only pay us to do so, you must show us your coin before we start."

Cheers and laughter from the villagers, Bertran pale with rage. "When Sir Gardrad returns from Wales, he will restore you to obedience and your lowly estate, an estate ordained by God. Even our king is ruled by God."

"God," says Haukyn, "has not to my knowledge issued a letter revoking the Great Seal." More laughter, which emboldens him to say, "You will bring out the manorial court rolls and lay them before us."

"I'll not!"

"You will. Or we'll take them by force—in London, rebels used axes and fire to win freedom for us all."

A number of men edge forward, hands to daggers: Walter, Blundred, Simon, Neuton, and Solomon. Bertran stands firm, and if ever Haukyn were to admire him, it was then. The bailiff says, "You alone will come to the manor with me to fetch them."

"You mistake the meaning of this meeting. Your days of giving orders are done. I will accompany you with four men, leaving the rest here to watch Saul and Mauld."

The men, Haukyn among them, soon come out laden with scrolls, Bertran in their wake. The scrolls are dumped on the green in a vast, untidy heap. Haukyn shouts, "Our rents, our customary lands, our merchet and chevage and leyrwite. Our trespasses, our fines, our boon works, our tallage."

"But also the ancient customs that are our protection," Edmund calls, "and records of those rents that are fixed."

Haukyn hesitates. His father by his own admission is a cautious old man, yet there is truth in what he says. Before he can speak, Blundred picks up a scroll and waves it in the air. "The king have given us a new custom—manumission. We got no need o' records."

Walter has pushed forward with a tinder box, and to more cheers, the old ways rise heavenward in smoke and the lick of flame.

The midsummer days slip by. Rain on the hay, weeds shooting toward the sky, and as Haukyn, Ilotte, and Alyce eat oatmeal after Mass, Rust barks and a light tap comes on the door. Jenet is standing outside, Jack-for-Short at her side, wagging his tail and bowing before Rust in an invitation to play. Hiding surprise, he says, "Out you go, Rust. And, Jenet, welcome."

Jenet drops a curtsey and says in a rush, "I come to tell you that Ivo been good to me 'n' Jack since you was there so I never moved from Dunstan's to Johanna's shed—I misses the ol' man sore. But Ivo still got hatred for you, Haukyn. I wish it were other."

Ilotte says, "I have a brew of mint tea, would you like a mug?"

"Aye. Aye, I'd like that." In another rush of words, her cheeks reddening, she says to Ilotte, "I were that jealous o' you but now I ain't. The cooper's youngest son, his name be Swithin, he be courting me, he pleases me though I ain't yet tol' Ivo."

"If Ivo gives you trouble, you come to me," Haukyn says. "I'm happy for you, I've always liked Swithin."

"Jack lays down, legs in the air, when he see him, 'n' I trusts Jack."

She gulps her tea and leaves in a flurry of thanks.

In the bright sunshine, Bertran, who knows the lord's hay must be harvested, stands at the edge of the meadow counting out pennies to men with scythes and women with rakes, each penny, Haukyn thinks mockingly, a knife to the bailiff's heart. When the crop has been dried and stored, he himself rides to Wiltshire, delivers the king's letter to James, and witnesses his staggered delight. He leaves for home, the reins lax. He feels blessed. *Blessed Mary* is a phrase he uses oft enough. But to apply the word to his own life? Freedom is at the heart of it, Ilotte also, and his sweet, mischievous daughter. Add his acres, to which he's attached after all these years; his crops, which need weeding, although not even that can dispel the smile on his face; his craft as bowyer; and *my cup runneth over*, and doesn't the psalm then say that goodness, or is it mercy, will follow him for the rest of his life, and mustn't God, that ever-mysterious distance, be both the source of his gratitude and its receptacle?

The death of a faraway priest exorcised by a force greater than itself?

That night, by candlelight, he and Ilotte couple, tenderness a word made flesh. If marriage is a sacrament, he thinks, resting his forehead on her breast and listening to her heartbeat, then he is most truly married.

On the third day of the new month, a London merchant gives a letter to Father Mortimer, who passes it on to Edmund to give to Haukyn, a long, much creased letter from Javyd. Even though Javyd must have hired a scribe, its wandering script and grammatical confusion take some deciphering. Its gist is devastating. The day after Haukyn left London, the rebels were summoned to Smithfield, where their leader, Wat Tyghler, laid hands on the king and was slaughtered by Richard's knights. When the rebels nocked their bows, Richard, alone and with great courage, led them toward Clerkenwell's fields. They were fast-surrounded by armed men from the city. Tyghler's head, stuck on a pole, was paraded in front of them, and Richard then ordered them to go home with their charters. A long straggle of dirty, confused, exhausted men trailing toward London Bridge, Haukyn can picture it. Back at Clerkenwell, the king knighted the mayor and three other rich merchants, out of gratitude for the murder of the rebels' leader and the quick assemblage of London's armed men.

Haukyn bites his lip. Did the king order Tyghler's death? At the very least, he'd wanted him dead. He also, understandably, wanted Kent gone from his city, and if it took armed men to frighten them into leaving, then armed men would be used.

He works his way through the remaining jumble of script. A commission of seven men has been set up. Swift reprisals on any suspected rebels, gibbets all over the city, a new block on Cheapside, heads lopped off after the most summary of trials. Then Javyd's voice cuts through the scribe's: "All in our ward forced to swear fealty. Me, a king's archer! Look to yer arse, Haukyn. The commission got powers outside the city, 'n' this ain't no game o' hide-'n'-seek."

His father says, "Bad news, Haukyn?"

Haukyn had forgotten his presence. He passes the letter over. "It only yields its bad news with effort."

Edmund reads it, brow furrowed. "Richard is young, he'd be easy swayed. But the rebels weren't slaughtered at Clerkenwell, as they could have been, and were permitted to take their charters of freedom with them."

"The punishments in the city, on whose orders were those, mayor or king or both? Am I to distrust our anointed king?" His brain spiked by questions, spiked like Sudbury's teetering mitre, and today is the Feast of St. Thomas, the apostle of doubt.

"We can only wait and see." Edmund passes the letter back, keeping hold of his son's hand. "Waiting is worse than weeding ragwort to you, I know, but wait we must."

At home, Haukyn shares the letter with Ilotte. "Them rich merchants, what loaned him coin for his wars, they holds the money bags, they got power. You keep your gob shut, Haukyn, no more stirring the pot."

What if Bertran also hears of gibbets and blocks? What if he, Haukyn, the leader of the vill, has led his neighbours into danger? That evening, he convenes the men closest to him, shares the contents of the letter, and asks them to pass the word around that there should be no further acts of rebellion. "Weeks til harvest and the next boon days…we must lie low til then."

They nod, uneasy. Are they, like him, remembering the leaping flames of a bonfire on the green, the charred circle it left in the grass?

A thunderstorm, days later, does not sever summer's heat. Haukyn weeds, forehead dripping, that evening begins the slow process of tillering an elm bow, and lies without covers beside Ilotte on their mattress.

Soon after Prime, she leaves with Alyce to deliver a potion to Catherine, the cooper's wife, for her headaches, and mid-morning another letter arrives, brought to his door by Solomon the Small. Creased like Javyd's, but dirtier, the ink blotched. "Solomon, tis from Sir Geoffrey in Essex, written in haste, I'd say. I'll read it to you. 'Haukyn, rebels in Kent, Norwich, and Essex executed by hanging and beheading. Essex rebels cut down near Billericay by Woodstock's army. The king north of there in Waltham…'" Haukyn's voice falters. "'He this day revoked all charters of manumission and pardon throughout the country, as if they had never been. Rebels are to be ferreted out, tried, and punished. I am gone into hiding and my lands forfeit. Gardrad was with Woodstock but may have left him by now. I urge you to hide for safety's sake. God's blessing on you and your family, and may we meet again in more peaceable times. Geoffrey.'

"Christ Jesus," Haukyn says softly, "the king has betrayed us, betrayed every one of his serfs throughout England, and now he hunts us down like beasts." His face anguished, he looks up. "At Mile End, I'd have trusted him with my life. I've been a fool, a blind, stupid fool, and I've led Flintbourne into danger."

"You must hide, Haukyn, but where?"

"I have a place. The less you know, the better. Go home, Solomon, and look to your wife and family."

And then he sees her, his Ilotte, running along the headlands toward him. When she reaches him, she's almost sobbing. "Haukyn, such heaviness come over me at Catherine's. Why, I can't tell, but—"

Swiftly he shares the contents of Sir Geoffrey's letter. "I'll hide in the woods toward Savernake, past where I found you last winter. If you'd fill my waterskin and pack some bread, I'll put a bedroll together. You mustn't—"

"Someone coming," she says, panicked, "look!"

He squints down the hill. At the ford, Ivo arguing with Amos— and a horseman crossing the river. "Tis Tirrell."

The constable takes the slope at a canter and pulls up his mount by their doorway. "Haukyn, a retinue of armed men stayed last night at an inn close to here, on the Bristol road. I pray they pass us by."

"Do they have hounds?"

"I heard no baying."

"Go home, you haven't seen me. Ilotte, if they come for me, tell my father, and take Alyce there. You know where I'll hide." He kisses her on the mouth. Then he races up the nearest baulk into the woods, along the ridge, down the slope to the river path, no waterskin, no bread, too little time should the armed men have Flintbourne as their destination. But why would they? The king has bigger fish to fry than one small vill on the Kennet.

The big oak beckons him. He darts around the clump of blackthorn, finds the entrance, already part overgrown, and slides into it on his belly. Spines snag his sleeves and hose as he drags himself into the circle of stones, turns around, then slithers back to the entrance to smooth over any signs of his passage.

His sanctuary.

He's safe.

Edmund sees Ilotte running toward the north field, where he and the twins are weeding. She stops at the field's edge. "Haukyn gone into hiding 'cause of a letter Solomon brought, 'n' Tirrell warned us there be a retinue on the Bristol road."

His gaze shifts to the green. "Those five men? Heading for Ivo and Amos?"

She gasps. "I'll hide in the woods so they can't ask me 'bout Haukyn. Alyce be at Catherine's."

He stays where he is. Talk at the ford, Ivo hitched up on one of the horses, then the retinue canters toward the river path, and he can't possibly reach the hideaway in time to save his son. Helpless, sick at heart, he picks up a chunk of flint and throws it with all his strength into the ditch.

Panting, Haukyn lies still, his whole body a wordless prayer that Ilotte and Alyce also be safe. The river ripples among the rocks, soothing and timeless. If the riders pass by on their way to Windsor, Tirrell will tell Ilotte and she'll come here. Until then, he'll stay where he is.

A kingfisher rattles its call from the riverbank, another answers, and then—*Jesu*—the thud of hoofs, closer and closer, jingle of harness, and a voice, Sir Gardrad's voice, he'd know it anywhere. "Is this the place?"

"Aye. Inside that clump of blackthorn."

Ivo. His brain flashes backward to the small boy who'd begun tunnelling into the blackthorn and who'd had, on occasion, the unnerving sensation of being watched. He *was* watched. By Ivo, Warty Ivo. Sir Gardrad says, "Come out, Haukyn."

He holds his breath, his heartbeat loud enough to alert an army on the move.

"One of my men has torch and tinder. Perhaps you'd rather roast to death."

The rebel pushed into the flames at the Sauvoye...any fate better than that. He crawls forward, a spine claws his cheek, he reaches the entrance and pushes himself to his feet, feeling blood trickle down his face. "God's greeting, Sir Gardrad," he says and looks from face to face. "This many men, in leather doublets and chain mail, for one lowly serf?" With a jar of recognition, he adds, "You with the broke nose, you were in France. Near Lalinde you held me down while my friend Piers was dying—and still you do your master's dirty work? For shame." His gaze shifts. "And this scut your servant? Ivo, you and the king, a fine pair, betrayers both."

Ivo stares at him, unblinking. Sir Gardrad urges his big chestnut so close Haukyn is forced to back up. "Enough! Take him."

Two men dismount and approach him, one holding a thick length of rope, Broke-nose a truncheon. No escaping them. Is he meekly to hold out his wrists to be trussed like a chicken? He steps nearer to the one with the rope, ups his knee to the man's groin, and whirls toward Broke-nose. The truncheon slams into his shoulder, he cries out with the pain, and through a red mist of rage grabs for it, throwing his whole weight forward. A barked order and before he's ready two more men surge toward him and he falls beneath a hail of blows. Boots to his ribs; he curls into himself on the ground. Sir Gardrad shouts, "Don't kill the bastard! Rope him to the bay mare."

He's hauled to his feet. He's bleeding, he thinks muzzily, from more than a blackthorn spine, and every bone in his body hurts. Hands bound, mouth gagged, both with cruel strength, he's tugged like a sack of grain onto the mare, upright in front of its rider, praise God, not slung across the saddle as he'd thought he might be.

Ivo is still standing, as if carved in stone, beside the blackthorn. His greasy red curls, his scars—horseshoe, oxshoe. Ivo, the outlaw in his own vill...*Sir Gardrad would have found me sooner or later, and the longer the search, the greater the danger to my neighbours.*

Back along the river path, only wide enough for two horses side by side, his and Sir Gardrad's in the vanguard. Through the overhanging leaves of willow and sallow, he sees a woman walking toward them. Ilotte. His heart quails. *Run, run away...*She approaches his mare, her gaze steady, a hand outstretched to stroke its muzzle, and the horse halts, head lowered.

Sir Gardrad says, "Go home! Or I'll have the ropes around his wrist so tight his hands will drop off before we reach Newbury's gaol."

Her other hand cups the muzzle of the knight's gelding and it too stands quietly. She looks up at Haukyn. "I have called a curse upon this knight and all his company. They will find out its nature soon enough." Sir Gardrad shifts in his saddle. One of the retainers hawks and spits. In the same calm voice she says, "Alyce will be well cared for, my dearest Haukyn, as will your son. May she o' the criss-crossed blackthorns be with you."

A last stroke to the horses' muzzles and she steps aside into the bracken along the path. Sir Gardrad spurs his horse, it kicks out, he flops forward in the saddle, and Haukyn is nearly unseated as the bay mare backs up, snorting. He'd laugh were he not gagged. He fastens his eyes on Ilotte's face, and then they pass her, and he doesn't look back.

Standing like a man stunned, Edmund watches the five horses appear from the river path, walk past the well, and splash across the ford. His son roped and gagged on the mare alongside the knight.

Tirrell, also at the ford, grabs for the knight's reins. The horse swerves, knocking him off his feet onto the grass, and the retinue trots up the track that leads out of Flintbourne.

Edmund thinks about killing Ivo; thinks, wearily, *I am too late.*

The retinue has turned east and speeded to a canter, each lurch of the saddle sending a shaft of agony through Haukyn's chest: one of his ribs, he's almost certain, is cracked. He tries not to groan, can't always succeed.

The gaol in Newbury. If ever he needed courage, tis now.

Ilotte again arrives at the field's edge. "Sir Gardrad 'n' his men, they're taking Haukyn to Newbury's gaol."

The furrows waver in Edmund's vision. "I must talk to Tirrell."

His legs can still carry him at a run, Ilotte at his side holding up her skirts. The constable's horse is drinking from the river, Solomon nearby. Tirrell tugs on the reins. "I'll ride to Newbury, Edmund, see what I can find out."

"I'll be in the north field."

Before he can go, Solomon gives him Sir Geoffrey's crumpled letter. He reads it quickly, the colour draining from his face. "Haukyn known as the leader of rebellion in Flintbourne. A trial, aye. But if Sir Gardrad is the judge, twill be a travesty."

He and Ilotte trail across the baulks. She says, "I sees things, you knows that, dark things, afore they happen. But today it come too late to help Haukyn—too late! Ma couldn't even give me the sight whole, what did she ever give me but naught?" She catches herself. "Tirrell will do all he can, Edmund."

She leaves him at the field and goes up the hill to Catherine's. Edmund picks up his hoe, stares at it, drops it to the ground, and stares at his feet. His boots coated in mud. His wife never so far away.

The gaol is underground, no sconces for a torch. Two of the retinue half-push, half-lift Haukyn toward the far wall where long shackles are bolted into the stone; a third holds a torch. Broke-nose saws through the rope around his wrists, where the the skin is already raw, cuts the gag loose, then slices through his tunic and shirt. "Take 'em off. Braies 'n' hose. Shoes too."

He knows enough to obey without question. Broke-nose kicks the clothes against the far wall. "Cold in here year-round," he says as he clamps the manacles around Haukyn's wrists. Bending, he shackles his ankles. "That'll hold you."

Sir Gardrad walks into the gaol's foul air, a kerchief to his nose. "Aye," he says, "that will hold you. Tomorrow morning, early, you'll be drawn through the streets and hanged until dead, your body buried in quicklime."

His wrist shackles rattle. Haukyn says hoarsely, "King Richard's proclamation says I am entitled to a trial by law."

"The king will never know the difference, and we both know you are guilty of inciting Flintbourne to rebellion." He smiles his thin smile. "A night to repent of your sins. A priest will arrive shortly, to confess you. Never say that I am not a merciful man."

All three leave, taking the torch with them, and the door bangs shut. He slides his bare back down the wall, sits, and closes his eyes. *Annabel died without me at her side. And now I will die alone.* God's justice, is it, or His vengeance, and does it matter?

Sharper than any dagger, grief pierces him. He'll never see his daughter again, he'll never meet his unborn son, he won't be there to watch them grow, he won't be able to protect them from the world's wounds. Never again will he lie with Ilotte, his courageous, vibrant Ilotte, whose depths foretell darkness. The twins, gentle Ralf and tough-minded Gil. His beloved father, scarred by war...all lost to him.

No rebellion is worth such penalty.

When Tirrell returns three hours later, Edmund straightens, his back aching, and crosses to the edge of the field. "What news?"

"The worst. Haukyn is to be hanged early tomorrow morning. Without trial."

Edmund grabs his sleeve. "Can Gardrad do that?"

"Ain't he always bent the law to suit hisself?"

"I must go to Newbury. To see Haukyn. To beg Sir Gardrad for mercy."

"No one allowed in the gaol 'cepting a priest." Tirrell hesitates. "Not enough time before the hanging for me to find the sheriff and ride back with the ruling for a trial, tis why the hurry." Another hesitation, longer this time. "M' cousin's house be close to the gaol. You can see the scaffold too, a distance away. He be in Bristol and I got the key."

"You'll give it to me?"

"Don't go, Edmund, don't. Twill tear the heart from yer body."

"I have to. I can't let Haukyn die alone—I have to bear witness. Alyce will stay with Ilotte, neither of them must be there."

"You ain't going nowheres on yer own. I'll ride with you, watch over the horses in the woods west o' Newbury."

And so it is left.

Edmund trudges to his son's house. Alyce is outside tugging at buttercups in her little garden patch, Rust watching, head cocked. He lifts the child and holds her close, her curls tickling his face. She wriggles to be put down. "Lotte be inside," she says.

Ilotte is at the table, bending withies to weave another hive. "I has to keep m' hands busy…the news be bad."

He nods and tell her of the hanging. She rests her forehead on the hive's frame. "How'll we live without him? Yet he wouldn't have been true to hisself had he done naught."

"Tirrell's cousin has a house in Newbury near the scaffold. I'll go there at dawn, as the vill's witness."

Her voice jagged, she says, "We has to walk toward our darknesses, then through 'em, your son taught me so." She gets up and does something she has never done before: kisses him on both cheeks, the scarred and the unscarred. "You raised a good man," she says. "Our blessed Mother go with you on the morrow 'n' bring you comfort. Will you take Trefoil?"

"I thought to."

"I'll bring her over at dusk, with her saddle."

Before dusk, news of a hanging has travelled the vill and, with it, the name of the man who betrayed Haukyn's hiding place. Almost nightfall when the house that was Dunstan's burns to the ground, Jenet and Jack-for-Short both at the cooper's. Shortly afterward, the vill learns that Swithin Cooper is betrothed to Jenet Smyth, the marriage to take place after the banns are read by Father Mortimer, Jack-for-Short part of her dowry.

Ivo was not in the house either, his whereabouts as unknown as the cause of the fire.

The priest, his hood pulled forward, is accompanied by a guard holding a torch. "Stay by the door," the priest says tersely, waddles closer to Haukyn—a well-fed priest—and waits. Clumsily Haukyn kneels. "*Benedicite*," he says.

"*Dominus vobiscum.* Do you confess to knowing the Creed and believing that the Host brings us the Real Presence of Our Saviour?"

With difficulty, Haukyn stands up; the shackles are heavy and any movement a stab to his ribs. "*Confiteor Deo omnipotenti*...I confess to trusting the word of our anointed king. I confess that I may have led the villagers, my neighbours, into error and danger, to my most sincere regret. I confess my deep devotion for my father and repent my unkind words to him in the past. I confess to loving my daughter, Alyce, with all my heart. I confess my love for Ilotte, whom I have swived for the sheer joy of the act, without thought for the making of son or daughter. I confess that I have not killed, other than in France in a time of war, and among those dead, a French priest. And I confess that I have never in my life felt the presence of God."

The priest's pudgy cheeks are as purple as a bishop's cassock. "Be silent!"

"I was ready to be so."

"You feel too little sorrow, too little remorse, for these sins. Repent, or I cannot absolve you, and you will be damned for eternity."

"Do you believe a serf's soul has the same value as a king's?" The pause lasts too long. "So you do not. Then we have no more to say to each other. God bless you, sir priest."

The door slams shut behind priest and guard. Exhausted, Haukyn sinks to the ground. Cold, darkness, and damp envelop him, God never more distant. His sister who died in the plague, little Margaret, he scarce remembers her...will it be thus for Alyce, her father receding into conjured memory, *father* a word with no heft?

He's jerked awake—was he sleeping?—by a harsh whisper. "Be you there?"

He's alone. He knows it. The Devil's come for him and he can't even cross himself.

Again the whisper pierces the darkness. "I be yer neighbour. M' name be Cobb."

"The walls are thick stone," Haukyn says stupidly, "how is it I hear you?"

"Some poor bugger afore us gaoled long enough to dig out the mortar. I ain't shackled 'cause I be in fer theft. Trial at the next assizes." Haukyn can almost hear the shrug. "The rope after, likely. What be your name?"

"Haukyn. Of Flintbourne. Rebellion my crime."

"Word o' warning. They—"

"Hush! Someone's coming."

A key grating in the lock, the door opens and light floods in. He winces from it. Broke-nose and the man he kicked in the groin. "Stand up," Broke-nose says.

Slowly he does so, his chains clinking. They use bare fists, boots when he collapses against the wall. It goes on too long.

Broke-nose laughs. "Sleep well."

Naught but pain.

Later, separate hurts. In his mouth, the taste of his own blood.

Later still, he doesn't know when, Cobb whispers, "You there?"

He spits out a broken tooth and finds his voice. "Aye."

"Be God inside this Devil's lair? I'll hedge m' bets, say a prayer or two."

Ill-spoke Latin. Haukyn's head falls forward.

Edmund keeps vigil all night, Ralf and Gil sleeping, his candle holding darkness at bay; he has not shared his plan with any but Tirrell and Ilotte. Before dawn, he chalks a note on his slate for the twins, leaves it on the table, saddles Trefoil, and meets Tirrell at the ford. They ride in silence and dismount in the thick woods to the west of the town. Tirrell passes him a key. "For the back door. Go down the second alley behind the main street, Northbrook, tis the third door in. A window on the second floor where you can see the gaol. Scaffold farther away. I'll be here, Edmund, waiting for you." His voice breaks. "God be with you."

Briefly Edmund presses Tirrell's shoulder. "With you also," he says and picks his way through the trees, his cloak pulled around him, its hood hiding his scarred face.

Dawn, Haukyn senses, is close.

Terror has him in its grip, terror and pain. His life to end at the sun's rising, him drawn naked through the streets for the entertainment of the crowd—he's in no doubt there will be a crowd. Pray God Ilotte not be among them, nor his father. And then the noose, the agonized search for air, the clawing and kicking for air...*I cannot do this, I am not man enough.*

Through the wall, Cobb's voice. "Be you awake?"

"Aye." He gulps breath while he can. "Cobb, they took my clothes." An odd thing to complain about, given the rest.

"You still got two feet 'n' yer pride. Up with you."

Pride. He seeks it in his body's wreckage. "I'm afeard."

"O' course you be afeard. Now you listen to me. You got one task, Haukyn o' Flintbourne—be rebel to the end."

"Cobb, have you wife or little-uns?"

"Me, a vagrant with a chin what didn't grow to fit m' face and not a cut farthing to m' name? If you has 'em, tis another reason to hold yer head high, ain't it?"

"Aye. It is...it is, you're right." He gulps more air. "I can't be huddling on the floor when Gardrad comes for me."

"Lonesome here when you be gone."

"You've been a true friend to me, Cobb, and I pray you can hold to your courage when your time comes. God bless you and keep you."

God, he thinks. *The God of distance has spoken through the stone wall of a gaol. A thief has spoken to me, such as hung at the side of Christ, Cobb his name, he has offered me all he has to give, and is that not another word for love?*

"*I have never in my life felt the presence of God*"...*perhaps I have, and knew it not.*

Love, he thinks, humbled. *Love and courage, a word that has* heart *within it.*

His little Alyce, she must grow up in the knowledge her father stood tall before a mob that clamoured for his death. His unborn son must also have a father to be proud of. Ilotte, who fled the horrors of her home, made a life for herself and her bees, and gave herself to him, withholding naught, she will tell stories of him to his children, keeping him alive. His father, his dear father, a man of kindness and great courage. His mother, who'd skin him with one of her looks should he quiver and quake his way to the scaffold. The twins, he prays strength for Ralf of the easy-bruised heart, prays honey will temper easy-aroused Gil.

Robert, his elder brother, still missed. Annabel, loving mother of Alyce, her chatter, her single, perfect word. Piers and Willem, Javyd and Petronilla, Solomon and Lucy, Modge and Trefoil...and now Cobb.

A strange time to be shrouded in peace.

Through the window's open shutters, Edmund can see the gaol, the stout door and small, barred windows. The street is lined with people, a hawker selling meat pies, a stall for ale, the mood that of a high holiday. A horse with strong hocks and tufted hoofs stands patiently; from its girth, two long ropes dangle to the ground. So Haukyn, his son, is to be drawn without benefit of hurdle over every cobble, every sharp stone.

In the distance he sees the scaffold, its wooden ladder, its noose, the masked executioner, waiting. As he waits.

His hands are clammy. The pounding of his heart is so insistent he's surprised no one looks up. But why would they? They want spectacle: a man's inglorious death played out on a summer's morning.

It takes forever, or so it seems, for Haukyn to get to his feet. One ankle won't bear his weight, so he props himself against the wall. He won't whimper like Jackdawe. He won't beg for mercy.

Footsteps. He draws on all that is within him and stands tall in his shackles. Broke-nose, three others, and Sir Gardrad. "I ordered you to beat him," the knight says sharply.

"We done so."

"Not enough. Keep hold of him until you fasten him behind the horse. Face up, I think, so all can see him. Now, gag and blindfold him."

Haukyn says, "You don't want me proclaiming you hang me without trial?"

"The rabble wants blood, not sermons." To his men, he says, "Hurry up."

"In case the sheriff should arrive?"

"Gag him!"

Broke-nose is unravelling a tangled length of cloth, cursing under his breath. Haukyn holds the knight's eyes with his. "A man is easy to kill. But rebellion won't die with me."

The gag is fastened cruelly tight against loosened teeth and an aching jaw. The blindfold pulled as tight. Despite himself, he sways on his feet. His leg shackles are unfastened from the wall. His elbows are seized and he's hustled forward, doing his best not to limp. Terror like fire to flesh. *Nay, I won't give in to it, I won't, let Alyce and my son be proud of their father, Edmund of his son, let Ilotte know her beloved showed courage to the end*...he's half-lifted, half-dragged up a flight of cold stone stairs.

From his perch, Edmund sees the gaol door open.

Even behind the blindfold Haukyn knows when he emerges into daylight. He's pushed in the small of his back, nearly falls, hears laughter, shouts, and crude insults. Sir Gardrad says, "Bring the horse. Now!"

A stone strikes his cracked rib, his cry stifled by the cloth. A second stone, thrown harder, glances off his cheekbone, and into his mind drops the long-ago image of Ilotte in the stocks, the defiance in her sloe-black eyes. Deliberately, impeded by his sore ankle, he shuffles around to face the one who threw it.

Edmund in one glance has taken in the gag, the blindfold, his son's blotched, grazed skin, caked with blood: Haukyn has been beaten, and more than once. Rage rises in his chest and steadies him. His movements unhurried, he wipes his hands down his hose and strings his bow, its stave short enough that his cloak kept it hidden. He nocks the arrow and as Haukyn turns to face the man who threw the stone, he raises the bow, takes careful aim, and shoots. The arrow strikes Haukyn in the chest.

Shocked gasps. The thud of a body hitting the cobbles.

Back from the window, unstring the bow, tuck it beneath his cloak, hood forward, and he takes the stairs at a run. Lock the door with the key. Down the alley, away from Northbrook, no one around to see him, they're all near the gaol or the scaffold. Into the shelter of the trees, hood back so he doesn't trip, Tirrell and the two horses waiting for him. "I shot him," he says. "We must ride hard. Gardrad will guess twas someone from Flintbourne." Too little change in the constable's face as Tirrell swings himself up on his horse. "You suspected?"

"I been to hangings. I wondered."

They spur the horses forward. Tirrell says choppily, "Ivo trussed to a chunk of iron in the Swallowbend smithy upriver, how that come about, no one knows. More strange doings—hooded men with masks stole Bertran's keys 'n' locked him, Mauld, and Saul in the manor gaol." As they leave the woods for the road, he adds, "This horse ain't mine. Belongs to the atte Medes' ol' grandfer. They'll hide it after."

"Ilotte will calm Trefoil. I left a note for the twins of my whereabouts, with instructions to rub it out once read."

Ride hard they do, along the road, across the shallow slide of the river east of the vill, and into the lord's woods. Tirrell says, patting his mount's neck, "Walter atte Mede will lead this-un into the forest beyond the ridge. No witnesses, Edmund. Gardrad can do naught."

"God's blessing on you, Tirrell, for all you've done."

Trefoil trots fast through the trees along the ridge, then down the hill. Smoke rising in blue puffs from the smithy. Edmund shouts for Sim, and when he appears, says, "Is your fire hot enough to burn this bow and my second arrow before Sir Gardrad arrives in the vill?"

"Give 'em to me. Not even ashes'll be left by the time that scut come."

"My thanks."

On his approach to Haukyn's house, he sees to his surprise that the acre above the orchard is part-ploughed, the coulter still in the ground, the handles damp from last night's rain; unlike Ilotte to be careless of tools, he thinks, and dismounts. Ilotte comes out of the open door, this woman who made his son so happy. She looks into his eyes, and what she sees there brings to her body a stillness like that of death. "I felt him gone," she says, "'n' hoped I were wrong."

"One of my arrows was all it took."

"I thought it might be so."

His words drop to the ground like shards of flint. "He was blindfolded and gagged, and he'd been sorely beaten. Yet he showed great fortitude."

"As did his da," she says. "I'll harness Trefoil to the plough 'n' that way there be a reason she be sweaty should anyone ask."

If he were to weep, it would be now. His eyes burn in his skull. "My thanks, Ilotte."

My thanks, my thanks…he hurries along the headlands. A group of men armed with bows and arrows line the river's edge near the ford, women and children converging behind them. Jackdaws circle the church tower.

His house is in sight. He stands still, whispers into the morning air, "My son is dead. By my own hand."

Ranulf lopes across the grass to meet him. Alyce, who was playing in the dirt with a little horse Haukyn had carved for her, puts it down and rolls down the hill, giggling, Ranulf now chasing her and trying to lick her face. Ralf and Gil flank the doorway. He says, wondering if he repeats it often enough it will make sense, "Your brother is dead. I shot him to save him from being drawn and hanged. Should Sir Gardrad come after me, the bow is now ashes in the forge, and Trefoil in a sweat from dragging the plough in Haukyn's upper field, Ilotte her guide. I'll join the men at the ford."

The twins look stricken, but unsurprised; they would have noticed the absence of the short bow that rested below the rafters. Ralf says, implacable, "I'm going to the ford with you."

"You mustn't do anything there that will harm you!"

"I won't. But I won't sit quiet by the fire either."

Gil the one with tears on his cheeks. "We made pottage."

Edmund says, "I'll eat later. Ralf, you'll come to the ford with me. Will you watch Alyce, Gil? I can't tell her about her father until Sir Gardrad's gone."

He takes his long bow from its rack and strings it, the bow he can no longer draw to full compass, pushes two arrows through his belt, and together he and Ralf hasten to the ford. His neighbours nod at him and let him through. One of Haukyn's legacies, this crowd, he thinks, a hard lump lodged in his throat as he stations himself at the front.

Rhythmic beat of hoofs, clink of harness, and five men canter down the slope toward them: Sir Gardrad and his retainers. Edmund holds his bowstave firmly in front of him as the knight hauls his mount's head around and stops so close that he can smell the horse's sweat. He says, "Sir Gardrad. Have you come to tell me my son is dead? Hanged without trial at your command?"

"You shot him."

"I was once champion archer of the shire. But not even I can shoot an arrow from Flintbourne to Newbury."

"You loosed your arrow from a house near the gaol!"

"I was here, with my young sons."

"Where's the oaf who led us to Haukyn's hiding place?"

"The vill outlawed him."

"Then where's my bailiff?"

Edmund looks around. "He seems to be absent. You must calm yourself, sir, too much choler will unbalance your humours."

"Once you're in Newbury's gaol, you'll sing a different tune."

Someone shouts, "Four hirelings 'n' a knight, it'd only take five arrows."

"Five more for their nags."

"I'll scour the vill from end to end," Sir Gardrad says, "someone will have seen you leave the vill with your bow. Where's your constable?"

Tirrell edges through the crowd. "The sheriff don't like hangings without due trial. The sheriff what overrules you, Sir Gardrad."

"Haukyn was murdered by his father!"

There is a time to speak truth and a time to circle it. Edmund says, spacing his words, "Your two sons are dead, sir, and for that I am sorry—they must have suffered from their crooked bones before they died. Yet you could not have murdered them any more than I could murder my son, flesh of my flesh, blood of my blood."

The knight shrinks, visibly, in his saddle, cheeks that were red now wraith-pale. "How do you know of my sons? You, a common serf?"

"John of Gaunt told Haukyn about them, urging him to have compassion toward you. Haukyn told me. I too have now lost two sons, Sir Gardrad. Go in peace, and your men with you. Haukyn of Flintbourne will be buried in quicklime in unconsecrated ground, let that be enough."

For a long moment, a moment out of time, the knight and he stare at each other. Then Sir Gardrad, his shoulders bowed, pulls on the reins, kicks his horse, and without a backward look rides toward the track that leads out of the vill. His retainers, perforce, follow. The men in the crowd lower their bows, and Edmund lets out his breath in a long sigh.

Tirrell says, "You got no need o' bow 'n' arrow with words like them at your command. I'll see that Bertran be released. Go home, Edmund."

Twas Ilotte told him about the knight's two sons; she had it from Sir Geoffrey. What matter a small untruth when he did commit murder? He stumbles homeward, Ralf gripping him by the elbow. Alyce comes to meet them, flourishing long strands of bindweed. Ilotte is running across the field toward them. No need for her and Trefoil to plough, he thinks numbly, not with Gardrad gone.

He crouches, his knees protesting, holds his granddaughter close, and waits until Ilotte kneels beside them. "Alyce," he says, "we are all very sad. Your father is dead. Killed by an arrow in Newbury. He won't be coming home, not today. Nor ever."

Bewilderment, denial, tears, one after the other; she throws herself at Ilotte and sobs into her apron. *Alyce is more hers than mine,* Edmund thinks, *and so it should be.*

After they have left, hand in hand along the headland, he chokes down some of Gil's pottage and walks to the church. The faded paintings fail to console him. He broke his oath this day, for after he left France he swore never to kill again.

Hawise, were she here, would have lifted the short bow from the rafters and passed it to him, she would have tested the two arrowheads for sharpness, and her green eyes would have burned into his.

Father, I pray you, may my son rest in peace.

...that which is immutable...

The vill goes about its business. The last of the hay is stooked, reeds are cut in the river and bundled with string, weeds uprooted, ragwort burnt. The twins are discovered behind the byre doing their best to thrash each other, and when Edmund drags one off the other, each of them is weeping. Alyce has nightmares. Ilotte has dark circles under her eyes.

Edmund works from dawn til dusk, blunting axes against trees, shooting with his long bow any of the lord's rabbits foolish enough to stray onto his fields, breaking the handle of his old spade when he tries to lever flint from a new patch of garden that he doesn't need. He mends the handle, he takes his mattock and smashes the flint, he helps Swithin clear wasteland and Sim collect firewood and Solomon pull ragwort. He welcomes Ilotte for her lessons and begins to teach the alphabet to Alyce, drawing them in the dirt for her, she tracing them with dirty fingers.

He talks. He even laughs.

He cannot lie down and die as, too often, he wants to; his family, what is left of it, needs him. He cannot sit beside Haukyn's grave, for Haukyn is buried who knows where.

The Feast of St. Felicity, and Haukyn dead a month. Three days before the Feast of St. Mary Magdalene, Tirrell returns from a visit with his uncle, the sheriff. Sir Gardrad, he reports, has been chided most strongly for disobeying the king's dictum that there be fair trial in London of any accused rebel. "He should have been outlawed," Edmund says and neglects to thank the constable.

He had sent word to Javyd and Petronilla of Haukyn's death, and reads the reply, written by a scribe who made no attempt to blunt Javyd's ripe curses or his sorrow.

Alyce asks why war left her da's face smooth and why did God shoot him.

Ilotte brings the twins an early honeycomb. Solomon visits with gossip, Neuton with a fine cabbage, Walter with beans. They mean well. He is careful to thank them.

In the byre one afternoon—where else can he hide? —when he's sitting on the piled hay, back bent like a drawn bow, eyes dry, Ilotte enters with herbs for his cow. As he hurriedly pushes himself to his feet, she puts her arms around him. "We holds Haukyn," she whispers, "can you not feel him?"

He cannot. He nods, not wanting to disappoint her.

Another week passes. Tirrell receives a letter from his uncle and gives it to Edmund to read. John of Gaunt is to travel south and meet with the king in Reading, a reconciliation, says the sheriff, though why tis needed you would have to ask the king. Edmund smooths the parchment, his fingers shaky.

The sixth day of the new month finds him in Sonning, at the gateway of the bishop's palace where, he's been told, John of Gaunt is lodging. "Tell the duke that Edmund of Flintbourne, father of Haukyn, has a gift for him," he says in his loftiest voice to the servant who greets him, "and would you see that my horse is given water?"

Rather to his surprise, he is soon ushered into a room of tapestries and brocaded chairs. The duke is seated at a desk, frowning at a book of accounts. "Your Highness," Edmund says and bows.

"Haukyn didn't accompany his father to visit an out-of-favour duke?"

"Haukyn is dead. He was accused of rebellion, confined in Newbury's gaol, beaten by Sir Gardrad's thugs, then was to be drawn naked to the scaffold, also at Sir Gardrad's orders. All without benefit of the trial mandated by our king."

"Was the sentence carried out?"

"He was killed by a single arrow before he could be tied behind the horse. He is buried in quicklime in unconsecrated ground."

"He once told me you were an archer at Crécy."

"I trust your highness never discovers how old arms cannot draw a bow to full compass, or old eyes focus on a target."

"You have my full attention," the duke says wryly. His bejewelled fingers tap the top of the desk. "Haukyn was a common soldier, yet he looked at me as though—can you not hear God laugh?—we were equals."

"Two men mired in the mud of the Auvergne." The words spill from him. "Haukyn envisaged power stripped of its trappings, without comprehending its will to maintain itself regardless of means or consequence. Power will bury London's four days of rebellion in quicklime, and no one can tell me otherwise."

"I warned your son his fires would one day scorch him."

"He didn't heed you." Edmund steadies his voice. "I would he had."

The duke shrugs. "I am not in favour of the rebels. The Sauvoye burned to the ground and everything in it destroyed."

"But you are in favour of the due process of law. An execution without trial? Sir Gardrad broke the law. I would ask you to distrain his lands in my shire and send him and his bailiff elsewhere. Perhaps then I can forgive him."

"There was mention of a gift."

"I don't resort to bribery! Tis a gift and freely given." With scant ceremony, Edmund pulls the small package from his pouch and drops it on the desk. "Haukyn was in the Sauvoye that day, saw the destruction, and at the risk of his life rescued this."

The duke unwraps the linen around the book. "I can still smell the smoke."

"The fires of rebellion linger."

But the duke is not listening. He opens the book and turns the pages, stroking them as he might stroke a mistress's skin, pausing to smile at some of the images and to read the decorative script. He says softly, "Tis the Book of Hours that belonged to my first wife, Blanche, whom I dearly loved. I kept it in my chamber at the Sauvoye for safe-keeping." He sighs, letting the leather cover close. "I am grateful to your son for rescuing it, and to you for giving it to me. As for Sir Gardrad, he has a habit of disregarding royal law. His lands in Berkshire will revert to the Crown. I have property in Northumberland that will suit him, and his line dies with him." He reaches for parchment, scratches instructions on it, and calls for a servant. "Have this delivered immediately. Take six of my retainers."

Edmund stands very still. As the door closes behind the servant, he says, "I thank you, Your Highness."

"Will your village now return to the rule of fealty?"

"My vill is forever changed."

"Do your part to ensure obedience to your new lord. Now, begone, I have more important matters on my mind than a rebellious archer and his possibly murderous father."

"God's blessing on you." Edmund bows and walks out of the room.

Trefoil, wet-whiskered, tosses her head when she sees him. He mounts her. The reins loose, the sun on his face, they amble along, one league, then a second, and gradually his inner turmoil settles. Before he can forgive Sir Gardrad, he has to forgive Haukyn, who saved from rebellion's flames a book of prayer, who died of his own fires, who thought to overturn that which is immutable: the moon in its orbit, the stars in their course.

His dearly loved son.

Ah Edmund, would you placate with words the release of an arrow?

Is it enough, oh Lord, that I will repent that act for the rest of my days, and yet, for the sake of mercy, would do it again?

The following winter, as snow blankets the vill, Ilotte gives birth, with the assistance of Lucy, to a healthy son. Haukyn's son, a half-brother to Alyce.

Haukyn's bastard son, born a freeman.

Edmund's grandson, red-faced and squalling.

Ilotte, with care, places the infant in his arms. The squalling stops. The weight of him. The mop of damp, dark hair, the spiked, dark lashes, the dark, solemn eyes. Fists flailing empty air. Tears stream down Edmund's cheeks, tears that have been locked in his chest for months, ever since he loosed that single arrow.

How is it he can weep from sorrow and from joy?

Glossary

Pronunciation

A number of people asked, after the publication of *The Arrows of Mercy*, how to pronounce Hawise's name. Here is my attempt at a pronunciation guide for names in *The Arrows of Fealty*:

Alyce: Alice
Gil: a hard *G*
Haukyn: Haw/kin (accent on first syllable)
Hawise: Hah/wees (accent on second syllable)
Ilotte: Ee/lot (accent on second syllable)
Mauld: rhymes with Saul
Trefoil: Tree/foil (accent on first syllable)

I have used medieval spelling for a number of words: waggon, serjeant, byelaw, All Hallowes, mede (meadow), Sauvoye Palace (which was on the site of the present-day Savoy Hotel), and Wat Tyghler.

Hours of the Day

A mechanical clock is installed in Westminster in the 1360s, audible outside London's city walls, but not within. By 1376 a clock is in place on the tower of St. Pancras Church on Soper Lane. Haukyn hears this hourly bell on his visits to London, hours that are all of the same length: the regulation of time in a busy city.

For the Flintbourne villagers, time is told by the placement of the sun in its arc through the sky, the relative length of shadows, and the ringing of church bells.

The bell of St. Edmund's Church tolls the liturgical hours, approximately as follows:

Vigils (Matins): midnight
Lauds: 3 a.m.
Prime: 6 a.m. or daybreak, the first hour
Terce: 9 a.m., the third hour

Sext: noon, the sixth hour
None: 3 p.m., the ninth hour
Vespers: 6 p.m., the hour of the lighting of the lamps
Compline: 9 p.m., the hour of retiring

Money
The silver penny is the coin in circulation. After the late 1200s, half-penny (ha'penny) and quarter-penny (farthing) coins are minted. Fourpence is a groat, twelve-pence is a shilling, and twenty shillings is a pound. Haukyn is paid sixpence a day as a horse archer in John of Gaunt's army. Edward III's annual royal revenues are between £30,000 and £50,000.

Saints' Days
Because Haukyn's story covers several years, I sometimes used saints' days to suggest a particular month.
St. Andrew: November 30
St. Cecilia: November 22
St. Felicity: July 10
St. James the Less: May 3
St. John the Baptist: June 24
St. Jude: October 28
St. Mary Magdalene: July 22
St. Sebastian: January 20
St. Stephen: December 26
St. Swithin: July 15
St. Thomas: July 3
St. Valentine: February 14
Christ's Mass: December 25
Corpus Christi: June 13 in 1381
Feast of All Saints: November 1
Feast of the Holy Innocents: December 28

absolvat me Deus: may God forgive me

amercement: a fine for an offence, paid to the lord at the manor court, whereby the person fined is "in mercy"

ancient demesne: lands that made up Edward the Confessor's estate (he reigned from 1042 to 1066). A serf who lives on ancient demesne is free of obligations to his lord.

Ash Wednesday: the first day of Lent and seventh Wednesday before Easter; the foreheads of penitents were sprinkled with ashes on that day

assart: tract of forest or wasteland cleared for cultivation

assize of bread and ale: the regulating, in accordance with the law, of the price and quality of bread and ale that are to be sold

bailiff: a freeman appointed by the lord who acts as an officer for justice below the sheriff, with the power to call hallmotes. He also manages the lord's estate, with authority over the reeve.

basinet: a metal helmet

baulk: strip of grass between ploughed fields

bay: a room in a peasant's house

benedicite: a blessing

bole: the trunk of a tree

boon works: labour services such as harvest and hay-making that villeins are required to perform on the lord's demesne, in theory as a boon or favour; by custom, the lord provides food.

bowyer: someone who practices the craft of making bows. In London, the Bowyers' Guild has been recognized since 1371.

braies: loose linen underwear, tied with a cord at the waist

butt: a target, a mark to be shot at by archers

byre: a cowshed, often attached to the peasant's house and opening into it, for the sake of winter warmth

chain mail, mail: flexible, interlinked metal rings riveted into panels, which give protection from attack

Chancery and the Exchequer: Chancery issues charters and writs in the king's name; the Exchequer deals with the Crown's revenues.

chasuble: an outer vestment worn by a priest to celebrate Mass

chattels: personal property that is moveable (i.e., not land)

chevage: annual payment a villein makes to the lord for permission to live off the manor

chevauchées: mounted raids that destroy property, food supplies, and morale and disrupt the economy. They are considered less risky than battles.

childwyte: the fine paid by a villein to the lord of the manor for the birth of a child out of wedlock

clouts: diapered cloths for an infant

cob: a strong, short-legged horse

cog: a single-masted, square-sailed ship

common fields: land where the tenants (serfs or freemen) have certain rights

Commons: one of the Houses of Parliament, with representatives from the shires and the boroughs

commutation: a money payment from serf to lord, freeing the serf from boon works and other labours

conduit: the taps on Cheapside that were a source of fresh water

confiteor Deo omnipotenti: I confess to Almighty God

constable: a man elected by the vill to keep order and peace in the vill

cordwainer: a shoemaker

costard: an old variety of English apple

cot: small dwelling or cottage

coulter: an iron blade on a plough that cuts into the soil

croft: enclosed land usually adjacent to a house and including outbuildings and garden

curvet: quick moves made by a frisky horse

customary (unfree/villein) land: land rented from the lord that comes with terms and obligations enforceable by hallmote

daub: see wattle and daub

dead-hedge: woven from stakes and brush (not "live" in the sense of a modern privet hedge)

demesne: land within the manor held by the lord for his own use, and in Flintbourne worked by villeins

destrier: a knight's war horse, bred for size and the ability to carry a man in full armour, and hence costly

Dieu vous bénisse: God bless you

Deus vobiscum: God be with you

distrain, distraint: confiscation of land or chattels to enforce a court decision; dispossession

Domesday Book: compiled in 1068 under William the Conqueror, to ascertain the ownership and value of lands at the end of Edward the Confessor's reign. Serfs revere it, calling it Domesday (a reference to the Day of Judgement; pronounced *doomz/day* with the accent on first syllable); appeals to it should not lightly be dismissed.

doublet: any short, padded jacket. When made of leather, the doublet, together with chain mail and basinet, comprises an archer's armour.

drawknife: a knife with an eight- to ten-inch blade used by bowyers

ell: a measure for cloth. The English ell is forty-five inches.

exemplifications: writs purchased by serfs (via lawyers or counsellors) from the royal courts. In Haukyn's case, the writ is based on Domesday, in the hope that Flintbourne's land was ancient demesne and therefore free of manorial obligations.

faggot: a bundle of small branches used for fuel

fealty: a serf's obligation of fidelity toward his lord. The definition of fidelity includes devotion, loyalty, and constancy.

fleur-de-lys: a gold, three-petalled lily on a blue field, the royal arms of France

Flintbourne: an imaginary village on the banks of the Kennet River between Hungerford and Newbury, in southwestern Berkshire

gates of London: London is a walled city of about a square mile, with seven gates: Ludgate, Newgate, Aldersgate, Cripplegate, Moorgate, Bishop's Gate, and Aldgate (above which Chaucer has a dwelling; he might have seen Haukyn passing beneath it, one of the many rebels walking to Mile End to meet Richard II).

gauntlet: a glove made of leather, mail, or metal

gibbet: gallows

gong-fermour: a worker hired by the city and/or by private households to clean latrines and cesspits

goodwife: a woman who is the head of a household; the wife of a family

Great Seal: this seal bears the authority of king and state and is thus a very powerful symbol

greaves: armour that protects the shin

groat: fourpence

grout: the particular flavour given to home-brewed ale by the addition of herbs

hallmote: the manorial court held by the lord or one of his officials (in Flintbourne, the bailiff) to deal with local byelaws, transfers of land, servile labour, theft, slander, brawls, minor assaults, and minor offences against morality. The manor court, indirectly, guards "the custom of the manor" and hence prevents sudden, harmful policy changes.

hayward: the official who oversees the harvest and hay-making, a lesser official than the reeve

headland: unploughed land at the ends of adjoining strips of arable land where oxen can turn the plough

heriot: the surrender of the best live beast or of chattels to the lord upon a tenant's death

Hocktide: On Hocktide Tuesday, the Tuesday after Easter Sunday, the young women of the vill can capture the young men they have their eyes on, after which the men must pay for their freedom ("hock" themselves). The money goes to the parish.

hue and cry, the hue: an obligatory outcry by the tenants of a manor, warning of a misdemeanour and causing pursuit of the suspect

in nomine Patris, et Filii, et Spiritus sancti: in the name of the Father and the Son and the Holy Ghost

Jacquerie: an uprising of French peasants against the nobility in 1358, centred north of Paris. After over a month of violence, it was brutally suppressed.

jupon: a short garment worn over armour, displaying a coat of arms

knight banneret: a knight of high rank, who can display his coat of arms on a square banner

league: a league is about three and a half miles (or about five and a half kilometres)

leyrwite: a fine paid at hallmote by a woman who has sexual intercourse outside wedlock

manumission: a serf's attainment of free status, by charter, upon payment of a fee to the lord

maslin: bread made from a mixture of rye and wheat

mattock: a tool for loosening the soil, with a flat blade on one or both sides

mazer: a drinking cup made from maple wood

mede: a meadow (as in the atte Mede family)

men-at-arms: a variable term, by which Haukyn means soldiers wearing metal armour, hence not archers or infantry with leather armour

merchet: a fine due to the lord when a serf's daughter or son marries

midden: a heap of dung or rubbish

midguard: the middle position in an army's column, as compared to the vanguard (at the front) and the rearguard (at the back)

mizzle: drizzle, a light rain

murrain: a general name for animal disease

nocks: the ends of a bowstave where the string is attached, often covered with horn. Also, each arrow has a nock to fit the string; the archer "nocks" the arrow, by sight or by feel.

outlawry: the state of being outlawed, which places the person outside the protection of the law

pattens: clogs or shoes whose soles raise the wearer's feet above the mud

pennon: a long narrow flag, carried by some of the rebels in London

piss-a-bed: dandelion, so named for its diuretic properties

pizzle: see **tarse**

poll tax: a tax levied on all those over the age of fourteen or fifteen (i.e., on every "head," the meaning of "poll"). It brings with it the possibility of a census.

popinjay: a feathered, bird-like target for archers that is strung to a pole so it can move freely. The word is used years later to refer to a conceited man.

reeve: a local official, usually a villein, elected from among the manor's tenants and responsible for the day-to-day management of the manor; his status is below that of bailiff.

right-side sickness: appendicitis

russet: a coarse woollen cloth, undyed

sallow: a small species of willow

sard: to copulate, more or less the equivalent of "fuck," which is of early sixteenth-century origin. Words such as cunt, sard, tarse, and bollocks are in common usage, bear little or no taboo, and hence carry little charge, although they can be used in an insulting manner. It is considered a more serious offence to take God's name in vain.

scrofulous: having a disease with glandular swellings, probably tuberculosis

se'night: seven nights, or a week

serf (also called a **villein**): an unfree peasant who rents land on the manor, is not permitted to leave the manor without the lord's consent, is required to pay taxes such as chevage, merchet, and tallage, and owes the lord labour on the demesne; he is not permitted access to the royal courts.

Shambles, the: an open-air slaughterhouse and meat market near Spitalfield inside the London wall

sharkskin: the skin of a shark, used as we would use sandpaper

shrive: to hear confession, assign penance, and grant absolution

sloe: a shrub also known as blackthorn, with sour blue-black berries

Southwark's stews: Southwark is a borough of London on the south bank of the Thames, with many brothels, or stews.

squats: dysentery, which causes severe diarrhea with blood and mucus

starlings: the boat-shaped foundations that in Haukyn's day hold up the stone arches of London Bridge, which has nineteen starlings. Sharp-pointed logs were rammed into the river bottom and the wooden foundations around them filled with rubble, all this to prevent tidal erosion—an astonishing feat of engineering, given that the bridge was completed in 1209.

Statute of Labourers, 1351: royal legislation that attempted to freeze prices and wages (especially the latter) to low pre-plague levels, despite the shortage of workers

string follow: the tendency of a bow to stay bent when it is unstrung, which can cause the bow "to lose cast," that is, to shoot less hard and less fast

subsidy of fifteenths: a direct tax on the value of moveable goods, one-fifteenth in the case of rural serfs

swive: to copulate, the equivalent, more or less, of our term "to make love"

tallage: a lord's right to tax his serfs at any time and for whatever reason

tarse (also **pizzle**)**:** an Old English word for penis

tithe: a tenth of all a serf's profits and produce (corn, livestock, fruit, etc.), which is owed to the church

toft: site on which the house is built (hence, toft and croft)

tuppence: two pennies

verjuice: the sour fermented juice of crabapples or other fruit

villein: see **serf**

virgate: a holding of land, usually about thirty acres

wattle and daub: a method of construction using upright stakes interwoven with branches of hazel and covered on both sides with daub, a mix of mud, dung, lime, animal hair, and straw; the finished walls are waterproof and can be white-washed.

withershins: counter-clockwise, contrary to the course of the sun

withies: tough, flexible twigs of hazel used for wattle; also willow and osier twigs

woodbote: wood granted to his tenants by the lord

woodward: the official who watches over the manor's woodland and hedges

writ: a legal document ordering or prohibiting a certain action

Author's Note

Two quick comments. First, *The Arrows of Fealty* can, I think, stand on its own, although it would perhaps be enhanced if you've read its predecessor, *The Arrows of Mercy*, the story of Haukyn's father, Edmund. Second, when I write historical fiction, I'm guided by Hilary Mantel's Reith Lectures, striving, within my limits, for historical accuracy.

A campaign in France that began too late in the season, a rebellion in London that paralyzed king and Commons, and a young serf named Haukyn caught up in both: therein lie the seeds of *The Arrows of Fealty*.

The so-called Hundred Years War between France and England, long-time rivals, started in 1337 and ended in defeat for the English in 1453. Edward III of England, with some justification, was convinced he had a solid claim to the French throne. He conducted his first campaign in France in 1339 and formally declared himself King of England and France in 1340. At first, the war went well for England (Edmund was one of the archers at the battle of Crécy in 1346, a huge victory for the English and for the bow and arrow, the weapon of commoners); however, after the accession of wily Charles V of France, who eschewed battles for guerilla warfare, matters deteriorated, and from 1369 onward, the English suffered setbacks on land and at sea. Armed raids that devastated the French countryside (*chevauchées*), such as John of Gaunt's in 1373, for which Haukyn volunteered, did nothing to establish permanent garrisons or reclaim contested territory. In 1377 and again in 1380, the French attacked ports on England's southern coast, sacking and burning, and by 1380 Charles V had reclaimed the greater part of the lands won by Edward III.

John of Gaunt, son of Edward III and the richest man in the country, was perceived as the leader of England's war efforts from the 1370s onward; he became, perhaps not always fairly, the scapegoat for these failures and the most hated man in England. I've based my estimation of his character on a number of sources, including two recent biographies, both, as it happens, by female scholars, Helen Carr and Kathryn Warner.

Originally, the 1373 *chevauchée* was to have embarked from Plymouth in May, with a landing in Brittany near Saint-Malo; from there it would have crossed the Loire and invaded Aquitaine. By mid-May, however, the news had reached Westminster that Brittany was now almost entirely in French hands. The landing place was changed to Calais, which would necessitate crossing the Loire in the Massif Central. The fleet of 200 transports already in or near Plymouth was redirected to Dover, as were the 4,500 men marching toward Plymouth; the result was chaos. In consequence, Gaunt's army did not leave Calais until August 10, nearly three months later than first planned.

During the campaign, Haukyn made an enemy of a knight whose demesne was in Berkshire; Sir Gardrad is an entirely fictional character, and I've strayed from historical truth by placing him as the lord of Faircross Hundred in southern Berkshire in 1381.

Along the six-hundred-mile route of the *chevauchée*, I have omitted any number of raids, ambushes, and skirmishes—I didn't want Part One of the novel to turn into a military travelogue.

And now, a little background on the English setting of Parts Two and Three, with apologies to those of you who have already read about this in *The Arrows of Mercy*. Both novels are set in Berkshire because I was born there. A few years ago, in the county's southwest, my son drove me along the "wrong" side of many of its back lanes—narrow, winding lanes, with high hedgerows—and Flintbourne evolved as an imaginary village between the market towns of Hungerford and Newbury, on the banks of the River Kennet. The Kennet is a chalkstream that has its source in Wiltshire, chalkstreams being known for clear, pure water whose temperature changes very little from winter to summer.

The paintings that were familiar to Haukyn in the Flintbourne church can be seen in St. Clement's Church in Ashampstead, Berkshire, and date from 1230 to 1240.

The Kennet valley in medieval times consisted of sparsely settled lowlands, which were a combination of managed woods, common pastureland, arable land, and heath (wasteland). Some of the fields were small, irregular in shape, and hedged. In the open, "common" fields, villeins left one-third of the land fallow every year and had to agree on the type of crop grown on the rest. For their crofts and assarts they could choose arable, pasture, orchard, or all three.

In the ninth century, King Alfred had divided the population of England into three orders considered to be divinely ordained and therefore beyond challenge: aristocrats who fought; clergy who prayed; and peasants who worked. Dukes, earls, and barons held their lands directly from the king and granted land to local lords of the manor, who were either knights or gentry; the manor was thus the basic secular organization of English rural society. Two-thirds of them, like Flintbourne, had fewer than five hundred acres of arable land, their peasantry made up of freemen and unfree serfs, who owed fealty to their lord. The lord, in return, granted his tenants land and his protection. His income resulted from yearly rents, sales of excess produce, tolls for the use of the mill, fines collected at manor courts, and a wide array of customary taxes. Although the serf didn't own his land, it was heritable on payment of an entry fee by his successor. His servile duties included seasonal boon works and the holding of offices like reeve, hayward, constable, and woodward, which could be demanding and often led to unpopularity in the village.

The manor court enabled the lord to maintain control over his tenants and their lands, fine miscreants, issue byelaws, and further enrich himself. I've ignored the difference between the ordinary manorial court (hallmote) and the leet court, held for the assize of bread and ale and for more serious offences such as rape and assault, because in practice the distinction was not always maintained. In both courts, cases were decided by an all-male jury. Misogyny was rampant, biblically based, and legally entrenched: a woman moved from the authority of her father to that of her husband, her happiness and sometimes her life depending on whether she married a peaceable man or one prone to violence.

The number of Christian names, often those of saints, was limited—I've varied my characters' names for the sake of clarity. Surnames were stabilizing by the mid-fourteenth century for taxation and record-keeping purposes, although children did not necessarily assume a parent's surname, the mother's or the father's. Surnames were often based on occupation, like Cooper and Smyth, or could derive from location, as atte Mede and under Woode.

Canon law was frequently ignored on the manor. In theory, no one should work on Sunday or any holy day, of which there were about fifty in the year, a combined loss of more than fourteen weeks of labour. Even bishops' manors were known to permit work on Sundays. The church preached that the recurrences of bubonic plague from 1348 onward were sent by God as punishment for sin, and although the plague did not necessarily cause a loss of belief, religious dogma was questioned, as were clerical shortcomings.

The factors leading to revolt in England in 1381 were complex. The socially inequitable Statute of Labourers of 1351, which followed the initial outbreak of plague in 1348, blamed the workers for labour shortages that were a direct result of the horrific death rate; and in the mid-1370s it was still universally hated. The quality of royal justice had declined, becoming so multi-layered as to be both unmanageable and easily corruptible. Constant taxation, coupled with the perception that the government was wasting the money on a war that was going nowhere, added to the unrest, especially in southern England, as did excessive tolls on commerce. While serfdom was not, in general, at the forefront of the issues, one-fifth of England's population were serfs; serfdom could be onerous and bore a severe social stigma, even though literacy was on the rise and peasants were by no means politically uninformed. The Great Rumour, which arose in 1376 in ten southern counties, including Berkshire, and which mistakenly regarded the Domesday Book as an infallible source for manumission, is not nearly as well-known as the revolt of 1381. It did, however, demonstrate the craving for freedom in the lowest rank of society and undoubtedly unsettled Parliament.

Wars are expensive. In the first four years after ten-year-old Richard II acceded to his grandfather Edward III's throne in 1377, a double subsidy of fifteenths and three poll taxes were levied by Parliament to pay for the war, the burden falling disproportionately on the peasants. The last poll tax of 1380, a shilling per head ("poll"), regardless if the head were serf or noble, set off the Great Revolt of 1381. More commonly, and not altogether accurately, it has been known as the Peasants' Revolt: peasants were certainly involved, serfs and freemen, but so also were town and city dwellers, merchants and gentry, and even a few noblemen. Unrest began in Essex and Kent, spread to other counties in the south, and culminated in a coordinated march on London.

On June 12, Kentish rebels destroyed prisons and brothels in Southwark and sacked Lambeth Palace, seat of Archbishop Sudbury, the loathed chancellor of England. The next day, June 13, the Feast of Corpus Christi, the drawbridge was lowered on London Bridge (it remains a mystery who was responsible), and Kent streamed into London; shortly afterward, Aldgate was opened, allowing the rebels from Essex to enter the city. Haukyn arrived in London that afternoon. I have described only those events on June 13 and 14 where he was witness or participant. He left late on June 14, hence did not observe Wat Tyghler's murder at Smithfield on June 15 and the subsequent events at Clerkenwell when the rebels were ousted from the city.

On their way to and from Mile End, Haukyn, Javyd, and the rebels passed under Aldgate's archway, where Chaucer rented rooms. As an experienced diplomat for the English Crown, I doubt the poet looked upon the rebels with any empathy; his sole comment in "The Nun's Priest's Tale" is not complimentary.

The Great Revolt was England's first popular rebellion (the events leading up to Magna Carta were spearheaded by barons); it foreshadowed the French revolution by almost four hundred years, and it did not, of course, go unpunished.

For a variety of reasons, mostly related to the economics of the peasant land market, serfdom gradually disappeared in England during the next century. Haukyn, I like to think, would have been gratified to know this.

Acknowledgements

My warm thanks are extended to:

Michael Langan of The Literary Consultancy in London UK, for his acute readings of a draft of *The Arrows of Fealty*, his encouragement, and his thoughtful and insightful suggestions for improvement.

Anne Louise O'Connell, publisher, and Marianne Ward, associate publisher and editor, of OC Publishing, for their faith in my writing, their pragmatic and ongoing support, and their sheer hard work, from contract to promotion to launch and beyond. Particular thanks to Marianne, whose encouragement and unfailingly prompt attention have been vital.

Paula Sarson, for her thorough proofreading of the manuscript and her appreciation of the story.

Helen Carr, author of *The Red Prince: The Life of John of Gaunt, Duke of Lancaster* (Oneworld 2021), for a very helpful email exchange, which included the link to John of Gaunt's Register of 1379 to 1383. This register enabled me to place the duke with reasonable accuracy in Sonning, Berkshire, in early August of 1381.

Kathy Cawsey, of the English department, Dalhousie University, for reading excerpts to me in Middle English from two medieval poems, *Pearl* and *Sir Gawain and the Green Knight*, allowing me to hear how Haukyn might actually have spoken. Kathy also passed on an essay by Caroline Barron about the transition from canonical to clock time in London (hence the clock of St. Pancras on Soper Lane), suggested books about the trauma caused by the plague in England and about the link between writing and rebellion, and alerted me to a few anachronisms in the manuscript before it went to layout. Thank you, Kathy!

Lance Bishop and Sarah Clarke, of Seawinds Horse Archers, near Canning, Nova Scotia. Lance invited me to attend one of their competitions, they both met with me so I could ask questions (a lot of questions), and later Lance read, for accuracy, the pages in *The Arrows of Fealty* where I describe how Haukyn learned the art of horse archery.

John Large, of the Maritime Traditional Archery Group, former president of the Traditional Archers Association of Nova Scotia (TAANS), for technical advice and some great photographs when it came to the bowyer's art, especially tillering.

Marsha Amanova, for her support of my website.

Ted Tupper for (much-needed!) technical support.

The scholars whose books I have so heavily leaned upon, and whose knowledge has illumined my path. I've already mentioned the title of Helen Carr's biography of John of Gaunt; Kathryn Warner's is called *John of Gaunt: Son of One King, Father of Another.* Jonathan Sumption's third volume about the Hundred Years War, *Divided Houses*, was invaluable, as were Juliet Barker's *England, Arise: The People, The King & the Great Revolt of 1381*, Dan Jones's *Summer of Blood*, and R. B. Dobson's *The Peasants' Revolt of 1381*. For life on the manor, Mark Bailey's *The English Manor* and *The Decline of Serfdom in Late Medieval England* were particularly valuable and made me aware that a bastard son of a serf was born a freeman. *Going to Church in Medieval England* by Nicholas Orme is a wonderfully informative book. Any historical errors are my own.

Michelle Butler Hallett, Kathy Cawsey, Sarah Emsley, Anne Fleming, Trudy Morgan-Cole, and Julie Strong, for taking time in their busy lives to read *The Arrows of Fealty* and write such thoughtful testimonials.

Susan Atkinson, who has read two drafts of the novel, offered her thoughts and reactions, in particular with the chapters about the 1381 revolt. She is another insightful reader and a friend whose encouragement has been constant. Some great beach walks too!

The Abbey Girls and Sister Kate, constant companions along the way.

The many friends who offered encouragement, conversation, tea, wine, and meals (all greatly appreciated) during the the writing and revision of *The Arrows of Fealty*. You've helped me keep the faith, trust the process, all the clichés that attempt to deal with the joys and the sheer hard work of being immersed in the fourteenth century.

Finally, my family, as always, for being there.

I discovered Budge Row on a copy of a medieval map of London and chose it as the street on which Javyd and his sister lived, in loving memory of Budge Wilson, who was both a mentor and a dear friend.

About the Author

Photo credit: Nicola Davison, Snickerdoodle Photography

Jill MacLean has a BSc with honours from Dalhousie University, and a master's in theological studies from the Atlantic School of Theology.

Her years of writing genre fiction taught her the basics of storytelling. An excellent, and demanding, full-year poetry course at St. Mary's University in Halifax and a three-year mentorship with a professor of English and much-published poet in Winnipeg honed her love of language and her respect for the power of words.

Her poetry collection, *The Brevity of Red*, was shortlisted for two awards. Her eight-year-old grandson then asked her to write him a book, which, three years and three rejections later, was published as *The Nine Lives of Travis Keating*. Two more middle-grade and two young adult novels followed. Altogether these books won four awards and received many nominations, four international, including the prestigious White Ravens Honour List in Munich for *Nix Minus One*. Two of the novels are in the Nova Scotia school system.

Wanting a change and the challenge of an adult audience, Jill delved into her long-time fascination with the medieval period. In 2023 *The Arrows of Mercy* was a finalist for the Whistler Independent Book Award sponsored by The Writers' Union of Canada.

Jill loves canoeing, gardening, listening to classical music, and, of course, reading. She lives in Bedford, Nova Scotia, near her family.

You can read more about Jill and her publications on her website: jillmaclean.mywriting.network.